William Henry Herndon, Jesse William Weik

Abraham Lincoln; the true story of a great life

William Henry Herndon, Jesse William Weik

Abraham Lincoln; the true story of a great life

ISBN/EAN: 9783743658097

Printed in Europe, USA, Canada, Australia, Japan

Cover: Foto ©Raphael Reischuk / pixelio.de

More available books at **www.hansebooks.com**

LINCOLN DURING THE DEBATE WITH DOUGLAS.

*After an ambrotype taken by C. Jackson, at Pittsfield, Illinois,
October 1, 1858.*

ABRAHAM LINCOLN

The True Story of a Great Life

BY

WILLIAM H. HERNDON AND JESSE W. WEIK

WITH AN INTRODUCTION
By HORACE WHITE

ILLUSTRATED

IN TWO VOLUMES
VOL. II

NEW YORK
D. APPLETON AND COMPANY
1892

Printed at the
Appleton Press, U.S.A.

CONTENTS.

CHAPTER IV.

CHAPTER V.

CHAPTER VI.

CHAPTER XI.

APPENDIX.

LIST OF ILLUSTRATIONS.

VOL. II.

THE LIFE OF LINCOLN.

CHAPTER I.

A LAW office is a dull, dry place so far as pleasurable or interesting incidents are concerned. If one is in search of stories of fraud, deceit, cruelty, broken promises, blasted homes, there is no better place to learn them than a law office. But to the majority of persons these painful recitals are anything but attractive, and it is well perhaps that it should be so. In the office, as in the court room, Lincoln, when discussing any point, was never arbitrary or insinuating. He was deferential, cool, patient, and respectful. When he reached the office, about nine o'clock in the morning, the first thing he did was to pick up a newspaper, spread himself out on an old sofa, one leg on a chair, and read aloud, much to my discomfort. Singularly enough Lincoln never read any other way but aloud. This habit used to annoy me almost beyond the point of endurance. I once asked him why he did so. This was his explanation: " When I read aloud two senses catch the idea: first, I see what I read ; second, I hear it, and therefore I can remember it better." He never studied law books unless a case was on hand for consideration—never followed up the decisions of the supreme courts, as other lawyers did. It seemed as if he depended for his effectiveness in managing a lawsuit entirely on the stimulus and inspiration of the final hour. He paid but little attention to the fees and money matters of the firm—usually leaving all such to me. He never entered an item in the account book. If any one paid money to him which belonged to the firm, on arriving at the office he divided it with me. If I was not there, he would wrap up my share in a piece of paper and place it in my drawer—marking it with a pencil, " Case of Roe *vs.* Doe.—Herndon's half."

On many topics he was not a good conversationalist, because he felt that he was not learned enough. Neither was he a good listener. Putting it a little strongly, he was often not even polite. If present with others, or participating in a conversation, he was rather abrupt, and in his anxiety to say something apt or to illustrate the subject under discussion, would burst in with a story. In our office I have known him to consume the whole forenoon relating stories. If a man came to see him for the purpose of finding out something which he did not care to let him know and at the same time did not want to refuse him, he was very adroit. In such cases Lincoln would do most of the talking, swinging around what he suspected was the vital point, but never nearing it, interlarding his answers with a seemingly endless supply of stories and jokes. The interview being both interesting and pleasant, the man would depart in good humor, believing he had accomplished his mission. After he had walked away a few squares and had cooled off, the

question would come up, " Well, what did I find
out?" Blowing away the froth of Lincoln's humorous narratives he would find nothing substantial left.

"As he entered the trial," relates one of his colleagues at the bar,* " where most lawyers would object he would say he ' reckoned ' it would be fair to
let this in, or that ; and sometimes, when his adversary could not quite prove what Lincoln knew to
be the truth, he 'reckoned ' it would be fair to admit
the truth to be so-and-so. When he did object to
the court, and when he heard his objections answered, he would often say, ' Well, I reckon I must
be wrong.' Now, about the time he had practised
this three-fourths through the case, if his adversary
didn't understand him, he would wake up in a few
minutes learning that he had feared the Greeks too
late, and find himself beaten. He was wise as a
serpent in the trial of a cause, but I have had too
many scares from his blows to certify that he was
harmless as a dove. When the whole thing was
unravelled, the adversary would begin to see that
what he was so blandly giving away was simply
what he couldn't get and keep. By giving away
six points and carrying the seventh he carried his
case, and the whole case hanging on the seventh,
he traded away everything which would give him
the least aid in carrying that. Any man who took
Lincoln for a simple-minded man would very soon
wake up with his back in a ditch."

---

* Leonard Swett.

Lincoln's restless ambition found its gratification only in the field of politics. He used the law merely as a stepping-stone to what he considered a more attractive condition in the political world. In the allurements held out by the latter he seemed to be happy. Nothing in Lincoln's life has provoked more discussion than the question of his ability as a lawyer. I feel warranted in saying that he was at the same time a very great and a very insignificant lawyer. Judge David Davis, in his eulogy on Lincoln at Indianapolis, delivered at the meeting of the bar there in May, 1865, said this: " In all the elements that constituted a lawyer he had few equals. He was great at *nisi prius* and before an appellate tribunal. He seized the strong points of a cause and presented them with clearness and great compactness. His mind was logical and direct, and he did not indulge in extraneous discussion. Generalities and platitudes had no charm for him. An unfailing vein of humor never deserted him, and he was able to claim the attention of court and jury when the cause was most uninteresting by the appropriateness of his anecdotes. His power of comparison was large, and he rarely failed in a legal discussion to use that mode of reasoning. The framework of his mental and moral being was honesty, and a wrong case was poorly defended by him. The ability which some eminent lawyers possess of explaining away the bad points of a cause by ingenious sophistry was denied him. In order to bring into full activity his great powers it was necessary that he should be convinced of the right and justice of the matter which he advocated. When so convinced, whether the cause was great or small he was usually successful." *

This statement of Judge Davis in general is correct, but in some particulars is faulty. It was intended as a eulogy on Lincoln, and as such would not admit of as many limitations and modifications as if spoken under other circumstances. In 1866 Judge Davis said in a statement made to me in his home at Bloomington, which I still have, " Mr. Lincoln had no managing faculty nor organizing power ; hence a child could conform to the simple and technical rules, the means and the modes of getting at justice, better than he. The law has its own rules, and a student could get at them or keep with them better than Lincoln. Sometimes he was forced to study these if he could not get the rubbish of a case removed. But all the way through his lack of method and organizing ability was clearly apparent." The idea that Mr. Lincoln was a great lawyer in the higher courts and a good *nisi prius* lawyer, and yet that a child or student could manage a case in court better than he, seems strangely inconsistent, but the facts of his life as a lawyer will reconcile this and other apparent contradictions.

I was not only associated with Mr. Lincoln in Springfield, but was frequently on the circuit with

---

* He never took advantage of a man's low character to prejudice the jury. Mr. Lincoln thought his duty to his client extended to what was honorable and high-minded, just and noble—nothing further. Hence the meanest man at the bar always paid great deference and respect to him.—David Davis, Sept. 10, 1866, MS.

him, but of course not so much as Judge Davis, who held the court, and whom Lincoln followed around on the circuit for at least six months out of the year. I easily realized that Lincoln was strikingly deficient in the technical rules of the law. Although he was constantly reminding young legal aspirants to study and "work, work," yet I doubt if he ever read a single elementary law book through in his life. In fact, I may truthfully say, I never knew him to read through a law book of any kind. Practically, he knew nothing of the rules of evidence, of pleading, or practice, as laid down in the text-books, and seemed to care nothing about them. He had a keen sense of justice, and struggled for it, throwing aside forms, methods, and rules, until it appeared pure as a ray of light flashing through a fog-bank. He was not a general reader in any field of knowledge, but when he had occasion to learn or investigate any subject he was thorough and indefatigable in his search. He not only went to the root of a question, but dug up the root, and separated and analyzed every fibre of it. He was in every respect a case lawyer, never cramming himself on any question till he had a case in which the question was involved. He thought slowly and acted slowly; he must needs have time to analyze all the facts in a case and wind them into a connected story. I have seen him lose cases of the plainest justice, which the most inexperienced member of the bar would have gained without effort. Two things were essential to his success in managing a case. One was time;

the other a feeling of confidence in the justice of the cause he represented. He used to say, "If I can free this case from technicalities and get it properly swung to the jury, I'll win it." But if either of these essentials were lacking, he was the weakest man at the bar. He was greatest in my opinion as a lawyer in the Supreme Court of Illinois. There the cases were never hurried. The attorneys generally prepared their cases in the form of briefs, and the movements of the court and counsel were so slow that no one need be caught by surprise. I was with Lincoln once and listened to an oral argument by him in which he rehearsed an extended history of the law. It was a carefully prepared and masterly discourse, but, as I thought, entirely useless. After he was through and we were walking home I asked him why he went so far back in the history of the law. I presumed the court knew enough history. "That's where you're mistaken," was his instant rejoinder. "I dared not trust the case on the presumption that the court knows everything—in fact I argued it on the presumption that the court didn't know anything," a statement which, when one reviews the decision of our appellate courts, is not so extravagant as one would at first suppose.

I used to grow restless at Lincoln's slow movements and speeches in court. "Speak with more vim," I would frequently say, "and arouse the jury —talk faster and keep them awake." In answer to such a suggestion he one day made use of this illustration : "Give me your little pen-knife, with its short blade, and hand me that old jack-knife, lying

25

on the table." Opening the blade of the pen-knife
he said : "You see, this blade at the point travels
rapidly, but only through a small portion of space
till it stops ; while the long blade of the jack-knife
moves no faster but through a much greater space
than the small one. Just so with the long,
labored movements of my mind. I may not emit
ideas as rapidly as others, because I am compelled
by nature to speak slowly, but when I do throw off
a thought it seems to me, though it comes with
some effort, it has force enough to cut its own way
and travel a greater distance." This was said to
me when we were alone in our office simply for
illustration. It was not said boastingly.

As a specimen of Lincoln's method of reasoning
I insert here the brief or notes of an argument used
by him in a lawsuit as late as 1858. I copy from
the original :

"Legislation and adjudication must follow and
conform to the progress of society.

"The progress of society now begins to produce
cases of the transfer for debts of the entire
property of railroad corporations; and to enable
transferees to use and enjoy the transferred property
legislation and *adjudication* begin to be necessary.

"Shall this class of legislation just now beginning
with us be *general* or *special ?*

"Section Ten of our Constitution requires that it
should be general, if possible, (Read the Section.)

"Special legislation always trenches upon the judicial department ; and in so far violates Section Two
of the Constitution. (Read it.)

"Just reasoning—policy—is in favor of general
legislation—else the legislature will be *loaded* down

with the investigation of smaller cases—a work which the courts *ought* to perform, and can perform much more perfectly. How can the Legislature rightly decide the facts between P. & B. and S. C. & Co.

"It is said that under a general law, whenever a R. R. Co. gets tired of its debts, it may transfer *fraudulently* to get rid of them. So they may—so may individuals ; and which—the *Legislature* or the *courts*—is best suited to try the question of fraud in either case ?

"It is said, if a purchaser have acquired legal rights, let him not be robbed of them, but if he needs *legislation* let him submit to just terms to obtain it.

"Let him, say we, have general law in advance (guarded in every possible way against fraud), so that, when he acquires a legal right, he will have no occasion to wait for additional legislation ; and if he has practiced fraud let the courts so decide.''

David Davis said this of Lincoln: "When in a lawsuit he believed his client was oppressed,—as in the Wright case,—he was hurtful in denunciation. When he attacked meanness, fraud, or vice, he was powerful, merciless in his castigation." The Wright case referred to was a suit brought by Lincoln and myself to compel a pension agent to refund a portion of a fee which he had withheld from the widow of a revolutionary soldier. The entire pension was $400, of which sum the agent had retained one-half. The pensioner, an old woman crippled and bent with age, came hobbling into the office and told her story. It stirred Lincoln up, and he walked over to the agent's office and made a demand for a return of the money, but without success. Then suit was brought. The day before the trial I hunted up for Lincoln, at his request, a history of the Revolutionary War, of which he read a good portion. He told me to remain during the trial until I had heard his address to the jury. " For," said he, " I am going to skin Wright, and get that money back." The only witness we introduced was the old lady, who through her tears told her story. In his speech to the jury, Lincoln recounted the causes leading to the outbreak of the Revolutionary struggle, and then drew a vivid picture of the hardships of Valley Forge, describing with minuteness the men, barefooted and with bleeding feet, creeping over the ice. As he reached that point in his speech wherein he narrated the hardened action of the defendant in fleecing the old woman of her pension his eyes flashed, and throwing aside his handkerchief, which he held in his right hand, he fairly launched into him. His speech for the next five or ten minutes justified the declaration of Davis, that he was " hurtful in denunciation and merciless in castigation." There was no rule of court to restrain him in his argument, and I never, either on the stump or on other occasions in court, saw him so wrought up. Before he closed, he drew an ideal picture of the plaintiff's husband, the deceased soldier, parting with his wife at the threshold of their home, and kissing their little babe in the cradle, as he started for the war. " Time rolls by," he said, in conclusion ; " the heroes of '76 have passed away and are encamped on the other shore. The soldier has gone to rest, and now, crippled, blinded, and broken, his widow comes to you and to me, gentlemen of the jury, to right her wrongs. She was not always thus. She was once a beautiful young woman. Her step was as elastic, her face as fair, and her voice as sweet as any that rang in the mountains of old Virginia. But now she is poor and defenceless. Out here on the prairies of Illinois, many hundreds of miles away from the scenes of her childhood, she appeals to us, who enjoy the privileges achieved for us by the patriots of the Revolution, for our sympathetic aid and manly protection. All I ask is, shall we befriend her?" The speech made the desired impression on the jury. Half of them were in tears, while the defendant sat in the court room, drawn up and writhing under the fire of Lincoln's fierce invective. The jury returned a verdict in our favor for every cent we demanded. Lincoln was so much interested in the old lady that he became her surety for costs, paid her way home, and her hotel bill while she was in Springfield. When the judgment was paid we remitted the proceeds to her and made no charge for our services. Lincoln's notes for the argument were unique: " No contract.—Not professional services.—Unreasonable charge.—Money retained by Def't not given by Pl'ff.—Revolutionary War.—Describe Valley Forge privations.—Ice—Soldier's bleeding feet.—Pl'ff's husband.—Soldier leaving home for army.—*Skin Def't.*—Close."

It must not be inferred from this that Lincoln was in the habit of slopping over. He never

hunted up acts of injustice, but if they came to him
he was easily enlisted. In 1855 he was attending
court at the town of Clinton, Illinois. Fifteen
ladies from a neighboring village in the county had
been indicted for trespass. Their offence consisted in sweeping down on one Tanner, the
keeper of a saloon in the village, and knocking in
the heads of his barrels. Lincoln was not employed
in the case, but sat watching the trial as it proceeded. In defending the ladies their attorney
seemed to evince a little want of tact, and this
prompted one of the former to invite Mr. Lincoln to
add a few words to the jury, if he thought he could
aid their cause. He was too gallant to refuse and,
their attorney having consented, he made use of
the following argument: "In this case I would
change the order of indictment and have it read
The State *vs.* Mr. Whiskey, instead of The State *vs.*
The Ladies; and touching these there are three laws:
The law of self-protection; the law of the land, or
statute law; and the moral law, or law of God.
First, the law of self-protection is a law of necessity,
as evinced by our forefathers in casting the tea
overboard and asserting their right to the pursuit
of life, liberty, and happiness. In this case it is
the only defense the ladies have, for Tanner neither
feared God nor regarded man. Second, the law
of the land, or statute law, and Tanner is recreant
to both. Third, the moral law, or law of God, and
this is probably a law for the violation of which
the jury can fix no punishment." Lincoln gave
some of his own observations on the ruinous

effects of whiskey in society, and demanded its early suppression. After he had concluded, the Court, without awaiting the return of the jury, dismissed the ladies, saying : " Ladies, go home. I will require no bond of you, and if any fine is ever wanted of you, we will let you know."

After Lincoln's death a fellow-lawyer paid this tribute to him :* " He was wonderfully kind, careful, and just. He had an immense stock of common-sense, and he had faith enough in it to trust it in every emergency. Mr. Lincoln's love of justice and fair-play was his predominating trait. I have often listened to him when I thought he would certainly state his case out of court. It was not in his nature to assume or attempt to bolster up a false position.† He would abandon his case first.

---

* Joseph Gillespie, MS., Letter, Oct. 8, 1886.

† " Early in 1858 at Danville, Ill., I met Lincoln, Swett, and others who had returned from court in an adjoining county, and were dis-cussing the various features of a murder trial in which Lincoln had made a vigorous fight for the prosecution and Swett had defended. The plea of the defense was insanity. On inquiring the name of the defendant I was surprised to learn that it was my old friend Isaac Wyant, formerly of Indiana. I told them that I had been Wyant's counsel frequently and had defended him from almost every charge in the calendar of crimes ; and that he was a weak brother and could be led into almost everything. At once Lincoln began to manifest great interest in Wyant's history, and had to be told all about him. The next day on the way to the court-house he told me he had been greatly troubled over what I related about Wyant ; that his sleep had been disturbed by the fear that he had been too bitter and unre-lenting in his prosecution of him. " I acted," he said, " on the the-ory that he was 'possuming insanity, and now I fear I have been too severe and that the poor fellow may be insane after all. If he cannot realize the wrong of his crime, then I was wrong in aiding to punish him.'''—Hon. Joseph E. McDonald, August, 1888. State-ment to J. W. W.

He did so in the case of Buckmaster for the use of Dedham *vs.* Beems and Arthur, in our Supreme Court, in which I happened to be opposed to him. Another gentleman, less fastidious, took Mr. Lincoln's place and gained the case."

A widow who owned a piece of valuable land employed Lincoln and myself to examine the title to the property, with the view of ascertaining whether certain alleged tax liens were just or not. In tracing back the title we were not satisfied with the description of the ground in one of the deeds of conveyance. Lincoln, to settle the matter, took his surveying instruments and surveyed the ground himself. The result proved that Charles Matheney, a former grantor, had sold the land at so much per acre, but that in describing it he had made an error and conveyed more land than he received pay for. This land descended to our client, and Lincoln after a careful survey and calculation, decided that she ought to pay to Matheney's heirs the sum which he had shown was due them by reason of the erroneous conveyance. To this she entered strenuous objections, but when assured that unless she consented to this act of plain justice we would drop the case, she finally, though with great reluctance, consented. She paid the required amount, and this we divided up into smaller sums proportioned to the number of heirs. Lincoln himself distributed these to the heirs, obtaining a receipt from each one.*

---

* "DEAR HERNDON:

"One morning, not long before Lincoln's nomination—a year perhaps—I was in your office and heard the following: Mr. Lincoln,

While Mr. Lincoln was no financier and had no propensity to acquire property,—no avarice of the get,—yet he had the capacity of retention, or the avarice of the keep. He never speculated in lands or anything else. In the days of land offices and " choice lots in a growing town " he had many opportunities to make safe ventures promising good returns, but he never availed himself of them. His brother lawyers were making good investments and lucky turns, some of them, Davis, for example, were rapidly becoming wealthy; but Lincoln cared nothing for speculation ; in fact there was no ventursome spirit in him. His habits were very simple. He was not fastidious as to food or dress. His hat was brown, faded, and the nap usually worn or rubbed off. He wore a short cloak and sometimes a shawl. His coat and vest hung loosely on his gaunt frame, and his trousers were invariably too short. On the

---

seated at the baize-covered table in the center of the office, listened attentively to a man who talked earnestly and in a low tone. After being thus engaged for some time Lincoln at length broke in, and I shall never forget his reply. ' Yes,' he said, ' we can doubtless gain your case for you ; we can set a whole neighborhood at loggerheads ; we can distress a widowed mother and her six fatherless children and thereby get for you six hundred dollars to which you seem to have a legal claim, but which rightfully belongs, it appears to me, as much to the woman and her children as it does to you. You must remember that some things legally right are not morally right. We shall not take your case, but will give you a little advice for which we will charge you nothing. You seem to be a sprightly, energetic man ; we would advise you to try your hand at making six hundred dollars in some other way.'

" Yours,

" LORD."

From undated MS., about 1866.

circuit he carried in one hand a faded green umbrella, with "A. Lincoln" in large white cotton or muslin letters sewed on the inside. The knob was gone from the handle, and when closed a piece of cord was usually tied around it in the middle to keep it from flying open. In the other hand he carried a literal carpet-bag, in which were stored the few papers to be used in court, and undercloth-ing enough to last till his return to Springfield. He slept in a long, coarse, yellow flannel shirt, which reached half-way between his knees and ankles. It probably was not made to fit his bony figure as completely as Beau Brummel's shirt, and hence we can somewhat appreciate the sensation of a young lawyer who, on seeing him thus arrayed for the first time, observed afterwards that, "He was the ungodliest figure I ever saw."

"He never complained of the food, bed, or lodg-ings. If every other fellow grumbled at the bill-of-fare which greeted us at many of the dingy tav-erns," says David Davis, "Lincoln said nothing." He was once presiding as judge in the absence of Davis, and the case before him was an action brought by a merchant against the father of a minor son for a suit of clothes sold to the son without parental authority. The real question was whether the clothes were necessary, and suited to the condition of the son's life. The father was a wealthy farmer; the bill for the clothing was twenty-eight dollars. I happened in court just as Lincoln was rendering his decision. He ruled against the plea of necessity. "I have rarely in my life," said he, "worn a suit of clothes costing twenty-eight dollars."

"Several of us lawyers," remarked one of his colleagues, "in the eastern end of the circuit annoyed Lincoln once while he was holding court for Davis by attempting to defend against a note to which there were many makers. We had no legal, but a good moral defense, but what we wanted most of all was to stave it off till the next term of court by one expedient or another. We bothered "the court" about it till late on Saturday, the day of adjournment. He adjourned for supper with nothing left but this case to dispose of. After supper he heard our twaddle for nearly an hour, and then made this odd entry : ' L. D. Chaddon *vs.* J. D. Beasley *et al.* April Term, 1856. Champaign County Court. Plea in abatement by B. Z. Green, a defendant not served, filed Saturday at 11 o'clock A. M., April 24, 1856, stricken from the files by order of court. Demurrer to declaration, if there ever was one, overruled. Defendants who are served now, at 8 o'clock, P. M., of the last day of the term, ask to plead to the merits, which is denied by the court on the ground that the offer comes too late, and therefore, as by *nil dicet*, judgment is rendered for Pl'ff. Clerk assess damages. A. Lincoln, Judge *pro tem.*' " The lawyer who reads this singular entry will appreciate its oddity if no one else does. After making it one of the lawyers, on recovering his astonishment, ventured to enquire, " Well, Lincoln,

---

how can we get this case up again?" Lincoln eyed him quizzically a moment, and then answered, "You have all been so 'mighty smart about this case you can find out how to take it up again yourselves."*

The same gentleman who furnishes this last incident, and who was afterward a trusted friend of Mr. Lincoln, Henry C. Whitney, has described most happily the delights of a life on the circuit. A bit of it, referring to Lincoln, I apprehend, cannot be deemed out of place here. "In October, 1854, Abraham Lincoln," he relates, " drove into our town (Urbana) to attend court. He had the appearance of a rough, intelligent farmer, and his rude, home-made buggy and raw-boned horse enforced this belief. I had met him for the first time in June of the same year. David Davis and Leonard Swett had just preceded him. The next morning he

---

* " During my first attendance at court in Menard County," relates a lawyer who travelled the circuit with Lincoln, "some thirty young men had been indicted for playing cards, and Lincoln and I were employed in their defense. The prosecuting attorney, in framing the indictments, alternately charged the defendants with playing a certain game of cards called 'seven-up,' and in the next bill charged them with playing cards at a certain game called 'old sledge.' Four defendants were indicted in each bill. The prosecutor, being entirely unacquainted with games at cards, did not know the fact that both 'seven-up' and 'old sledge' were one and the same. Upon the trial on the bills describing the game as 'seven-up' our witnesses would swear that the game played was 'old sledge,' and vice versa on the bills alleging the latter. The result was an acquittal in every case under the instructions of the Court. The prosecutor never found out the dodge until the trials were over, and immense fun and rejoicing were indulged in at the result."

started North, on the Illinois Central Railroad, and as he went in an old omnibus he played on a boy's harp all the way to the depot. I used to attend the Danville court, and while there, usually roomed with Lincoln and Davis. We stopped at McCormick's hotel, an old-fashioned frame country tavern. Jurors, counsel, prisoners, everybody ate at a long table. The judge, Lincoln, and I had the ladies' parlor fitted up with two beds. Lincoln, Swett, McWilliams, of Bloomington, Voorhees, of Covington, Ind., O. L. Davis, Drake, Ward Lamon, Lawrence, Beckwith, and O. F. Harmon, of Danville, Whiteman, of Iroquois County, and Chandler, of Williamsport, Ind., constituted the bar. Lincoln, Davis, Swett, I, and others who came from the western part of the state would drive from Urbana. The distance was thirty-six miles. We sang and exchanged stories all the way. We had no hesitation in stopping at a farm-house and ordering them to kill and cook a chicken for dinner. By dark we reached Danville. Lamon would have whiskey in his office for the drinking ones, and those who indulged in petty gambling would get by themselves and play till late in the night. Lincoln, Davis, and a few local wits would spend the evening in Davis's room, talking politics, wisdom, and fun. Lincoln and Swett were the great lawyers, and Lincoln always wanted Swett in jury cases. We who stopped at the hotel would all breakfast together and frequently go out into the woods and hold court. We were of more consequence than a court and bar is now. The feelings were those of great fraternity in the bar, and if we desired to restrict our circle it was no trouble for Davis to freeze out any disagreeable persons. Lincoln was fond of going all by himself to any little show or concert. I have known him to slip away and spend the entire evening at a little magic lantern show intended for children. A travelling concert company, calling themselves the 'Newhall Family,' were sure of drawing Lincoln. One of their number, Mrs. Hillis, a good singer, he used to tell us was the only woman who ever seemed to exhibit any liking for him. I attended a negro-minstrel show in Chicago, where we heard Dixie sung. It was entirely new, and pleased him greatly. In court he was irrepressible and apparently inexhaustible in his fund of stories. Where in the world a man who had travelled so little and struggled amid the restrictions of such limited surroundings could gather up such apt and unique yarns we never could guess. Davis appreciated Lincoln's talent in this direction, and was always ready to stop business to hear one of his stories. Lincoln was very bashful when in the presence of ladies. I remember once we were invited to take tea at a friend's house, and while in the parlor I was called to the front gate to see a client. When I returned, Lincoln, who had undertaken to entertain the ladies, was twisting and squirming in his chair, and as bashful as a schoolboy. Everywhere, though we met a hard crowd at every court, and though things were free and easy, we were treated with great respect."

Probably the most important lawsuit Lincoln

and I conducted was one in which we defended the
Illinois Central Railroad in an action brought by
McLean County, Illinois, in August, 1853, to recover
taxes alleged to be due the county from the road.
The Legislature had granted the road immunity
from taxation, and this was a case intended
to test the constitutionality of the law. The
road sent a retainer fee of $250. In the lower court
the case was decided in favor of the railroad. An
appeal to the Supreme Court followed, and there it
was argued twice, and finally decided in our favor.
This last decision was rendered some time in 1855.
Mr. Lincoln soon went to Chicago and presented
our bill for legal services. We only asked for
$2000 more. The official to whom he was referred,
—supposed to have been the superintendent George
B. McClellan who afterwards became the eminent
general,— looking at the bill expressed great surprise. " Why, sir," he exclaimed, " this is as much
as Daniel Webster himself would have charged.
We cannot allow such a claim." Stung by the re-
buff, Lincoln withdrew the bill, and started for
home. On the way he stopped at Bloomington.
There he met Grant Goodrich, Archibald Williams,
Norman B. Judd, O. H. Browning, and other
attorneys, who, on learning of his modest charge
for such valuable services rendered the railroad,
induced him to increase the demand to $5000,
and to bring suit for that sum. This was done at
once. On the trial six lawyers certified that the
bill was reasonable, and judgment for that sum
went by default. The judgment was promptly paid.

Lincoln gave me my half, and much as we deprecated the avarice of great corporations, we both thanked the Lord for letting the Illinois Central Railroad fall into our hands.

In the summer of 1857 Lincoln was employed by Mr. Manny, of Rockford, Ill., to defend him in an action brought by McCormick,* who was one of the inventors of the reaping machine, for infringement of patent. Lincoln had been recommended to Manny by E. B. Washburne, then a member of Congress from northern Illinois. The case was to be tried before Judge McLean at Cincinnati, in the Circuit Court of the United States. The counsel for McCormick was Reverdy Johnson. Edwin M. Stanton and George Harding, of Philadelphia, were associated on the other side with Lincoln. The latter came to Cincinnati a few days before the argument took place, and stopped at the house of a friend. " The case was one of great importance pecuniarily," relates a lawyer † in Cincinnati, who was a member of the bar at the time, "and in the law questions involved. Reverdy Johnson represented the plaintiff. Mr. Lincoln had prepared himself with the greatest care ; his ambition was up to speak in the case and to measure swords with the renowned lawyer from Baltimore. It was understood between his client and himself before his coming that Mr. Harding, of Philadelphia, was to be associated with him in the case, and was to make the ' mechanical argument.'

---

* The case, McCormick *vs.* Manny, is reported in 6 McLean's Rep., p. 539.

† W. M. Dickson.

After reaching Cincinnati, Mr. Lincoln was a little surprised and annoyed to learn that his client had also associated with him Mr. Edwin M. Stanton, of Pittsburg, and a lawyer of our own bar, the reason assigned being that the importance of the case required a man of the experience and power of Mr. Stanton to meet Mr. Johnson. The Cincinnati lawyer was appointed for his 'local influence.' These reasons did not remove the slight conveyed in the employment without consultation with him of this additional counsel. He keenly felt it, but acquiesced. The trial of the case came on; the counsel for defense met each morning for consultation. On one of these occasions one of the counsel moved that only two of them should speak in the case. This matter was also acquiesced in. It had always been understood that Mr. Harding was to speak to explain the mechanism of the reapers. So this motion excluded either Mr. Lincoln or Mr. Stanton, —which? By the custom of the bar, as between counsel of equal standing, and in the absence of any action of the client, the original counsel speaks. By this rule Mr. Lincoln had precedence. Mr. Stanton suggested to Mr. Lincoln to make the speech. Mr. Lincoln answered, 'No, you speak.' Mr. Stanton replied, 'I will,' and taking up his hat, said he would go and make preparation. Mr. Lincoln acquiesced in this, but was greatly grieved and mortified; he took but little more interest in the case, though remaining until the conclusion of the trial. He seemed to be greatly depressed, and gave evidence of that tendency to melancholy

26

which so marked his character. His parting on leaving the city cannot be forgotten. Cordially shaking the hand of his hostess he said: ' You have made my stay here most agreeable, and I am a thousand times obliged .to you ; but in reply to your request for me to come again, I must say to you I never expect to be in Cincinnati again. I have nothing against the city, but things have so happened here as to make it undesirable for me ever to return.' Lincoln felt that Stanton had not only been very discourteous to him, but had purposely ignored him in the case, and that he had received rather rude, if not unkind, treatment from all hands. Stanton, in his brusque and abrupt way, it is said, described him as a ' long, lank creature from Illinois, wearing a dirty linen duster for a coat, on the back of which the perspiration had splotched wide stains that resembled a map of the continent. Mr. Lincoln," adds Mr. Dickson, " remained in Cincinnati about a week, moving freely around, yet not twenty men knew him personally or knew he was here ; not a hundred would have known who he was had his name been given to them. He came with the fond hope of making fame in a forensic contest with Reverdy Johnson. He was pushed aside, humiliated and mortified. He attached to the innocent city the displeasure that filled his bosom, and shook its dust from his feet." On his return to Springfield he was somewhat reticent regarding the trial, and, contrary to his custom, communicated to his associates at the bar but few of its incidents. He told me that he had been "roughly handled by that man Stanton"; that he overheard the latter from an adjoining room, while the door was slightly ajar, referring to Lincoln, inquire of another, "Where did that long-armed creature come from, and what can he expect to do in this case?" During the trial Lincoln formed a poor opinion of Judge McLean. He characterized him as an "old granny," with considerable vigor of mind, but no perception at all. " If you were to point your finger at him," he put it, " and a darning needle at the same time he never would know which was the sharpest."

As Lincoln grew into public favor and achieved such marked success in the profession, half the bar of Springfield began to be envious of his growing popularity. I believe there is less jealousy and bitter feeling among lawyers than professional men of any other class ; but it should be borne in mind that in that early day a portion of the bar in every county seat, if not a majority of the lawyers everywhere, were politicians. Stuart frequently differed from Lincoln on political questions, and was full of envy. Likewise those who coincided with Lincoln in his political views were disturbed in the same way. Even Logan was not wholly free from the degrading passion. But in this respect Lincoln suffered no more than other great characters who preceded him in the world's history.

That which Lincoln's adversaries in a lawsuit feared most of all was his apparent disregard of custom or professional propriety in managing a case before a jury. He brushed aside all rules, and very often resorted to some strange and strategic performance which invariably broke his opponent down or exercised some peculiar influence over the jury. Hence the other side in a case were in constant fear of one of his dramatic strokes, or trembled lest he should "ring in" some ingeniously planned interruption not on the programme. In a case where Judge Logan—always earnest and grave—opposed him, Lincoln created no little merriment by his reference to Logan's style of dress. He carried the surprise in store for the latter, till he reached his turn before the jury. Addressing them, he said: "Gentlemen, you must be careful and not permit yourselves to be overcome by the eloquence of counsel for the defense. Judge Logan, I know, is an effective lawyer. I have met him too often to doubt that; but shrewd and careful though he be, still he is sometimes wrong. Since this trial has begun I have discovered that, with all his caution and fastidiousness, he hasn't knowledge enough to put his shirt on right." Logan turned red as crimson, but sure enough, Lincoln was correct, for the former had donned a new shirt, and by mistake had drawn it over his head with the pleated bosom behind. The general laugh which followed destroyed the effect of Logan's eloquence over the jury—the very point at which Lincoln aimed.

The trial of William Armstrong* for the murder

---

* This incident in Lincoln's career has been most happily utilized by Dr. Edward Eggleston in his story "The Graysons," recently published in the *Century Magazine.*

of James P. Metzger, in May, 1858, at Beardstown, Illinois, in which Lincoln secured the acquittal of the defendant, was one of the gratifying triumphs in his career as a lawyer. Lincoln's defense, wherein he floored the principal prosecuting witness, who had testified positively to seeing the fatal blow struck in the moonlight, by showing from an almanac that the moon had set, was not more convincing than his eloquent and irresistible appeal in his client's favor. The latter's mother, old Hannah Armstrong, the friend of his youth, had solicited him to defend her son. "He told the jury," relates the prosecuting attorney, " of his once being a poor, friendless boy ; that Armstrong's parents took him into their house, fed and clothed him, and gave him a home. There were tears in his eyes as he spoke. The sight of his tall, quivering frame, and the particulars of the story he so pathetically told, moved the jury to tears also, and they forgot the guilt of the defendant in their admiration of his advocate. It was the most touching scene I ever witnessed." * Before passing it may be well to listen to the humble tribute of old Hannah Armstrong, the defendant's mother : "Lincoln had said to me, ' Hannah, your son will be cleared before sundown.' I left the court-room, and they came and told me that my son was cleared and a free man. I went up to the court-house. The jury shook hands with me ; so did the judge and Lincoln ; tears streamed down Lincoln's eyes . . . . After the trial I asked him

---

* J. Henry Shaw, letter, Aug. 22, 1866, MS.

what his fee would be; told him I was poor. 'Why, Hannah,' he said, 'I sha'n't charge you a cent, and anything else I can do for you, will do it willingly and without charge.' He afterwards wrote to me about a piece of land which certain men were trying to get from me, and said: 'Hannah, they can't get your land. Let them try it in the Circuit Court, and then you appeal it; bring it to the Supreme Court and I and Herndon will attend to it for nothing.' " *

The last suit of any importance in which Lincoln was personally engaged, was known as the Johnson sand-bar case. It involved the title to certain lands, the accretion on the shores of Lake Michigan, in or near Chicago. It was tried in the United States Circuit Court at Chicago in April and May, 1860. During the trial, the Court—Judge Drummond—and all the counsel on both sides dined at the residence of Isaac N. Arnold, afterwards a member of Congress. "Douglas and Lincoln," relates Mr. Arnold, "were at the time both candidates for the nomination for President. There were active and ardent political friends of each at the table, and when the sentiment was proposed, 'May Illinois furnish the next President,' it was drank with enthusiasm by the friends of both Lincoln and Douglas."†

I could fill this volume with reminiscences of Lincoln's career as a lawyer, but lest the reader should tire of what must savor in many cases of monotony

---

* From statement, Nov. 24, 1865.

† Arnold's "Lincoln," p. 90.

it is best to move on. I have made this portion of
the book rather full ; but as Lincoln's individuality
and peculiarities were more marked in the law office
and court-room than anywhere else it will play its
part in making up the picture of the man. Enough
has been told to show how, in the face of adverse
fortune and the lack of early training, and by force
of his indomitable will and self-confidence, he gained
such ascendency among the lawyers of Illinois.
The reader is enabled thereby to understand the
philosophy of his growth.

But now another field is preparing to claim him.
There will soon be great need for his clear reason,
masterly mind and heroic devotion to principle.
The distant mutterings of an approaching contest
are driving scattered factions into a union of sentiment and action. As the phalanxes of warriors are
preparing for action, amid the rattle of forensic
musketry, Lincoln, their courageous leader, equipped
for battle, springs into view.

CHAPTER II.

WHILE Lincoln in a certain sense was buried in the law from the time his career in Congress closed till, to use his own words, " the repeal of the Missouri Compromise aroused him again," yet he was a careful student of his times and kept abreast of the many and varied movements in politics. He was generally on the Whig electoral tickets, and made himself heard during each successive canvas,*

* In the campaign of 1852, when Pierce was the Democratic candidate for President, Douglas made speeches for him in almost every State in the Union. His "key-note" was sounded at Richmond, Va. Lincoln, whose reputation was limited by the boundaries of Illinois, was invited by the Scott Club of Springfield to answer it, but his soul and heart were not in the undertaking. He had not yet been awakened, and, considering it entire, the speech was a poor effort. Another has truthfully said of it, " If it was distinguished by one quality above another it was by its attempts at humor, and all those attempts were strained and affected, as well as very coarse. He displayed a jealous and petulant temper from the first to the last, wholly beneath the dignity of the occasion and the importance of the topic. Considered as a whole it may be said that none of his public performances was more unworthy of its really noble author than this one. The closing paragraph will serve as a fair sample of the entire speech: " Let us stand by our candidate [Gen. Scott] as faithfully as he has always stood by our country, and I much doubt if we do not perceive a slight abatement of Judge Douglas's confidence in Providence as well as the people. I suspect that confidence is not more firmly fixed with the Judge than it was with the old woman whose horse ran away with her in a buggy. She said

but he seemed to have lost that zealous interest in politics which characterized his earlier days. He plodded on unaware of, and seemingly without ambition for, the great distinction that lay in store for him. John T. Stuart relates* that, as he and Lincoln were returning from the court in Tazewell county in 1850, and were nearing the little town of Dillon, they engaged in a discussion of the political situation. " As we were coming down the hill," are Stuart's words, " I said, ' Lincoln, the time is coming when we shall have to be all either Abolitionists or Democrats.' He thought a moment and then answered, ruefully and emphatically, ' When that time comes my mind is made up, for I believe the slavery question can never be successfully compromised.' I responded with equal emphasis, ' My mind is made up too.' " Thus it was with Lincoln. But he was too slow to suit the impetuous demand of the few pronounced Abolitionists whom he met in his daily walks. The sentiment of the majority in Springfield tended in the other direction, and, thus environed, Lincoln lay down like the sleeping lion. The future would yet arouse him. At that time I was an ardent Abolitionist in sentiment. I used to warn Lincoln against his apparent conservatism when the needs of the hour were so great ; but his only answer would be, ' Billy, you're

---

she trusted in Providence till the ' britchen' broke, and then she didn't know what on ' airth' to do. The chance is the Judge will see the ' britchen' broke, and then he can at his leisure bewail the fate of Locofocoism as the victim of misplaced confidence."

* Statement, J. T. S., MS., July 21, 1865.

too rampant and spontaneous.' I was in correspondence with Sumner, Greeley, Phillips, and Garrison, and was thus thoroughly imbued with all the
rancor drawn from such strong anti-slavery sources.
I adhered to Lincoln, relying on the final outcome of
his sense of justice and right. Every time a good
speech on the great issue was made I sent for it.
Hence you could find on my table the latest utterances of Giddings, Phillips, Sumner, Seward, and
one whom I considered grander than all the others
—Theodore Parker. Lincoln and I took such
papers as the Chicago *Tribune*, New York *Tribune*,
Anti-Slavery Standard, *Emancipator*, and *National
Era*. On the other side of the question we took the
Charleston *Mercury* and the Richmond *Enquirer*.
I also bought a book called " Sociology," written
by one Fitzhugh, which defended and justified
slavery in every conceivable way. In addition I purchased all the leading histories of the slavery movement, and other works which treated on that subject.
Lincoln himself never bought many books, but he
and I both read those I have named. After reading them we would discuss the questions they
touched upon and the ideas they suggested, from
our different points of view. I was never conscious
of having made much of an impression on Mr. Lincoln, nor do I believe I ever changed his views.
I will go further and say, that, from the profound
nature of his conclusions and the labored method
by which he arrived at them, no man is entitled to
the credit of having either changed or greatly modified them. I remember once, after having read one

of Theodore Parker's sermons on slavery, saying
to Mr. Lincoln substantially this: "I have always
noticed that ill-gotten wealth does no man any good.
This is as true of nations as individuals. I believe
that all the ill-gotten gain wrenched by us from the
negro through his enslavement will eventually be
taken from us, and we will be set back where we
began." Lincoln thought my prophecy rather dire-
ful. He doubted seriously if either of us would
live to see the righting of so great a wrong ; but
years after, when writing his second Inaugural address, he endorsed the idea. Clothing it in the most
beautiful language, he says: "Yet if God wills that
it [the war] continue till all the wealth piled by
the bondsman's two hundred and fifty years of unrequited toil shall be sunk, and until every drop of
blood drawn by the lash shall be paid by another
drawn by the sword, as was said three thousand
years ago, so still it must be said, 'The judgments
of the Lord are true and righteous altogether.'"

The passage in May, 1854, of the Kansas-
Nebraska bill swept out of sight the Missouri Compromise and the Compromise measures of 1850. This
bill, designed and carried through by Douglas, was
regarded by him as the masterpiece of all his varied
achievements in legislation. It served to prove
more clearly than anything he had ever before
done his flexibility and want of political conscience.
Although in years gone before he had invoked the
vengeance of Heaven on the ruthless hand that
should dare to disturb the sanctity of the compact
of 1821, yet now he was the arrogant and audacious

leader in the very work he had so heartily condemned. When we consider the bill and the unfortunate results which followed it in the border States we are irresistibly led to conclude that it was, all things considered, a great public wrong and a most lamentable piece of political jugglery. The stump speech which Thomas H. Benton charged that Douglas had " injected into the belly of the bill " contains all there was of Popular Sovereignty—" It being the true intent and meaning of this act not to legislate slavery into any Territory or State nor to exclude it therefrom, but to leave the people thereof perfectly free to form and regulate their domestic institutions in their own way, subject only to the Constitution of the United States," an argument which, using Lincoln's words, " amounts to this: That if any one man chooses to enslave another no third man shall be allowed to object." The widespread feeling the passage of this law aroused everywhere over the Union is a matter of general history. It stirred up in New England the latent hostility to the aggression of slavery; it stimulated to extraordinary endeavors the derided Abolitionists, arming them with new weapons; it sounded the death-knell of the gallant old Whig party; it drove together strange, discordant elements in readiness to fight a common enemy; it brought to the forefront a leader in the person of Lincoln.

The revolt of Cook, Judd, and Palmer, all young and progressive, from the Democratic majority in the Legislature was the first sign of discontent in Illinois. The rude and partly hostile reception of

Douglas, on his arrival in Chicago, did not in any degree tend to allay the feeling of disapproval so general in its manifestation. The warriors, young and old, removed their armor from the walls, and began preparations for the impending conflict. Lincoln had made a few speeches in aid of Scott during the campaign of 1852, but they were efforts entirely unworthy of the man. Now, however, a live issue was presented to him. No one realized this sooner than he. In the office discussions he grew bolder in his utterances. He insisted that the social and political difference between slavery and freedom was becoming more marked; that one must overcome the other; and that postponing the struggle between them would only make it the more deadly in the end. "The day of compromise," he still contended, " has passed. These two great ideas have been kept apart only by the most artful means. They are like two wild beasts in sight of each other, but chained and held apart. Some day these deadly antagonists will one or the other break their bonds, and then the question will be settled." In a conversation with a fellow-lawyer * he said of slavery: "It is the most glittering, ostentatious, and displaying property in the world, and now, if a young man goes courting, the only inquiry is how many negroes he or his lady-love owns. The love for slave property is swallowing up every other mercenary possession. Slavery is a great and crying injustice—an enormous national crime." At another time he made the

---

* Joseph Gillespie, MS. letter, June 9, '66.

observation that it was "singular that the courts would hold that a man never lost his right to his property that had been stolen from him, but that he instantly lost his right to himself if he was stolen." It is useless to add more evidence—for it could be piled mountain high—showing that at the very outset Mr. Lincoln was sound to the core on the injustice and crime of human slavery.

After a brief rest at his home in Chicago Mr. Douglas betook himself to the country, and in October, during the week of the State Fair, we find him in Springfield. On Tuesday he made a speech in the State House which, in view of the hostile attitude of some of his own party friends, was a labored defense of his position. It was full of ingenious sophistry and skilful argument. An unprecedented concourse of people had gathered from all parts of the State, and Douglas, fresh from the halls of Congress, was the lion of the hour. On the following day Mr. Lincoln, as the champion of the opponents of Popular Sovereignty, was selected to represent those who disagreed with the new legislation, and to answer Douglas. His speech encouraged his friends no less than it startled his enemies. At this time I was zealously interested in the new movement, and not less so in Lincoln. I frequently wrote the editorials in the Springfield *Journal*, the editor, Simeon Francis, giving to Lincoln and to me the utmost liberty in that direction. Occasionally Lincoln would write out matter for publication, but I believe I availed myself of the privilege oftener than he. The editorial in the issue containing the speeches of Lincoln and Douglas on this occasion was my own, and while in description it may seem rather strongly imbued with youthful enthusiasm, yet on reading it in maturer years I am still inclined to believe it reasonably faithful to the facts and the situation. "The anti-Nebraska speech of Mr. Lincoln," says the article, "was the profoundest in our opinion that he has made in his whole life. He felt upon his soul the truths burn which he uttered, and all present felt that he was true to his own soul. His feelings once or twice swelled within, and came near stifling utterance. He quivered with emotion. The whole house was as still as death. He attacked the Nebraska bill with unusual warmth and energy; and all felt that a man of strength was its enemy, and that he intended to blast it if he could by strong and manly efforts. He was most successful, and the house approved the glorious triumph of truth by loud and continued huzzas. Women waved their white handkerchiefs in token of woman's silent but heartfelt assent. Douglas felt the sting; the animal within him was roused because he frequently interrupted Mr. Lincoln. His friends felt that he was crushed by Lincoln's powerful argument, manly logic, and illustrations from nature around us. The Nebraska bill was shivered, and like a tree of the forest was torn and rent asunder by the hot bolts of truth. Mr. Lincoln exhibited Douglas in all the attitudes he could be placed, in a friendly debate. He exhibited the bill in all its aspects to show its humbuggery and falsehood, and, when thus torn to rags, cut into slips, held up to the gaze of the vast crowd, a kind of scorn and mockery was visible upon the face of the crowd and upon the lips of their most eloquent speaker. At the conclusion of this speech every man and child felt that it was unanswerable. He took the heart captive and broke like a sun over the understanding."

Anent the subject of editorial writing it may not be inappropriate to relate that Lincoln and I both kept on furnishing political matter of many varieties for the Springfield *Journal* until 1860. Many of the editorials that I wrote were intended directly or indirectly to promote the interest of Lincoln. I wrote one on the advisability of annexing Cuba to the United States, taking the rather advanced ground that slavery would be abolished in Cuba before it would in this country—a position which aroused no little controversy with other papers. One little incident occurs to me in this connection which may not be without interest to newspaper men. A newspaper had been started in Springfield called the *Conservative*, which, it was believed, was being run in the interest of the Democratic party. While pretending to support Fillmore it was kept alive by Buchanan men and other kindred spirits, who were somewhat pro-slavery in their views. The thing was damaging Lincoln and the friends of freedom more than an avowed Democratic paper could. The editor, an easy, good-natured fellow, simply placed in charge to execute the will of those who gave the paper its financial backing, was a good friend of mine, and by means of this friendship I was always well informed of matters in the *Conservative* editorial room. One day I read in the Richmond *Enquirer* an article endorsing slavery, and arguing that from principle the enslavement of either whites or blacks was justifiable and right. I showed it to Lincoln, who remarked that it was "rather rank doctrine for Northern Democrats to endorse. I should like to see," he said, with emphasis, "some of these Illinois newspapers champion that." I told him if he would only wait and keep his own counsel I would have a pro-slavery organ in Springfield publish that very article. He doubted it, but when I told him how it was to be done he laughed and said, "Go in." I cut the slip out and succeeded in getting it in the paper named. Of course it was a trick, but it acted admirably. Its appearance in the new organ, although without comment, almost ruined that valuable journal, and my good-natured friend the editor was nearly overcome by the denunciation of those who were responsible for the organ's existence. My connection, and Lincoln's too,—for he endorsed the trick,—with the publication of the condemned article was eventually discovered, and we were thereafter effectually prevented from getting another line in the paper. The anti-slavery people quoted the article as having been endorsed by a Democratic newspaper in Springfield, and Lincoln himself used it with telling effect. He joined in the popular denunciation, expressing great astonishment that such a sentiment could find lodgment in any paper in Illinois,

27

although he knew full well how the whole thing
had been carried through.

During the remainder of the State-Fair week,
speeches were made by Lyman Trumbull, Sidney
Breese, E. D. Taylor, and John Calhoun, none of
which unfortunately have been preserved. Among
those who mingled in the crowd and listened to
them was Owen Lovejoy, a radical, fiery, brave,
fanatical man, it may be, but one full of the virus of
Abolitionism. I had been thoroughly inoculated
with the latter myself, and so had many others, who
helped to swell the throng. The Nebraska movement had kindled anew the old zeal, and inspired us
with renewed confidence to begin the crusade. As
many of us as could, assembled together to organ-
ize for the campaign before us. As soon therefore
as Lincoln finished his speech in the hall of the
House of Representatives, Lovejoy, moving forward
from the crowd, announced a meeting in the same
place that evening of all the friends of Freedom.
That of course meant the Abolitionists with whom
I had been in conference all the day. Their plan
had been to induce Mr. Lincoln to speak for them
at their meeting. Strong as I was in the faith, yet
I doubted the propriety of Lincoln's taking any
stand yet. As I viewed it, he was ambitious to
climb to the United States Senate, and on grounds
of policy it would not do for him to occupy at that
time such advanced ground as we were taking. On
the other hand, it was equally as dangerous to
refuse a speech for the Abolitionists. I did not
know how he felt on the subject, but on learning

that Lovejoy intended to approach him with an invitation, I hunted up Lincoln and urged him to avoid meeting the enthusiastic champion of Abolitionism. "Go home at once," I said. "Take Bob with you and drive somewhere into the country and stay till this thing is over." Whether my admonition and reasoning moved him or not I do not know, but it only remains to state that under pretence of having business in Tazewell county he drove out of town in his buggy, and did not return till the apostles of Abolitionism had separated and gone to their homes.* I have always believed this little arrangement—it would dignify it too much to call it a plan—saved Lincoln. If he had endorsed the resolutions passed at the meeting, or spoken simply in favor of freedom that night, he would have been identified with all the rancor and extremes of Abolitionism. If, on the contrary, he had been invited to join them, and then had refused to take a position as advanced as theirs, he would have lost their support. In either event he was in great danger; and so he who was aspiring to succeed his old rival, James Shields, in the United States Senate was forced to avoid the issue by driving hastily in his one horse buggy to the court in Tazewell county. A singular coincidence suggests itself in the fact that, twelve years before, James Shields and a friend drove hastily in the same direction, and destined for the same point, to force Lincoln to take issue in another and entirely different matter.

---

* See Lincoln's Speech, Joint Debate, Ottawa, Ills., Aug. 20, 1858.

By request of party friends Lincoln was induced to follow after Douglas and, at the various places where the latter had appointments to speak, reply to him. On the 16th of October they met at Peoria, where Douglas enjoyed the advantages of an "open and close." Lincoln made an effective speech, which he wrote out and furnished to the Sangamon *Journal* for publication, and which can be found among his public utterances. His party friends in Springfield and elsewhere, who had urged him to push after Douglas till he cried, "enough,' .were surprised a few days after the Peoria debate to find him at home, with the information that by an agreement with the latter they were both to return home and speak no more during the campaign. Judge of his astonishment a few days later to find that his rival, instead of going direct to his home in Chicago, had stopped at Princeton and violated his express agreement by making a speech there! Lincoln was much displeased at this action of Douglas, which tended to convince him that the latter was really a man devoid of fixed political morals. I remember his explanation in our office made to me, William Butler, William Jayne, Ben. F. Irwin, and other friends, to account for his early withdrawal from the stump. After the Peoria debate Douglas approached him and flattered him by saying that he was giving him more trouble on the territorial and slavery questions than all the United States Senate, and he therefore proposed to him that both should abandon the field and return to their homes. Now Lincoln could never refuse a polite request—one in which no principle was involved. I have heard him say, "It's a fortunate thing I wasn't born a woman, for I cannot refuse anything, it seems." He therefore consented to the cessation of debate proposed by Douglas, and the next day both went to the town of Lacon, where they had been billed for speeches. Their agreement was kept from their friends, and both declined to speak—Douglas, on the ground of hoarseness, and Lincoln gallantly refusing to take advantage of "Judge Douglas's indisposition." Here they separated, Lincoln going directly home, and Douglas, as before related, stopping at Princeton and colliding in debate with Owen Lovejoy. Upon being charged afterwards with his breach of agreement Douglas responded that Lovejoy "bantered and badgered" him so persistently he could not gracefully resist the encounter. The whole thing thoroughly displeased Lincoln.*

During this campaign Lincoln was nominated and elected to the Legislature. This was done in the face of his unwillingness and over his protest. On

----

* In a letter from Princeton, Ill., March 15, 1866, John H. Bryant, brother of the poet William Cullen Bryant, writes: "I have succeeded in finding an old file of our Princeton papers, from which I learn that Mr. Douglas spoke here on Wednesday, Oct. 18, 1854. This fixes the date. I recollect that he staid at Tiskilwa, six miles south of this, the night before, and a number of our Democrats went down the next morning and escorted him to this place. Douglas spoke first one half-hour and was answered by Lovejoy one half-hour, when Douglas talked till dark, giving no opportunity for reply.

"Yours truly,

"JOHN H. BRYANT."

the ticket with him was Judge Logan. Both were elected by a majority of about 600 votes. Lincoln, being ambitious to reach the United States Senate, and warmly encouraged in his aspirations by his wife, resigned his seat in the Legislature in order that he might the more easily be elected to succeed his old rival James Shields, who was then one of the senators from Illinois. His canvass for that exalted office was marked by his characteristic activity and vigilance. During the anxious moments that intervened between the general election and the assembling of the Legislature he slept, like Napoleon, with one eye open. While attending court at Clinton on the 11th of November, a few days after the election, he wrote to a party friend in the town of Paris: " I have a suspicion that a Whig has been elected to the Legislature from Edgar. If this is not so, why then, '*nix cum arous ;*' but if it is so, then could you not make a mark with him for me for U. S. Senator? I really have some chance. Please write me at Springfield giving me the names, post-offices, and political positions of your Representative and Senator, whoever they may be. Let this be confidential."*

That man who thinks Lincoln calmly sat down and gathered his robes about him, waiting for the people to call him, has a very erroneous knowledge of Lincoln. He was always calculating, and always planning ahead. His ambition was a little engine that knew no rest. The vicissitudes of a

---

* Robert Mosely, November 11, 1855, MS.

political campaign brought into play all his **tact** and management and developed to its fullest extent his latent industry. In common with other politicians he never overlooked a newspaper man who had it in his power to say a good or bad thing of him. The press of that day was not so powerful an institution as now, but ambitious politicians courted the favor of a newspaper man with as much zeal as the same class of men have done in later days. I remember a letter Lincoln once wrote to the editor of an obscure little country newspaper in southern Illinois in which he warms up to him in the following style.* " Friend Harding: I have been reading your paper for three or four years and have paid you nothing for it." He then encloses ten dollars and admonishes the editor with innocent complacency: " Put it into your pocket, saying nothing further about it." Very soon thereafter, he prepared an article on political matters and sent it to the rural journalist, requesting its publication in the editorial columns of his " valued paper," but the latter, having followed Lincoln's directions and stowed the ten dollars away in his pocket, and alive to the importance of his journal's influence, declined, " because," he said, " I long ago made it a rule to publish nothing as editorial matter not written by myself." Lincoln read the editor's answer to me. Although the laugh was on Lincoln he enjoyed the joke heartily. " That editor," he said, " has a rather lofty but proper conception of true journalism."

---

* Jacob Harding, May 25, 1855, MS.

Meanwhile the Legislature had convened and the Senatorial question came on for solution. The history of this contest is generally understood, and the world has repeatedly been told how Lincoln was led to expect the place and would have won but for the apostasy of the five anti-Nebraska men of Democratic antecedents who clung to and finally forced the election of Lyman Trumbull. The student of history in after years will be taught to revere the name of Lincoln for his exceeding magnanimity in inducing his friends to abandon him at the critical period and save Trumbull, while he himself disappeared beneath the waves of defeat.*

This frustration of Lincoln's ambition had a

---

* "After a number of ballots—Judd of Cook, Cook of La Salle, Palmer of Macoupin, and Allen and Baker of Madison voting for Trumbull—I asked Mr. Lincoln what he would advise us to do. He answered, 'Go for Trumbull by all means.' We understood the case to be that Shields was to be run by the Democrats at first and then to be dropped, and Joel A. Matteson put up; and it was calculated that certain of our men who had been elected on the 'Free Soil' issue would vote for him after they had acted with us long enough to satisfy their consciences and constituents. Our object was to force an election before they got through with their programme. We were savagely opposed to Matteson, and so was Mr. Lincoln, who said that if we did not drop in and unite upon Trumbull the five men above-named would go for Matteson and elect him, which would be an everlasting disgrace to the State. We reluctantly complied; went to Trumbull and elected him. I remember that Judge S. T. Logan gave up Lincoln with great reluctance. He begged hard to try him on one or two ballots more, but Mr. Lincoln urged us not to risk it longer. I never saw the latter more earnest and decided. He congratulated Trumbull warmly, although of course greatly disappointed and mortified at his own want of success."—Joseph Gillespie, letter, September 19, 1866, MS.

LYMAN TRUMBULL.
Photographed in 1891.

marked effect on his political views. It was plain to him now that the "irrepressible conflict" was not far ahead. With the strengthening of his faith in a just cause so long held in abeyance he became more defiant each day. But in the very nature of things he dared not be as bold and outspoken as I. With him every word and sentence had to be weighed and its effects calculated, before being uttered: but with me that operation had to be reversed if done at all. An incident that occurred about this time will show how his views were broadening. Some time after the election of Trumbull a young negro, the son of a colored woman in Springfield known as Polly, went from his home to St. Louis and there hired as a hand on a lower Mississippi boat,—for what special service, I do not recollect,—arriving in New Orleans without what were known as free papers. Though born free he was subjected to the tyranny of the " black code," all the more stringent because of the recent utterances of the Abolitionists in the North, and was kept in prison until his boat had left. Then, as no one was especially interested in him, he was forgotten. After a certain length of time established by law, he would inevitably have been sold into slavery to defray prison expenses had not Lincoln and I interposed our aid. The mother came to us with the story of the wrong done her son and induced us to interfere in her behalf. We went first to see the Governor of Illinois, who, after patient and thorough examination of the law, responded that he had no right or power to interfere. Recourse was then had to the Governor of Louisiana, who responded in like manner. We were sorely perplexed. A second interview with the Governor of Illinois resulting in nothing favorable Lincoln rose from his chair, hat in hand, and exclaimed with some emphasis: " By God, Governor, I'll make the ground in this country too hot for the foot of a slave, whether you have the legal power to secure the release of this boy or not." Having exhausted all legal means to recover the negro we dropped our relation as lawyers to the case. Lincoln drew up a subscription-list, which I circulated, collecting funds enough to purchase the young man's liberty. The money we sent to Col. A. P. Fields, a friend of ours in New Orleans, who applied it as directed, and it restored the prisoner to his overjoyed mother.

The political history of the country, commencing in 1854 and continuing till the outbreak of the Rebellion, furnishes the student a constant succession of stirring and sometimes bloody scenes. No sooner had Lincoln emerged from the Senatorial contest in February, 1855, and absorbed himself in the law, than the outrages on the borders of Missouri and Kansas began to arrest public attention. The stories of raids, election frauds, murders, and other crimes were moving eastward with marked rapidity. These outbursts of frontier lawlessness, led and sanctioned by the avowed pro-slavery element, were not only stirring up the Abolitionists to fever heat, but touching the hearts of humanity in general. In Illinois an association was formed to aid the cause of " Free-Soil" men in Kansas. In the meetings of these bands the Abolitionists of course took the most prominent part. At Springfield we were energetic, vigilant, almost revolutionary. We recommended the employment of any means, however desperate, to promote and defend the cause of freedom. At one of these meetings Lincoln was called on for a speech. He responded to the request, counselling moderation and less bitterness in dealing with the situation before us. We were belligerent in tone, and clearly out of patience with the Government. Lincoln opposed the notion of coercive measures with the possibility of resulting bloodshed, advising us to eschew resort to the bullet. "You can better succeed," he declared, "with the ballot. You can peaceably then redeem the Government and preserve the liberties of mankind through your votes and voice and moral influence. . . . . Let there be peace. Revolutionize through the ballot box, and restore the Government once more to the affections and hearts of men by making it express, as it was intended to do, the highest spirit of justice and liberty. Your attempt, if there be such, to resist the laws of Kansas by force is criminal and wicked; and all your feeble attempts will be follies and end in bringing sorrow on your heads and ruin the cause you would freely die to preserve!" These judicious words of counsel, while they reduced somewhat our ardor and our desperation, only placed before us in their real colors the grave features of the situation. We raised a neat sum of money, Lincoln showing his sincerity by joining in the subscription, and forwarded it to our friends in Kansas.

The Whig party, having accomplished its mission in the political world, was now on the eve of a great break-up. Lincoln realized this and, though proverbially slow in his movements, prepared to find a firm footing when the great rush of waters should come and the maddening freshet sweep former landmarks out of sight. Of the strongest significance in this connection is a letter written by him at this juncture to an old friend in Kentucky,* who called to his attention their differences of views on the wrong of slavery. Speaking of his observation of the treatment of the slaves, he says: " I confess I hate to see the poor creatures hunted down and caught and carried back to their unrequited toils; but I bite my lips and keep quiet. In 1841 you and I had rather a tedious low-water trip on a steamboat from Louisville to St. Louis. You may remember, as I well do, that from Louisville to the mouth of the Ohio, there were on board ten or a dozen slaves shackled together with irons. That sight was a continued torment to me; and I see something like it every time I touch the Ohio or any slave border. It is not fair for you to assume that I have no interest in a thing which has, and continually exercises, the power of making me miserable. You ought rather to appreciate how much the great body of the Northern people do crucify their feelings in order to maintain their loyalty to the Constitution and the Union. I do oppose the extension of slavery because my judgment and feel-

---

* Letter to Joshua F. Speed, August 24, 1855, MS.

ing so prompt me; and I am under no obligations to the contrary. If for this you and I must differ, differ we must."

Finding himself drifting about with the disorganized elements that floated together after the angry political waters had subsided, it became apparent to Lincoln that if he expected to figure as a leader he must take a stand himself. Mere hatred of slavery and opposition to the injustice of the Kansas-Nebraska legislation were not all that were required of him. He must be a Democrat, Know-Nothing, Abolitionist, or Republican, or forever float about in the great political sea without compass, rudder, or sail. At length he declared himself. Believing the times were ripe for more advanced movements, in the spring of 1856 I drew up a paper for the friends of freedom to sign, calling a county convention in Springfield to select delegates for the forthcoming Republican State convention in Bloomington. The paper was freely circulated and generously signed. Lincoln was absent at the time and, believing I knew what his " feeling and judgment " on the vital questions of the hour were, I took the liberty to sign his name to the call. The whole was then published in the Springfield *Journal.* No sooner had it appeared than John T. Stuart, who, with others, was endeavoring to retard Lincoln in his advanced movements, rushed into the office and excitedly asked if " Lincoln had signed that Abolition call in the *Journal?* " I answered in the negative, adding that I had signed his name myself. To the question, " Did Lincoln authorize you to sign it?" I returned an emphatic "No." "Then," exclaimed the startled and indignant Stuart, " you have ruined him." But I was by no means alarmed at what others deemed inconsiderate and hasty action. I thought I understood Lincoln thoroughly, but in order to vindicate myself if assailed I immediately sat down, after Stuart had rushed out of the office, and wrote Lincoln, who was then in Tazewell County attending court, a brief account of what I had done and how much stir it was creating in the ranks of his conservative friends. If he approved or disapproved my course I asked him to write or telegraph me at once. In a brief time came his answer: " All right ; go ahead. Will meet you— radicals and all." Stuart subsided, and the conservative spirits who hovered around Springfield no longer held control of the political fortunes of Abraham Lincoln.

The Republican party came into existence in Illinois as a party at Bloomington, May 29, 1856. The State convention of all opponents of anti-Nebraska legislation, referred to in a foregoing paragraph, had been set for that day. Judd, Yates, Trumbull, Swett, and Davis were there ; so also was Lovejoy, who, like Otis of colonial fame, was a flame of fire. The firm of Lincoln and Herndon was represented by both members in person. The gallant William H. Bissell, who had ridden at the head of the Second Illinois Regiment at the battle of Buena Vista in the Mexican war, was nominated as governor. The convention adopted a platform ringing with strong anti-Nebraska sentiments, and then and

there gave the Republican party its official christ-
ening. The business of the convention being over,
Mr. Lincoln, in response to repeated calls, came
forward and delivered a speech of such earnestness and power that no one who heard it will ever
forget the effect it produced. In referring to this
speech some years ago I used the following rather
graphic language : " I have heard or read all of Mr.
Lincoln's great speeches, and I give it as my
opinion that the Bloomington speech was the
grand effort of his life. Heretofore he had
simply argued the slavery question on grounds
of policy,—the statesman's grounds,—never reaching the question of the radical and the eternal
right. Now he was newly baptized and freshly
born ; he had the fervor of a new convert ; the
smothered flame broke out ; enthusiasm unusual to
him blazed up ; his eyes were aglow with an inspiration ; he felt justice ; his heart was alive to the
right ; his sympathies, remarkably deep for him,
burst forth, and he stood before the throne of the
eternal Right. His speech was full of fire and
energy and force ; it was logic ; it was pathos ; it
was enthusiasm ; it was justice, equity, truth, and
right set ablaze by the divine fires of a soul mad-
dened by the wrong; it was hard, heavy, knotty,
gnarly, backed with wrath. I attemped for about
fifteen minutes as was usual with me then to take
notes, but at the end of that time I threw pen and
paper away and lived only in the inspiration of the
hour. If Mr. Lincoln was six feet, four inches high
usually, at Bloomington that day he was seven feet,

and inspired at that. From that day to the day of his death he stood firm in the right. He felt his great cross, had his great idea, nursed it, kept it, taught it to others, in his fidelity bore witness of it to his death, and finally sealed it with his precious blood." The foregoing paragraph, used by me in a lecture in 1866, may to the average reader seem somewhat vivid in description, besides inclining to extravagance in imagery, yet although more than twenty years have passed since it was written I have never seen the need of altering a single sentence. I still adhere to the substantial truthfulness of the scene as described. Unfortunately Lincoln's speech was never written out nor printed, and we are obliged to depend for its reproduction upon personal recollection.

The Bloomington convention and the part Lincoln took in it met no such hearty response in Springfield as we hoped would follow. It fell flat, and in Lincoln's case drove from him many persons who had heretofore been his warm political friends. A few days after our return we announced a meeting at the court-house to ratify the action of the Bloomington convention. After the usual efforts to draw a crowd, however, only three persons had temerity enough to attend. They were Lincoln, the writer, and a courageous man named John Pain. Lincoln, in answer to the " deafening calls " for a speech, responded that the meeting was larger than he *knew* it would be, and that while he knew that he himself and his partner would attend he was not sure anyone else would, and yet another man had been found brave enough to come out. "While all seems dead," he exhorted, "the age itself is not. It liveth as sure as our Maker liveth. Under all this seeming want of life and motion, the world does move nevertheless. Be hopeful, and now let us adjourn and appeal to the people."

Not only in Springfield but everywhere else the founders of the Republican party—the apostles of freedom—went out to battle for the righteousness of their cause. Lincoln, having as usual been named as one of the Presidental electors, canvassed the State, making in all about fifty speeches. He was in demand everywhere. I have before me a package of letters addressed to him, inviting him to speak at almost every county seat in the State. Yates wanted him to go to one section of the State, Washburne to another, and Trumbull still another; while every cross-roads politician and legislative aspirant wanted him "down in our country, where we need your help." Joshua R. Giddings wrote him words of encouragement. "You may start," said the valiant old Abolitionist in a letter from Peoria,* "on the one great issue of restoring Kansas and Nebraska to freedom, or rather of restoring the Missouri Compromise, and in this State no power on earth can withstand you on that issue." The demand for Lincoln was not confined to his own State. Indiana sent for him, Wisconsin also, while Norman B. Judd and Ebenezer Peck, who were stumping Iowa, sent for him to come there.

---

* J. R. Giddings, MS. letter, Sept. 18, 1855.

28

A town committee invited him to come during "our Equestrian Fair on the 9th, 10th, and 11th," evidently anticipating a three days' siege. An enthusiastic officer in a neighboring town urges him: "Come to our place, because in you do our people place more confidence than in any other man. Men who do not read want the story told as you only can tell it. Others may make fine speeches, but it would not be 'Lincoln said so in his speech.'" A jubilant friend in Chicago writes: "Push on the column of freedom. Give the Buck Africans plenty to do in Egypt. The hour of our redemption draweth nigh. We are coming to Springfield with 20,000 majority!" A postmaster, acting under the courage of his convictions, implores him to visit his neighborhood. "The Democrats here," he insists, "are dyed in the wool. Thunder and lightning would not change their political complexion. I am postmaster here," he adds, confidentially, "for which reason I must ask you to keep this private, for if old Frank [President Pierce] were to hear of my support of Frémont I would get my walking papers sure enough." A settlement of Germans in southern Indiana asked to hear him ; and the president of a college, in an invitation to address the students under his charge, characterizes him as "one providentially raised up for a time like this, and even should defeat come in the contest, it would be some consolation to remember we had Hector for a leader."

And thus it was everywhere. Lincoln's importance in the conduct of the campaign was apparent to all, and his canvass was characterized by his usual vigor and effectiveness. He was especially noted for his attempt to break down the strength of Fillmore, who was nominated as a third party candidate and was expected to divide the Republican vote. He tried to wean away Fillmore's adherents by an adroit and ingenious letter * sent

---

* One of these letters which Lincoln wrote to counteract the Fillmore movement is still in my possession. As it is more or less characteristic I copy it entire:

"SPRINGFIELD, September 8, 1856.

"HARRISON MALTBY, Esq.

"*Dear Sir:*

"I understand you are a Fillmore man. Let me prove to you that every vote withheld from Frémont and given to Fillmore in this State actually lessens Fillmore's chance of being President.

"Suppose Buchanan gets all the slave States and Pennsylvania and any other one State besides; then he is elected, no matter who gets all the rest. But suppose Fillmore gets the two slave States of Maryland and Kentucky, then Buchanan is not elected; Fillmore goes into the House of Representatives and may be made President by a compromise. But suppose again Fillmore's friends throw away a few thousand votes on him in Indiana and Illinois; it will inevitably give these States to Buchanan, which will more than compensate him for the loss of Maryland and Kentucky; it will elect him, and leave Fillmore no chance in the House of Representatives or out of it.

"This is as plain as adding up the weight of three small hogs. As Mr. Fillmore has no possible chance to carry Illinois for himself it is plainly to his interest to let Frémont take it and thus keep it out of the hands of Buchanan. Be not deceived. Buchanan is the hard horse to beat in this race. Let him have Illinois, and nothing can beat him; and he will get Illinois if men persist in throwing away votes upon Mr. Fillmore. Does some one persuade you that Mr. Fillmore can carry Illinois? Nonsense! There are over seventy newspapers in Illinois opposing Buchanan, only three or four of which support Mr. Fillmore, all the rest going for Frémont. Are not these newspapers a fair index of the proportion of the votes? If not, tell me why.

"Again, of these three or four Fillmore newspapers, two at least are supported in part by the Buchanan men, as I understand. Do not they know where the shoe pinches? They know the Fillmore movement helps them, and therefore they help it.

"Do think these things over and then act according to your judgment.

"Yours very truly,

[Confidential.] "A. LINCOLN."

to those suspected of the latter's support, and marked confidential, in which he strove to show that in clinging to their candidate they were really aiding the election of Buchanan. But the effort proved unavailing, for in spite of all his arguments and appeals a large number of the Fillmore men clung tenaciously to their leader, resulting in Buchanan's election. The vote in Illinois stood, Buchanan 105,344, Frémont 96,180, and Fillmore 37,451. At the same time Bissell was elected governor by a majority of 4729 over W. A. Richardson, Democrat. After the heat and burden of the day Lincoln returned home, bearing with him more and greater laurels than ever. The signs of the times indicated, and the result of the canvass demonstrated, that he and he alone was powerful enough to meet the redoubtable Little Giant in a greater conflict yet to follow.

CHAPTER III.

I SHALL be forced to omit much that happened during the interval between the election of Buchanan and the campaign of 1858, for the reason that it would not only swell this work to undue proportions, but be a mere repetition of what has been better told by other writers. It is proper to note in passing, however, that Mr. Lincoln's reputation as a political speaker was no longer bounded by the border lines of Illinois. It had passed beyond the Wabash, the Ohio, and the Mississippi rivers, and while his pronounced stand on the slavery question had increased the circle of his admirers in the North it provoked a proportionate amount of execration in the South. He could not help the feeling that he was now the leading Republican in his State, and he was therefore more or less jealous of his prerogative. Formidable in debate, plain in speech, without pretence of literary acquirements, he was none the less self-reliant. He already envied the ascendancy and domination Douglas exercised over his followers, and felt keenly the slight given him by others of his own faith whom he conceived were disposed to prevent his attaining the leadership of his party. I remember early in 1858 of his coming into the office one morning and speaking in very dejected terms of the treatment he was receiving at the hands of Horace Greeley. " I think Greeley," he complained, " is not doing me right. His conduct, I believe, savors a little of injustice. I am a true Republican and have been tried already in the hottest part of the anti-slavery fight, and yet I find him taking up Douglas, a veritable dodger,—once a tool of the South, now its enemy,—and pushing him to the front. He forgets that when he does that he pulls me down at the same time. I fear Greeley's attitude will damage me with Sumner, Seward, Wilson, Phillips, and other friends in the East." This was said with so much of mingled sadness and earnestness that I was deeply impressed. Lincoln was gloomy and restless the entire day. Greeley's letters were driving the enthusiasm out of him.* He seemed unwilling to attend to any business, and finally, just before noon, left the office, going over to the United States Court room to play a game of chess with Judge Treat, and did not return again

---

* Greeley's letters were very pointed and sometimes savage. Here is one :

" I have not proposed to instruct the Republicans of Illinois in their political duties, and I doubt very much that even so much as is implied in your letter can be fairly deduced from anything I have written. Now let me make one prediction. If you run a candidate [for Congress] against Harris and he is able to canvass *he will beat you badly*. He is more of a man at heart and morally than Douglas, and has gone into this fight with more earnestness and less calculation. Of the whole Douglas party he is the truest and best. I never spoke a dozen words with him in my life, having met him but once, but if I lived in his district I should vote for him. As I have never spoken of him in my paper, and suppose I never shall, I take the liberty to say this much to you. Now paddle your own dug-out !
" Yours,
" HORACE GREELEY."

that day. I pondered a good deal over Lincoln's dejection, and that night, after weighing the matter well in mind, resolved to go to the eastern States myself and endeavor to sound some of the great men there. The next day, on apprising Lincoln of my determination, he questioned its propriety. Our relations, he insisted, were so intimate that a wrong construction might be put upon the movement. I listened carefully to him, but as I had never been beyond the Alleghanies I packed my valise and went, notwithstanding his objections. I had been in correspondence on my own account with Greeley, Seward, Sumner, Phillips, and others for several years, had kept them informed of the feelings of our people and the political campaigns in their various stages, but had never met any of them save Greeley. I enjoyed heartily the journey and the varied sights and scenes that attended it. Aside from my mission, the trip was a great success. The magnificent buildings, the display of wealth in the large cities and prosperous manufacturing towns, broadened the views of one whose vision had never extended beyond the limits of the Illinois prairies. In Washington I saw and dined with Trumbull, who went over the situation with me. Trumbull had written to Lincoln shortly before* that he thought it " useless to speculate upon the further course of Douglas or the effect it is to have in Illinois or other States. He himself does not know where he is going or where he will come out." At my interview with Trumbull, however, he directed me to

---

* Letter, December 25, 1857, MS.

assure Mr. Lincoln that Douglas did not mean to join the Republican party, however great the breach between himself and the administration might be. "We Republicans here," he said exultingly in another letter to Lincoln, "are in good spirits, and are standing back to let the fight go on between Douglas and his former associates. Lincoln will lose nothing by this if he can keep the attention of our Illinois people from being diverted from the great and vital question of the day to the minor and temporary issues which are now being discussed."* In Washington I saw also Seward, Wilson, and others of equal prominence. Douglas was confined to his house by illness, but on receiving my card he directed me to be shown up to his room. We had a pleasant and interesting interview. Of course the conversation soon turned on Lincoln. In answer to an inquiry regarding the latter I remarked that Lincoln was pursuing the even tenor of his way. "He is not in anybody's way," I contended, "not even in yours, Judge Douglas." He was sitting up in a chair smoking a cigar. Between puffs he responded that neither was he in the way of Lincoln or any one else, and did not intend to invite conflict. He conceived that he had achieved what he had set out to do, and hence did not feel that his course need put him in opposition to Mr. Lincoln or his party. "Give Mr. Lincoln my regards," he said, rather warmly, "when you return, and tell him I have crossed the river and

---

* Letter, December 27, 1857, MS.

burned my boat." Leaving Washington, my next point was New York, where I met the editor of the *Anti-Slavery Standard*, Horace Greeley, Henry Ward Beecher, and others. I had a long talk with Greeley, who, I noticed, leaned towards Douglas. I found, however, he was not at all hostile to Lincoln. I presented the latter's case in the best phase I knew how, but while I drew but little from him, I left feeling that he hadn't been entirely won over. He introduced me to Beecher, who, as everybody else did, inquired after Lincoln and through me sent him words of encouragement and praise.* From New York I went to Boston, and from the latter place I wrote Lincoln a letter which happily I found not long since in a bundle of Lincoln's letters, and which I insert here, believing it affords a better reflex of the situation at the time than anything I might see fit to say now. Here it is:

"REVERE HOUSE,
"BOSTON, MASS., March 24, 1858.

"FRIEND LINCOLN.

"I am in this city of notions, and am well—very well indeed. I wrote you a hasty letter from Washington some days ago, since which time I have been in Philadelphia, Baltimore, New York, and now here. I saw Greeley, and so far as any of our conversation is interesting to you I will relate. And we talked, say twenty minutes. He evidently

---

* Lincoln's greatest fear was that Douglas might be taken up by the Republicans. Senator Seward, when I met him in Washington, assured me there was no danger of it, insisting that the Republicans nor any one else could place any reliance on a man so slippery as Douglas.

wants Douglas sustained and sent back to the Senate. He did not say so in so many words, yet his *feelings* are with Douglas. I *know* it from the spirit and drift of his conversation. He talked bitterly—somewhat so—against the papers in Illinois, and said they were fools. I asked him this question, 'Greeley, do you want to see a third party organized, or do you want Douglas to ride to power through the North, which he has so much abused and betrayed?' and to which he replied, 'Let the future alone; it will all come right. Douglas is a brave man. Forget the past and sustain the *right-eous.*' Good God, *righteous*, eh!

"Since I have landed in Boston I have seen much that was entertaining and interesting. This morning I was introduced to Governor Banks. He and I had a conversation about Republicanism and especially about Douglas. He asked me this question, 'You will sustain Douglas in Illinois, wont you?' and to which I said '*No, never!*' He affected to be much surprised, and so the matter dropped and turned on Republicanism, or in general—Lincoln. Greeley's and other sheets that laud Douglas, Harris, *et al.*, want them sustained, and will *try* to do it. Several persons have asked me the same question which Banks asked, and evidently they get their cue, ideas, or what not from Greeley, Seward, *et al.* By-the-bye, Greeley remarked to me this, 'The Republican standard is too high; we want something practical.'

"This may not be interesting to you, but, however it may be, it is my duty to state what is going on, so that you may head it off—counteract it in some way. I hope it can be done. The Northern men are cold to me—somewhat repellent.

"Your friend,

"W. H. HERNDON."

On my return home I had encouraging news to relate. I told Lincoln of the favorable mention I had heard of him by Phillips, Sumner, Seward, Garrison, Beecher, and Greeley. I brought with me additional sermons and lectures by Theodore Parker, who was warm in his commendation of Lincoln. One of these was a lecture on "The Effect of Slavery on the American People," which was delivered in the Music Hall in Boston, and which I gave to Lincoln, who read and returned it. He liked especially the following expression, which he marked with a pencil, and which he in substance afterwards used in his Gettysburg address: "Democracy is direct self-government, over all the people, for all the people, by all the people."

Meanwhile, passing by other events which have become interwoven in the history of the land, we reach April, 1858, at which time the Democratic State convention met and, besides nominating candidates for State offices, endorsed Mr. Douglas' services in the Senate, thereby virtually renominating him for that exalted office. In the very nature of things Lincoln was the man already chosen in the hearts of the Republicans of Illinois for the same office, and therefore with singular appropriateness they passed, with great unanimity, at their convention in Springfield on the 16th of June, the characteristic resolution: "That Hon. Abraham Lincoln is our first and only choice for United States Senator to fill the vacancy about to be created by the expiration of Mr. Douglas' term of office." There was of course no surprise in this for Mr. Lincoln. He had been all along led to expect it, and with that in view had been earnestly and quietly at work preparing a speech in acknowledgment of the honor about to be conferred on him. This speech he wrote on stray envelopes and scraps of paper, as ideas suggested themselves, putting them into that miscellaneous and convenient receptacle, his hat. As the convention drew near he copied the whole on connected sheets, carefully revising every line and sentence, and fastened them together, for reference during the delivery of the speech, and for publication. The former precaution, however, was unnecessary, for he had studied and read over what he had written so long and carefully that he was able to deliver it without the least hesitation or difficulty. A few days before the convention, when he was at work on the speech, I remember that Jesse K. Dubois,* who was Auditor of State, came into the office and, seeing Lincoln busily writing, inquired what he was doing or what he was writing. Lincoln answered gruffly, "It's something you may see or hear some time, but I'll not let you see it now." I myself knew what he was writing, but having asked neither my opinion nor that of anyone else, I did not venture to

----

* "After the convention Lincoln met me on the street and said, 'Dubois, I can tell you now what I was doing the other day when you came into my office. I was writing that speech, and I knew if I read the passage about the " house divided against itself " to you, you would ask me to change or modify it, and that I was determined not to do. I had willed it so, and was willing if necessary to perish with it."—Statement of Jesse K. Dubois, MS.

offer any suggestions. After he had finished the final draft of the speech, he locked the office door, drew the curtain across the glass panel in the door, and read it to me. At the end of each paragraph he would halt and wait for my comments. I remember what I said after hearing the first paragraph, wherein occurs the celebrated figure of the house divided against itself: "It is true, but is it wise or politic to say so?" He responded: "That expression is a truth of all human experience, 'a house divided against itself cannot stand,' and 'he that runs may read.' The proposition also is true, and has been for six thousand years. I want to use some universally known figure expressed in simple language as universally well-known, that may strike home to the minds of men in order to raise them up to the peril of the times. I do not believe I would be right in changing or omitting it. I would rather be defeated with this expression in the speech, and uphold and discuss it before the people, than be victorious without it." This was not the first time Lincoln had endorsed the dogma that our Government could not long endure part slave and part free. He had incorporated it in a speech at Bloomington in 1856, but in obedience to the emphatic protest of Judge T. Lyle Dickey and others, who conceived the idea that its "delivery would make Abolitionists of all the North and slavery propagandists of all the South, and thereby precipitate a struggle which might end in disunion," he consented to suspend its repetition, but only for that campaign.* Now, however, the situation had changed somewhat. There had been a shifting of scenes, so to speak. The Republican party had gained some in strength and more in moral effectiveness and force. Nothing could keep back in Lincoln any longer, sentiments of right and truth, and he prepared to give the fullest expression to both in all future contests.

Before delivering his speech he invited a dozen or so of his friends over to the library of the State House, where he read and submitted it to them. After the reading he asked each man for his opinion. Some condemned and not one endorsed it. One man, more forcible than elegant, characterized it as a "d——d fool utterance ;" another said the doctrine was "ahead of its time ;" and still another contended that it would drive away a good many voters fresh from the Democratic ranks. Each man attacked it in his criticism. I was the last to respond. Although the doctrine announced was

* " After the meeting was over Mr. Lincoln and I returned to the Pike House, where we occupied the same room. Immediately on reaching the room I said to him, ' What in God's name could induce you to promulgate such an opinion?' He replied familiarly, ' Upon my soul, Dickey, I think it is true.' I reasoned to show it was not a correct opinion. He argued strenuously that the opinion was a sound one. At length I said, ' Suppose you are right, that our Government cannot last part free and part slave, what good is to be accomplished by inculcating that opinion (or truth, if you please) in the minds of the people?' After some minutes reflection he rose and approached me, extending his right hand to take mine, and said, ' From respect for your judgment, Dickey, I'll promise you I won't teach the doctrine again during this campaign.' " —Letter, T. Lyle Dickey, MS., December 8, 1866.

HALL OF REPRESENTATIVES, STATE-HOUSE, SPRINGFIELD.

Room in which Lincoln delivered his "house-divided-against-itself" speech.

Photographed in 1888.

rather rank, yet it suited my views, and I said, "Lincoln, deliver that speech as read and it will make you President." At the time I hardly realized the force of my prophecy. Having patiently listened to these various criticisms from his friends —all of which with a single exception were adverse—he rose from his chair, and after alluding to the careful study and intense thought he had given the question, he answered all their objections substantially as follows: "Friends, this thing has been retarded long enough. The time has come when these sentiments should be uttered; and if it is decreed that I should go down because of this speech, then let me go down linked to the truth— let me die in the advocacy of what is just and right." The next day, the 17th, the speech was delivered just as we had heard it read. Up to this time Seward had held sway over the North by his "higher-law" sentiments, but the "house-divided-against-itself" speech by Lincoln in my opinion drove the nail into Seward's political coffin.*

Lincoln had now created in reality a more profound impression than he or his friends anticipated. Many Republicans deprecated the advanced ground he had taken, the more so as the Democrats rejoiced that it afforded them an issue clear and

---

* If any student of oratorical history, after reading Lincoln's speech on this occasion, will refer to Webster's reply to Hayne in the Senate, he will be struck with the similarity in figure and thought in the opening lines of both speeches. In fact, it may not be amiss to note that, in this instance, Webster's effort was carefully read by Lincoln and served in part as his model.

well-defined.   Numbers of his friends distant from Springfield, on reading his speech, wrote him censorious letters ; and one well-informed co-worker * predicted his defeat, charging it to the first ten lines of the speech.   These complaints, coming apparently from every quarter, Lincoln bore with great patience.   To one complainant who followed him into his office he said proudly, " If I had to draw a pen across my record, and erase my whole life from sight, and I had one poor gift or choice left as to what I should save from the wreck, I should choose that speech and leave it to the world unerased."

Meanwhile Douglas had returned from Washington to his home in Chicago.   Here he rested for a few days until his friends and co-workers had arranged the details of a public reception on the 9th of July, when he delivered from the balcony of the Tremont House a speech intended as an answer to the one made by Lincoln in Springfield.   Lincoln was present at this reception, but took no part in it. The next day, however, he replied.   Both speeches were delivered at the same place.   Leaving Chicago, Douglas passed on down to Bloomington and Springfield, where he spoke on the 16th and 17th of July respectively.   On the evening of the latter day Lincoln responded again in a most effective and convincing effort.   The contest now took on a different phase.   Lincoln's Republican friends urged him to draw Douglas into a joint debate, and he accordingly sent him a challenge on the 24th of

---

* Leonard Swett.

Springfield, June 25. 1858

A. Campbell, Esq,
My dear Sir

In 1856 you gave me
authority to draw on you for any sum
not exceeding five hundred dollars—
I see clearly, that such a privilege
would be now available, than it was then.
I am aware that times are tighter now
than they were then— Please write me at
all events; and whether you can now do
anything or not, I shall continue grateful for the past— Yours very truly,
A. Lincoln

July.   It is not necessary, I suppose, to reproduce here the correspondence that passed between these great leaders.   On the 30th Douglas finally accepted the proposition to " divide time, and address the same audiences," naming seven different places, one in each Congressional district, outside of Chicago and Springfield, for joint meetings.* The places and dates were, Ottawa, August 21; Freeport, August 27; Jonesboro, September 15; Charleston, September 18; Galesburg, October 7; Quincy,

---

* Among the items of preparation on Lincoln's part hitherto withheld is the following letter, which explains itself:

"SPRINGFIELD, June 28, 1858.

" A. CAMPBELL, Esq.

" MY DEAR SIR:—In 1856 you gave me authority to draw on you for any sum not exceeding five hundred dollars. I see clearly that such a privilege would be more available now than it was then. I am aware that times are tighter now than they were then. Please write me at all events, and whether you can now do anything or not I shall continue grateful for the past.

" Yours very truly,
" A. LINCOLN."

* The following recent letter from Mr. Campbell is not without interest :

LA SALLE, ILL., Dec. 12th, 1888.

" JESSE W. WEIK, Esq.

"MY DEAR SIR :—I gave Mr. Lincoln some money in the office of Lincoln & Herndon in Springfield in 1856, but I do not remember the exact amount. It was, however, between two and three hundred dollars. I never had Mr. Lincoln's obligation for the payment of any money. I never kept any account of nor charged my memory with any money I gave him. It was given to defray his personal expenses and otherwise promote the interest of a cause which I sincerely believed to be for the public good, and without the thought or expectation of a dollar of it ever being returned. From what I knew and learned of his careful habits in money matters in the campaign of 1856 I am entirely confident that every dollar and dime I ever gave was carefully and faithfully applied to the uses and purposes for which it was given.

" Sincerely yours,
" A. CAMPBELL."

October 13 ; and Alton, October 15. " I agree to your suggestion, " wrote Douglas, "that we shall alternately open and close the discussion. I will speak at Ottawa one hour, you can reply, occupying an hour and a half, and I will then follow for half an hour. At Freeport you shall open the discussion and speak one hour, I will follow for an hour and a half, and you can then reply for half an hour. We will alternate in like manner in each successive place." To this arrangement Lincoln on the 31st gave his consent, " although, " he wrote, " by the terms as you propose you take four openings and closes to my three."

History furnishes few characters whose lives and careers were so nearly parallel as those of Lincoln and Douglas. They met for the first time at the Legislature in Vandalia in 1834, where Lincoln was a member of the House of Representatives and Douglas was in the lobby. The next year Douglas was also a member. In 1839 both were admitted to practice in the Supreme Court of Illinois on the same day.* In 1841 both courted the same young lady. In 1846 both represented Illinois in Congress at Washington, the one in the upper and the other in the lower House. In 1858 they were opposing candidates for United States Senator ; and finally, to complete the remarkable counterpart, both were candidates for the Presidency in 1860. While it is true that their ambitions ran in parallel lines, yet they were exceedingly unlike in all other particulars.

----

* December 3d.

Douglas was short,—something over five feet high,—heavy set, with a large head, broad shoulders, deep chest, and striking features. He was polite and affable, but fearless. He had that unique trait, magnetism, fully developed in his nature, and that attracted a host of friends and readily made him a popular idol. He had had extensive experience in debate, and had been trained by contact for years with the great minds and orators in Congress. He was full of political history, well informed on general topics, eloquent almost to the point of brilliancy, self-confident to the point of arrogance, and a dangerous competitor in every respect. What he lacked in ingenuity he made up in strategy, and if in debate he could not tear down the structure of his opponent's argument by a direct and violent attack, he was by no means reluctant to resort to a strained restatement of the latter's position or to the extravagance of ridicule. Lincoln knew his man thoroughly and well.* He had often met Douglas on the stump; was familiar with his tactics, and though fully aware of his " want of

---

* An erroneous impression has grown up in recent years concerning Douglas's ability and standing as a lawyer. One of the latest biographies of Lincoln credits him with many of the artifices of the "shyster." This is not only unfair, but decidedly untrue. I always found Douglas at the bar to be a broad, fair, and liberal-minded man. Although not a thorough student of the law his large fund of good common-sense kept him in the front rank. He was equally generous and courteous, and he never stooped to gain a case. I know that Lincoln entertained the same view of him. It was only in politics that Douglas demonstrated any want of inflexibility and rectitude, and then only did Lincoln manifest a lack of faith in his morals.

fixed political morals," was not averse to measuring swords with the elastic and flexible " Little Giant."

Lincoln himself was constructed on an entirely different foundation. His base was plain common-sense, direct statement, and the inflexibility of logic. In physical make-up he was cold—at least not magnetic—and made no effort to dazzle people by his bearing. He cared nothing for a following, and though he had often before struggled for a political prize, yet in his efforts he never had strained his well-known spirit of fairness or open love of the truth. He analyzed everything, laid every statement bare, and by dint of his broad reasoning powers and manliness of admission inspired his hearers with deep conviction of his earnestness and honesty. Douglas may have electrified the crowds with his eloquence or charmed them with his majestic bearing and dexterity in debate, but as each man, after the meetings were over and the applause had died away, went to his home, his head rang with Lincoln's logic and appeal to manhood.

A brief description of Mr. Lincoln's appearance on the stump and of his manner when speaking may not be without interest. When standing erect he was six feet four inches high. He was lean in flesh and ungainly in figure. Aside from the sad, pained look due to habitual melancholy, his face had no characteristic or fixed expression. He was thin through the chest, and hence slightly stoop-shouldered. When he arose to address courts, juries, or crowds of people, his body inclined forward to a slight degree. At first he was very awkward, and it seemed a real labor to adjust himself to his surroundings. He struggled for a time under a feeling of apparent diffidence and sensitiveness, and these only added to his awkwardness. I have often seen and sympathized with Mr. Lincoln during these moments. When he began speaking, his voice was shrill, piping, and unpleasant. His manner, his attitude, his dark, yellow face, wrinkled and dry, his oddity of pose, his diffident movements—everything seemed to be against him, but only for a short time. After having arisen, he generally placed his hands behind him, the back of his left hand in the palm of his right, the thumb and fingers of his right hand clasped around the left arm at the wrist. For a few moments he played the combination of awkwardness, sensitiveness, and diffidence. As he proceeded he became somewhat animated, and to keep in harmony with his growing warmth his hands relaxed their grasp and fell to his side. Presently he clasped them in front of him, interlocking his fingers, one thumb meanwhile chasing another. His speech now requiring more emphatic utterance, his fingers unlocked and his hands fell apart. His left arm was thrown behind, the back of his hand resting against his body, his right hand seeking his side. By this time he had gained sufficient composure, and his real speech began. He did not gesticulate as much with his hands as with his head. He used the latter frequently, throwing it with vim this way and that. This movement was a significant one when he sought to enforce his statement. It sometimes came with a quick jerk, as if throwing off electric sparks into combustible material. He never sawed the air nor rent space into tatters and rags as some orators do. He never acted for stage effect. He was cool, considerate, reflective—in time self-possessed and self-reliant. His style was clear, terse, and compact. In argument he was logical, demonstrative, and fair. He was careless of his dress, and his clothes, instead of fitting neatly as did the garments of Douglas on the latter's well-rounded form, hung loosely on his giant frame. As he moved along in his speech he became freer and less uneasy in his movements ; to that extent he was graceful. He had a perfect naturalness, a strong individuality; and to that extent he was dignified. He despised glitter, show, set forms, and shams. He spoke with effectiveness and to move the judgment as well as the emotions of men. There was a world of meaning and emphasis in the long, bony finger of his right hand as he dotted the ideas on the minds of his hearers. Sometimes, to express joy or pleasure, he would raise both hands at an angle of about fifty degrees, the palms upward, as if desirous of embracing the spirit of that which he loved. If the sentiment was one of detestation— denunciation of slavery, for example—both arms, thrown upward and fists clenched, swept through the air, and he expressed an execration that was truly sublime. This was one of his most effective gestures, and signified most vividly a fixed determination to drag down the object of his hatred and trample it in the dust. He always stood squarely on his feet, toe even with toe; that is, he never put one foot before the other. He neither touched nor leaned on anything for support. He made but few changes in his positions and attitudes. He never ranted, never walked backward and forward on the platform. To ease his arms he frequently caught hold, with his left hand, of the lapel of his coat, keeping his thumb upright and leaving his right hand free to gesticulate. The designer of the monument recently erected in Chicago has happily caught him in just this attitude. As he proceeded with his speech the exercise of his vocal organs altered somewhat the tone of his voice. It lost in a measure its former acute and shrilling pitch, and mellowed into a more harmonious and pleasant sound. His form expanded, and, notwithstanding the sunken breast, he rose up a splendid and imposing figure. In his defence of the Declaration of Independence—his greatest inspiration—he was "tremendous in the directness of his utterances; he rose to impassioned eloquence, unsurpassed by Patrick Henry, Mirabeau, or Vergniaud, as his soul was inspired with the thought of human right and Divine justice." * His little gray eyes flashed in a face aglow with the fire of his profound thoughts; and his uneasy movements and diffident manner sunk themselves beneath the wave of righteous indignation that came sweeping over him. Such was Lincoln the orator.

* Horace White, who was present and reported the speech for his paper, the Chicago *Tribune.* Letter, June 9, 1865, MS.

We can somewhat appreciate the feeling with which Douglas, aggressive and fearless though he was, welcomed a contest with such a man as Lincoln. Four years before, in a joint debate with him, he had asked for a cessation of forensic hostilities, conceding that his opponent of rail-splitting fame had given him " more trouble than all the United States Senate together." Now he was brought face to face with him again.*

It is unnecessary and not in keeping with the purpose of this work to reproduce here the speeches made by either Lincoln or Douglas in their justly renowned debate. Briefly stated, Lincoln's position was announced in his opening speech at Springfield : " 'A house divided against itself cannot stand.' I believe this Government cannot endure permanently half slave and half free. I do not expect the Union to be dissolved, I do not expect the house to fall—but I do expect it will cease to be divided. It will become all the one thing or the other. Either the opponents of slavery will arrest the further spread of it and place it where the public mind shall rest in the belief that it is in the course of ultimate extinction ; or its advocates will push it forward till it becomes alike lawful in all the states, old as well as new, North as well as South." The position of Douglas on the question of slavery was one of indifference. He advocated

---

* " Douglas and I, for the first time this canvass, crossed swords here yesterday. The fire flew some, and I am glad to know I am yet alive."—Lincoln to J. O. Cunningham, Ottawa, Ill., August 22, 1858, MS.

with all his power the doctrine of "Popular Sovereignty," a proposition, as quaintly put by Lincoln, which meant that, "if one man chooses to enslave another, no third man has a right to object." At the last joint discussion in Alton, Lincoln, after reflecting on the patriotism of any man who was so indifferent to the wrong of slavery that he cared not whether it was voted up or down, closed his speech with this stirring summary: "That [slavery] is the real issue. That is the issue that will continue in this country when these poor tongues of Judge Douglas and myself shall be silent. It is the eternal struggle between these two principles —right and wrong—throughout the world. They are the two principles that have stood face to face from the beginning of time, and will ever continue to struggle. The one is the common right of humanity, and the other the divine right of kings. It is the same principle, in whatever shape it develops itself. It is the same spirit that says: 'You work and toil and earn bread, and I eat it.' No matter in what shape it comes, whether from the mouth of a king who seeks to bestride the people of his own nation and live by the fruit of their labor, or from one race of men as an apology for enslaving another race, it is the same tyrannical principle."

It is unnecessary, I presume, to insert here the seven questions which Douglas propounded to Lincoln at their first meeting at Ottawa, nor the historic four which Lincoln asked at Freeport. It only remains to say that in answering Lincoln at

Freeport, Douglas accomplished his own political downfall. He was swept entirely away from his former foundation, and even the glory of a subsequent election to the Senate never restored him to it.

During the canvass Mr. Lincoln, in addition to the seven meetings with Douglas, filled thirty-one appointments made by the State Central Committee, besides speaking at many other times and places not previously advertised. In his trips to and fro over the State, between meetings, he would stop at Springfield sometimes, to consult with his friends or to post himself up on questions that occurred during the canvass. He kept me busy hunting up old speeches and gathering facts and statistics at the State library. I made liberal clippings bearing in any way on the questions of the hour from every newspaper I happened to see, and kept him supplied with them; and on one or two occasions, in answer to letters and telegrams, I sent books forward to him. He had a little leather bound book, fastened in front with a clasp, in which he and I both kept inserting newspaper slips and newspaper comments until the canvass opened. In arranging for the joint meetings and managing the crowds Douglas enjoyed one great advantage. He had been United States Senator for several years, and had influential friends holding comfortable government offices all over the State. These men were on hand at every meeting, losing no opportunity to applaud lustily all the points Douglas made and to lionize him in every conceivable way. The ingeniously contrived display of their enthusiasm had a marked effect on certain crowds—a fact of which Lincoln frequently complained to his friends. One who accompanied him during the canvass* relates this: " Lincoln and I were at the Centralia agricultural fair the day after the debate at Jonesboro. Night came on and we were tired, having been on the fair grounds all day. We were to go north on the Illinois Central railroad. The train was due at midnight, and the depot was full of people. I managed to get a chair for Lincoln in the office of the superintendent of the railroad, but small politicans would intrude so that he could scarcely get a moment's sleep. The train came and was filled instantly. I got a seat near the door for Lincoln and myself. He was worn out, and had to meet Douglas the next day at Charleston. An empty car, called a saloon car, was hitched on to the rear of the train and locked up. I asked the conductor, who knew Lincoln and myself well,—we were both attorneys of the road,—if Lincoln could not ride in that car; that he was exhausted and needed rest; but the conductor refused. I afterwards got him in by a stratagem. At the same time George B. McClellan in person was taking Douglas around in a special car and special train; and that was the unjust treatment Lincoln got from the Illinois Central railroad. Every interest of that road and every employee was against Lincoln and for Douglas."

The heat and dust and bonfires of the campaign

---

* Henry C. Whitney, MS., July 21, 1865.

at last came to an end.   The election took place on the second of November, and while Lincoln received of the popular vote a majority of over four thousand, yet the returns from the legislative districts foreshadowed his defeat.   In fact, when the Senatorial election took place in the Legislature, Douglas received fifty-four and Lincoln forty-six votes—one of the results of the lamentable apportionment law then in operation.*

The letters of Lincoln at this period are the best evidence of his feelings now obtainable, and of how he accepted his defeat.   To Henry Asbury, a friend who had written him a cheerful letter ad-

---

* Horace Greeley was one of the most vigilant men during the debate.   He wrote to Lincoln and me many letters which I still retain. In a letter to me during the campaign, October 6, he says with reference to Douglas: "In his present position I could not of course support him, but he need not have been in this position had the Republicans of Illinois been as wise and far-seeing as they are earnest and true. . . . but seeing things are as they are, I do not wish to be quoted as authority for making trouble and division among our friends."   Soon after hearing of the result of November election he again writes : "I advise you privately that Mr. Douglas would be the strongest candidate that the Democratic party could present for President ; but they will not present him.   The old leaders wouldn't endorse it.   As he is doomed to be slaughtered at Charleston it is good policy to fatten him meantime.   He will cut up the better at killing time."   An inquiry for his preference as to Presidential timber elicited this response, December 4th.   "As to President, my present judgment is Edward Bates, with John M. Read for Vice ; but I am willing to go anything that looks strong.   I don't wish to load the team heavier than it will pull through.   As to Douglas, he is like the man's boy who (he said) 'didn't weigh so much as he expected, and he always knew he wouldn't.'   I never thought him very sound coin ; but I didn't think it best to beat him on the back of his anti-Lecompton fight, and I am still of that opinion."

monishing him not to give up the battle, he responded ;

"Springfield, November 19, 1858.

"Mr. Henry Asbury,

"*My Dear Sir:*—Yours of the 13th was received some days ago. The fight must go on.
The cause of civil liberty must not be surrendered
at the end of one or even one hundred defeats.
Douglas had the ingenuity to be supported in the
late contest both as the best means to break down
and to uphold the slave interest. No ingenuity can
keep these antagonistic elements in harmony long.
Another explosion will soon come.

"Yours truly,

"A. Lincoln.

To another friend* on the same day he writes :
"I am glad I made the late race. It gave me a
hearing on the great and durable questions of the
age which I could have had in no other way ; and
though I now sink out of view and shall be forgotten, I believe I have made some marks which will
tell for the cause of liberty long after I am gone."

Before passing to later events in Mr. Lincoln's
life it is proper to include in this chapter, as a specimen of his oratory at this time, his eloquent reference to the Declaration of Independence found
in a speech delivered at Beardstown, August 12,
and not at Lewiston five days later, as many biographers have it. Aside from its concise reasoning, the sublime thought it suggests entitles it to
rank beside that great masterpiece, his Gettysburg

---

* Dr. Henry.

address. After alluding to the suppression by the Fathers of the Republic of the slave trade, he says : " These by their representatives in old Independence Hall said to the whole race of men : ' We hold these truths to be self-evident : that all men are created equal ; that they are endowed by their Creator with certain inalienable rights ; that among these are life, liberty, and the pursuit of happiness.' This was their majestic interpretation of the economy of the universe. This was their lofty, and wise, and noble understanding of the justice of the Creator to his creatures—yes, gentlemen, to all his creatures, to the whole great family of man. In their enlightened belief, nothing stamped with the divine image and likeness was sent into the world to be trodden on and degraded and imbruted by its fellows. They grasped not only the whole race of man then living, but they reached forward and seized upon the farthest posterity. They erected a beacon to guide their children, and their children's children, and the countless myriads who should inhabit the earth in other ages. Wise statesmen as they were, they knew the tendency of prosperity to breed tyrants, and so they established these great self-evident truths, that when in the distant future some man, some faction, some interest, should set up the doctrine that none but rich men, none but white men, or none but Anglo-Saxon white men were entitled to life, liberty, and the pursuit of happiness, their posterity might look up again to the Declaration of Independence and take courage to renew the battle which their fathers began, so that truth and justice and mercy and all the humane and Christian virtues might not be extinguished from the land; so that no man would hereafter dare to limit and circumscribe the great principles on which the temple of liberty was being built.

" Now, my countrymen, if you have been taught doctrines conflicting with the great landmarks of the Declaration of Independence ; if you have listened to suggestions which would take away from its grandeur and mutilate the fair symmetry of its proportions; if you have been inclined to believe that all men are not created equal in those inalienable rights enumerated by our chart of liberty : let me entreat you to come back. Return to the fountain whose waters spring close by the blood of the Revolution. Think nothing of me ; take no thought for the political fate of any man whomsoever, but come back to the truths that are in the Declaration of Independence. You may do anything with me you choose, if you will but heed these sacred principles. You may not only defeat me for the Senate, but you may take me and put me to death. While pretending no indifference to earthly honors, I do claim to be actuated in this contest by something higher than an anxiety for office. I charge you to drop every paltry and insignificant thought for any man's success. It is nothing ; I am nothing ; Judge Douglas is nothing. But do not destroy that immortal emblem of humanity—the Declaration of American Independence."

One of the newspaper men* who heard this majestic oration wrote me as follows: "The apostrophe to the Declaration of Independence to which you refer was written by myself from a vivid recollection of Mr. Lincoln's speech at Beardstown, August 12, 1858. On the day following the delivery of the speech, as Mr. Lincoln and I were proceeding by steamer from Beardstown to Havana, I said to him that I had been greatly impressed by his concluding remarks of the day previous, and that if he would write them out for me I felt confident their publication would be highly beneficial to our cause as well as honorable to his own fame. He replied that he had but a faint recollection of any portion of the speech ; that, like all his campaign speeches, it was necessarily extemporaneous ; and that its good or bad effect depended upon the inspiration of the moment. He added that I had probably over-estimated the value of the remarks referred to. In reply to my question whether he had any objection to my writing them out from memory and putting them in the form of a verbatim report, he said, ' None at all.' I accordingly did so. I felt confident then and I feel equally assured now that I transcribed the peroration with absolute fidelity as to ideas and commendable fidelity as to language. I certainly aimed to reproduce his exact words, and my recollection of the passage as spoken was very clear. After I had finished writing I read it to Mr. Lincoln. When I had finished the reading he said,

---

* Horace White, MS., May 17, 1865.

' Well, those are my views, and if I said anything on the subject I must have said substantially that, but not nearly so well as that is said.' I remember this remark quite distinctly, and if the old steamer *Editor* is still in existence I could show the place where we were sitting. Having secured his assent to the publication I forwarded it to our paper, but inasmuch as my report of the Beardstown meeting had been already mailed I incorporated the remarks on the Declaration of Independence in my letter from Lewiston two or three days subsequently.

. . . . I do not remember ever having related these facts before, although they have often recurred to me as I have seen the peroration resuscitated again and again, and published (with good effect, I trust) in the newspapers of this country and England."

CHAPTER IV.

THE importance of a more accurate and elaborate history of the debate between Lincoln and Douglas has induced Mr. Weik and me to secure, for publication in these pages, the account by Horace White, of this world-renowned forensic contest. Mr. White's means of knowledge, as fully set forth in the article, are exceptional, and his treatment of the subject is not less entertaining than truthful. It is certainly a great contribution to history and we insert it without further comment:

"It was my good fortune to accompany Mr. Lincoln during his political campaign against Senator Douglas in 1858, not only at the joint debates but also at most of the smaller meetings where his competitor was not present. We traveled together many thousands of miles. I was in the employ of the Chicago *Tribune*, then called the *Press and Tribune*. Senator Douglas had entered upon his campaign with two short-hand reporters, James B. Sheridan and Henry Binmore, whose duty it was to 'write it up' in the columns of the Chicago *Times*. The necessity of counteracting or matching that force became apparent very soon, and I was chosen to write up Mr. Lincoln's campaign.

"I was not a short-hand reporter. The verbatim reporting for the Chicago *Tribune* in the joint debates was done by Mr. Robert R. Hitt, late Assistant Secretary of State, and the present Representative in Congress from the 6th District of Illinois. Verbatim reporting was a new feature in journalism in Chicago, and Mr. Hitt was the pioneer thereof. The publication of Senator Douglas's opening speech in that campaign, delivered on the evening of July 9th, by the *Tribune* the next morning, was a feat hitherto unexampled in the West, and most mortifying to the Democratic newspaper, the *Times*, and to Sheridan and Binmore, who, after taking down the speech as carefully as Mr. Hitt had done, had gone to bed intending to write it out next day, as was then customary.

"All of the seven joint debates were reported by Mr. Hitt for the *Tribune*, the manuscript passing through my hands before going to the printers, but no changes were made by me except in a few cases where confusion on the platform, or the blowing of the wind, had caused some slight hiatus or evident mistake in catching the speaker's words. I could not resist the temptation to *italicise* a few passages in Mr. Lincoln's speeches, where his manner of delivery had been especially emphatic.

"The volume containing the debates, published in 1860 by Follett, Foster & Co., of Columbus, Ohio, presents Mr. Lincoln's speeches as they appeared in the Chicago *Tribune*, and Mr. Douglas's as they appeared in the Chicago *Times*. Of course, the speeches of both were published simultaneously in both papers. The Chicago *Times'* reports of Mr. Lincoln's speeches were not at all satisfactory to Mr. Lincoln's friends, and this led to a charge that they were purposely mutilated in order to give his competitor a more

scholarly appearance before the public—a charge in-
dignantly denied by Sheridan and Binmore.   There
was really no foundation for this charge.   Of course,
Sheridan and Binmore took more pains with Mr.
Douglas's speeches than with those of his opponent.
That was their business.   It was what they were paid
for, and what they were expected to do.   The debates
were all held in the open air, on rude platforms hastily
put together, shaky, and overcrowded with people.
The reporters' tables were liable to be jostled and
their manuscript agitated by the wind.   Some gaps
were certain to occur in the reporters' notes and these,
when occurring in Mr. Douglas's speeches, would certainly be straightened out by his own reporters, who
would feel no such responsibility for the rough places
in Mr. Lincoln's.   Then it must be added that there
were fewer involved sentences in Mr. Douglas's *ex-
tempore* speeches than in Mr. Lincoln's.   Douglas
was the more practiced and more polished speaker of
the two, and it was easier for a reporter to follow him.
All his sentences were round and perfect in his mind
before he opened his lips.   This was not always the
case with Mr. Lincoln's.

"My acquaintance with Mr. Lincoln began four
years before the campaign of which I am writing, in
October, 1854.   I was then in the employ of the Chicago *Evening Journal.*   I had been sent to Springfield
to report the political doings of State Fair week for
that newspaper.   Thus it came about that I occupied
a front seat in the Representatives' Hall, in the old
State House, when Mr. Lincoln delivered the speech
already described in this volume.   The impression
made upon me by the orator was quite overpowering.

I had not heard much political speaking up to that time. I have heard a great deal since. I have never heard anything since, either by Mr. Lincoln, or by anybody, that I would put on a higher plane of oratory. All the strings that play upon the human heart and understanding were touched with masterly skill and force, while beyond and above all skill was the overwhelming conviction pressed upon the audience that the speaker himself was charged with an irresistible and inspiring duty to his fellow men. This conscientious impulse drove his arguments through the heads of his hearers down into their bosoms, where they made everlasting lodgment. I had been nurtured in the Abolitionist faith, and was much more radical than Mr. Lincoln himself on any point where slavery was concerned, yet it seemed to me, when this speech was finished, as though I had had a very feeble conception of the wickedness of the Kansas-Nebraska Bill. I was filled, as never before, with the sense of my own duty and responsibility as a citizen toward the aggressions of the slave power.

"Having, since then, heard all the great public speakers of this country subsequent to the period of Clay and Webster, I award the palm to Mr. Lincoln as the one who, although not first in all respects, would bring more men, of doubtful or hostile leanings, around to his way of thinking by talking to them on a platform, than any other.

"Although I heard him many times afterward I shall longest remember him as I then saw the tall, angular form with the long, angular arms, at times bent nearly double with excitement, like a large flail animating two smaller ones, the mobile face wet with perspiration which he discharged in drops as he threw his head this way and that like a projectile—not a graceful figure, yet not an ungraceful one. After listening to him a few minutes, when he had got well warmed with his subject, nobody would mind whether he was graceful or not. All thought of grace or form would be lost in the exceeding attractiveness of what he was saying.

"Returning to the campaign of 1858—I was sent by my employers to Springfield to attend the Republican State Convention of that year. Again I sat at a short distance from Mr. Lincoln when he delivered the 'house-divided-against-itself' speech, on the 17th of June. This was delivered from manuscript, and was the only one I ever heard him deliver in that way. When it was concluded he put the manuscript in my hands and asked me to go to the *State Journal* office and read the proof of it. I think it had already been set in type. Before 1 had finished this task Mr. Lincoln himself came into the composing room of the *State Journal* and looked over the revised proofs. He said to me that he had taken a great deal of pains with this speech, and that he wanted it to go before the people just as he had prepared it. He added that some of his friends had scolded him a good deal about the opening paragraph and 'the house divided against itself,' and wanted him to change it or leave it out altogether, but that he believed he had studied this subject more deeply than they had, and that he was going to stick to that text whatever happened.

"On the 9th of July, Senator Douglas returned to Chicago from Washington City. He had stopped a few days at Cleveland, Ohio, to allow his friends to arrange a grand *entrée* for him. It was arranged that he should arrive about eight o'clock in the evening by the Michigan Central Railway, whose station was at the foot of Lake street, in which street the principal hotel, the Tremont House, was situated, and that he should be driven in a carriage drawn by six horses to the hotel, where he should make his first speech of the campaign. To carry out this arrangement it was necessary that he should leave the Michigan Southern Railway at Laporte and go to Michigan City, at which place the Chicago committee of reception took him in charge. It was noted by the Chicago *Times* that some malicious person at Michigan City had secretly spiked the only cannon in the town, so that the Douglas men were obliged to use an anvil on the occasion.

"When Mr. Douglas and his train arrived at the Lake street station, the crowd along the street to the hotel, four or five blocks distant, was dense, and, for the Chicago of that day, tremendous. It was with great difficulty that the six-horse team got through it at all. Banners, bands of music, cannon and fireworks added their various inspiration to the scene. About nine o'clock Mr. Douglas made his appearance on a balcony on the Lake street side of the hotel and made his speech. Mr. Lincoln sat in a chair just inside the house, very near the speaker, and was an attentive listener.

"Mr. Douglas's manner on this occasion was courtly and conciliatory. His argument was plausible but worthless—being, for the most part, a rehash of his 'popular sovereignty' dogma ; nevertheless, he made a good impression. He could make more out of a bad case, I think, than any other man this country has ever produced, and I hope the country will never produce his like again in this particular. If his fate had been cast in the French Revolution, he would have out-demagogued the whole lot of them. I consider the use he made of this chip called popular sovereignty, riding upon it safely through some of the stormiest years in our history, and having nothing else to ride upon, a feat of dexterity akin to genius. But mere dexterity would not alone have borne him along his pathway in life. He had dauntless courage, unwearied energy, engaging manners, boundless ambition, unsurpassed powers of debate, and strong personal magnetism. Among the Democrats of the North his ascendency was unquestioned and his power almost absolute. He was exactly fitted to hew his way to the Presidency, and he would have done so infallibly if he had not made the mistake of coquetting with slavery. This was a mistake due to the absence of moral principle. If he had been as true to freedom as Lincoln was he would have distanced Lincoln in the race. It was, in fact, no easy task to prevent the Republicans from flocking after him in 1858, when he had, for once only, sided with them, in reference to the Lecompton Constitution. There are some reasons for believing that Douglas would have separated himself from the slave-holders entirely after the Lecompton fight, if he had thought that the Republicans would join in re-electing him to the Senate. Yet the position taken by the party in Illinois was perfectly sound. Douglas was too slippery to make a bargain with. He afterward redeemed himself in the eyes of his opponents by an immense service to the Union, which no other man could have rendered ; but, up to this time, there was nothing for anti-slavery men to do but to beat him if they could.

"I will add here that I had no personal acquaintance with Mr. Douglas, although my opportunities for meeting him were frequent. I regarded him as the most dangerous enemy of liberty, and, therefore, as my enemy. I did not want to know him. Accordingly, one day when Mr. Sheridan courteously offered to present me to his chief, I declined without giving any reason. Of course, this was a mistake ; but, at the age of twenty-four, I took my politics very seriously. I thought that all the work of saving the country had to be done then and there. I have since learned to leave something to time and Providence.

"Mr. Lincoln's individual campaign began at Beardstown, Cass county, August 12th. Douglas had been there the previous day, and I had heard him. His speech had consisted mainly of tedious repetitions of 'popular sovereignty,' but he had taken occasion to notice Lincoln's conspiracy charge, and had called it 'an infamous lie.' He had also alluded to Senator Trumbull's charge that he (Douglas) had, two years earlier, been engaged in a plot to force a bogus constitution on the people of Kansas without giving them an opportunity to vote upon it. 'The miserable, craven-hearted wretch,' said Douglas, 'he would rather have both ears cut off than to use that language in my presence, where I could call him to account.' Before entering upon this subject, Douglas turned to his reporters and said 'Take this down.' They did so and it was published a few days later in the St. Louis *Republican.* This incident furnished the text of the Charleston joint debate on the 18th of September.

"Mr. Douglas's meeting at Beardstown was large and enthusiastic, but was composed of a lower social stratum than the Republican meeting of the following day. Mr. Lincoln came up the Illinois River from the town of Naples in the steamer *Sam Gaty.* Cass county and the surrounding region was by no means hopeful Republican ground. Yet Mr. Lincoln's friends mustered forty horsemen and two bands of music, beside a long procession on foot to meet him at the landing. Schuyler county sent a delegation of three hundred, and Morgan county was well represented. These were mostly Old Line Whigs who had followed Lincoln in earlier days. Mr. Lincoln's speech at Beardstown was one of the best he ever made in my hearing, and was not a repetition of any other. In fact, he never repeated himself except when some remark or question from the audience led him back upon a subject that he had already discussed. Many times did I marvel to see him get on a platform at some out-of-the-way place and begin an entirely new speech, equal, in all respects, to any of the joint debates, and continue for two hours in a high strain of argumentative power and eloquence, without saying anything that I had heard before. After the Edwardsville meeting I said to him that it was wonderful to me that he could find new things to say everywhere, while Douglas was parroting his popular sovereignty speech at every place. He replied that Douglas was not lacking in versatility, but that he had a theory that the popular sovereignty speech was the one to win on, and that the audiences whom he addressed would hear it only once and would never know whether he made the same speech elsewhere or not, and would never care. Most likely, if their attention were called to the subject, they would think that was the proper thing to do. As for himself, he said that he could not repeat to-day what he had said yesterday. The subject kept enlarging and widening in his mind as he went on, and it was much easier to make a new speech than to repeat an old one.

"It was at Beardstown that Mr. Lincoln uttered the glowing words that have come to be known as the apostrophe to the Declaration of Independence, the circumstances attending which are narrated in another part of this book. Probably the apostrophe, as printed, is a trifle more florid than as delivered, and, therefore, less forcible.

"The following passage, from the Beardstown speech, was taken down by me on the platform by long-hand notes and written out immediately afterward:

THE CONSPIRACY CHARGE.

"'I made a speech in June last in which I pointed out, briefly and consecutively, a series of public measures leading directly to the nationalization of slavery —the spreading of that institution over all the Territories and all the States, old as well as new, North as well as South. I enumerated the repeal of the Missouri Compromise, which, every candid man must acknowledge, conferred upon emigrants to Kansas and Nebraska the right to carry slaves there and hold them in bondage, whereas formerly they had no such right; I alluded to the events which followed that repeal, events in which Judge Douglas's name figures quite prominently; I referred to the Dred Scott decision and the extraordinary means taken to prepare the public mind for that decision; the efforts put forth by President Pierce to make the people believe that, in the election of James Buchanan, they had endorsed the doctrine that slavery may exist in the free Territories of the Union — the earnest exhortation put forth by President Buchanan to the people to stick to that decision whatever it might be — the close-fitting niche in the Nebraska bill, wherein the right of the people to govern themselves is made 'subject to the constitution of the United States'—the extraordinary haste made by Judge Douglas to give this decision an endorsement at the capitol of Illinois. I alluded to other concurring circumstances, which I need not repeat now, and I said that, though I could not open the bosoms of men and find out their secret motives, yet, when I found the framework of a barn, or a bridge, or any other structure, built by a number of carpenters — Stephen and Franklin and Roger and James — and so built that each tenon had its proper mortice, and the whole forming a symmetrical piece of workmanship, I should say that those carpenters all worked on an intelligible plan, and understood each other from the beginning. This embraced the main argument in my speech before the Republican State Convention in June. Judge Douglas received a copy of my speech some two weeks before his return to Illinois. He had ample time to examine and reply to it if he chose to do so. He did examine and he did reply to it, but he wholly overlooked the body of my argument, and said nothing about the 'conspiracy charge,' as he terms it. He made his speech up of complaints against our tendencies to negro equality and amalgamation. Well, seeing that Douglas had had the process served on him, that he had taken notice of the process, that he had come into court and pleaded to a part of the complaint, but had ignored the main issue, I took a default on him. I held that he had no plea to make to the general charge. So when I was called on to reply to him, twenty-four hours afterward, I renewed the charge as explicitly as I could. My speech was reported and published on the following morning, and, of course, Judge Douglas saw it. He went from Chicago to Bloomington and there made another and longer speech, and yet took no notice of the 'conspiracy charge.' He then went to Springfield and made another elaborate argument, but was not prevailed upon to know anything about the outstanding indictment. I made another speech at Springfield, this time taking it for granted that Judge Douglas was satisfied to take his chances in the campaign with the imputation of the conspiracy hanging over him. It was not until he went into a small town, Clinton, in De Witt county, where he delivered his fourth or fifth regular speech, that he found it convenient to notice this matter at all. At that place (I was standing in the crowd when he made his speech), he bethought himself that he was charged with something, and his reply was that his ' self-respect alone prevented him from calling it a falsehood.' Well, my friends, perhaps he so far lost his self-respect in Beardstown as to actually call it a falsehood.

" ' But now I have this reply to make: that while the Nebraska bill was pending, Judge Douglas helped to vote down a clause giving the people of the Territories the right to exclude slavery if they chose; that neither while the bill was pending, nor at any other time, would he give his opinion whether the people had the right to exclude slavery, though respectfully asked; that he made a report, which I hold in my hand, from the Committee on Territories, in which he said the rights of the people of the Territories, in this regard, are 'held in abeyance,' and cannot be immediately exercised; that the Dred Scott decision expressly denies any such right, but declares that neither Congress nor the Territorial Legislature can keep slavery out of Kansas and that Judge Douglas endorses that decision. All these charges are new; that is, I did not make them in my original speech. They are additional and cumulative testimony. I bring them forward now and dare Judge Douglas to deny one of them. Let him do so and I will prove them by such testimony as shall confound him forever. I say to you, that it would be more to the purpose for Judge Douglas to say that he did not repeal the Missouri Compromise; that he did not make slavery possible where it was impossible before; that he did not leave a niche in the Nebraska bill for the Dred Scott decision to rest in; that he did not vote down a clause giving the people the right to exclude slavery if they wanted to; that he did not refuse to give his individual opinion whether a Territorial Legislature could exclude slavery; that he did not make a report to the Senate, in which he said that the rights of the people, in this regard, were held in abeyance and could not be immediately exercised; that he did not make a hasty endorsement of the Dred Scott decision over at Springfield;* that he does not now endorse that decision;

---

* This refers to Douglas's speech of June 12, 1857.

that that decision does not take away from the Territorial Legislature the right to exclude slavery; and that he did not, in the original Nebraska bill, so couple the words State and Territory together that what the Supreme Court has done in forcing open all the Territories to slavery it may yet do in forcing open all the States. I say it would be vastly more to the point for Judge Douglas to say that he did not do some of these things; that he did not forge some of these links of testimony, than to go vociferating about the country that possibly he may hint that somebody is a liar.'

"The next morning, August 13th, we boarded the steamer *Editor* and went to Havana, Mason county. Mr. Lincoln was in excellent spirits. Several of his old Whig friends were on board, and the journey was filled up with politics and story-telling. In the latter branch of human affairs, Mr. Lincoln was most highly gifted. From the beginning to the end of our travels the fund of anecdotes never failed, and, wherever we happened to be, all the people within ear-shot would begin to work their way up to this inimitable story-teller. His stories were always *apropos* of something going on, and oftenest related to things that had happened in his own neighborhood. He was constantly being reminded of one, and, when he told it, his facial expression was so irresistibly comic that the bystanders generally exploded in laughter before he reached what he called the 'nub' of it. Although the intervals between the meetings were filled up brimful with mirth in this way, Mr. Lincoln indulged very sparingly in humor in his speeches. I asked him one day why he did not oftener turn the laugh on Douglas. He replied that he was too much in earnest, and that it was doubtful whether turning the laugh on anybody really gained any votes.

"We arrived at Havana while Douglas was still speaking. The deputation that met Mr. Lincoln at the landing suggested that he should go up to the grove where the Democratic meeting was going on and hear what Douglas was saying. But he declined to do so, saying: 'The Judge was so put out by my listening to him at Bloomington and Clinton that I promised to leave him alone at his own meetings for the rest of the campaign. I understand that he is calling Trumbull and myself liars, and if he should see me in the crowd he might be so ashamed of himself as to omit the most telling part of his argument.' I strolled up to the Douglas meeting just before its conclusion, and there met a friend who had heard the whole. He was in a state of high indignation. He said that Douglas must certainly have been drinking before he came on the platform, because he had called Lincoln 'a liar, a coward, a wretch and a sneak.'

"When Mr. Lincoln replied, on the following day, he took notice of Douglas's hard words in this way:

"'I am informed that my distinguished friend yesterday became a little excited, nervous (?) perhaps, and that he said something about fighting, as though looking to a personal encounter between himself and me. Did anybody in this audience hear him use such language? (Yes, Yes.) I am informed, further, that somebody in his audience, rather more excited or nervous than himself, took off his coat and offered to take the job off Judge Douglas's hands and fight Lincoln himself. Did anybody here witness that war-

like proceeding ? (Laughter and cries of 'yes.') Well,
I merely desire to say that I shall fight neither Judge
Douglas nor his second. I shall not do this for two
reasons, which I will explain. In the first place a fight
would prove nothing which is in issue in this election
It might establish that Judge Douglas is a more muscular man than myself, or it might show that I am a
more muscular man than Judge Douglas. But this
subject is not referred to in the Cincinnati platform,
nor in either of the Springfield platforms. Neither
result would prove him right or me wrong. And so of
the gentleman who offered to do his fighting for him.
If my fighting Judge Douglas would not prove any
thing, it would certainly prove nothing for me to fight
his bottle-holder. My second reason for not having a
personal encounter with Judge Douglas is that I don't
believe he wants it himself. He and I are about the
best friends in the world, and when we get together
he would no more think of fighting me than of fighting
his wife. Therefore, when the Judge talked about
fighting he was not giving vent to any ill-feeling of his
own, but was merely trying to excite—well, let us say
enthusiasm against me on the part of his audience.
And, as I find he was tolerably successful in this, we
will call it quits.'

"At Havana I saw Mrs. Douglas (*née* Cutts)
standing with a group of ladies a short distance from
the platform on which her husband was speaking, and
I thought I had never seen a more queenly face and
figure. I saw her frequently afterward in this campaign, but never personally met her till many years
later, when she had become the wife of General Williams of the regular army, and the mother of children

who promised to be as beautiful as herself. There is no doubt in my mind that this attractive presence was very helpful to Judge Douglas in the campaign. It is certain that the Republicans considered her a dangerous element.

" From Havana we went to Lewistown and thence to Peoria, still following on the heels of the Little Giant, but nothing of special interest happened at either place. As we came northward Mr. Lincoln's meetings grew in size, but at Lewistown the Douglas gathering was much the larger of the two and was the most considerable in point of numbers I had yet seen.

"The next stage brought us to Ottawa, the first joint debate, August 21st. Here the crowd was enormous. The weather had been very dry and the town was shrouded in dust raised by the moving populace. Crowds were pouring into town from sunrise till noon in all sorts of conveyances, teams, railroad trains, canal boats, cavalcades, and processions on foot, with banners and inscriptions, stirring up such clouds of dust that it was hard to make out what was underneath them. The town was covered with bunting, and bands of music were tooting around every corner, drowned now and then by the roar of cannon. Mr. Lincoln came by railroad and Mr. Douglas by carriage from La Salle. A train of seventeen passenger cars from Chicago attested the interest felt in that city in the first meeting of the champions. Two great processions escorted them to the platform in the public square. But the eagerness to hear the speaking was so great that the crowd had taken possession of the square and the platform, and had climbed on the wooden awning overhead, to such an extent that the speakers and the committees and reporters could not get to their places. Half an hour was consumed in a rough-and-tumble skirmish to make way for them, and, when finally this was accomplished, a section of the awning gave way with its load of men and boys, and came down on the heads of the Douglas committee of reception. But, fortunately, nobody was hurt.

"Here I was joined by Mr. Hitt and also by Mr. Chester P. Dewey of the New York *Evening Post*, who remained with us until the end of the campaign. Hither, also, came quite an army of young newspaper men, among whom was Henry Villard, in behalf of Forney's Philadelphia *Press*. I have preserved Mr. Dewey's sketch of the two orators as they appeared on the Ottawa platform, and I introduce it here as a graphic description by a new hand:

"'Two men presenting wider contrasts could hardly be found, as the representatives of the two great parties. Everybody knows Douglas, a short, thick-set, burly man, with large, round head, heavy hair, dark complexion, and fierce, bull-dog look. Strong in his own real power, and skilled by a thousand conflicts in all the strategy of a hand-to-hand or a general fight; of towering ambition, restless in his determined desire for notoriety, proud, defiant, arrogant, audacious, unscrupulous, 'Little Dug' ascended the platform and looked out impudently and carelessly on the immense throng which surged and struggled before him. A native of Vermont, reared on a soil where no slave stood, he came to Illinois a teacher, and from one post to another had risen to his present eminence. Forgetful of the ancestral hatred of slavery to which he was the heir, he had come to be a holder of slaves, and to owe much of his fame to continued subservience to Southern influence.

"'The other—Lincoln— is a native of Kentucky, of poor white parentage, and, from his cradle, has felt the blighting influence of the dark and cruel shadow which rendered labor dishonorable and kept the poor in poverty, while it advanced the rich in their possessions. Reared in poverty, and to the humblest aspirations, he left his native State, crossed the line into Illinois, and began his career of honorable toil. At first a laborer, splitting rails for a living—deficient in education, and applying himself even to the rudiments of knowledge—he, too, felt the expanding power of his American manhood, and began to achieve the greatness to which he has succeeded. With great difficulty, struggling through the tedious formularies of legal lore, he was admitted to the bar, and rapidly made his way to the front ranks of his profession. Honored by the people with office, he is still the same honest and reliable man. He volunteers in the Black Hawk war, and does the State good service in its sorest need. In every relation of life, socially and to the State, Mr. Lincoln has been always the pure and honest man. In physique he is the opposite to Douglas. Built on the Kentucky type, he is very tall, slender and angular, awkward even in gait and attitude. His face is sharp, large-featured and unprepossessing. His eyes are deep-set under heavy brows, his forehead is high and retreating, and his hair is dark and heavy. In repose, I must confess that 'Long Abe's' appearance is *not* comely. But stir him up and the fire of his genius plays on every feature. His eye glows and sparkles; every lineament, now so ill-formed, grows brilliant and expressive, and you have before you a man of rare power and of strong magnetic influence. He *takes* the people every time, and there is no getting away from his sturdy good sense, his unaffected sincerity and the unceasing play of his good humor, which accompanies his close logic and smoothes the way to conviction. Listening to him on Saturday, calmly and unprejudiced, I was convinced that he had no superior as a stump-speaker. He is clear, concise and logical, his language is eloquent and at perfect command. He is altogether a more fluent speaker than Douglas, and in all the arts of debate fully his equal. The Republicans of Illinois have chosen a champion worthy of their heartiest support, and fully equipped for the conflict with the great Squatter Sovereign.'

"One trifling error of fact will be noticed by the readers of these volumes in Mr. Dewey's sketch. It relates to Douglas, and it is proper to correct it here. Mr. Douglas was never a slave-holder. As a trustee or guardian, he held a plantation in Louisiana with the slaves thereon, which had belonged to Col. Robert Martin, of North Carolina, the maternal grandfather of his two sons by his first marriage. It is a fact that Douglas refused to accept this plantation and its belongings as a gift to himself from Colonel Martin in the life-time of the latter. It was characteristic of him that he declined to be an owner of slaves, not because he sympathized with the Abolitionists, but because, as he said once in a debate with Senator Wade, 'being a Northern man by birth, by education and residence, and intending always to remain such, it was impossible for me to know, understand, and provide for the happiness of those people.'

"At the conclusion of the Ottawa debate, a circumstance occurred which, Mr. Lincoln said to me afterwards, was extremely mortifying to him. Half a dozen Republicans, roused to a high pitch of enthusiasm for their leader, seized him as he came down from the platform, hoisted him upon their shoulders and marched off with him, singing the 'Star Spangled Banner,' or 'Hail Columbia,' until they reached the place where he was to spend the night. What use Douglas made of this incident, is known to the readers of the joint debates. He said a few days later, at Joliet, that Lincoln was so used up in the discussion that his knees trembled, and he had to be carried from the platform, and he caused this to be printed in the newspapers of his own party. Mr. Lincoln called him to account for this fable at Jonesboro.

"The Ottawa debate gave great satisfaction to our side. Mr. Lincoln, we thought, had the better of the argument, and we all came away encouraged. But the Douglas men were encouraged also. In his concluding half hour, Douglas spoke with great rapidity and animation, and yet with perfect distinctness, and his supporters cheered him wildly.

"The next joint debate was to take place at Freeport, six days later. In the interval, Mr. Lincoln addressed meetings at Henry, Marshall county; Augusta, Hancock county, and Macomb, McDonough county. During this interval he prepared the answers to the seven questions put to him by Douglas at Ottawa, and wrote the four questions which he propounded to Douglas at Freeport. The second of these, viz.: 'Can the people of a United States Territory, in any lawful way, against the wish of any citizen of the United States, exclude slavery from its limits prior to the formation of a State Constitution?' was made the subject of a conference between Mr. Lincoln and a number of his friends from Chicago, among whom were Norman B. Judd and Dr. C. H. Ray, the latter the chief editor of the *Tribune*. This conference took place at the town of Dixon. I was not present, but Doctor Ray told me that all who were there counseled Mr. Lincoln not to put that question to Douglas, because he would answer it in the affirmative and thus probably secure his re-election. It was their opinion that Lincoln should argue strongly from the Dred Scott decision, which Douglas endorsed, that the people of the Territories could not lawfully exclude slavery prior to the formation of a State Constitution, but that he should not force Douglas to say yes or no. They believed that the latter would let that subject alone as much as possible in order not to offend the South, unless he should be driven into a corner. Mr. Lincoln replied that to draw an affirmative answer from Douglas on this question was exactly what he wanted, and that his object was to make it impossible for Douglas to get the vote of the Southern States in the next Presidential election. He considered that fight much more important than the present one and he would be willing to lose this in order to win that.*

---

* Mr. Lincoln's words are given in Mr. Arnold's biography thus: "I am after larger game ; the battle of 1860 is worth a hundred of this." Mr. Arnold's authority is not mentioned, but these are exactly the words that Doctor Ray repeated to me.

"The result justified Mr. Lincoln's prevision. Douglas did answer in the affirmative. If he had answered in the negative he would have lost the Senatorial election, and that would have ended his political career. He took the chance of being able to make satisfactory explanations to the slaveholders, but they would have nothing to do with him afterward.

"The crowd that assembled at Freeport on the 27th of August was even larger than that at Ottawa. Hundreds of people came from Chicago and many from the neighboring State of Wisconsin. Douglas came from Galena the night before the debate, and was greeted with a great torch-light procession. Lincoln came the following morning from Dixon, and was received at the railway station by a dense crowd, filling up all the adjacent streets, who shouted themselves hoarse when his tall form was seen emerging from the train. Here, again, the people had seized upon the platform, and all the approaches to it, an hour before the speaking began, and a hand-to-hand fight took place to secure possession.

"After the debate was finished, we Republicans did not feel very happy. We held the same opinion that Mr. Judd and Doctor Ray had—that Douglas's answer had probably saved him from defeat. We did not look forward, and we did not look South, and even if we had done so, we were too much enlisted in this campaign to swap it for another one which was two years distant. Mr. Lincoln's wisdom was soon vindicated by his antagonist, one of whose earliest acts, after he returned to Washington City, was to make a speech (February 23, 1859) defending himself against attacks upon the 'Freeport heresy,' as the Southerners called it. In that debate Jefferson Davis was particularly aggravating, and Douglas did not reply to him with his usual spirit.

"It would draw this chapter out to unreasonable length, if I were to give details of all the small meetings of this campaign. After the Freeport joint debate, we went to Carlinville, Macoupin county, where John M. Palmer divided the time with Mr. Lincoln. From this place we went to Clinton, De Witt county, via Springfield and Decatur. During this journey an incident occurred which gave unbounded mirth to Mr. Lincoln at my expense.

"We left Springfield about nine o'clock in the evening for Decatur, where we were to change cars and take the north-bound train on the Illinois Central Railway. I was very tired and I curled myself up as best I could on the seat to take a nap, asking Mr. Lincoln to wake me up at Decatur, which he promised to do. I went to sleep, and when I did awake I had the sensation of having been asleep a long time. It was daylight and I knew that we should have reached Decatur before midnight. Mr. Lincoln's seat was vacant. While I was pulling myself together, the conductor opened the door of the car and shouted, 'State Line.' This was the name of a shabby little town on the border of Indiana. There was nothing to do but to get out and wait for the next train going back to Decatur. About six o'clock in the evening I found my way to Clinton. The meeting was over, of course, and the Chicago *Tribune* had lost its expected report, and I was out of pocket for railroad fares. I wended my way to the house of Mr. C. H. Moore, where Mr. Lincoln was staying, and where I, too, had been an expected guest. When Mr. Lincoln saw me coming up the garden path, his lungs began to crow like a chanticleer, and I thought he would laugh, *sans* intermission, an hour by his dial. He paused long enough to say that he had fallen asleep, also, and did not wake up till the train was starting *from* Decatur. He had very nearly been carried past the station himself, and, in his haste to get out, had forgotten all about his promise to waken me. Then he began to laugh again. The affair was so irresistibly funny, in his view, that he told the incident several times in Washington City when I chanced to meet him, after he became President, to any company who might be present, and with such contagious drollery that all who heard it would shake with laughter.

"Our course took us next to Bloomington, McLean county; Monticello, Piatt county, and Paris, Edgar county. At the last-mentioned place (September 8th) we were joined by Owen Lovejoy, who had never been in that part of the State before. The fame of Lovejoy as an Abolitionist had preceded him, however, and the people gathered around him in a curious and hesitating way, as though he were a witch who might suddenly give them lock-jaw or bring murrain on their cattle, if he were much provoked. Lovejoy saw this and was greatly amused by it, and when he made a speech in the evening, Mr. Lincoln having made his in the day-time, he invited the timid ones to come up and feel of his horns and examine his cloven foot and his forked tail. Lovejoy was one of the most effective orators of his time. After putting his audience in good humor in this way, he made one of his impassioned speeches which never failed to gain votes where human hearts were responsive to the wrongs of slavery. Edgar county was in the Democratic list, but this year it gave a Republican majority on the legislative and congressional tickets, and I think Lovejoy's speech was largely accountable for the result.

"My notes of the Paris meeting embrace the following passage from Mr. Lincoln's speech :

WHAT IS POPULAR SOVEREIGNTY?

"'Let us inquire what Judge Douglas really invented when he introduced the Nebraska Bill? He called it Popular Sovereignty. What does that mean ? It means the sovereignty of the people over their own affairs—in other words, the right of the people to govern themselves. Did Judge Douglas invent this ? Not quite. The idea of Popular Sovereignty was floating about several ages before the author of the Nebraska Bill was born—indeed, before Columbus set foot on this continent. In the year 1776 it took form in the noble words which you are all familiar with: 'We hold these truths to be self-evident, that all men are created equal,' etc. Was not this the origin of Popular Sovereignty as applied to the American people? Here we are told that governments are instituted among men deriving their just powers from the consent of the governed. If that is not Popular Sovereignty, then I have no conception of the meaning of words. If Judge Douglas did not invent this kind of Popular Sovereignty, let us pursue the inquiry and find out what kind he did invent. Was it the right of emigrants to Kansas and Nebraska to govern themselves, and a lot of 'niggers,' too, if they wanted them? Clearly this was no invention of his, because General Cass put forth the same doctrine in 1848 in his so-called Nicholson letter, six years before Douglas thought of such a thing. Then what was it that the 'Little Giant' invented? It never occurred to General Cass to call his discovery by the odd name of Popular Sovereignty. He had not the face to say that the right of the people to govern 'niggers' was the right of the people to govern themselves. His notions of the fitness of things were not moulded to the brazenness of calling the right to put a hundred 'niggers' through under the lash in Nebraska a 'sacred right of self-government.' And here, I submit to you, was Judge Douglas's discovery, and the whole of it. He discovered that the right to breed and flog negroes in Nebraska was Popular Sovereignty.'

"The next meetings in their order were Hillsboro, Montgomery county; Greenville, Bond county, and Edwardsville, Madison county. At Edwardsville (September 13th) I was greatly impressed with Mr. Lincoln's speech, so much so, that I took down the following passages, which, as I read them now, after the lapse of thirty-one years, bring back the whole scene with vividness before me—the quiet autumn day in the quaint old town; the serious people clustered around the platform; Joseph Gillespie officiating as chairman, and the tall, gaunt, earnest man, whose high destiny and tragic death were veiled from our eyes, appealing to his old Whig friends, and seeking to lift them up to his own level:

"'I have been requested,' he said, 'to give a concise statement of the difference, as I understand it, between the Democratic and the Republican parties on the leading issues of the campaign. This question has been put to me by a gentleman whom I do not know. I do not even know whether he is a friend of mine or a supporter of Judge Douglas in this contest, nor does that make any difference. His question is a proper one. Lest I should forget it, I will give you my answer before proceeding with the line of argument I have marked out for this discussion.

" ' The difference between the Republican and the Democratic parties on the leading issues of this contest, as I understand it, is that the former consider slavery a moral, social and political wrong, while the latter do not consider it either a moral, a social or a political wrong; and the action of each, as respects the growth of the country and the expansion of our population, is squared to meet these views. I will not affirm that the Democratic party consider slavery morally, socially and politically right, though their tendency to that view has, in my opinion, been constant and unmistakable for the past five years. I prefer to take, as the accepted maxim of the party, the idea put forth by Judge Douglas, that he 'don't care whether slavery is voted down or voted up.' I am quite willing to believe that many Democrats would prefer that slavery should be always voted down, and I know that some prefer that it be always 'voted up;' but I have a right to insist that their action, especially if it be their constant action, shall determine their ideas and preferences on this subject. Every measure of the Democratic party of late years, bearing directly or indirectly on the slavery question, has corresponded with this notion of utter indifference, whether slavery or freedom shall outrun in the race of empire across to the Pacific—every measure, I say, up to the Dred Scott decision, where, it seems to me, the idea is boldly suggested that slavery is better than freedom. The Republican party, on the contrary, hold that this government was instituted to secure the blessings of freedom, and that slavery is an unqualified evil to the negro, to the white man, to the soil, and to the State. Regarding it as an evil, they will not molest it in the States where it exists, they will not overlook the constitutional guards which our fathers placed around it; they will do nothing that can give proper offense to those who hold slaves by legal sanction; but they will use every constitutional method to prevent the evil from becoming larger and involving more negroes, more white men, more soil, and more States in its deplorable consequences. They will, if possible, place it where the public mind shall rest in the belief that it is in course of ultimate peaceable extinction in God's own good time. And to this end they will, if possible, restore the government to the policy of the fathers— the policy of preserving the new Territories from the baneful influence of human bondage, as the north- western Territories were sought to be preserved by the ordinance of 1787, and the Compromise Act of 1820. They will oppose, in all its length and breadth, the modern Democratic idea, that slavery is as good as freedom, and ought to have room for expansion all over the continent, if people can be found to carry it. All, or nearly all, of Judge Douglas's arguments are logical, if you admit that slavery is as good and as right as freedom, and not one of them is worth a rush if you deny it. This is the difference, as I understand it, between the Republican and Democratic parties.

*   *   *   *   *   *   *   *   *   *

"' My friends, I have endeavored to show you the logical consequences of the Dred Scott decision, which holds that the people of a Territory cannot prevent the establishment of slavery in their midst. I have stated what cannot be gainsaid, that the grounds upon which this decision is made are equally applicable to the free States as to the free Territories, and that the peculiar reasons put forth by Judge Douglas for endorsing this decision, commit him, in advance, to the next decision and to all other decisions coming from the same source. And when, by all these means, you have succeeded in dehumanizing the negro; when you have put him down and made it impossible for him to be but as the beasts of the field; when you have extinguished his soul in this world and placed him where the ray of hope is blown out as in the darkness of the damned, are you quite sure that the demon you have roused will not turn and rend you? What constitutes the bulwark of our own liberty and independence? It is not our frowning battlements, our bristling sea coasts, our army and our navy. These are not our reliance against tyranny. All of those may be turned against us without making us weaker for the struggle. Our reliance is in the love of liberty which God has planted in us. Our defense is in the spirit which prizes liberty as the heritage of all men, in all lands everywhere. Destroy this spirit and you have planted the seeds of despotism at your own doors. Familiarize yourselves with the chains of bondage and you prepare your own limbs to wear them. Accustomed to trample on the rights of others, you have lost the genius of your own independence and become the fit subjects of the first cunning tyrant who rises among you. And let me tell you, that all these things are prepared for you by the teachings of history, if the elections shall promise that the next Dred Scott decision and all future decisions will be quietly acquiesced in by the people.'

"From Edwardsville we went to the Jonesboro joint debate. The audience here was small, not more than 1,000 or 1,500, and nearly all Democrats. This was in the heart of Egypt. The country people came into the little town with ox teams mostly, and a very stunted breed of oxen, too. Their wagons were old-fashioned, and looked as though they were ready to fall in pieces. A train with three or four carloads of Douglas men came up, with Douglas himself, from Cairo. All who were present listened to the debate with very close attention, and there was scarcely any cheering on either side. Of course we did not expect any in that place. The reason why Douglas did not get much, was that Union county was a stronghold of the 'Danites,' or Buchanan Democrats. These were a pitiful minority everywhere except in the two counties of Union and Bureau. The reason for this peculiarity in the two counties named, must lie in the fact that Union county was the home of the United States Marshal for the Southern District, W. L. Dougherty; and Bureau, that of the Marshal for the Northern District, Charles N. Pine. Evidently both these men worked their offices for all they were worth, and the result would seem to show that Marshalships are peculiarly well fitted to the purpose of turning voters from their natural leanings. In Bureau county the 'Danites' polled more votes than the Douglas Democrats. In Union, they divided the party into two nearly equal parts. In no other county did they muster a corporal's guard; James W. Sheahan, the editor of the *Times*, told me, with great glee, after the election, that at one of the voting places in Chicago, where the two Democratic judges of election were Irish, a few 'Danite' votes were offered, but that the judges refused to receive them, saying gravely, 'We don't take that kind.' They thought it was illegal voting.

"The only thing noteworthy that I recall at Jonesboro was not political and not even terrestrial. It was the splendid appearance of Donati's comet in the sky, the evening before the debate. Mr. Lincoln greatly admired this strange visitor, and he and I sat for an hour or more in front of the hotel looking at it.

"From Jonesboro we went to Centralia, where a great State Fair was sprawling over the prairie, but there was no speaking there. It was not good form to have political bouts at State Fairs, and I believe that the managers had prohibited them. After one day at this place, where great crowds clustered around both Lincoln and Douglas whenever they appeared on the grounds, we went to Charleston, Coles county, September 18th, where the fourth joint debate took place.

"This was a very remarkable gathering, the like of which we had not seen elsewhere. It consisted of a great outpouring (or rather inpouring) of the rural population, in their own conveyances. There was only one line of railroad here, and only one special train on it. Yet, to my eye, the crowd seemed larger than at either Ottawa or Freeport, in fact the largest of the series, except the one at Galesburg, which

32

came later. The campaign was now at its height, the previous debates having stirred the people into a real fever. ' It is astonishing,' said Mr. Dewey, in his letter from Charleston to the *Evening Post*, ' how deep an interest in politics this people take. Over long weary miles of hot, dusty prairie, the processions of eager partisans come on foot, on horseback, in wagons drawn by horses or mules; men, women and children, old and young; the half-sick just out of the last ' shake,' children in arms, infants at the maternal fount; pushing on in clouds of dust under a blazing sun, settling down at the town where the meeting is, with hardly a chance for sitting, and even less oppor- tunity for eating, waiting in anxious groups for hours at the places of speaking; talking, discussing, litig- ious, vociferous, while the roar of artillery, the mu- sic of bands, the waving of banners, the huzzas of the crowds, as delegation after delegation appears; the cry of peddlers vending all sorts of wares, from an infallible cure for ' agur ' to a monster water-melon in slices to suit purchasers — combine to render the occasion one scene of confusion and commotion. The hour of one arrives, and a perfect rush is made for the grounds; a column of dust rising to the heavens, and fairly deluging those who are hurrying on through it. Then the speakers come, with flags and banners and music, surrounded by cheering partisans. Their arrival at the grounds and immediate approach to the stand, is the signal for shouts that rend the heavens. They are introduced to the audience amid prolonged and enthusiastic cheers, they are interrupted by frequent applause and they sit down finally among the same uproarious demonstrations. The audience sit or stand patiently, throughout, and, as the last word is spoken, make a break for their homes, first hunting up lost members of their families, gathering their scattered wagon loads together, and, as the daylight fades away, entering again upon the broad prairies and slowly picking their way back to the place of beginning.'

"Both Lincoln and Douglas left the train at Mattoon, distant some ten miles from Charleston, to accept the escort of their respective partisans. Mattoon was then a comparatively new place, a station on the Illinois Central Railway peopled by Northern men. Nearly the whole population of this town turned out to escort Mr. Lincoln along the dusty highway to Charleston. In his procession was a chariot containing thirty-two young ladies, representing the thirty-two States of the Union, and carrying banners to designate the same. Following this, was one young lady on horseback holding aloft a banner inscribed, 'Kansas — I will be free.' As she was very good looking, we thought that she would not remain free always. The muses had been wide awake also, for, on the side of the chariot, was the stirring legend:

'Westward the star of empire takes its way;
The girls link-on to Lincoln, as their mothers did to Clay.'

"The Douglas procession was likewise a formidable one. He, too, had his chariot of young ladies, and, in addition, a mounted escort. The two processions stretched an almost interminable distance along the road, and were marked by a moving cloud of dust.

"Before the Charleston debate, Mr. Lincoln had received (from Senator Trumbull, I suppose) certain official documents to prove that Douglas had attempted, in 1856, to bring Kansas into the Union without allowing the people to vote upon her constitution, and with these he put the Little Giant on the defensive, and pressed him so hard that we all considered that our side had won a substantial victory.

"The Democrats seemed to be uneasy and dissatisfied, both during the debate and afterward. Mr. Isaac N. Arnold, in his biography of Lincoln, page 148, relates an incident in the Charleston debate on the authority of 'a spectator' (not named), to this effect: that near the end of Mr. Lincoln's closing speech, Douglas became very much excited and walked rapidly up and down the platform behind Lincoln, holding a watch in his hand; that the instant the watch showed the half hour, he called out 'Sit down! Lincoln, sit down! Your time is up.'

"This must be a pure invention. My notes show nothing of the kind. I sat on the platform within ten feet of Douglas all the time that Lincoln was speaking. If any such dramatic incident had occurred, I should certainly have made a note of it, and even without notes I think I should have remembered it. Douglas was too old a campaigner to betray himself in this manner, whatever his feelings might have been.

'After the debate was ended and the country people had mostly dispersed, the demand for speeches was still far from being satisfied. Two meetings were started in the evening, with blazing bonfires in the street to mark the places. Richard J. Oglesby, the Republican nominee for Congress (afterward General, Governor and Senator), addressed one of them. At the Douglas meeting, Richard T. Merrick and U. F. Linder were the speakers. Merrick was a young lawyer from Maryland, who had lately settled in Chicago, and a fluent and rather captivating orator. Linder was an Old Line Whig, of much natural ability, who had sided with the Democrats on the break-up of his own party. Later in the campaign Douglas wrote him a letter saying: 'For God's sake, Linder, come up here and help me.' This letter got into the newspapers, and, as a consequence, the receiver of it was immediately dubbed, 'For-God's-Sake Linder,' by which name he was popularly know all the rest of his days.

"There was nothing of special interest between the Charleston debate and that which took place at Galesburg, October 7th. Here we had the largest audience of the whole series and the worst day, the weather being very cold and raw, notwithstanding which, the people flocked from far and near. One feature of the Republican procession was a division of one hundred ladies and an equal number of gentlemen on horseback as a special escort to the carriage containing Mr. Lincoln. The whole country seemed to be swarming and the crowd stood three hours in the college grounds, in a cutting wind, listening to the debate. Mr. Lincoln's speech at Galesburg was, in my judgment, the best of the series.

"At Quincy, October 13th, we had a fine day and a very large crowd, although not so large as at Galesburg. The usual processions and paraphernalia were on hand. Old Whiggery was largely represented here, and, in front of the Lincoln procession, was a live raccoon on a pole, emblematic of a by-gone day and a by-gone party. When this touching reminder of the past drew near the hotel where we were staying, an old weather-beaten follower of Henry Clay, who was standing near me, was moved to tears. After mopping his face he made his way up to Mr. Lincoln, wrung his hand and burst into tears again. The wicked Democrats carried at the head of their procession a dead 'coon, suspended by its tail. This was more in accord with existing facts than the other specimen, but our prejudices ran in favor of live 'coons in that part of Illinois. Farther north we did not set much store by them. Here I saw Carl Schurz for the first time. He was hotly in the fray, and was an eager listener to the Quincy debate. Another rising star, Frank P. Blair, Jr., was battling for Lincoln in the southern part of the State.

"The next day both Lincoln and Douglas, and their retainers, went on board the steamer *City of Louisiana*, bound for Alton. Here the last of the joint debates took place, October 15th. The day was pleasant but the audience was the smallest of the series, except the one at Jonesboro. The debate passed off quietly and without any incident worthy of note.

"The campaign was now drawing to a close. Everybody who had borne an active part in it was pretty well fagged out, except Mr. Lincoln. He showed no signs of fatigue. Douglas's voice was worn down to extreme huskiness. He took great pains to save what was left of his throat, but to listen to him moved one's pity. Nevertheless, he went on doggedly, bravely, and with a jaunty air of confidence. Mr. Lincoln's voice was as clear and far-reaching as it was the day he spoke at Beardstown, two months before—a high-pitched tenor, almost a falsetto, that could be heard at a greater distance than Douglas's heavy basso. The battle continued till the election (November 2d), which took place in a cold, pelting rainstorm, one of the most uncomfortable in the whole year. But nobody minded the weather. The excitement was intense all day in all parts of the State. The Republican State ticket was elected by a small plurality, the vote being as follows:

FOR STATE TREASURER.

MILLER (Republican), - - - - 125,430
FONDEY (Douglas Democrat), - - 121,609
DOUGHERTY (Buchanan Democrat), - - 5,079

"The Legislature consisted of twenty-five Senators and seventy-five Representatives. Thirteen Senators held over from the preceding election. Of these, eight were Democrats and five Republicans. Of the twelve Senators elected this year, the Democrats elected six and the Republicans six. So the new Senate was composed of fourteen Democrats and eleven Republicans.

"Of the seventy-five members of the House of Representatives, the Democrats elected forty and the Republicans thirty-five.

"On joint ballot, therefore, the Democrats had fifty-four and the Republicans forty-six. And by this vote was Mr. Douglas re-elected Senator.

"Mr. Isaac N. Arnold, in his biography, says that Mr. Lincoln lost the election because a number of the holding-over Senators, representing districts that actually gave Republican majorities in this election, were Democrats. This is an error, and an inexcusable one for a person who is writing history. The apportionment of the State into Legislative districts had become, by the growth and movement of population, unduly favorable to the Democrats; that is, it required fewer votes on the average to elect a member in a Democratic district than in a Republican district. But ideal perfection is never attained in such matters. By the rules of the game Douglas had fairly won. The Republicans claimed that the Lincoln members of the Lower House of the Legislature received more votes, all told, than the Douglas members. These figures are not, at this writing, accessible to me, but my recollection is that, even on this basis, Douglas scored a small majority. There were five thousand Democratic votes to be accounted for, which had been cast for Dougherty for State Treasurer, and of these, the Douglas candidates for the Legislature would naturally get more than the Lincoln candidates.

"What is more to the purpose, is that the Republicans gained 29,241 votes, as against a Democratic gain of 21,332 (counting the Douglas and Buchanan vote together), over the presidential election of 1856. There were 37,444 votes for Fillmore in that year, and there was also an increase of the total vote of 13,129. These 50,573 votes, or their equivalents, were divided between Lincoln and Douglas in the ratio of 29 to 21.

"Mr. Lincoln, as he said at the Dixon Conference, had gone after 'larger game,' and he had bagged it to a greater extent than he, or anybody, then, imagined. But the immediate prize was taken by his great rival.

"I say great rival, with a full sense of the meaning of the words. I heard Mr. Douglas deliver his speech to the members of the Illinois Legislature, April 25, 1861, in the gathering tumult of arms. It was like a blast of thunder. I do not think that it is possible for a human being to produce a more prodigious effect with spoken words, than he produced on those who were within the sound of his voice. He was standing in the same place where I had first heard Mr. Lincoln. The veins of his neck and forehead were swollen with passion, and the perspiration ran down his face in streams. His voice had recovered its clearness from the strain of the previous year, and was frequently broken with emotion. The amazing force that he threw into the words: 'When hostile armies are marching under new and odious banners against the government of our country, the shortest way to peace is the most stupendous and unanimous preparation for war,' seemed to shake the whole building. That speech hushed the breath of treason in every corner of the State. Two months later he was in his grave. He was only forty-eight years old.

"The next time I saw Mr. Lincoln, after the election, I said to him that I hoped he was not so much disappointed as I had been. This, of course, 'reminded him of a little story.' I have forgotten the story, but it was about an over-grown boy who had met with some mishap, 'stumped' his toe, perhaps, and who said that 'it hurt too much to laugh, and he was too big to cry.'

"Mention has been made of the 'Danites' in the campaign. They were the Buchanan office-holders and their underlings, and, generally, a contemptible lot. The chief dispenser of patronage for Illinois was John Slidell, Senator from Louisiana. He took so much interest in his vocation that he came to Chicago as early as the month of July, to see how the post-masters were doing their work. He hated Douglas intensely, and slandered him vilely, telling stories about the cruel treatment and dreadful condition of the negroes on the Douglas plantation in Louisiana. These stories were told to Dr. Daniel Brainard, the surgeon of the U. S. Marine Hospital. Brainard was a Buchanan Democrat, like all the other federal office-holders, but was a very distinguished surgeon ; in fact, at the head of his profession, and a man of wealth and social standing. He became convinced that Slidell's story about the Douglas negroes was true, and he communicated it to Doctor Ray, and urged him to publish it in the *Tribune.* Doctor Ray did so, without, however, giving any names. It made no little commotion. Presently, the New Orleans *Picayune* denied the truth of the statement, concerning the condition and treatment of the negroes, and called it ' an election canard.' Then the Chicago *Times* called for the authority, and the *Tribune* gave the names of Brainard and Slidell. The latter at once published a card in the Washington *Union*, denying that he had ever made the statements attributed to him by Brainard. The latter was immediately in distress. He first denied that he had made the statements imputed to him, but afterward admitted that he had had conversations with a Republican editor about the hardships of the Douglas negroes, but denied that he had given Slidell as authority. Nobody doubted that the authorship of the story was correctly stated in the first publication. It was much too circumstantial to have been invented, and Doctor Ray was not the man to publish lies knowingly.

" The ' Danites ' held a State convention at Springfield, September 8th, or, rather, they had called one for that date, but the attendance was so small that they organized it as a convention of the Sixth Congressional District. John C. Breckinridge and Daniel S. Dickinson had been announced as speakers for the occasion, but neither of them appeared. Breckinridge took no notice of this meeting, or of his invitation to be present. A telegram was read from Dickinson, sending 'a thousand greetings,' and this, the Douglas men said, was liberal, being about ten to each delegate. Ex-Gov. John Reynolds was the principal speaker. Douglas was in Springfield the same day. He met his enemies by chance at the railway station, and glared defiance at them.

"Mention should be made of the services of Senator Trumbull in the campaign. Mr. Trumbull was a political debator, scarcely, if at all, inferior to either Lincoln or Douglas. He had given Douglas more trouble in the Senate, during the three years he had been there, than anybody else in that body. He had known Douglas from his youth, and he knew all the joints in his armor. He possessed a courage equal to any occasion, and he wielded a blade of tempered steel. He was not present at any of the joint debates, or at any of Mr. Lincoln's separate meetings, but addressed meetings wherever the State Central Committee sent him. Mr. Lincoln often spoke of him to me, and always in terms of admiration. That Mr. Lincoln was sorely disappointed at losing the Senatorship in 1855, when Trumbull was elected, is quite true, but he knew, as well as anybody, that in the then condition of parties, such a result could not be avoided. Judd, Palmer and Cook had been elected to the Legislature as Democrats. The Republican party was not yet born. The political elements were in the boiling stage. These men could not tell what kind of crystallization would take place. The only safe course for them, looking to their constituencies, was to vote for a Democrat who was opposed to the extension of slavery. Such a man they found in Lyman Trumbull, and they knew that no mistake would be made in choosing him. I say that Mr. Lincoln knew all this as fully as anybody could. I do not remember having any talk with him on that subject, for it was then somewhat stale. But I do remember the hearty good feeling that he cherished toward Trumbull and the three men here mentioned, who were chiefly instrumental in securing Trumbull's election.

" Douglas scented danger when Trumbull took the field, and, with his usual adroitness, sought to gain sympathy by making it appear that it was no fair game. At Havana, in the speech already alluded to, he made a rather moving remonstrance against this ' playing of two upon one,' as he called it. Mr. Lincoln, in his speech at the same place, thought it worth while to reply :

" 'I understand,' he said, 'that Judge Douglas, yesterday, referred to the fact that both Judge Trumbull and myself are making speeches throughout the State to beat him for the Senate, and that he tried to create sympathy by the suggestion that this was playing *two upon one* against him. It is true that Judge Trumbull has made a speech in Chicago, and I believe he intends to co-operate with the Republican Central Committee in their arrangements for the campaign, to the extent of making other speeches in different parts of the State. Judge Trumbull is a Republican like myself, and he naturally feels a lively interest in the success of his party. Is there anything wrong about that? But I will show you how little Judge Douglas's appeal to your sympathies amounts to. At the next general election, two years from now, a Legislature will be elected, which will have to choose a successor to Judge Trumbull. Of course, there will be an effort to fill his place with a Democrat. This person, whoever he may be, is probably out making stump-speeches against me, just as Judge Douglas is. He may be one of the present Democratic members of the Lower House of Congress—but, whoever he is, I can tell you that he has got to make some stump-speeches now, or his party will not nominate him for the seat occupied by Judge Trumbull. Well, are not Judge Douglas and this man playing *two upon one* against me, just as much as Judge Trumbull and I are playing *two upon one* against Judge Douglas? And, if it happens that there are two Democratic aspirants for Judge Trumbull's place, are they not playing *three upon one* against me, just as we are playing *two upon one* against Judge Douglas?'

"Douglas had as many helpers as Lincoln had. His complaint implied that there was nobody on the Democratic side who was anywhere near being a match for Trumbull, and this was the fact.

" I think that this was the most important intellectual wrestle that has ever taken place in this country, and that it will bear comparison with any which history mentions. Its consequences we all know. It gave Mr. Lincoln such prominence in the public eye that his nomination to the Presidency became possible and almost inevitable. It put an apple of discord in the Democratic party which hope-lessly divided it at Charleston, thus making Republi-can success in 1860 morally certain. This was one of Mr. Lincoln's designs, as has been already shown. Perhaps the Charleston schism would have taken place, even if Douglas had not been driven into a corner at Freeport, and compelled to proclaim the doctrine of 'unfriendly legislation,' but it is more likely that the break would have been postponed a few years longer.

"Everything stated in this chapter is taken from memoranda made at the time of occurrence. I need not say that I conceived an ardent attachment to Mr. Lincoln.   Nobody could be much in his society with-out being strongly drawn to him.

" HORACE WHITE."

NEW YORK, *February 27, 1890.*

CHAPTER V.

BEFORE Mr. Lincoln surrenders himself completely
to the public—for it is apparent he is fast approaching the great crisis of his career—it may not be
entirely inappropriate to take a nearer and more personal view of him. A knowledge of his personal
views and actions, a glimpse through the doorway
of his home, and a more thorough acquaintance
with his marked and strong points as they developed, will aid us greatly in forming our general estimate of the man. When Mr. Lincoln entered the
domain of investigation he was a severe and persistent thinker, and had wonderful endurance ; hence
he was abstracted, and for that reason at times was
somewhat unsocial, reticent, and uncommunicative.
After his marriage it cannot be said that he liked
the society of ladies ; in fact, it was just what he did
not like, though one of his biographers says otherwise. Lincoln had none of the tender ways that
please a woman, and he could not, it seemed, by any
positive act of his own make her happy. If his
wife was happy, she was naturally happy, or made
herself so in spite of countless drawbacks. He was,
however, a good husband in his own peculiar way,
and in his own way only.

If exhausted from severe and long-continued

thought, he had to touch the earth again to renew his strength. When this weariness set in he would stop thought, and get down and play with a little dog or kitten to recover; and when the recovery came he would push it aside to play with its own tail. He treated men and women in much the same way. For fashionable society he had a marked dislike, although he appreciated its value in promoting the welfare of a man ambitious to succeed in politics. If he was invited out to dine or to mingle in some social gathering, and came in contact with the ladies, he treated them with becoming politeness; but the consciousness of his shortcomings as a society man rendered him unusually diffident, and at the very first opportunity he would have the men separated from their ladies and crowded close around him in one corner of the parlor, listening to one of his characteristic stories. That a lady * as proud and as ambitious to exercise the rights of supremacy in society as Mary Todd should repent of her marriage to the man I have just described surely need occasion no surprise in the mind of anyone. Both she and the man whose hand she accepted acted along the lines of human conduct, and both reaped the bitter harvest of conjugal infelicity. In dealing with Mr. Lincoln's home life perhaps I am revealing an element of his character that has here-

---

* Mrs. Lincoln was decidedly pro-slavery in her views. One day she was invited to take a ride with a neighboring family, some of whose members still reside in Springfield. "If ever my husband dies," she ejaculated during the ride, "his spirit will never find me living outside the limits of a slave State."

tofore been kept from the world; but in doing so I feel sure I am treading on no person's toes, for all the actors in this domestic drama are dead, and the world seems ready to hear the facts. As his married life, in the opinion of all his friends, exerted a peculiar influence over Mr. Lincoln's political career there can be no impropriety, I apprehend, in throwing the light on it now. Mrs. Lincoln's disposition and nature have been dwelt upon in another chapter, and enough has been told to show that one of her greatest misfortunes was her inability to control her temper. Admit that, and everything can be explained. However cold and abstracted her husband may have appeared to others, however impressive, when aroused, may have seemed his indignation in public, he never gave vent to his feelings at home. He always meekly accepted as final the authority of his wife in all matters of domestic concern.* This may explain somewhat the statement of Judge Davis that, " as a general rule, when all the lawyers of a Saturday evening would go home and see their families and friends, Lincoln would find some excuse and refuse to go. We said nothing, but it seemed to us all he was not domestically happy." He exercised no government of any kind over his household. His children did much as

---

* One day a man making some improvements in Lincoln's yard suggested to Mrs. Lincoln the propriety of cutting down one of the trees, to which she willingly assented. Before doing so, however, the man came down to our office and consulted Lincoln himself about it. "What did Mrs. Lincoln say?" enquired the latter. "She consented to have it taken away." " Then, in God's name," exclaimed Lincoln, " cut it down to the roots!"

33

they pleased. Many of their antics he approved, and he restrained them in nothing. He never reproved them or gave them a fatherly frown. He was the most indulgent parent I have ever known. He was in the habit, when at home on Sunday, of bringing his two boys, Willie and Thomas—or "Tad"—down to the office to remain while his wife attended church. He seldom accompanied her there. The boys were absolutely unrestrained in their amusement. If they pulled down all the books from the shelves, bent the points of all the pens, overturned inkstands, scattered law-papers over the floor, or threw the pencils into the spittoon, it never disturbed the serenity of their father's good-nature. Frequently absorbed in thought, he never observed their mischievous but destructive pranks—as his unfortunate partner did, who thought much, but said nothing—and, even if brought to his attention, he virtually encouraged their repetition by declining to show any substantial evidence of parental disapproval. After church was over the boys and their father, climbing down the office stairs, ruefully turned their steps homeward. They mingled with the throngs of well-dressed people returning from church, the majority of whom might well have wondered if the trio they passed were going to a fireside where love and white-winged peace reigned supreme. A near relative of Mrs. Lincoln, in explanation of the unhappy condition of things in that lady's household, offered this suggestion: " Mrs. Lincoln came of the best stock, and was raised like a lady. Her husband was her opposite,

THE LINCOLN RESIDENCE, SPRINGFIELD.

Photographed about 1870.

in origin, in education, in breeding, in everything ; and it is therefore quite natural that she should complain if he answered the door-bell himself instead of sending the servant to do so ; neither is she to be condemned if, as you say, she raised ' merry war ' because he persisted in using his own knife in the butter, instead of the silver-handled one intended for that purpose." * Such want of social polish on the part of her husband of course gave Mrs. Lincoln great offense, and therefore in commenting on it she cared neither for time nor place. Her frequent outbursts of temper precipitated many an embarrassment from which Lincoln with great difficulty extricated himself.

Mrs. Lincoln, on account of her peculiar nature, could not long retain a servant in her employ. The sea was never so placid but that a breeze would ruffle its waters. She loved show and attention, and if, when she glorified her family descent or indulged in one of her strange outbreaks, the servant could simulate absolute obsequiousness or had tact enough to encourage her social pretensions, Mrs.

---

* A lady relative who lived for two years with the Lincolns told me that Mr. Lincoln was in the habit of lying on the floor with the back of a chair for a pillow when he read. One evening, when in this position in the hall, a knock was heard at the front door and although in his shirt-sleeves he answered the call. Two ladies were at the door whom he invited into the parlor, notifying them in his open familiar way, that he would " trot the women folks out." Mrs. Lincoln from an adjoining room witnessed the ladies' entrance and overheard her husband's jocose expression. Her indignation was so instantaneous she made the situation exceedingly interesting for him, and he was glad to retreat from the mansion. He did not return till very late at night and then slipped quietly in at a rear door.

Lincoln was for the time her firmest friend. One servant, who adjusted herself to suit the lady's capricious ways, lived with the family for several years. She told me that at the time of the debate between Douglas and Lincoln she often heard the latter's wife boast that she would yet be mistress of the White House. The secret of her ability to endure the eccentricities of her mistress came out in the admission that Mr. Lincoln gave her an extra dollar each week on condition that she would brave whatever storms might arise, and suffer whatever might befall her, without complaint. It was a rather severe condition, but she lived rigidly up to her part of the contract. The money was paid secretly and without the knowledge of Mrs. Lincoln. Frequently, after tempestuous scenes between the mistress and her servant, Lincoln at the first opportunity would place his hand encouragingly on the latter's shoulder with the admonition, " Mary, keep up your courage." It may not be without interest to add that the servant afterwards married a man who enlisted in the army. In the spring of 1865 his wife managed to reach Washington to secure her husband's release from the service. After some effort she succeeded in obtaining an interview with the President. He was glad to see her, gave her a basket of fruit, and directed her to call the next day and obtain a pass through the lines and money to buy clothes for herself and children. That night he was assassinated.

The following letter to the editor of a newspaper in Springfield will serve as a specimen of the perplexities which frequently beset Mr. Lincoln when his wife came in contact with others. What in this instance she said to the paper carrier we do not know; we can only intelligently infer. I have no personal recollection of the incident, although I knew the man to whom it was addressed quite well. The letter only recently came to light. I insert it without further comment.

[Private.]

"SPRINGFIELD, ILL., February 20, 1857.

"JOHN E. ROSETTE, Esq.

"*Dear Sir :*—Your note about the little paragraph in the *Republican* was received yesterday, since which time I have been too unwell to notice it. I had not supposed you wrote or approved it. The whole originated in mistake. You know by the conversation with me that I thought the establishment of the paper unfortunate, but I always expected to throw no obstacle in its way, and to patronize it to the extent of taking and paying for one copy. When the paper was brought to my house, my wife said to me, 'Now are you going to take another worthless little paper ?' I said to her *evasively*, 'I have not directed the paper to be left.' From this, in my absence, she sent the message to the carrier. This is the whole story.

"Yours truly,

"A. LINCOLN."

A man once called at the house to learn why Mrs. Lincoln had so unceremoniously discharged his niece from her employ. Mrs. Lincoln met him at the door, and being somewhat wrought up, gave vent to her feelings, resorting to such violent gestures and emphatic language that the man was glad to beat a hasty retreat. He at once started out to find Lincoln, determined to exact from him proper satisfaction for his wife's action. Lincoln was entertaining a crowd in a store at the time. The man, still laboring under some agitation, called him to the door and made the demand. Lincoln listened for a moment to his story. "My friend," he interrupted, "I regret to hear this, but let me ask you in all candor, can't you endure for a few moments what I have had as my daily portion for the last fifteen years?" These words were spoken so mournfully and with such a look of distress that the man was completely disarmed. It was a case that appealed to his feelings. Grasping the unfortunate husband's hand, he expressed in no uncertain terms his sympathy, and even apologized for having approached him. He said no more about the infuriated wife, and Lincoln afterward had no better friend in Springfield.

Mr. Lincoln never had a confidant, and therefore never unbosomed himself to others. He never spoke of his trials to me or, so far as I knew, to any of his friends. It was a great burden to carry, but he bore it sadly enough and without a murmur. I could always realize when he was in distress, without being told. He was not exactly an early riser, that is, he never usually appeared at the office till about nine o'clock in the morning. I usually preceded him an hour. Sometimes, however, he would come down as early as seven o'clock—in fact, on one occasion I remember he came down before daylight. If, on arriving at the office, I found him in, I knew instantly that a breeze had sprung up over the domestic sea, and that the waters were troubled. He would either be lying on the lounge looking skyward, or doubled up in a chair with his feet resting on the sill of a back window. He would not look up on my entering, and only answered my "Good morning" with a grunt. I at once busied myself with pen and paper, or ran through the leaves of some book; but the evidence of his melancholy and distress was so plain, and his silence so significant, that I would grow restless myself, and finding some excuse to go to the court-house or elsewhere, would leave the room.

The door of the office opening into a narrow hall-way was half glass, with a curtain on it working on brass rings strung on wire. As I passed out on these occasions I would draw the curtain across the glass, and before I reached the bottom of the stairs I could hear the key turn in the lock, and Lincoln was alone in his gloom. An hour in the clerk's office at the court-house, an hour longer in a neigh-boring store having passed, I would return. By that time either a client had dropped in and Lincoln was propounding the law, or else the cloud of despondency had passed away, and he was busy in the recital of an Indiana story to whistle off the recollections of the morning's gloom. Noon hav-ing arrived I would depart homeward for my dinner. Returning within an hour, I would find him still in the office,—although his house stood but a few squares away,—lunching on a slice of cheese and a handful of crackers which, in my absence, he had brought up from a store below. Separating for the day at five or six o'clock in the evening, I would still leave him behind, either sitting on a box at the foot of the stairway, entertaining a few loungers, or killing time in the same way on the court-house steps. A light in the office after dark attested his presence there till late along in the night, when, after all the world had gone to sleep, the tall form of the man destined to be the nation's President could have been seen strolling along in the shadows of trees and buildings, and quietly slipping in through the door of a modest frame house, which it pleased the world, in a conventional way, to call his home.

Some persons may insist that this picture is too highly colored. If so, I can only answer, they do not know the facts. The majority of those who have a personal knowledge of them are persistent in their silence. If their lips could be opened and all could be known, my conclusions and statements, to say the least of them, would be found to be fair, reasonable, and true. A few words more as to Lincoln's domestic history, and I pass to a different phase of his life. One of his warmest and closest friends, who still survives, maintains the theory that, after all, Lincoln's political ascendancy and final elevation to the Presidency were due more to the' influence of his wife than to any other person or cause. " The fact," insists this friend, "that Mary Todd, by her turbulent nature and unfortunate manner, prevented her husband from becoming a domestic man, operated largely in his favor; for he was thereby kept out in the world of business and politics. Instead of spending his evenings at home, reading the papers and warming his toes at his own fireside, he was constantly out with the common people, was mingling with the politicians, discussing public questions with the farmers who thronged the offices in the court-house and state house, and exchanging views with the loungers who surrounded the stove of winter evenings in the village store. The result of this continuous contact with the world was, that he was more thoroughly known than any other man in his community. His wife, therefore, was one of the unintentional means of his promotion. If, on the other hand, he had married some less ambitious but more domestic woman, some honest farmer's quiet daughter,—one who would have looked up to and worshipped him because he uplifted her,—the result might have been different. For, although it doubtless would have been her pride to see that he had clean clothes whenever he needed them ; that his slippers were always in their place ; that he was warmly clad and had plenty to eat ; and, although the privilege of ministering to his every wish and whim might have been to her a pleasure rather than a duty; yet I fear he would have been buried in the pleasures of a loving home, and the country would never have had Abraham Lincoln for its President."

In her domestic troubles I have always sympathized with Mrs. Lincoln. The world does not know what she bore, or how ill-adapted she was to bear it. Her fearless, witty, and austere nature shrank instinctively from association with the calm, imperturbable, and simple ways of her thoughtful and absent-minded husband. Besides, who knows but she may have acted out in her conduct toward her husband the laws of human revenge? The picture of that eventful evening in 1841, when she stood at the Edwards mansion clad in her bridal robes, the feast prepared and the guests gathered, and when the bridegroom came not, may have been constantly before her, and prompted her to a course of action which kept in the background the better elements of her nature. In marrying Lincoln she did not look so far into the future as Mary Owens, who declined his proposal because " he was deficient in those little links which make up the chain of woman's happiness." *

---

* Mrs. Lincoln died at the residence of her sister Mrs. Ninian W. Edwards, in Springfield, July 16, 1882. Her physician during her last illness says this of her : " In the late years of her life certain mental peculiarities were developed which finally culminated in a slight apoplexy, producing paralysis, of which she died. Among the peculiarities alluded to, one of the most singular was the habit she had during the last year or so of her life of immuring herself in a perfectly dark room and, for light, using a small candle-light, even when the sun was shining bright out-of-doors. No urging would induce her to go out into the fresh air. Another peculiarity was the accumulation of large quantities of silks and dress goods in trunks and by the cart-load, which she never used and which accumulated until it was really feared that the floor of the store-room would give way. She was bright and sparkling in conversation, and her memory remained singularly good up to the very close of her life. Her face was animated and pleasing ; and to me she was always an interesting woman ; and while the whole world was finding fault with her tem-

By reason of his practical turn of mind Mr. Lincoln never speculated any more in the scientific and philosophical than he did in the financial world. He never undertook to fathom the intricacies of psychology and metaphysics.* Investigation into first causes, abstruse mental phenomena, the science of being, he brushed aside as trash—mere scientific absurdities. He discovered through experience that his mind, like the minds of other men, had its limitations, and hence he economized his forces and his time by applying his powers in the field of the practical. Scientifically regarded he was a realist as opposed to an idealist, a sensationist as opposed to an intuitionist, a materialist as opposed to a spiritualist.

There was more or less superstition in his nature, and, although he may not have believed implicitly in the signs of his many dreams, he was constantly endeavoring to unravel them. His mind was readily impressed with some of the most absurd superstitions. His visit to the Voodoo fortune-

---

per and disposition, it was clear to me that the trouble was really a cerebral disease."—Dr. Thomas W. Dresser, letter, January 3, 1889, MS.

* "He was contemplative rather than speculative. He wanted something solid to rest upon, and hence his bias for mathematics and the physical sciences. He bestowed more attention on them than upon metaphysical speculations. I have heard him descant upon the problem whether a ball discharged from a gun in a horizontal position would be longer in reaching the ground than one dropped at the instant of discharge from the muzzle. He said it always appeared to him that they would both reach the ground at the same time, even before he had read the philosophical explanation."—Joseph Gillespie, letter, December 8, 1866, MS.

teller in New Orleans in 1831 ; his faith in the virtues of the mad-stone, when he took his son Robert to Terre Haute, Indiana, to be cured of the bite of a rabid dog ; and the strange double image of himself which he told his secretary, John Hay, he saw reflected in a mirror just after his election in 1860, strongly attest his inclination to superstition. He held most firmly to the doctrine of fatalism all his life. His wife, after his death, told me what I already knew, that " his only philosophy was, what is to be will be, and no prayers of ours can reverse the decree." He always contended that he was doomed to a sad fate, and he repeatedly said to me when we were alone in our office: " I am sure I shall meet with some terrible end." In proof of his strong leaning towards fatalism he once quoted the case of Brutus and Cæsar, arguing that the former was forced by laws and conditions over which he had no control to kill the latter, and, *vice versâ*, that the latter was specially created to be disposed of by the former. This superstitious view of life ran through his being like the thin blue vein through the whitest marble, giving the eye rest from the weariness of continued unvarying color. *

For many years I subscribed for and kept on our office table the *Westminster* and *Edinburgh Review* and a number of other English periodicals. Besides them I purchased the works of Spencer, Darwin,

---

* I have heard him frequently quote the couplet,

> " There's a divinity that shapes our ends,
> Rough-hew them how we will."

and the utterances of other English scientists, all of
which I devoured with great relish. I endeavored,
but had little success in inducing Lincoln to read
them. Occasionally he would snatch one up and
peruse it for a little while, but he soon threw it down
with the suggestion that it was entirely too heavy
for an ordinary mind to digest.* A gentleman in
Springfield gave him a book called, I believe,
"Vestiges of Creation," which interested him so
much that he read it through. The volume was pub-

---

* In 1856 I purchased in New York a life of Edmund Burke. I
have forgotten now who the author was, but I remember I read it
through in a short time. One morning Lincoln came into the office
and, seeing the book in my hands, enquired what I was reading. I
told him, at the same time observing that it was an excellent work
and handing the book over to him. Taking it in his hand he threw
himself down on the office sofa and hastily ran over its pages, reading a little here and there. At last he closed and threw it on the
table with the exclamation, " No, I've read enough of it. It's like
all the others. Biographies as generally written are not only mis-
leading, but false. The author of this life of Burke makes a wonderful hero out of his subject. He magnifies his perfections—if he
had any—and suppresses his imperfections. He is so faithful in his
zeal and so lavish in praise of his every act that one is almost driven
to believe that Burke never made a mistake or a failure in his life."
He lapsed into a brown study, but presently broke out again, " Billy,
I've wondered why book-publishers and merchants don't have blank
biographies on their shelves, always ready for an emergency; so
that, if a man happens to die, his heirs or his friends, if they wish to
perpetuate his memory, can purchase one already written, but with
blanks. These blanks they can at their pleasure fill up with rosy
sentences full of high-sounding praise. In most instances they com-
memorate a lie, and cheat posterity out of the truth. History,"
he concluded, " is not history unless it is the truth." This emphatic avowal of sentiment from Mr. Lincoln not only fixes his estimate of ordinary biography, but is my vindication in advance if
assailed for telling the truth.

lished in Edinburgh, and undertook to demonstrate the doctrine of development or evolution. The treatise interested him greatly, and he was deeply impressed with the notion of the so-called "universal law"—evolution; he did not extend greatly his researches, but by continued thinking in a single channel seemed to grow into a warm advocate of the new doctrine. Beyond what I have stated he made no further investigation into the realm of philosophy. "There are no accidents," he said one day, "in my philosophy. Every effect must have its cause. The past is the cause of the present, and the present will be the cause of the future. All these are links in the endless chain stretching from the finite to the infinite." From what has been said it would follow logically that he did not believe, except in a very restricted sense, in the freedom of the will. We often argued the question, I taking the opposite view; he changed the expression, calling it the freedom of the mind, and insisted that man always acted from a motive. I once contended that man was free and could act without a motive. He smiled at my philosophy, and answered that it was impossible, because the motive was born before the man."

The foregoing thoughts are prefatory to the much-mooted question of Mr. Lincoln's religious belief. For what I have heretofore said on this subject, both in public lectures and in letters which have frequently found their way into the newspapers, I have been freely and sometimes bitterly assailed, but I do not intend now to reopen the discussion or to answer the many persons who have risen up and asked to measure swords with me. I merely purpose to state the bare facts, expressing no opinion of my own, and allowing each and every one to put his or her construction on them.

Inasmuch as he was so often a candidate for public office Mr. Lincoln said as little about his religious opinions as possible, especially if he failed to coincide with the orthodox world. In illustration of his religious code I once heard him say that it was like that of an old man named Glenn, in Indiana, whom he heard speak at a church meeting, and who said: "When I do good I feel good, when I do bad I feel bad, and that's my religion." In 1834, while still living in New Salem and before he became a lawyer, he was surrounded by a class of people exceedingly liberal in matters of religion. Volney's "Ruins" and Paine's "Age of Reason" passed from hand to hand, and furnished food for the evening's discussion in the tavern and village store. Lincoln read both these books and thus assimilated them into his own being. He prepared an extended essay—called by many, a book—in which he made an argument against Christianity, striving to prove that the Bible was not inspired, and therefore not God's revelation, and that Jesus Christ was not the son of God. The manuscript containing these audacious and comprehensive propositions he intended to have published or given a wide circulation in some other way. He carried it to the store, where it was read and freely discussed. His friend and employer, Samuel Hill, was among the listeners, and, seriously questioning the propriety of a promising young man like Lincoln fathering such unpopular notions, he snatched the manuscript from his hands and thrust it into the stove. The book went up in flames, and Lincoln's political future was secure. But his infidelity and his sceptical views were not diminished. He soon removed to Springfield, where he attracted considerable notice by his rank doctrine. Much of what he then said may properly be credited to the impetuosity and exuberance of youth. One of his closest friends, whose name is withheld, narrating scenes and reviewing discussions that in 1838 took place in the office of the county clerk, says: "Sometimes Lincoln bordered on atheism. He went far that way, and shocked me. I was then a young man, and believed what my good mother told me. . . . He would come into the clerk's office where I and some young men were writing and staying, and would bring the Bible with him; would read a chapter and argue against it. . . . Lincoln was enthusiastic in his infidelity. As he grew older he grew more discreet; didn't talk much before strangers about his religion; but to friends, close and bosom ones, he was always open and avowed, fair and honest; to strangers, he held them off from policy." John T. Stuart, who was Lincoln's first partner, substantially endorses the above. "He was an avowed and open infidel," declares Stuart, "and sometimes bordered on atheism; . . . . went further against Christian beliefs and doctrines and principles than any man I ever heard;

he shocked me. I don't remember the exact line of his argument; suppose it was against the inherent defects, so-called, of the Bible, and on grounds of reason. Lincoln always denied that Jesus was the Christ of God—denied that Jesus was the son of God as understood and maintained by the Christian Church." David Davis tells us this : "The idea that Lincoln talked to a stranger about his religion or religious views, or made such speeches and remarks about it as are published, is to me absurd. I knew the man so well; he was the most reticent, secretive man I ever saw or expect to see. He had no faith, in the Christian sense of the term—had faith in laws, principles, causes and effects." Another man * testifies as follows : " Mr. Lincoln told me that he was a kind of immortalist ; that he never could bring himself to believe in eternal punishment ; that man lived but a little while here ; and that if eternal punishment were man's doom, he should spend that little life in vigilant and ceaseless preparation by never-ending prayer." Another intimate friend † furnishes this : " In my intercourse with Mr. Lincoln I learned that he believed in a Creator of all things, who had neither beginning nor end, possessing all power and wisdom, established a principle in obedience to which worlds move and are upheld, and animal and vegetable life come into existence. A reason he gave for his belief was that in view of the order and harmony of all nature which we behold, it would have been more miraculous to have come about by

---

* William H. Hannah.   † I. W. Keys.

chance than to have been created and arranged by some great thinking power. As to the Christian theory that Christ is God or equal to the Creator, he said that it had better be taken for granted; for by the test of reason we might become infidels on that subject, for evidence of Christ's divinity came to us in a somewhat doubtful shape; but that the system of Christianity was an ingenious one at least, and perhaps was calculated to do good." Jesse W. Fell, to whom Lincoln first confided the details of his biography, furnishes a more elaborate account of the latter's religious views than anyone else. In a statement made September 22, 1870, Fell says: " If there were any traits of character that stood out in bold relief in the person of Mr. Lincoln they were those of truth and candor. He was utterly incapable of insincerity or professing views on this or any other subject he did not entertain. Knowing such to be his true character, that insincerity, much more duplicity, were traits wholly foreign to his nature, many of his old friends were not a little surprised at finding in some of the biographies of this great man statements concerning his religious opinions so utterly at variance with his known sentiments. True, he may have changed or modified these sentiments*

---

* " EXECUTIVE MANSION, WASHINGTON, May 27, 1865.

" FRIEND HERNDON :

" Mr. Lincoln did not to my knowledge in any way change his religious ideas, opinions, or beliefs from the time he left Springfield to the day of his death. I do not know just what they were, never having heard him explain them in detail; but I am very sure he gave no outward indication of his mind having undergone any change in that regard while here.   " Yours truly,
                              " JNO. G. NICOLAY."

after his removal from among us, though this is hardly reconcilable with the history of the man, and his entire devotion to public matters during his four years' residence at the national capital. It is possible, however, that this may be the proper solution of this conflict of opinions; or it may be that, with no intention on the part of any one to mislead the public mind, those who have represented him as believing in the popular theological views of the times may have misapprehended him, as experience shows to be quite common where no special effort has been made to attain critical accuracy on a subject of this nature. This is the more probable from the well-known fact, that Mr. Lincoln seldom communicated to any one his views on this subject; but be this as it may, I have no hesitation whatever in saying that whilst he held many opinions in common with the great mass of Christian believers, he did not believe in what are regarded as the orthodox or evangelical views of Christianity.

"On the innate depravity of man, the character and office of the great Head of the Church, the atonement, the infallibility of the written revelation, the performance of miracles, the nature and design of present and future rewards and punishments (as they are popularly called), and many other subjects he held opinions utterly at variance with what are usually taught in the Church. I should say that his expressed views on these and kindred topics were such as, in the estimation of most believers, would place him outside the Christian pale. Yet, to my mind, such was not the true position, since his principles and practices and the spirit of his whole life were of the very kind we universally agree to call Christian; and I think this conclusion is in no wise affected by the circumstance that he never attached himself to any religious society whatever.

"His religious views were eminently practical, and are summed up, as I think, in these two propositions: the Fatherhood of God, and the brotherhood of man. He fully believed in a superintending and overruling Providence that guides and controls the operations of the world, but maintained that law and order, and not their violation or suspension, are the appointed means by which this Providence is exercised.*

"I will not attempt any specification of either his belief or disbelief on various religious topics, as derived from conversations with him at different times during a considerable period; but as conveying a general view of his religious or theological opinions, will state the following facts. Some eight or ten years prior to his death, in conversing with him upon this subject, the writer took occasion to refer, in terms of approbation, to the sermons and writings generally of Dr. W. E. Channing; and, find-

---

* "A convention of preachers held, I think, at Philadelphia, passed a resolution asking him to recommend to Congress an amendment to the Constitution directly recognizing the existence of God. The first draft of his message prepared after this resolution was sent him did contain a paragraph calling the attention of Congress to the subject. When I assisted him in reading the proof he struck it out, remarking that he had not made up his mind as to its propriety."—MS. letter, John D. Defrees, December 4, 1866.

ing he was considerably interested in the statement I made of the opinions held by that author, I proposed to present him (Lincoln) a copy of Channing's entire works, which I soon after did. Subsequently the contents of these volumes, together with the writings of Theodore Parker, furnished him, as he informed me, by his friend and law partner, William H. Herndon, became naturally the topics of conversation with us ; and, though far from believing there was an entire harmony of views on his part with either of those authors, yet they were generally much admired and approved by him.

" No religious views with him seemed to find any favor except of the practical and rationalistic order ; and if, from my recollections on this subject, I was called upon to designate an author whose views most nearly represented Mr. Lincoln's on this subject, I would say that author was Theodore Parker."

The last witness to testify before this case is submitted to the reader is no less a person than Mrs. Lincoln herself. In a statement made at a time and under circumstances detailed in a subsequent chapter she said this : " Mr. Lincoln had no faith and no hope in the usual acceptation of those words. He never joined a Church ; but still, as I believe, he was a religious man by nature. He first seemed to think about the subject when our boy Willie died, and then more than ever about the time he went to Gettysburg ; but it was a kind of poetry in his nature, and he was never a technical Christian."

No man had a stronger or firmer faith in Providence—God—than Mr. Lincoln, but the continued use by him late in life of the word God must not be interpreted to mean that he believed in a personal God. In 1854 he asked me to erase the word God from a speech which I had written and read to him for criticism because my language indicated a personal God, whereas he insisted no such personality ever existed.

My own testimony, however, in regard to Mr. Lincoln's religious views may perhaps invite discussion. The world has always insisted on making an orthodox Christian of him, and to analyze his sayings or sound his beliefs is but to break the idol. It only remains to say that, whether orthodox or not, he believed in God and immortality ; and even if he questioned the existence of future eternal punishment he hoped to find a rest from trouble and a heaven beyond the grave. If at any time in his life he was sceptical of the divine origin of the Bible he ought not for that reason to be condemned ; for he accepted the practical precepts of that great book as binding alike upon his head and his conscience. The benevolence of his impulses, the seriousness of his convictions, and the nobility of his character are evidences unimpeachable that his soul was ever filled with the exalted purity and sublime faith of natural religion.

CHAPTER VI

THE result of the campaign of 1858 wrought more disaster to Lincoln's finances than to his political prospects. The loss of over six months from his business, and the expenses of the canvass, made a severe drain on his personal income. He was anxious to get back to the law once more and earn a little ready money. A letter written about this time to his friend Norman B. Judd, Chairman of the Republican State Committee, will serve to throw some light on the situation he found himself in. "I have been on expenses so long, without earning anything," he says, "that I am absolutely without money now for even household expenses. Still, if you can put in $250 for me towards discharging the debt of the committee, I will allow it when you and I settle the private matter between us. This, with what I have already paid, with an outstanding note of mine, will exceed my subscription of $500. This, too, is exclusive of my ordinary expenses during the campaign, all of which, being added to my loss of time and business, bears prettily heavily upon one no better off than I am. But as I had the post of honor, it is not for me to be over-nice." At the time this letter was written his property consisted of the house and lot on which he lived, a few law books and some household furniture. He owned a small tract of land in Iowa which yielded him nothing, and the annual income from his law practice did not exceed $3,000; yet the party's committee in Chicago were dunning their late standard-bearer, who, besides the chagrin of his defeat, his own expenses, and the sacrifice of his time, was asked to aid in meeting the general expenses of the campaign. At this day one is a little surprised that some of the generous and wealthy members of the party in Chicago or elsewhere did not come forward and volunteer their aid. But they did not, and whether Lincoln felt in his heart the injustice of this treatment or not, he went straight ahead in his own path and said nothing about it.

Political business being off his hands, he now conceived the idea of entering the lecture field. He began preparations in the usual way by noting down ideas on stray pieces of paper, which found a lodgment inside his hat, and finally brought forth in connected form a lecture on " Inventions." He recounted the wonderful improvements in machinery, the arts, and sciences. Now and then he indulged in a humorous paragraph, and witticisms were freely sprinkled throughout the lecture. During the winter he delivered it at several towns in the central part of the State, but it was so commonplace, and met with such indifferent success, that he soon dropped it altogether.* The effort met with

---

* " As we were going to Danville court I read to Lincoln a lecture by Bancroft on the wonderful progress of man, delivered in the pre-

the disapproval of his friends, and he himself was filled with disgust. If his address in 1852, over the death of Clay, proved that he was no eulogist, then this last effort demonstrated that he was no lecturer. Invitations to deliver the lecture—prompted no doubt by the advertisement given him in the contest with Douglas—came in very freely; but beyond the three attempts named, he declined them all. "Press of business in the courts" afforded him a convenient excuse, and he retired from the field.*

During the fall of 1859 invitations to take part in the canvass came from over half-a-dozen States where elections were to be held. Douglas, fresh from the Senate, had gone to Ohio, and thither in September Lincoln, in response to the demands of party friends everywhere, followed.† He delivered

---

ceding November. Sometime later he told us—Swett and me—that he had been thinking much on the subject and believed he would write a lecture on 'Man and His Progress.' Afterwards I read in a paper that he had come to either Bloomington or Clinton to lecture and no one turned out. The paper added, 'That doesn't look much like his being President.' I once joked him about it; he said good-naturedly, 'Don't; that plagues me.'"—Henry C. Whitney, letter, Aug. 27, 1867, MS.

* "SPRINGFIELD, March 28, 1859.
" W. M. MORRIS, Esq.,
"DEAR SIR:—Your kind note inviting me to deliver a lecture at Galesburg is received. I regret to say I cannot do so now; I must stick to the courts awhile. I read a sort of lecture to three different audiences during the last month and this; but I did so under circumstances which made it a waste of no time whatever.
"Yours very truly,
"A. LINCOLN."

† "He returned to the city two years after with a fame as wide as the continent, with the laurels of the Douglas contest on his brow, and the Presidency in his grasp. He returned, greeted with the

telling and impressive speeches at Cincinnati and Columbus,* following Douglas at both places. He made such a favorable impression among his Ohio friends that, after a glorious Republican victory, the State committee asked the privilege of publishing his speeches, along with those of Douglas, to be used and distributed as a campaign document. This request he especially appreciated, because after some effort he had failed to induce any publisher in

thunder of cannon, the strains of martial music, and the joyous plaudits of thousands of citizens thronging the streets. He addressed a vast concourse on Fifth Street Market; was entertained in princely style at the Burnet House, and there received with courtesy the foremost citizens come to greet this rising star. With high hope and happy heart he left Cincinnati after a three days' sojourn. But a perverse fortune attended him and Cincinnati in their intercourse. Nine months after Mr. Lincoln left us, after he had been nominated for the Presidency, when he was tranquilly waiting in his cottage home at Springfield the verdict of the people, his last visit to Cincinnati and the good things he had had at the Burnet House were rudely brought to his memory by a bill presented to him from its proprietors. Before leaving the hotel he had applied to the clerk for his bill; was told that it was paid, or words to that effect. This the committee had directed, but afterwards neglected its payment. The proprietors shrewdly surmised that a letter to the nominee for the Presidency would bring the money. The only significance in this incident is in the letter it brought from Mr. Lincoln, revealing his indignation at the seeming imputation against his honor, and his greater indignation at one item of the bill. 'As to wines, liquors, and cigars, we had none, absolutely none. These last may have been in Room 15 by order of committee, but I do not recollect them at all.'" —W. M. Dickson, "Harper's Magazine," June, 1884.

* Douglas had written a long and carefully prepared article on "Popular Sovereignty in the Territories," which appeared for the first time in the September (1859) number of "Harper's Magazine." It went back some distance into the history of the government, recounting the proceedings of the earliest Congresses, and sought to

Springfield to undertake the enterprise,* thus proving anew that " a prophet is not without honor, save in his own country."   In December he visited Kansas, speaking at Atchison, Troy, Leavenworth, and other towns near the border.   His speeches there served to extend his reputation still further westward.   Though his arguments were repetitions of the doctrine laid down in the contest with Douglas, yet they were new to the majority of his Kansas †

---

mark out more clearly than had heretofore been done " the dividing line between Federal and Local authority."   In a speech at Columbus, O, Lincoln answered the " copy-right essay" categorically. After alluding to the difference of position between himself and Judge Douglas on the doctrine of Popular Sovereignty, he said : " Judge Douglas has had a good deal of trouble with Popular Sovereignty. His explanations, explanatory of explanations explained, are interminable.   The most lengthy and, as I suppose, the most maturely considered of his long series of explanations is his great essay in " Harper's Magazine."

* A gentleman is still living, who at the time of the debate between Lincoln and Douglas, was a book publisher in Springfield. Lincoln had collected newspaper slips of all the speeches made during the debate, and proposed to him their publication in book form ; but the man declined, fearing there would be no demand for such a book.   Subsequently, when the speeches were gotten out in book form in Ohio, Mr. Lincoln procured a copy and gave it to his Springfield friend, writing on the fly-leaf, " Compliments of A. Lincoln."

† How Mr. Lincoln stood on the questions of the hour, after his defeat by Douglas, is clearly shown in a letter written on the 14th of May, 1859, to a friend in Kansas, who had forwarded him an invitation to attend a Republican convention there.   " You will probably adopt resolutions," he writes, " in the nature of a platform.   I think the only danger will be the temptation to lower the Republican standard in order to gather recruits.   In my judgment such a step would be a serious mistake, and open a gap through which more would pass out than pass in.   And this would be the same whether the letting down should be in deference to Douglasism or to the

hearers and were enthusiastically approved. By the close of the year he was back again in the dingy law office in Springfield.

The opening of the year 1860 found Mr. Lincoln's name freely mentioned in connection with the Republican nomination for the Presidency. To be classed with Seward, Chase, McLean, and other celebrities was enough to stimulate any Illinois lawyer's pride; but in Mr. Lincoln's case, if it had any such effect, he was most artful in concealing it. Now and then some ardent friend, an editor, for example, would run his name up to the mast-head, but in all cases he discouraged the attempt. "In regard to the matter you spoke of," he answered one man who proposed his name, "I beg that you will not give it a further mention. Seriously, I do not think I am fit for the Presidency." *

The first effort in his behalf as a Presidential aspi-

Southern opposition element; either would surrender the object of the Republican organization—the preventing of the spread and nationalization of slavery. This object surrendered, the organization would go to pieces. I do not mean by this that no Southern man must be placed upon our national ticket for 1860. There are many men in the slave states for any one of whom I could cheerfully vote, to be either President or Vice-president, provided he would enable me to do so with safety to the Republican cause, without lowering the Republican standard. This is the indispensable condition of a union with us; it is idle to talk of any other. Any other would be as fruitless to the South as distasteful to the North, the whole ending in common defeat. Let a union be attempted on the basis of ignoring the slavery question, and magnifying other questions which the people are just now caring about, and it will result in gaining no single electoral vote in the South, and losing every one in the North."—MS. letter to M. W. Delahay.

* Letter, March 5, 1859, to Thomas J. Pickett.

rant was the action taken by his friends at a meet-ing held in the State House early in 1860, in the rooms of O. M. Hatch, then Secretary of State. Besides Hatch there were present Norman B. Judd, chairman of the Republican State Committee, Ebenezer Peck, Jackson Grimshaw, and others of equal prominence in the party. "We all expressed a personal preference for Mr. Lincoln," relates one who was a participant in the meeting,[*] "as the Illinois candidate for the Presidency, and asked him if his name might be used at once in connection with the nomination and election. With his char-acteristic modesty he doubted whether he could get the nomination even if he wished it, and asked until the next morning to answer us whether his name might be announced. Late the next day he authorized us, if we thought proper to do so, to place him in the field." To the question from Mr. Grimshaw whether, if the nomination for President could not be obtained, he would accept the post of Vice-president, he answered that he would not; that his name having been used for the office of President, he would not permit it to be used for any other office, however honorable it might be. This meeting was preliminary to the Decatur con-vention, and was also the first concerted action in his behalf on the part of his friends.

In the preceding October he came rushing into the office one morning, with the letter from New York City, inviting him to deliver a lecture there, and

---

[*] Jackson Grimshaw. Letter, Quincy, Ill., April 28, 1866, MS.

asked my advice and that of other friends as to the subject and character of his address. We all recommended a speech on the political situation. Remembering his poor success as a lecturer himself, he adopted our suggestions. He accepted the invitation of the New York committee, at the same time notifying them that his speech would deal entirely with political questions, and fixing a day late in February as the most convenient time. Meanwhile he spent the intervening time in careful preparation. He searched through the dusty volumes of congressional proceedings in the State library, and dug deeply into political history. He was painstaking and thorough in the study of his subject, but when at last he left for New York we had many misgivings—and he not a few himself—of his success in the great metropolis. What effect the unpretentious Western lawyer would have on the wealthy and fashionable society of the great city could only be conjectured. A description of the meeting at Cooper Institute, a list of the names of the prominent men and women present, or an account of Lincoln in the delivery of the address would be needless repetitions of well-known history.* It only remains to say that his speech was

---

* On his return home Lincoln told me that for once in his life he was greatly abashed over his personal appearance. The new suit of clothes which he donned on his arrival in New York were ill-fitting garments, and showed the creases made while packed in the valise; and for a long time after he began his speech and before he became "warmed up" he imagined that the audience noticed the contrast between his Western clothes and the neat-fitting suits of Mr. Bryant and others who sat on the platform. The collar of his coat on the

devoid of all rhetorical imagery, with a marked suppression of the pyrotechnics of stump oratory. It was constructed with a view to accuracy of statement, simplicity of language, and unity of thought. In some respects like a lawyer's brief, it was logical, temperate in tone, powerful—irresistibly driving conviction home to men's reasons and their souls. No former effort in the line of speech-making had cost Lincoln so much time and thought as this one. It is said by one of his biographers, that those afterwards engaged in getting out the speech as a campaign document were three weeks in verifying the statements and finding the historical records referred to and consulted by him. This is probably a little over-stated as to time, but unquestionably the work of verification and reference. was in any event a very labored and extended one.* The day following the Cooper Institute meeting, the leading New York dailies published the speech in full, and made favorable editorial mention of it and of the speaker as well. It was plain now that Lincoln had captured the metropolis. From New York he travelled to New England to visit his son Robert, who

----

right side had an unpleasant way of flying up whenever he raised his arm to gesticulate. He imagined the audience noticed that also. After the meeting closed, the newspaper reporters called for slips of his speech. This amused him, because he had no idea what slips were, and besides, didn't suppose the newspapers cared to print his speech verbatim.

* Mr. Lincoln obtained most of the facts of his Cooper Institute speech from Eliott's " Debates on the Federal Constitution." There were six volumes, which he gave to me when he went to Washington in 1861.

was attending college. In answer to the many calls and invitations which showered on him, he spoke at various places in Connecticut, Rhode Island, and New Hampshire. In all these places he not only left deep impressions of his ability, but he convinced New England of his intense earnestness in the great cause. The newspapers treated him with no little consideration. One paper* characterized his speech as one of "great fairness," delivered with "great apparent candor and wonderful interest. For the first half hour his opponents would agree with every word he uttered; and from that point he would lead them off little by little until it seemed as if he had got them all into his fold. He is far from prepossessing in personal appearance, and his voice is disagreeable; and yet he wins your attention from the start. He indulges in no flowers of rhetoric, no eloquent passages. . . . . He displays more shrewdness, more knowledge of the masses of mankind than any public speaker we have heard since Long Jim Wilson left for California."

Lincoln's return to Springfield after his dazzling success in the East was the signal for earnest congratulations on the part of his friends. Seward was the great man of the day, but Lincoln had demonstrated to the satisfaction of his friends that he was tall enough and strong enough to measure swords with the Auburn statesman. His triumph in New York and New England had shown that the idea of a house divided against itself induced as strong

---

* Manchester *Mirror.*

coöperation and hearty support in prevention of a great wrong in the East as the famous "irrepressible conflict" attracted warriors to Seward's standard in the Mississippi valley. It was apparent now to Lincoln that the Presidential nomination was within his reach. He began gradually to lose his interest in the law and to trim his political sails at the same time. His recent success had stimulated his self-confidence to unwonted proportions. He wrote to influential party workers everywhere. I know the idea prevails that Lincoln sat still in his chair in Springfield, and that one of those unlooked-for tides in human affairs came along and cast the nomination into his lap; but any man who has had experience in such things knows that great political prizes are not obtained in that way. The truth is, Lincoln was as vigilant as he was ambitious, and there is no denying the fact that he understood the situation perfectly from the start. In the management of his own interests he was obliged to rely almost entirely on his own resources. He had no money with which to maintain a political bureau, and he lacked any kind of personal organization whatever. Seward had all these things, and, behind them all, a brilliant record in the United States Senate with which to dazzle his followers. But with all his prestige and experience the latter was no more adroit and no more untiring in pursuit of his ambition than the man who had just delivered the Cooper Institute speech. A letter written by Lincoln about this time to a friend in Kansas serves to illustrate his methods, and measures the extent

35

of his ambition.   The letter is dated March 10, and is now in my possession.   For obvious reasons I withhold the friend's name: "As to your kind wishes for myself," writes Lincoln, "allow me to say I cannot enter the ring on the money basis—first, because in the main it is wrong; and secondly, I have not and cannot get the money.   I say in the main the use of money is wrong; but for certain objects in a political contest the use of some is both right and indispensable.   With me, as with yourself, this long struggle has been one of great pecuniary loss.   I now distinctly say this: If you shall be appointed a delegate to Chicago I will furnish one hundred dollars to bear the expenses of the trip." There is enough in this letter to show that Lincoln was not only determined in his political ambition, but intensely practical as well.   His eye was constantly fastened on Seward, who had already freely exercised the rights of leadership in the party.   All other competitors he dropped out of the problem. In the middle of April he again writes his Kansas friend: "Reaching home last night I found yours of the 7th.   You know I was recently in New England.   Some of the acquaintances while there write me since the election that the close vote in Connecticut and the quasi-defeat in Rhode Island are a drawback upon the prospects of Governor Seward; and Trumbull writes Dubois to the same effect. Do not mention this as coming from me.   Both these States are safe enough in the fall."   But, while Seward may have lost ground near his home, he was acquiring strength in the West.   He had

As to your kind wishes for myself, allow
me to say I can not enter the ring on
the money basis—first, because, in the
main, it is wrong; and secondly, I
have not, and can not get, the money—
I say, in the main, the use of money
is wrong; but for certain objects, in a
political contest, the use of some, is both
right, and indispensable— With me,
as with yourself, this long struggle has
been one of great pecuniary loss. ~~[illegible]~~
I now distinctly say this— If you shall
be appointed a delegate to Chicago, I
will furnish one hundred dollars to
bear the expences of the trip—

Present my respects to Genl. Lane; and
say to him, I shall be pleased to hear from
him at any time— Your friend, as ever
A. Lincoln—

EXTRACT FROM LETTER TO KANSAS DELEGATE, MARCH 10, 1860.

(Slightly reduced.)

Original in possession of J. W. Weik.

invaded the very territory Lincoln was intending to retain by virtue of his course in the contest with Douglas. Lincoln's friend in Kansas, instead of securing that delegation for him, had suffered the Seward men to outgeneral him, and the prospects were by no means flattering. "I see by the dispatches," writes Lincoln, in a burst of surprise, "that, since you wrote, Kansas has appointed delegates and instructed for Seward. Don't stir them up to anger, but come along to the convention and I will do as I said about expenses." Whether the friend ever accepted Lincoln's generous offer I do not know,* but it may not be without interest to state that within ten days after the latter's inauguration he appointed him to a Federal office with comfortable salary attached, and even asked for his preferences as to other contemplated appointments in his own State.† In the rapid, stirring scenes that

---

* This case illustrates quite forcibly Lincoln's weakness in dealing with individuals. This man I know had written Lincoln, promising to bring the Kansas delegation to Chicago for him if he would only pay his expenses. Lincoln was weak enough to make the promise, and yet such was his faith in the man that he appointed him to an important judicial position and gave him great prominence in other ways. What President or candidate for President would dare do such a thing now?

† The following is in my possession:

"Executive Mansion, March 13, 1861.

"—— ——, Esq.

"My Dear Sir:

"You will start for Kansas before I see you again; and when I saw you a moment this morning I forgot to ask you about some of the Kansas appointments, which I intended to do. If you care much about them you can write, as I think I shall not make the appointments just yet.   "Yours in haste,

"A. Lincoln."

crowd upon each other from this time forward the individuality of Lincoln is easily lost sight of. He was so thoroughly interwoven in the issues before the people of Illinois that he had become a part of them. Among his colleagues at the bar he was no longer looked upon as the Circuit-Court lawyer of earlier days. To them it seemed as if the nation were about to lay its claim upon him. His tall form enlarged, until, to use a figurative expression, he could no longer pass through the door of our dingy office. Reference has already been made to the envy of his rivals at the bar, and the jealousy of his political contemporaries. Very few indeed were free from the degrading passion ; but it made no difference in Lincoln's treatment of them. He was as generous and deferred to them as much as ever. The first public movement by the Illinois people in his interest was the action of the State convention, which met at Decatur on the 9th and 10th of May. It was at this convention that Lincoln's friend and cousin, John Hanks, brought in the two historic rails which both had made in the Sangamon bottom in 1830, and which served the double purpose of electrifying the Illinois people and kindling the fire of enthusiasm that was destined to sweep over the nation. In the words of an ardent Lincoln delegate, " These rails were to represent the issue in the coming contest between labor free and labor slave ; between democracy and aristocracy. Little did I think," continues our jubilant and effusive friend, " of the mighty consequences of this little incident ; little did I think that the tall, and angular, and bony rail-splitter who stood in girlish diffidence bowing with awkward grace would fill the chair once filled by Washington, and that his name would echo in chants of praise along the corridor of all coming time." A week later the hosts were gathered for the great convention in Chicago. David Davis had rented rooms in the Tremont House and opened up "Lincoln's headquarters." I was not a delegate, but belonged to the contingent which had Lincoln's interests in charge. Judge Logan was the Springfield delegate, and to him Lincoln had given a letter authorizing the withdrawal of his name whenever his friends deemed such action necessary or proper. Davis was the active man, and had the business management in charge. If any negotiations were made, he made them. The convention was held in a monster building called the Wigwam. No one who has ever attempted a description of it has overdrawn its enthusiasm and exciting scenes. Amid all the din and confusion, the curbstone contentions, the promiscuous wrangling of delegates, the deafening roar of the assembled hosts, the contest narrowed down to a neck-and-neck race between the brilliant statesman of Auburn and the less pretentious, but manly rail-splitter from the Sangamon bottoms. With the proceedings of the convention the world is already well familiar. On the first ballot Seward led, but was closely followed by Lincoln; on the second Lincoln gained amazingly; on the third the race was an even one until the dramatic change by Carter, of Ohio, when Lincoln, swinging loose, swept grandly to the front. The cannon planted on the roof of the

Wigwam belched forth a boom across the Illinois prairies. The sound was taken up and reverberated from Maine to California. With the nomination of Hannibal Hamlin, of Maine, the convention adjourned. The delegates—victorious and vanquished alike—turned their steps homeward, and the great campaign of 1860 had begun. The day before the nomination the editor of the Springfield *Journal* arrived in Chicago with a copy of the Missouri *Democrat*, in which Lincoln had marked three passages referring to Seward's position on the slavery question. On the margin of the paper he had written in pencil, " I agree with Seward in his ' Irrepressible Conflict,' but I do not endorse his ' Higher Law ' doctrine." Then he added in words underscored, " Make no contracts that will bind me." This paper was brought into the room where Davis, Judd, Logan, and I were gathered, and was read to us. But Lincoln was down in Springfield, some distance away from Chicago, and could therefore not appreciate the gravity of the situation ; at least so Davis argued, and, viewing it in that light, the latter went ahead with his negotiations. What the consequences of these deals were will appear later on. The news of his nomination found Lincoln at Springfield in the office of the *Journal.* Naturally enough he was nervous, restless, and laboring under more or less suppressed excitement. He had been tossing ball—a pastime frequently indulged in by the lawyers of that day, and had played a few games of billiards to keep down, as another has expressed it, " the unnatural excitement that threatened to possess him." When the telegram containing the result of the last ballot came in, although apparently calm and undisturbed, a close observer could have detected in the compressed lip and serious countenance evidences of deep and unusual emotion. As the balloting progressed he had gone to the office of the *Journal*, and was sitting in a large arm-chair there when the news of his nomination came. What a line of scenes, stretching from the barren glade in Kentucky to the jubilant and enthusiastic throng in the Wigwam at Chicago, must have broken in upon his vision as he hastened from the newspaper office to " tell a little woman down the street the news !" In the evening his friends and neighbors called to congratulate him. He thanked them feelingly and shook them each by the hand. A day later the committee from the convention, with George Ashmun, of Massachusetts, at its head, called, and delivered formal notice of his nomination. This meeting took place at his house. His response was couched in polite and dignified language, and many of the committee, who now met him for the first time, departed with an improved impression of the new standard-bearer. A few days later he wrote his official letter of acceptance, in which he warmly endorsed the resolutions of the convention. His actions and utterances so far had begun to dissipate the erroneous notion prevalent in some of the more remote Eastern States, that he was more of a backwoods boor than a gentleman ; but with the arrival of the campaign in dead earnest, people paid less attention to the candidates and more to the great issues at stake. Briefly stated, the Republican platform was a declaration that "the new dogma, that the Constitution carries slavery into all the Territories, is a dangerous political heresy, revolutionary in tendency and subversive of the peace and harmony of the country; that the normal condition of all the Territories is that of freedom; that neither Congress, the territorial legislature, nor any individual can give legal existence to slavery in any territory; that the opening of the slave trade would be a crime against humanity." Resolutions favoring a homestead law, river and harbor improvements, and the Pacific railroad were also included in the platform. With these the Republicans, as a lawyer would say, went to the country. The campaign which followed was one with few parallels in American history. There was not only the customary exultation and enthusiasm over candidates, but there was patient listening and hard thinking among the masses. The slavery question, it was felt, must soon be decided. Threats of disunion were the texts of many a campaign speech in the South: in fact, as has since been shown, a deep laid conspiracy to overthrow the Union was then forming, and was only awaiting the election of a Republican President to show its hideous head. The Democratic party was struggling under the demoralizing effects of a split, in which even the Buchanan administration had taken sides. Douglas, the nominee of one wing, in his desperation had entered into the canvass himself, making speeches with all the power and eloquence at his command. The Republicans, cheered over the prospect, had joined hands with the Abolitionists, and both were marching to victory under the inspiration of Lincoln's sentiment, that "the further spread of slavery should be arrested, and it should be placed where the public mind shall rest in the belief of its ultimate extinction."

As the canvass advanced and waxed warm I tendered my services and made a number of speeches in the central part of the State. I remember, in the midst of a speech at Petersburg, and just as I was approaching an oratorical climax, a man out of breath came rushing up to me and thrust a message into my hand. I was somewhat frustrated and greatly alarmed, fearing it might contain news of some accident in my family; but great was my relief when I read it, which I did aloud. It was a message from Lincoln, telling me to be be of good cheer, that Ohio, Pennsylvania, and Indiana had gone Republican.*

These were then October States, and this was the first gun for the great cause. It created so much demonstration, such a burst of enthusiasm and confusion, that the crowd forgot they had any speaker; they ran yelling and hurrahing out of the hall, and I never succeeded in finishing the speech.

---

* The handwriting of the note was a little tremulous, showing that Lincoln was excited and nervous when he wrote it. Following is a copy of the original MS.:

"SPRINGFIELD, ILL., October 10, 1860.

"DEAR WILLIAM: I cannot give you details, but it is entirely certain that Pennsylvania and Indiana have gone Republican very largely. Pennsylvania 25,000, and Indiana 5000 to 10,000. Ohio of course is safe. "Yours as ever,

"A. LINCOLN."

As soon as officially notified of his nomination*
Mr. Lincoln moved his headquarters from our office
to a room in the State House building, and there,
with his secretary, John G. Nicolay, he spent the
busy and exciting days of his campaign. Of course
he attended to no law business, but still he loved to
come to our office of evenings, and spend an hour
with a few choice friends in a friendly privacy
which was denied him at his public quarters.
These were among the last meetings we had with
Lincoln as our friend and fellow at the bar; and
they are also the most delightful recollections any
of us have retained of him.† At last the turmoil

---

* Following is Lincoln's letter of acceptance:

"SPRINGFIELD, ILL., June 23, 1860.

"SIR: I accept the nomination tendered me by the convention over
which you presided, of which I am formally apprised in a letter of
yourself and others, acting as a committee of the convention for that
purpose. The declaration of principles which accompanies your
letter meets my approval, and it shall be my care not to violate it or
disregard it in any part. Imploring the assistance of Divine Providence, and with due regard to the views and feelings of all who were
represented in the convention, to the rights of all the states and
territories and people of the nation, to the inviolability of the Constitution, and the perpetual union, prosperity, and harmony of all, I
am most happy to coöperate for the practical success of the principles declared by the convention.

"Your obliged friend and fellow-citizen,
"HON. GEORGE ASHMUN." "ABRAHAM LINCOLN."

† One of what Lincoln regarded as the remarkable features of his
canvass for President was the attitude of some of his neighbors in
Springfield. A poll of the voters had been made in a little book and
given to him. On running over the names he found that the greater
part of the clergy of the city—in fact all but three—were against him.
This depressed him somewhat, and he called in Dr. Newton Bateman,
who as Superintendent of Public Instruction occupied the room
adjoining his own in the State House, and whom he habitually
addressed as "Mr. Schoolmaster." He commented bitterly on the

and excitement and fatigue of the campaign were over : the enthusiastic political workers threw aside their campaign uniforms, the boys blew out their torches, and the voter approached the polls with his ballot. On the morning of election day I stepped in to see Mr. Lincoln, and was surprised to learn that he did not intend to cast his vote. I knew of course that he did so because of a feeling that the candidate for a Presidential office ought not to vote for his own electors; but when I suggested the plan of cutting off the Presidential electors and voting for the State officers, he was struck with the idea, and at last consented. His appearance at the polls, accompanied by Ward Lamon, the lamented young Ellsworth, and myself, was the occasion of no little surprise because of the general impression which prevailed that he did not intend to vote. The crowd around the polls opened a gap as the distinguished voter approached, and some even removed their hats as he deposited his ticket and announced in a subdued voice his name, "Abraham Lincoln."

The election was held on the 6th of November. The result showed a popular vote of 1,857,610 for Lincoln; 1,291,574 for Douglas; 850,022 for Breckenridge; and 646,124 for Bell. In the elec-

---

attitude of the preachers and many of their followers, who, pretending to be believers in the Bible and God-fearing Christians, yet by their votes demonstrated that they cared not whether slavery was voted up or down. "God cares and humanity cares," he reflected, "and if they do not they surely have not read their Bible aright."

toral college Lincoln received 180 votes, Breckenridge 72, Bell 39, and Douglas 12.* Mr. Lincoln
having now been elected, there remained, before
taking up the reins of government, the details of his
departure from Springfield, and the selection of a
cabinet.

---

* Lincoln electors were chosen in seventeen of the free States, as
follows: Maine, New Hampshire, Massachusetts, Rhode Island, Connecticut, Vermont, New York, Pennsylvania, Ohio, Indiana, Illinois,
Michigan, Wisconsin, Minnesota, Iowa, California, Oregon; and in
one State,—New Jersey,—owing to a fusion between Democrats,
Lincoln secured four and Douglas three of the electors. Alabama,
Arkansas, Delaware, Florida, Georgia, Louisiana, Maryland, Mississippi, North, and South Carolina, and Texas went for Breckenridge;
Kentucky, Tennessee, and Virginia for Bell; while Douglas secured
only one entire State—Missouri.

And now God bless you; and
all good union-men.
Yours as ever
A. Lincoln

CHAPTER VII.

THE election over, Mr. Lincoln scarcely had time enough to take a breath until another campaign and one equally trying, so far as a test of his constitution and nerves was concerned, as the one through which he had just passed, opened up before him. I refer to the siege of the cabinet-makers and office-seekers. It proved to be a severe and protracted strain and one from which there seemed to be no relief, as the President-elect of this renowned democratic Government is by custom and precedent expected to meet and listen to everybody who calls to see him. " Individuals, deputations, and delegations," says one of Mr. Lincoln's biographers, "from all quarters pressed in upon him in a manner that might have killed a man of less robust constitution. The hotels of Springfield were filled with gentlemen who came with light baggage and heavy schemes. The party had never been in office. A clean sweep of the 'ins' was expected, and all the 'outs' were patriotically anxious to take the vacant places. It was a party that had never fed; and it was voraciously hungry. Mr. Lincoln and Artemus Ward saw a great deal of fun in it; and in all human probality it was the fun alone that enabled Mr. Lincoln to bear it."

His own election of course disposed of any claims Illinois might have had to any further representation in the cabinet, but it afforded Mr. Lincoln no relief from the argumentative interviews and pressing claims of the endless list of ambitious statesmen in the thirty-two other states, who swarmed into Springfield from every point of the compass. He told each one of them a story, and even if he failed to put their names on his slate they went away without knowing that fact, and never forgot the visit.*

---

* A newspaper correspondent who had been sent down from Chicago to "write up" Mr. Lincoln soon after his nomination, was kind enough several years ago to furnish me with an account of his visit. As some of his reminiscences are more or less interesting, I take the liberty of inserting a portion of his letter. "A what-not in the corner of the room," he relates, "was laden with various kinds of shells. Taking one in my hand, I said, 'This, I suppose, is called a Trocus by the geologist or naturalist.' Mr. Lincoln paused a moment as if reflecting and then replied, 'I do not know, for I never studied either geology or natural history.' I then took to examining the few pictures that hung on the walls, and was paying more than ordinary attention to one that hung above the sofa. He was immediately at my left and pointing to it said, 'That picture gives a very fair representation of my homely face.' . . . The time for my departure nearing, I made the usual apologies and started to go. 'You cannot get out of the town before a quarter past eleven,' remonstrated Mr. Lincoln, 'and you may as well stay a little longer.' Under pretence of some unfinished matters down town, however, I very reluctantly withdrew from the mansion. 'Well,' said Mr. Lincoln, as we passed into the hall, 'suppose you come over to the State House before you start for Chicago.' After a moment's deliberation I promised to do so. Mr. Lincoln, following without his hat, and continuing the conversation, shook hands across the gate, saying, 'Now, come over.' I wended my way to my hotel, and after a brief period was in his office at the State House. Resuming conversation, he said, 'If the man comes with the key before you go, I want to give you a book.' I certainly hoped the man *would* come

He had a way of pretending to assure his visitor that in the choice of his advisers he was "free to act as his judgment dictated," although David Davis, acting as his manager at the Chicago convention, had negotiated with the Indiana and Pennsylvania delegations, and assigned places in the cabinet to Simon Cameron and Caleb Smith, besides making other "arrangements" which Mr. Lincoln was expected to ratify. Of this he was undoubtedly aware, although in answer to a letter from Joshua R. Giddings, of Ohio, congratulating him

---

with the key. Some conversation had taken place at the house on which his book treated,—but I had forgotten this,—and soon Mr. Lincoln absented himself for perhaps two minutes and returned with a copy of the debates between himself and Judge Douglas. He placed the book on his knee, as he sat back on two legs of his chair, and wrote on the fly-leaf, 'J. S. Bliss, from A. Lincoln.' Besides this he marked a complete paragraph near the middle of the book. While sitting in the position described little Willie, his son, came in and begged his father for twenty-five cents. 'My son,' said the father, 'what do you want with twenty-five cents?' 'I want it to buy candy with,' cried the boy. 'I cannot give you twenty-five cents, my son, but will give you five cents,' at the same time putting his thumb and finger into his vest pocket and taking therefrom five cents in silver, which he placed upon the desk before the boy. But this did not reach Willie's expectations; he scorned the pile, and turning away clambered down-stairs and through the spacious halls of the Capitol, leaving behind him his five cents and a distinct reverberation of sound. Mr. Lincoln turned to me and said, 'He will be back after that in a few minutes.' 'Why do you think so?' said I. 'Because, as soon as he finds I will give him no more he will come and get it.' After the matter had been nearly forgotten and conversation had turned in an entirely different channel, Willie came cautiously in behind my chair and that of his father, picked up the specie, and went away without saying a word."—J. S. Bliss, letter, Jan. 29, 1867, MS.

on his nomination, he said,* "It is indeed most grateful to my feelings that the responsible position assigned me comes without conditions." Out of regard to the dignity of the exalted station he was about to occupy, he was not as free in discussing the matter of his probable appointments with some of his personal friends as they had believed he would be. In one or two instances, I remember, the latter were offended at his seeming disregard of the claims of old friendship. My advice was not asked for on such grave subjects, nor had I any right or reason to believe it would be; hence I never felt slighted or offended. On some occasions in our office, when Mr. Lincoln had come across from the State House for a rest or a chat with me, he would relate now and then some circumstance—generally an amusing one—connected with the settlement of the cabinet problem, but it was said in such a way that one would not have felt free to interrogate him about his plans. Soon after his election I received from my friend Joseph Medill, of Chicago, a letter which argued strongly against the appointment of Simon Cameron to a place in the cabinet, and which the writer desired I should bring to Mr. Lincoln's attention. I awaited a favorable opportunity, and one evening when we were alone in our office I gave it to him. It was an eloquent protest against the appointment of a corrupt and debased man, and coming from the source it did—the writer being one of Lincoln's best newspaper supporters—made a deep impression on him. Lincoln read

---

* Letter, May 21st, 1860, MS.

it over several times, but refrained from expressing any opinion. He did say however that he felt himself under no promise or obligation to appoint anyone ; that if his friends made any agreements for him they did so over his expressed direction and without his knowledge. At another time he said that he wanted to give the South, by way of placation, a place in his cabinet ; that a fair division of the country entitled the Southern States to a reasonable representation there, and if not interfered with he would make such a distribution as would satisfy all persons interested. He named three persons who would be acceptable to him. They were Botts, of Virginia; Stephens, of Georgia; and Maynard, of Tennessee. He apprehended no such grave danger to the Union as the mass of people supposed would result from Southern threats, and said he could not in his heart believe that the South designed the overthrow of the Government. This is the extent of my conversation about the cabinet. Thurlow Weed, the veteran in journalism and politics, came out from New York and spent several days with Lincoln. He was not only the representative of Senator Seward, but rendered the President-elect signal service in the formation of his cabinet. In his autobiography Mr. Weed relates numerous incidents of this visit. He was one day opposing the claims of Montgomery Blair, who aspired to a cabinet appointment, when Mr. Lincoln inquired of Weed whom he would recommend. " Henry Winter Davis," was the response. " David Davis, I see, has been posting you up on this question," retorted Lincoln. "He has Davis on the brain. I think Maryland must be a good State to move from." The President then told a story of a witness in court in a neighboring county, who on being asked his age replied, "Sixty." Being satisfied he was much older the question was repeated, and on receiving the same answer, the court admonished the witness, saying, "The court knows you to be much older than sixty." "Oh, I understand now," was the rejoinder ; "you're thinking of those ten years I spent on the eastern shore of Maryland ; that was so much time lost and don't count."

Before Mr. Lincoln's departure from Springfield, people who knew him personally were frequently asked what sort of man he was. I received many letters, generally from the Eastern States, showing that much doubt still existed in the minds of the people whether he would prove equal to the great task that lay in store for him. Among others who wrote me on the subject was the Hon. Henry Wilson, late Vice-president of the United States, whom I had met during my visit to Washington in the spring of 1858. Two years after Mr. Lincoln's death, Mr. Wilson wrote me as follows : "I have just finished reading your letter dated December 21, 1860, in answer to a letter of mine asking you to give me your opinion of the President just elected. In this letter to me you say of Mr. Lincoln what more than four years of observation confirmed. After stating that you had been his law partner for over eighteen years and his most intimate and bosom friend all that time you say, ' I

know him better than he does himself. I know
this seems a little strong, but I risk the assertion.
Lincoln is a man of heart—aye, as gentle as a
woman's and as tender—but he has a will strong as
iron. He therefore loves all mankind, hates slavery
and every form of despotism. Put these together
—love for the slave, and a determination, a will, that
justice, strong and unyielding, shall be done when
he has the right to act, and you can form your own
conclusion. Lincoln will fail here, namely, if a question of political economy—if any question comes
up which is doubtful, questionable, which no man
can demonstrate, then his friends can rule him ; but
when on justice, right, liberty, the Government,
the Constitution, and the Union, then you may
all stand aside: he will rule then, and no man can
move him—no set of men can do it. There is no
fail here. This is Lincoln, and you mark my prediction. You and I must keep the people right ;
God will keep Lincoln right.' These words of
yours made a deep impression upon my mind, and I
came to love and trust him even before I saw him.
After an acquaintance of more than four years I
found that your idea of him was in all respects correct—that he was the loving, tender, firm, and just
man you represented him to be ; while upon some
questions in which moral elements did not so
clearly enter he was perhaps too easily influenced
by others. Mr. Lincoln was a genuine democrat
in feelings, sentiments, and actions. How patiently
and considerately he listened amid the terrible
pressure of public affairs to the people who

thronged his ante-room!   I remember calling upon him one day during the war on pressing business. The ante-room was crowded with men and women seeking admission. He seemed oppressed, careworn, and weary. I said to him, ' Mr. President, you are too exhausted to see this throng waiting to see you ; you will wear yourself out and ought not see these people to-day.' He replied, with one of those smiles in which sadness seemed to mingle, ' They don't want much ; they get but little, and I must see them.'   During the war his heart was oppressed and his life burdened with the conflict between the tenderness of his nature and what seemed to be the imperative demands of duty. In the darkest hours of the conflict desertions from the army were frequent, and army officers urgently pressed the execution of the sentences of the law ; but it was with the greatest effort that he would bring himself to consent to the execution of the judgment of the military tribunals. I remember calling early one sabbath morning with a wounded Irish officer, who came to Washington to say that a soldier who had been sentenced to be shot in a day or two for desertion had fought gallantly by his side in battle.   I told Mr. Lincoln we had come to ask him to pardon the poor soldier. After a few moments' reflection he said, ' My officers tell me the good of the service demands the enforcement of the law ; but it makes my heart ache to have the poor fellows shot. I will pardon this soldier, and then you will all join in blaming me for it.   You censure me for granting pardons, and yet you all ask me to do so.'   I say again, no man had a more loving and tender nature than Mr. Lincoln."

Before departing for Washington Mr. Lincoln went to Chicago* for a few days' stay, and there by previous arrangement met his old friend, Joshua F. Speed. Both were accompanied by their wives, and while the latter were out shopping the two husbands repaired to Speed's room at the hotel. "For an hour or more," relates Speed, "we lived over again the scenes of other days. Finally Lincoln threw himself on the bed, and fixing his eyes on a spot in the ceiling asked me this question, ' Speed, what is your pecuniary condition? are you rich or poor?' I answered, addressing him by his new title, ' Mr. President, I think I can anticipate what you are going to say. I'll speak candidly to you on the subject. My pecuniary condition is satisfactory to me now; you would perhaps call it good. I do not think you have within your gift any office I could afford to take.' Mr. Lincoln then proposed to make Guthrie, of Kentucky, Secretary of War, but did not want to write to him— asked me to feel of him. I did as requested, but the Kentucky statesman declined on the ground of his advanced age, and consequent physical inability to fill the position. He gave substantial assurance

---

* A lady called one day at the hotel where the Lincolns were stopping in Chicago to take Mrs. Lincoln out for a promenade or a drive. She was met in the parlor by Mr. Lincoln, who, after a hurried trip upstairs to ascertain the cause of the delay in his wife's appearance, returned with the report that " She will be down as soon as she has all her trotting harness on."

of his loyal sentiments, however, and insisted that
the Union should be preserved at all hazards."

Late in January Mr. Lincoln informed me that he
was ready to begin the preparation of his inaugural
address. He had, aside from his law books and
the few gilded volumes that ornamented the centre-
table in his parlor at home, comparatively no
library. He never seemed to care to own or collect
books. On the other hand I had a very respectable
collection, and was adding to it every day. To my
library Lincoln very frequently had access. When,
therefore, he began on his inaugural speech he told
me what works he intended to consult. I looked
for a long list, but when he went over it I was
greatly surprised. He asked me to furnish him
with Henry Clay's great speech delivered in 1850;
Andrew Jackson's proclamation against Nullifica-
tion; and a copy of the Constitution. He afterwards called for Webster's reply to Hayne, a speech
which he read when he lived at New Salem, and
which he always regarded as the grandest specimen
of American oratory. With these few "volumes,"
and no further sources of reference, he locked himself
up in a room upstairs over a store across the street
from the State House, and there, cut off from all
communication and intrusion, he prepared the
address. Though composed amid the unromantic
surroundings of a dingy, dusty, and neglected back
room, the speech has become a memorable document. Posterity will assign to it a high rank
among historical utterances; and it will ever bear
comparison with the efforts of Washington, Jeffer-

son, Adams, or any that preceded its delivery from the steps of the national Capitol.

After Mr. Lincoln's rise to national prominence, and especially since his death, I have often been asked if I did not write this or that paper for him; if I did not prepare or help prepare some of his speeches. I know that other and abler friends of Lincoln have been asked the same question.* To people who made such enquiries I always responded, "You don't understand Mr. Lincoln. No man ever asked less aid then he; his confidence in his own ability to meet the requirements of every hour was so marked that his friends never thought of tendering their aid, and therefore no one could share his responsibilities. I never wrote a line for him; he never asked me to. I was never conscious of having exerted any influence over him. He often called out my views on some philosophical question, simply because I was a fond student of philosophy, and conceding that I had given the subject more attention than he; he often asked as to the use of a word or the turn of a sentence, but if I volunteered to recommend or even suggest a change of language which involved a change of sentiment I found him the most inflexible man I have ever seen."

One more duty—an act of filial devotion— remained to be done before Abraham Lincoln could

---

* "I know it was the general impression in Washington that I knew all about Lincoln's plans and ideas, but the truth is, I knew nothing. He never confided to me anything of his purposes."— David Davis, statement, September 20, 1866.

announce his readiness to depart for the city of Washington—a place from which it was unfortunately decreed he should never return. In the first week of February he slipped quietly away from Springfield and rode to Farmington in Coles County, where his aged step-mother was still living. Here, in the little country village, he met also the surviving members of the Hanks and Johnston families. He visited the grave of his father, old Thomas Lincoln, which had been unmarked and neglected for almost a decade, and left directions that a suitable stone should be placed there to mark the spot. Retracing his steps in the direction of Springfield he stopped over-night in the town of Charleston, where he made a brief address, recalling many of his boyhood exploits, in the public hall. In the audience were many persons who had known him first as the stalwart young ox-driver when his father's family drove into Illinois from southern Indiana. One man had brought with him a horse which the President-elect, in the earlier days of his law practice, had recovered for him in a replevin suit; another one was able to recite from personal recollection the thrilling details of the famous wrestling match between Lincoln the flat-boatman in 1830 and Daniel Needham; and all had some reminiscence of his early manhood to relate. The separation from his step-mother was particularly touching.*

---

* Lincoln's love for his second mother was a most filial and affectionate one. His letters show that he regarded the relation truly as that of mother and son. November 4, 1851, he writes her after the death of his father:

The parting, when the good old woman, with tears streaming down her cheeks, gave him a mother's benediction, expressing the fear that his life might be taken by his enemies, will never be forgotten by those who witnessed it. Deeply impressed by this farewell scene Mr. Lincoln reluctantly withdrew from the circle of warm friends who crowded around him, and, filled with gloomy forebodings of the future, returned to Springfield. The great questions of state having been pretty well settled in his own mind, and a few days yet remaining before his final departure, his neighbors and old friends called to take leave of him and pay their " best respects." Many of these callers were from New Salem, where he had made his start in life, and each one had some pleasant or amusing incident of earlier days to call up when they met. Hannah Armstrong, who had "foxed" his trowsers with buckskin in the days when he served as surveyor under John Calhoun, and whose son Lincoln had afterwards acquitted in the trial for murder at Beardstown, gave positive evidence of the interest she took in his continued rise in the world.

" DEAR MOTHER :

" Chapman tells me he wants you to go and live with him. If I were you I would try it awhile. If you get tired of it (as I think you will not) you can return to your own home. Chapman feels very kindly to you; and I have no doubt he will make your situation very pleasant.   "Sincerely your son,
     " A. LINCOLN."

On the 9th of the same month he writes his step-brother John D. Johnston : " If the land can be sold so that I can get three hundred dollars to put to interest for mother I will not object if she does not. But before I will make a deed the money must be had, or secured beyond all doubt at ten per cent."

She bade him good-bye, but was filled with a presentiment that she would never see him alive again. "Hannah," he said, jovially, "if they do kill me I shall never die again." Isaac Cogsdale, another New Salem pioneer, came, and to him Lincoln again admitted his love for the unfortunate Anne Rutledge. Cogsdale afterwards told me of this interview. It occurred late in the afternoon. Mr. Nicolay, the secretary, had gone home, and the throng of visitors had ceased for the day. Lincoln asked about all the early families of New Salem, calling up the peculiarities of each as he went over the list. Of the Rutledges he said: "I have loved the name of Rutledge to this day. I have kept my mind on their movements ever since." Of Anne he spoke with some feeling: "I loved her dearly. She was a handsome girl, would have made a good, loving wife; she was natural, and quite intellectual, though not highly educated. I did honestly and truly love the girl, and think often of her now."

Early in February the last item of preparation for the journey to Washington had been made. Mr. Lincoln had disposed of his household goods and furniture to a neighbor, had rented his house; and as these constituted all the property he owned in Illinois there was no further occasion for concern on that score. In the afternoon of his last day in Springfield he came down to our office to examine some papers and confer with me about certain legal matters in which he still felt some interest. On several previous occasions he had told me he was coming over to the office "to have a long talk with me," as he expressed it. We ran over the books and arranged for the completion of all unsettled and unfinished matters. In some cases he had certain requests to make—certain lines of procedure he wished me to observe. After these things were all disposed of he crossed to the opposite side of the room and threw himself down on the old office sofa, which, after many years of service, had been mveod against the wall for support. He lay for some moments, his face towards the ceiling, without either of us speaking. Presently he inquired, "Billy,"—he always called me by that name,—"how long have we been together?" "Over sixteen years," I answered. "We've never had a cross word during all that time, have we?" to which I returned a vehement, "No, indeed we have not." He then recalled some incidents of his early practice and took great pleasure in delineating the ludicrous features of many a lawsuit on the circuit. It was at this last interview in Springfield that he told me of the efforts that had been made by other lawyers to supplant me in the partnership with him. He insisted that such men were weak creatures, who, to use his own language, "hoped to secure a law practice by hanging to his coat-tail." I never saw him in a more cheerful mood. He gathered a bundle of books and papers he wished to take with him and started to go ; but before leaving he made the strange request that the sign-board which swung on its rusty hinges at the foot of the stairway should remain. "Let it hang there undisturbed,"* he said, with a significant lowering of his voice. " Give our clients to understand that the election of a President makes no change in the firm of Lincoln and Herndon. If I live I'm coming back some time, and then we'll go right on practising law as if nothing had ever happened." He lingered for a moment as if to take a last look at the old quarters, and then passed through the door into the narrow hallway. I accompanied him downstairs. On the way he spoke of the unpleasant features surrounding the Presidential office. " I am sick of office-holding already," he complained, "and I shudder when I think of the tasks that are still ahead." He said the sorrow of parting from his old associations was deeper than most persons would imagine, but it was more marked in his case because of the feeling which had become irrepressible that he would never return alive. I argued against the thought, characterizing it as an illusory notion not in harmory or keeping with the

---

* In answer to the many inquiries made of me, I will say here that during this last interview Mr. Lincoln, for the first time, brought up the subject of an office under his administration. He asked me if I desired an appointment at his hands, and, if so, what I wanted. I answered that I had no desire for a Federal office, that I was then holding the office of Bank Commissioner of Illinois under appointment of Governor Bissel, and that if he would request my retention in office by Yates, the incoming Governor, I should be satisfied. He made the necessary recommendation, and Governor Yates complied. I was present at the meeting between Yates and Lincoln, and I remember that the former, when Lincoln urged my claims for retention in office, asked Lincoln to appoint their mutual friend A. Y. Ellis postmaster at Springfield. I do not remember whether Lincoln promised to do so or not, but Ellis was never appointed.

popular ideal of a President. "But it is in keeping with my philosophy," was his quick retort. Our conversation was frequently broken in upon by the interruptions of passers-by, who, each in succession, seemed desirous of claiming his attention. At length he broke away from them all. Grasping my hand warmly and with a fervent "Good-bye," he disappeared down the street, and never came back to the office again. On the morning following this last interview, the 11th day of February, the Presidential party repaired to the railway station, where the train which was to convey them to Washington awaited the ceremony of departure. The intention was to stop at many of the principal cities along the route, and plenty of time had been allotted for the purpose. Mr. Lincoln had told me that a man named Wood had been recommended to him by Mr. Seward, and he had been placed in charge of the party as a sort of general manager. The party, besides the President, his wife, and three sons, Robert, William, and Thomas, consisted of his brother-in-law, Dr. W. S. Wallace, David Davis, Norman B. Judd, Elmer E. Ellsworth, Ward H. Lamon, and the President's two secretaries, John G. Nicolay and John Hay. Colonel E. V. Sumner and other army gentlemen were also in the car, and some friends of Mr. Lincoln—among them O. H. Browning, Governor Yates, and ex-Governor Moore—started with the party from Springfield, but dropped out at points along the way. The day was a stormy one, with dense clouds hanging heavily overhead. A goodly throng of Springfield people had gathered to see the distinguished party safely off. After the latter had entered the car the people closed about it until the President appeared on the rear platform. He stood for a moment as if to suppress evidences of his emotion, and removing his hat made the following brief but dignified and touching address: * " Friends: No one who has never been placed in a like position can understand my feelings at this hour, nor the oppressive sadness I feel at this parting. For more than a quarter of a century I have lived among you, and during all that time I have received nothing but kindness at your hands. Here I have lived from my youth until now I am an old man. Here the most sacred ties of earth were assumed. Here all my children were born; and here one of them lies buried. To you, dear friends, I owe all that I have, all that I am. All the strange, checkered past seems to crowd now upon my mind. To-day I leave you. I go to assume a task more difficult than that which devolved upon Washington. Unless the great God who assisted him shall be with and aid me, I must fail; but if the same omniscient mind and almighty arm that directed and protected him shall guide and support me I shall not fail—I shall succeed. Let us all pray that

---

* I was not present when Mr. Lincoln delivered his farewell at the depot in Springfield, and never heard what he said. I have adopted the version of his speech as published in our papers. There has been some controversy over the exact language he used on that occasion, and Mr. Nicolay has recently published the speech from what he says is the original MS., partly in his own and partly in the handwriting of Mr. Lincoln. Substantially, however, it is like the speech as reproduced here from the Springfield paper.

Springfield Passenger Station, Great Western Railway,

Where Mr. Lincoln delivered his farewell speech, February 11, 1861.

the God of our fathers may not forsake us now. To him I commend you all. Permit me to ask that with equal sincerity and faith you will invoke his wisdom and guidance for me. With these words I must leave you, for how long I know not. Friends, one and all, I must now bid you an affectionate farewell."

At the conclusion of this neat and appropriate farewell the train rolled slowly out, and Mr. Lincoln, still standing in the doorway of the rear car, took his last view of Springfield. The journey had been as well advertised as it had been carefully planned, and therefore, at every town along the route, and at every stop, great crowds were gathered to catch a glimpse of the President-elect.* Mr. Lincoln usu-

---

* " Before Mr. Lincoln's election in 1860 I, then a child of eleven years, was presented with his lithograph. Admiring him with my whole heart, I thought still his appearance would be much improved should he cultivate his whiskers. Childish thoughts must have utterance. So I proposed the idea to him, expressing as well as I was able the esteem in which he was held among honest men. A few days after I received this kind and friendly letter :

" ' SPRINGFIELD, ILL., October 19, 1860.

" ' MISS GRACE BEDELL.

" ' *My Dear Little Miss :*—Your very agreeable letter of the 15th is received. I regret the necessity of saying I have no daughter. I have three sons—one seventeen, one nine, and one seven. They with their mother constitute my whole family. As to the whiskers, as I have never worn any, do you not think that people would call it a piece of silly affectation were I to begin wearing them now?

" ' I am your true friend and sincere well-wisher,

" ' A. LINCOLN.'

" It appears I was not forgotten, for after his election to the Presidency, while on his journey to Washington, the train stopped at Westfield, Chautauqua County, at which place I then resided. Mr.

ally gratified the wishes of the crowds, who called him out for a speech whether it was down on the regular programme of movements or not. In all cases his remarks were well-timed and sensibly uttered. At Indianapolis, where the Legislature was in session, he halted for a day and delivered a speech the burden of which was an answer to the Southern charges of coercion and invasion. From Indianapolis he moved on to Cincinnati and Columbus, at the last-named place meeting the Legislature of Ohio. The remainder of the journey convinced Mr. Lincoln of his strength in the affections of the people. Many, no doubt, were full of curiosity to see the now famous rail-splitter, but all were outspoken and earnest in their assurances of support. At Steubenville, Pittsburg, Cleveland, Buffalo, Albany, New York, and Philadelphia he made manly and patriotic speeches. These speeches, plain in language and simple in illustration, made évery man who heard them a stronger friend than ever of the Government. He was skilful enough to warn the people of the danger ahead and to impress them with his ability to deal properly with the situation, without in any case outlining his intended policy or revealing the

---

Lincoln said, 'I have a correspondent in this place, a little girl whose name is Grace Bedell, and I would like to see her.' I was conveyed to him; he stepped from the cars, extending his hand and saying, 'You see I have let these whiskers grow for you, Grace,' kissed me, shook me cordially by the hand, and was gone. I was frequently afterward assured of his remembrance.'"—Grace G. Bedell, MS. letter, Dec. 14, 1866.

forces he held in reserve.* At Pittsburg he advised deliberation and begged the American people to keep their temper on both sides of the line. At Cleveland he insisted that "the crisis, as it is called, is an artificial crisis and has no foundation in fact;" and at Philadelphia he assured his listeners that under his administration there would be "no bloodshed unless it was forced upon the Government, and then it would be compelled to act in self-defence." This last utterance was made in front of Independence

---

* The following are extracts from Mr. Lincoln's letters written during the campaign in answer to his position with reference to the anticipated uprisings in the Southern States. They are here published for the first time:

[From a letter to L. Montgomery Bond, Esq., Oct. 15, 1860.]

"I certainly am in no temper and have no purpose to embitter the feelings of the South, but whether I am inclined to such a course as would in fact embitter their feelings you can better judge by my published speeches than by anything I would say in a short letter if I were inclined now, as I am not, to define my position anew."

[From a letter to Samuel Haycraft, dated, Springfield, Ill., June 4, 1860.]

"Like yourself I belonged to the old Whig party from its origin to its close. I never belonged to the American party organization, nor ever to a party called a Union party; though I hope I neither am or ever have been less devoted to the Union than yourself or any other patriotic man."

[Private and Confidential.]

SPRINGFIELD, ILL., Nov. 13, 1860.

"HON. SAMUEL HAYCRAFT.

"*My Dear Sir:*—Yours of the 9th is just received. I can only answer briefly. Rest fully assured that the good people of the South who will put themselves in the same temper and mood towards me which you do will find no cause to complain of me.

"Yours very truly,

"A. LINCOLN."

Hall, where, a few moments before, he had unfurled
to the breeze a magnificent new flag, an impressive
ceremony performed amid the cheers swelling from
the vast sea of upturned faces before him.   From
Philadelphia his journey took him to Harrisburg,
where he visited both branches of the Legislature
then in session.   For an account of the remainder
of this now famous trip I beg to quote from the
admirable narrative of Dr. Holland.   Describing
the welcome tendered him by the Legislature at
Harrisburg, the latter says : " At the conclusion of
the exercises of the day Mr. Lincoln, who was
known to be very weary, was permitted to pass
undisturbed to his apartments in the Jones House.
It was popularly understood that he was to start
for Washington the next morning, and the people
of Harrisburg supposed they had only taken a temporary leave of him.   He remained in his rooms
until nearly six o'clock, when he passed into the
street, entered a carriage unobserved in company
with Colonel Lamon, and was driven to a special
train on the Pennsylvania railroad in waiting for
him.   As a matter of precaution the telegraph
wires were cut the moment he left Harrisburg, so
that if his departure should be discovered intelligence
of it could not be communicated at a distance.   At
half-past ten the train arrived at Philadelphia, and
here Mr. Lincoln was met by a detective, who had
a carriage in readiness in which the party were
driven to the depot of the Philadelphia, Wilming-
ton, and Baltimore railroad.   At a quarter past
eleven they arrived and very fortunately found the

regular train, which should have left at eleven, delayed. The party took berths in the sleeping-car, and without change of cars passed directly through Baltimore to Washington, where Mr. Lincoln arrived at half-past six o'clock in the morning and found Mr. Washburne anxiously awaiting him. He was taken into a carriage and in a few minutes he was talking over his adventures with Senator Seward at Willard's Hotel." The remaining members of the Presidential party from whom Mr. Lincoln separated at Harrisburg left that place on the special train intended for him; and as news of his safe arrival in Washington had been already telegraphed over the country no attempt was made to interrupt their safe passage through Baltimore. As is now generally well known many threats had up to that time been made that Mr. Lincoln, on his way to Washington, should never pass through Baltimore alive. It was reported and believed that conspiracies had been formed to attack the train, blow it up with explosives or in some equally effective way dispose of the President-elect. Mr. Seward and others were so deeply impressed with the grave features of the reports afloat that Allan Pinkerton, the noted detective of Chicago, was employed to investigate the matter and ferret out the conspiracy, if any existed. This shrewd operator went to Baltimore, opened an office as a stock-broker, and through his assistants —the most adroit and serviceable of whom was a woman—was soon in possession of inside information. The change of plans and trains at Harrisburg was due to his management and advice. Some years before his death Mr. Pinkerton furnished me with a large volume of the written reports of his subordinates and an elaborate account by himself of the conspiracy and the means he employed to ferret it out. The narrative, thrilling enough in some particulars, is too extended for insertion here. It is enough for us to know that the tragedy was successfully averted and that Mr. Lincoln was safely landed in Washington.

In January preceding his departure from Springfield Mr. Lincoln, becoming somewhat annoyed, not to say alarmed, at the threats emanating from Baltimore and other portions of the country adjacent to Washington, that he should not reach the latter place alive, and that even if successful in reaching the Capitol his inauguration should in some way be prevented, determined to ascertain for himself what protection would be given him in case an effort should be made by an individual or a mob to do him violence. He sent a young military officer in the person of Thomas Mather, then Adjutant-General of Illinois, to Washington with a letter to General Scott, in which he recounted the threats he had heard and ventured to inquire as to the probability of any attempt at his life being made on the occasion of his inauguration. General Mather, on his arrival in Washington, found General Scott confined to his room by illness and unable to see visitors. On Mather calling a second time and sending in his letter he was invited up to the sick man's chamber. " Entering the room," related Mather in later years," I found the old warrior, grizzly and wrinkled, propped up in the bed by an embankment of pillows behind his back. His hair and beard were considerably disordered, the flesh seemed to lay in rolls across his warty face and neck, and his breathing was not without great labor. In his hand he still held Lincoln's letter. He was weak from long-continued illness, and trembled very perceptibly. It was evident that the message from Lincoln had wrought up the old veteran's feelings. 'General Mather,' he said to me, in great agitation, 'present my compliments to Mr. Lincoln when you return to Springfield, and tell him I expect him to come on to Washington as soon as he is ready. Say to him that I'll look after those Maryland and Virginia rangers myself; I'll plant cannon at both ends of Pennsylvania avenue, and if any of them show their heads or raise a finger I'll blow them to hell.' On my return to Springfield," concludes Mather, "I hastened to assure Mr. Lincoln that, if Scott were alive on the day of the inauguration, there need be no alarm lest the performance be interrupted by any one. I felt certain the hero of Lundy's Lane would give the matter the care and attention it deserved."

Having at last reached his destination in safety, Mr. Lincoln spent the few days preceding his inauguration at Willard's Hotel, receiving an uninterrupted stream of visitors and friends. In the few unoccupied moments allotted him, he was carefully revising his inaugural address. On the morning of the 4th of March he rode from his hotel with Mr. Buchanan in an open barouche to the Capitol.

There, slightly pale and nervous, he was introduced to the assembled multitude by his old friend Edward D. Baker, and in a fervid and impressive manner delivered his address. At its conclusion the customary oath was administered by the venerable Chief Justice Taney, and he was now clothed with all the powers and privileges of Chief Magistrate of the nation. He accompanied Mr. Buchanan to the White House, and here the historic bachelor of Lancaster bade him farewell, bespeaking for him a peaceful, prosperous, and successful administration.

One who witnessed the impressive scene left the following graphic description of the inauguration and its principal incidents: "Near noon I found myself a member of the motley crowd gathered about the side entrance to Willard's Hotel. Soon an open barouche drove up, and the only occupant stepped out. A large, heavy, awkward-moving man, far advanced in years, short and thin gray hair, full face, plentifully seamed and wrinkled, head curiously inclined to the left shoulder, a low-crowned, broad-brimmed silk hat, an immense white cravat like a poultice, thrusting the old-fashioned standing collar up to the ears, dressed in black throughout, with swallow-tail coat not of the newest style. It was President Buchanan, calling to take his successor to the Capitol. In a few minutes he reappeared, with Mr. Lincoln on his arm; the two took seats side-by-side, and the carriage rolled away, followed by a rather disorderly and certainly not very imposing procession. I had ample time to walk to the Capitol, and no difficulty in securing a place where everything could be seen and heard to the best advantage. The attendance at the inauguration was, they told me, unusually small, many being kept away by anticipated disturbance, as it had been rumored—truly, too—that General Scott himself was fearful of an outbreak, and had made all possible military preparations to meet the emergency. A square platform had been built out from the steps to the eastern portico, with benches for distinguished spectators on three sides. Douglas, the only one I recognized, sat at the extreme end of the seat on the right of the narrow passage leading from the steps. There was no delay, and the gaunt form of the President-elect was soon visible, slowly making his way to the front. To me, at least, he was completely metamorphosed—partly by his own fault, and partly through the efforts of injudicious friends and ambitious tailors. He was raising (to gratify a very young lady, it is said) a crop of whiskers, of the blacking-brush variety, coarse, stiff, and ungraceful; and in so doing spoiled, or at least seriously impaired, a face which, though never handsome, had in its original state a peculiar power and pathos. On the present occasion the whiskers were reinforced by brand-new clothes from top to toe; black dress-coat, instead of the usual frock, black cloth or satin vest, black pantaloons, and a glossy hat evidently just out of the box. To cap the climax of novelty, he carried a huge ebony cane, with a gold head the size of an egg. In these, to him, strange habiliments, he looked so miserably uncomfortable that I could not help pitying him. Reaching the platform, his discomfort was visibly increased by not knowing what to do with hat and cane; and so he stood there, the target for ten thousand eyes, holding cane in one hand and hat in the other, the very picture of helpless embarrassment. After some hesitation he pushed the cane into a corner of the railing, but could not find a place for the hat except on the floor, where I could see he did not like to risk it. Douglas, who fully took in the situation, came to rescue of his old friend and rival, and held the precious hat until the owner needed it again; a service which, if predicted two years before, would probably have astonished him. The oath of office was administered by Chief Justice Taney, whose black robes, attenuated figure, and cadaverous countenance reminded me of a galvanized corpse. Then the President came forward, and read his inaugural address in a clear and distinct voice. It was attentively listened to by all, but the closest listener was Douglas, who leaned forward as if to catch every word, nodding his head emphatically at those passages which most pleased him. There was some applause, not very much nor very enthusiastic. I must not forget to mention the presence of a Mephistopheles in the person of Senator Wigfall, of Texas, who stood with folded arms leaning against the doorway of the

Capitol, looking down upon the crowd and the ceremony with a contemptuous air, which sufficiently indicated his opinion of the whole performance. To him the Southern Confederacy was already an accomplished fact. He lived to see it the saddest of fictions."

CHAPTER VIII.

LINCOLN, the President, did not differ greatly from
Lincoln the lawyer and politician. In the latter
capacity only had his old friends in Illinois known
him. For a long time after taking his seat they
were curious to know what change, if any, his
exalted station had made in him. He was no
longer amid people who had seen him grow from
the village lawyer to the highest rank in the land,
and whose hands he could grasp in the confidence
of a time-tried friendship; but now he was surrounded by wealth, power, fashion, influence, by
adroit politicians and artful schemers of every sort.
In the past his Illinois and particularly his Springfield friends * had shared the anxiety and responsi-

---

* Lincoln, even after his elevation to the Presidency, always had
an eye out for his friends, as the following letters will abundantly
prove :

"EXECUTIVE MANSION, WASHINGTON, April 20, 1864.

"CALVIN TRUESDALE, ESQ.

"Postmaster, Rock Island, Ill. :

"Thomas J. Pickett, late agent of the Quarter-
master's Department for the Island of Rock Island, has been removed or suspended from that position on a charge of having sold
timber and stone from the island for his private benefit. Mr. Pickett
is an old acquaintance and friend of mine, and I will thank you, if
you will, to set a day or days and place on and at which to take
testimony on the point. Notify Mr. Pickett and one J. B. Danforth

bility of every step he had made; but now they were no longer to continue in the partnership. Many of them wanted no office, but all of them felt great interest as well as pride in his future. A few attempted to keep up a correspondence with him, but his answers were tardy and irregular. Because he did not appoint a goodly portion of his early associates to comfortable offices, and did not interest himself in the welfare of everyone whom he had known in Illinois, or met while on the circuit, the erroneous impression grew that his eleva-

---

(who as I understand makes the charge) to be present with their witnesses. Take the testimony in writing offered by both sides, and report it in full to me. Please do this for me.

> "Yours truly,
> "A. LINCOLN."

The man Pickett was formerly the editor of a newspaper in northern Illinois, and had, to use an expression of later days, inaugurated in the columns of his paper Lincoln's boom for the Presidency. When he afterwards fell under suspicion, no one came to his rescue sooner than the President himself.

The following letter needs no explanation:

> "EXECUTIVE MANSION, WASHINGTON, August 27, 1862.
> "Hon. WASH. TALCOTT.

> "*My Dear Sir:*—I have determined to appoint you collector. I now have a very special request to make of you, which is, that you will make no war upon Mr. Washburne, who is also my friend, and of longer standing than yourself. I will even be obliged if you can do something for him if occasion presents.

> "Yours truly,
> "A. LINCOLN."

Mr. Talcott, to whom it was addressed, was furnished a letter of introduction by the President, as follows:

> "The Secretary of the Treasury and the Commissioner of Internal Revenue will please see Mr. Talcott, one of the best men there is, and, if any difference, one they would like better than they do me.

> "A. LINCOLN."

August 18, 1862.

tion had turned his head. There was no foundation for such an unwarranted conclusion. Lincoln had not changed a particle. He was overrun with duties and weighted down with cares; his surroundings were different and his friends were new, but he himself was the same calm, just, and devoted friend as of yore. His letters were few and brief, but they showed no lack of gratitude or appreciation, as the following one to me will testify:

"EXECUTIVE MANSION, February 3, 1862.

"DEAR WILLIAM:

"Yours of January 30th is just received. Do just as you say about the money matters. As you well know, I have not time enough to write a letter of respectable length. God bless you, says
"Your friend,
"A. LINCOLN."*

His letters to others were of the same warm and generous tenor, but yet the foolish notion prevailed that he had learned to disregard the condition and claims of his Springfield friends. One of the latter who visited Washington returned somewhat displeased because Mr. Lincoln failed to inquire after the health and welfare of each one of his old neighbors. The report spread that he cared nothing for his home or the friends who had made him what he was. Those who entertained this opinion of the man forgot that he was not exactly the property of

---

* On February 19, 1863, I received this despatch from Mr. Lincoln:

"Would you accept a job of about a month's duration, at St. Louis, $5 a day and mileage. Answer.
"A. LINCOLN."

Springfield and Illinois, but the President of all the States in the Union.*

In this connection it may not be out of order to refer briefly to the settlement by Mr. Lincoln of the claims his leading Illinois friends had on him. As before observed his own election to the Presidency cancelled Illinois as a factor in the cabinet problem, but in no wise disposed of the friends whom the public expected and whom he himself intended should be provided for. Of these latter the oldest and most zealous and effective was David Davis.† It is not extravagance, taking their long association together in mind, to say that Davis had done more for Lincoln than any dozen other friends he had. Of course, after Lincoln was securely installed in office, the people, especially in Illinois, awaited his recognition of Davis. What was finally done is minutely told in a letter by Leonard Swett, which it is proper here to insert:

---

*The following letter from a disappointed Illinois friend will serve to illustrate the perplexities that beset Lincoln in disposing of the claims of personal friendship. It was written by a man of no inconsiderable reputation in Illinois, where he at one time filled a State office : " Lincoln is a singular man, and I must confess I never knew him. He has for twenty years past used me as a plaything to accomplish his own ends; but the moment he was elevated to his proud position he seems all at once to have entirely changed his whole nature and become altogether a new being. He knows no one, and the road to his favor is always open to his enemies, while the door is hermetically sealed to his old friends."

† " I had done Lincoln many, many favors, had electioneered for him, spent my money for him, worked and toiled for him." — David Davis, statement, September 20, 1866.

"CHICAGO, ILL., August 29, 1887.

" WILLIAM H. HERNDON.

" *My Dear Sir :*—Your inquiry in reference to the circumstances of the appointment of David Davis as one of the Justices of the Supreme Court reached me last evening. In reply I beg leave to recall the fact, that in 1860 the politicians of Illinois were divided into three divisions, which were represented in the Decatur convention by the votes on the nomination for Governor. The largest vote was for Norman B. Judd, of Chicago, his strength in the main being the northern part of the State. I was next in order of strength, and Richard Yates the third, but the divisions were not materially unequal. The result was Yates was nominated, his strength being about Springfield and Jacksonville, extending to Quincy on the west, and mine was at Bloomington and vicinity and south and southeast.

" These divisions were kept up awhile after Mr. Lincoln's election, and were considered in the distribution of Federal patronage. A vacancy in the United States Senate occurred early in 1861 by the death of Stephen A. Douglas, and Governor Yates appointed Oliver H. Browning, of Quincy, to fill the vacancy. There was also a vacancy upon the Supreme Bench of the United States to be filled from this general vicinity by Mr. Lincoln in the early part of his administration, and Judge Davis, of Bloomington, and Mr. Browning, of Quincy, were aspirants for the position. Mr. Browning had the advantage that Lincoln was new in his seat, and Senators were august personages; and, being in the Senate and a most courteous and able gentleman, Mr. Browning succeeded in securing nearly all the senatorial strength, and Mr. Lincoln was nearly swept off his feet by the current of influence. Davis' supporters were the circuit lawyers mainly in the eastern and central part of the State. These lawyers were at home, and their presence was not a living force felt constantly by the President at Washington.

"I was then living at Bloomington, and met Judge Davis every day. As months elapsed we used to get word from Washington in reference to the condition of things; finally, one day the word came that Lincoln had said, 'I do not know what I may do when the time comes, but there has never been a day when if I had to act I should not have appointed Browning.' Judge Davis, General Orme, and myself held a consultation in my law-office at Bloomington. We decided that the remark was too Lincolnian to be mistaken and no man but he could have put the situation so quaintly. We decided also that the appointment was gone, and sat there glum over the situation. I finally broke the silence, saying in substance, 'The appointment is gone and I am going to pack my carpet-sack for Washington.' 'No, you are not,' said Davis. 'Yes, I am,' was my reply. 'Lincoln is being swept off his feet by the influence of these Senators, and I will have the luxury of one more talk with him before he acts.'

"I did go home, and two days thereafter, in the morning about seven o'clock—for I knew Mr. Lincoln's habits well—was at the White House and spent most of the forenoon with him. I tried to impress upon him that he had been brought into prominence by the Circuit Court lawyers of the old eighth Circuit, headed by Judge Davis. 'If,' I said, 'Judge Davis, with his tact and force, had not lived, and all other things had been as they were, I believe you would not now be sitting where you are.' He replied gravely, 'Yes, that is so.' 'Now it is a common law of mankind,' said I, 'that one raised into prominence is expected to recognize the force that lifts him, or, if from a pinch, the force that lets him out. The Czar

Nicholas was once attacked by an assassin ; a kindly hand warded off the blow and saved his life. The Czar hunted out the owner of that hand and strewed his pathway with flowers through life. The Emperor Napoleon III. has hunted out everybody who even tossed him a biscuit in his prison at Ham and has made him rich. Here is Judge Davis, whom you know to be in every respect qualified for this position, and you ought in justice to yourself and public expectation to give him this place.' We had an earnest pleasant forenoon, and I thought I had the best of the argument, and I think he thought so too.

"I left him and went to Willard's Hotel to think over the interview, and there a new thought struck me. I therefore wrote a letter to Mr. Lincoln and returned to the White House. Getting in, I read it to him and left it with him. It was, in substance, that he might think if he gave Davis this place the latter when he got to Washington would not give him any peace until he gave me a place equally as good ; that I recognized the fact that he could not give this place to Davis, which would be charged to the Bloomington faction in our State politics, and then give me anything I would have and be just to the party there ; that this appointment, if made, should kill 'two birds with one stone ;' that I would accept it as one-half for me and one-half for the Judge ; and that thereafter, if I or any of my friends ever troubled him, he could draw that letter as a plea in bar on that subject. As I read it Lincoln said, 'If you mean that among friends as it reads I will take it and make the appointment.' He at once did as he said.

"He then made a request of the Judge after his appointment in reference to a clerk in his circuit, and wrote him a notice of the appointment, which Davis received the same afternoon I returned to Bloomington.

" Judge Davis was about fifteen years my senior. I had come to his circuit at the age of twenty-four, and between him and Lincoln I had grown up leaning in hours of weakness on their own great arms for support. I was glad of the opportunity to put in the mite of my claims upon Lincoln and give it to Davis, and have been glad I did it every day since.

" An unknown number of people have almost every week since, speaking perhaps extravagantly, asked me in a quasi-confidential manner, ' How was it that you and Lincoln were so intimate and he never gave you anything ? ' I have generally said, ' It seems to me that is my question, and so long as I don't complain I do not see why you should.' I may be pardoned also for saying that I have not considered every man not holding an office out of place in life. I got my eyes open on this subject before I got an office, and as in Washington I saw the Congressman in decline I prayed that my latter end might not be like his.

" Yours truly,
" LEONARD SWETT."

Before his departure for Washington, Mr. Lincoln had on several occasions referred in my presence to the gravity of the national questions that stared him in the face; yet from what he said I caught no definite idea of what his intentions were. He told me he would rely upon me to keep him informed of the situation about home, what his friends were saying of him, and whether his course was meeting with their approval. He suggested that I should write him frequently, and that arrangements would be made with his private secretary, Mr. Nicolay, that my letters should pass through the latter's hands unopened. This plan was adhered to, and I have every reason now to believe that all my letters to Lincoln, although they contained no great secrets of state, passed unread into his hands. I was what the newspaper men would call a "frequent contributor." I wrote oftener than he answered, sometimes remitting him his share of old fees, sometimes dilating on national affairs, but generally confining myself to local politics and news in and around Springfield. I remember of writing him two copious letters, one on the necessity of keeping up the draft, the other admonishing him to hasten his Proclamation of Emancipation. In the latter I was especially fervid, assuring him if he emancipated the slaves, he could "go down the other side of life filled with the consciousness of duty well done, and along a pathway blazing with eternal glory." How my rhetoric or sentiments struck him I never learned, for in the rush of executive business he never responded to either of the letters. Late in the summer of 1861, as elsewhere mentioned in these chapters, I made my first and only visit to Washington while he was President. My mission was intended to promote the prospects of a brother-in-law, Charles W. Chatterton, who desired to lay claim to an office in the Bureau of Indian Affairs. Mr. Lincoln accompanied me to the office of the Commissioner of Indian Affairs,— William P. Dole of Paris, Illinois,—told a good story, and made the request which secured the coveted office—an Indian agency—in an amazingly short time. This was one of the few favors I asked of Mr. Lincoln, and he granted it "speedily—without delay; freely—without purchase; and fully—without denial." I remained in Washington for several days after this, and, notwithstanding the pressure of business, he made me spend a good portion of the time at the White House. One thing he could scarcely cease from referring to was the persistence of the office-seekers. They slipped in, he said, through the half-opened doors of the Executive Mansion; they dogged his steps if he walked; they edged their way through the crowds and thrust their papers in his hands when he rode;* and, taking it all in all, they well-nigh worried him to death. He said that, if the Government passed through the Rebellion without dismemberment, there was the strongest danger of its falling a prey to the rapacity of the office-seeking class. "This human struggle and scramble for office," were his words, "for a way to live without work, will finally test the strength of our institutions." A good part of the day during my stay I would spend with him in his office or waiting-room. I saw the endless line of callers, and met the scores of dignitaries one usually meets at the White House, even now; but nothing took place worthy of special mention here. One day Horace Maynard and Andrew Johnson, both senators from Tennessee, came in arm-in-arm. They declined to sit down, but at

---

* He said that one day, as he was passing down Pennsylvania avenue, a man came running after him, hailed him, and thrust a bundle of papers in his hands. It angered him not a little, and he pitched the papers back, saying, "I'm not going to open shop here."

once set to work to discuss with the President his recent action in some case in which they were interested. Maynard seemed very earnest in what he said. "Beware, Mr. President," he said, "and do not go too fast. There is danger ahead." "I know that," responded Lincoln, good-naturedly, "but I shall go just so fast and only so fast as I think I'm right and the people are ready for the step." Hardly half-a-dozen words followed, when the pair wheeled around and walked away. The day following I left Washington for home. I separated from Mr. Lincoln at the White House. He followed me to the rear portico, where I entered the carriage to ride to the railroad depot. He grasped me warmly by the hand and bade me a fervent "Good-bye." It was the last time I ever saw him alive.

Mrs. Ninian Edwards, who, it will be remembered, was the sister of Mrs. Lincoln, some time before her death furnished me an account of her visit to Washington, some of the incidents of which are so characteristic that I cannot refrain from giving them room here. This lady, without endeavoring to suppress mention of her sister's many caprices and eccentricities while mistress of the White House, remarked that, having been often solicited by the Lincolns to visit them, she and her husband, in answer to the cordial invitation, at last made the journey to Washington. "One day while there," she relates, "in order to calm his mind, to turn his attention away from business and cheer him up, I took Mr. Lincoln down through the conservatory belonging to the Executive Mansion, and showed him the world of flowers represented there. He followed me patiently through. 'How beautiful these flowers are! how gorgeous these roses! Here are exotics,' I exclaimed, in admiration, 'gathered from the remotest corners of the earth, and grand beyond description.' A moody silence followed, broken finally by Mr. Lincoln with this observation: 'Yes, this whole thing looks like spring; but do you know I have never been in here before. I don't know why it is so, but I never cared for flowers; I seem to have no taste, natural or acquired, for such things.' I induced him one day," continued Mrs. Edwards, " to walk to the Park north of the White House. He hadn't been there, he said, for a year. On such occasions, when alone or in the company of a close friend, and released from the restraint of his official surroundings, he was wont to throw from his shoulders many a burden. He was a man I loved and respected. He was a good man, an honest and true one. Much of his seeming disregard, which has been tortured into ingratitude, was due to his peculiar construction. His habits, like himself, were odd and wholly irregular. He would move around in a vague, abstracted way, as if unconscious of his own or any one else's existence. He had no expressed fondness for anything, and ate mechanically. I have seen him sit down at the table absorbed in thought, and never, unless recalled to his senses, would he think of food. But, however peculiar and secretive he may have seemed, he was anything but cold. Beneath what the world saw lurked a nature as tender and poetic as any I ever knew. The death of his son Willie, which occurred in Washington, made a deep impression on him. It was the first death in his family, save an infant who died a few days after its birth in Springfield. On the evening we strolled through the Park he spoke of it with deep feeling, and he frequently afterward referred to it. When I announced my intention of leaving Washington he was much affected at the news of my departure. We were strolling through the White House grounds, when he begged me with tears in his eyes to remain longer. 'You have such strong control and such an influence over Mary,' he contended, 'that when troubles come you can console me.' The picture of the man's despair never faded from my vision. Long after my return to Springfield, on reverting to the sad separation, my heart ached because I was unable in my feeble way to lighten his burden."

In the summer of 1866 I wrote to Mrs. Lincoln, then in Chicago, asking for a brief account of her own and her husband's life or mode of living while at the White House. She responded as follows : *

"375 West Washington Street,
Chicago, Ill., August 28, 1866.

"Hon. Wm. H. Herndon.

"*My Dear Sir :*—Owing to Robert's absence from Chicago your last letter to him was only shown me last evening. The recollection of my

---

* From MSS. in Author's possession.

beloved husband's truly affectionate regard for you, and the knowledge of your great love and reverence for the best man that ever lived, would of itself cause you to be cherished with the sincerest regard by my sons and myself. In my overwhelming bereavement those who loved my idolized husband aside from disinterested motives are very precious to me and mine. My grief has been so uncontrollable that, in consequence, I have been obliged to bury myself in solitude, knowing that many whom I would see could not fully enter into the state of my feelings. I have been thinking for some time past I would like to see you and have a long conversation. I wish to know if you will be in Springfield next Wednesday week, September 4; if so, at ten o'clock in the morning you will find me at the St. Nicholas Hotel. Please mention this visit to Springfield to no one. It is a most sacred one, as you may suppose, to visit the tomb which contains my all in life—my husband. . . . If it will not be convenient, or if business at the time specified should require your absence, should you visit Chicago any day this week I will be pleased to see you. I remain,

> " Very truly,
> " MARY LINCOLN."

I met Mrs. Lincoln at the hotel in Springfield according to appointment. Our interview was somewhat extended in range, but none the less interesting. Her statement made at the time now lies before me. "My husband intended," she said, "when he was through with his Presidential term, to take me and our boys with him to Europe. After his return from Europe he intended to cross the Rocky Mountains and go to California, where the soldiers were to be digging out gold to pay the national debt. During his last days he and Senator Sumner became great friends, and were closely attached to each other. They were down the river after Richmond was taken—were full of joy and gladness at the thought of the war being over. Up to 1864 Mr. Lincoln wanted to live in Springfield, and if he died be buried there also ; but after that and only a short time before his death he changed his mind slightly, but never really settled on any particular place. The last time I remember of his referring to the matter he said he thought it would be good for himself and me to spend a year or more travelling. As to his nature, he was the kindest man, most tender husband, and loving father in the world. He gave us all unbounded liberty, saying to me always when I asked for anything, 'You know what you want, go and get it,' and never asking if it were necessary. He was very indulgent to his children. He never neglected to praise them for any of their good acts. He often said, ' It is my pleasure that my children are free and happy, and unrestrained by parental tyranny. Love is the chain whereby to bind a child to its parents.'

" My husband placed great reliance on my knowledge of human nature, often telling me, when about to make some important appointment, that he had no knowledge of men and their motives. It was his intention to remove Seward as soon as peace with the South was declared. He greatly disliked Andrew Johnson. Once the latter, when we were in company, followed us around not a little. It displeased Mr. Lincoln so much he turned abruptly and asked, loud enough to be heard by others, 'Why is this man forever following me?' At another time, when we were down at City Point, Johnson, still following us, was drunk. Mr. Lincoln in desperation exclaimed, 'For God's sake don't ask Johnson to dine with us.' Sumner, who was along, joined in the request. Mr. Lincoln was mild in his manners, but he was a terribly firm man when he set his foot down. None of us, no man or woman, could rule him after he had once fully made up his mind. I could always tell when in deciding anything he had reached the ultimatum. At first he was very cheerful, then he lapsed into thoughtfulness, bringing his lips together in a firm compression. When these symptoms developed I fashioned myself accordingly, and so did all others have to do sooner or later. When we first went to Washington many thought Mr. Lincoln was weak, but he rose grandly with the circumstances. I told him once of the assertion I had heard coming from the friends of Seward, that the latter was the power behind the throne; that he could rule him. He replied, 'I may not rule myself, but certainly Seward shall not. The only ruler I have is my conscience—following God in it—and these men will have to learn that yet.'

" Some of the newspaper attacks on him gave him great pain. I sometimes read them to him, but he would beg me to desist, saying, 'I have enough to bear now, but yet I care nothing for them. If I'm right I'll live, and if wrong I'll die anyhow; so let them fight at me unrestrained.' My playful response would be, ' The way to learn is to hear both sides.' I once assured him Chase and certain others who were scheming to supplant him ought to be restrained in their evil designs. ' Do good to them who hate you,' was his generous answer, 'and turn their ill-will into friendship.'

" I often told Mr. Lincoln that God would not let any harm come of him. We had passed through four long years—terrible and bloody years—unscathed, and I believed we would be released from all danger. He gradually grew into that belief himself, and the old gloomy notion of his unavoidable taking-off was becoming dimmer as time passed away. Cheerfulness merged into joyfulness. The skies cleared, the end of the war rose dimly into view when the great blow came and shut him out forever."

For a glimpse of Lincoln's habits while a resident of Washington and an executive officer, there is no better authority than John Hay, who served as one of his secretaries. In 1866, Mr. Hay, then a member of the United States Legation in Paris, wrote me an interesting account, which so faithfully delineates Lincoln in his public home that I cannot refrain from quoting it entire. Although the letter was written in answer to a list of questions I asked, and was prepared without any attempt at arrangement, still it is none the less interesting. " Lincoln went to bed ordinarily," it begins, " from ten to eleven o'clock, unless he happened to be kept up by important news, in which case he would frequently remain at the War Department till one or two. He rose early. When he lived in the country at the Soldiers' Home he would be up and dressed, eat his breakfast (which was extremely frugal, an egg, a piece of toast, coffee, etc.), and ride into Washington, all before eight o'clock. In the winter, at the White House, he was not quite so early. He did not sleep well, but spent a good while in bed. 'Tad' usually slept with him. He would lie around the office until he fell asleep, and Lincoln would shoulder him and take him off to bed. He pretended to begin business at ten o'clock in the morning, but in reality the ante-rooms and halls were full long before that hour—people anxious to get the first axe ground. He was extremely unmethodical; it was a four years' struggle on Nicolay's part and mine to get him to adopt some systematic rules. He would break through every regulation as fast as it was made. Anything that kept the people themselves away from him he disapproved, although they nearly annoyed the life out of him by unreasonable complaints and requests. He wrote very few letters, and did not read one in fifty that he received. At first we tried to bring them to his notice, but at last he gave the whole thing over to me, and signed, without reading them, the letters I wrote in his name. He wrote perhaps half-a-dozen a week himself—not more. Nicolay received members of Congress and other visitors who had business with the Executive office, communicated to the Senate and House the messages of the President, and exercised a general supervision over the business. I opened and read the letters, answered them, looked over the newspapers, supervised the clerks who kept the records, and in Nicolay's absence did his work also. When the President had any rather delicate matter to manage at a distance from Washington he rarely wrote, but sent Nicolay or me. The House remained full of people nearly all day. At noon the President took a little lunch—a biscuit, a glass of milk in winter, some fruit or grapes in summer. He dined between five and six, and we went off to our dinner also. Before dinner was over, members and Senators would come back and take up the whole evening. Sometimes, though rarely, he shut himself up and would see no one. Sometimes he would run away to a lecture, or concert, or theatre for the sake of a little rest. He was very abstemious—ate less than any man I know. He drank nothing but water, not from principle but because he did not like wine or spirits. Once, in rather dark days early in the war, a temperance committee came to him and said that the reason we did not win was because our army drank so much whiskey as to bring the curse of the Lord upon them. He said it was rather unfair on the part of the aforesaid curse, as the other side drank more and worse whiskey than ours did. He read very little. He scarcely ever looked into a newspaper unless I called his attention to an article on some special subject. He frequently said, ‘I know more about it than any of them.’ It is absurd to call him a modest man. No great man was ever modest. It was his intellectual arrogance and unconscious assumption of superiority that men like Chase and Sumner never could forgive. I believe that Lincoln is well understood by the people ; but there is a patent-leather, kid-glove set who know no more of him than an owl does of a comet blazing into his blinking eyes.* Their estimates of him are in many cases disgraceful exhibitions of ignorance and prejudice. Their effeminate natures shrink instinctively from the contact of a great reality like Lincoln's character. I consider Lincoln's republicanism incarnate—with all its faults and all its virtues. As, in spite of some rudeness, republicanism is the sole hope of a sick world, so Lincoln, with all his foibles, is the greatest character since Christ."

In 1863 Mr. Lincoln was informed one morning that among the visitors in the ante-room of the White House was a man who claimed to be his relative. He walked out and was surprised to find

---

* Bancroft's eulogy on Lincoln never pleased the latter's lifelong friends—those who knew him so thoroughly and well. February 16, 1866, David Davis, who had heard it, wrote me : " You will see Mr. Bancroft's oration before this reaches you. It is able, but Mr. Lincoln is in the background. His analysis of Mr. Lincoln's character is superficial. It did not please me. How did it satisfy you ? " On the 22d he again wrote : " Mr. Bancroft totally misconceived Mr. Lincoln's character in applying ' unsteadiness ' and confusion to it. Mr. Lincoln grew more steady and resolute, and his ideas were never confused. If there were any changes in him after he got here they were for the better. I thought him always master of his subject. He was a much more self-possessed man than I thought. He *thought* for himself, which is a rare quality nowadays. How could Bancroft know anything about Lincoln except as he judged of him as the public do ? He never saw him, and is himself as cold as an icicle. I should never have selected an old Democratic politician, and that one from Massachusetts, to deliver an eulogy on Lincoln."

his boyhood friend and cousin, Dennis Hanks. The latter had come to see his distinguished relative on a rather strange mission. A number of persons living in Coles County, in Illinois, offended at the presence and conduct of a few soldiers who were at home from the war on furlough at the town of Charleston, had brought about a riot, in which encounter several of the latter had been killed. Several of the civilian participants who had acted as leaders in the strife had been arrested and sent to Fort McHenry or some other place of confinement equally as far from their homes. The leading lawyers and politicians of central Illinois were appealed to, but they and all others who had tried their hands had been signally unsuccessful in their efforts to secure the release of the prisoners. Meanwhile some one of a sentimental turn had conceived the idea of sending garrulous old Dennis Hanks to Washington, fondly believing that his relationship to the President might in this last extremity be of some avail. The novelty of the project secured its adoption by the prisoners' friends, and Dennis, arrayed in a suit of new clothes, set out for the national capital. I have heard him describe this visit very minutely. How his appearance in Washington and his mission struck Mr. Lincoln can only be imagined. The President, after listening to him and learning the purpose of his visit, retired to an adjoining room and returned with an extremely large roll of papers labelled, "The Charleston Riot Case," which he carefully untied and gravely directed his now diplomatic cousin to read. Subsequently, and as if to continue the joke, he sent him down to confer with the Secretary of War. He soon returned from the latter's office with the report that the head of the War Department could not be found; and it was well enough that he did not meet that abrupt and oftentimes demonstrative official. In the course of time, however, the latter happened in at the Executive Mansion, and there, in the presence of Dennis, the President sought to reopen the now noted Charleston case. Adopting Mr. Hanks' version, the Secretary, with his characteristic plainness of speech, referring to the prisoners, declared that "every d——d one of them should be hung." Even the humane and kindly enquiry of the President, "If these men should return home and become good citizens, who would be hurt?" failed to convince the distinguished Secretary that the public good could be promoted by so doing. The President not feeling willing to override the judgment of his War Secretary in this instance, further consideration of the case ceased, and his cousin returned to his home in Illinois with his mission unaccomplished.*

Dennis retained a rather unfavorable impression of Mr. Stanton, whom he described as a "frisky little Yankee with a short coat-tail." "I asked Abe," he said to me once, "why he didn't kick him out. I told him he was too fresh altogether."

---

* The subsequent history of these riot cases I believe is that the prisoners were returned to Illinois to be tried in the State courts there ; and that by successive changes of venue and continuances the cases were finally worn out.

Lincoln's answer was, " If I did, Dennis, it would be difficult to find another man to fill his place."   The President's cousin * sat in the office during the endless interviews that take place between the head of the nation and the latter's loyal subjects. He saw modesty and obscurity mingling with the arrogance of pride and distinction. One day an attractive and handsomely dressed woman called to procure the release from prison of a relative in whom she professed the deepest interest. She was a good talker, and her winning ways seemed to be making a deep impression on the President. After listening to her story he wrote a few lines on a card, enclosing it in an envelope and directing her to take it to the Secretary of War. Before sealing it he showed it to Dennis. It read : " This woman, dear Stanton, is a little smarter than she looks to be.'' She had, woman-like, evidently overstated her case. Before night another woman called, more humble in appearance, more plainly clad. It was the old story. Father and son both in the army, the former in prison. Could not the latter be discharged from the army and sent home to help his mother? A few strokes of the pen, a gentle nod of the head, and the little woman, her eyes filling with tears and expressing a grateful acknowledgment her tongue could not utter, passed out.

* During this visit Mr. Lincoln presented Dennis with a silver watch, which the latter still retains as a memento alike of the donor and his trip to Washington.

CHAPTER IX.

BEFORE passing to a brief and condensed view of the great panorama of the war it will interest the reader and no doubt aid him greatly in drawing the portrait of Lincoln to call up for the purpose two friends of his, whose testimony is not only vivid and minute, but for certain reasons unusually appropriate and essential. The two were devoted and trusted friends of Lincoln; and while neither held office under him, both were offered and both declined the same. That of itself ought not to be considered as affecting or strengthening their statements, and yet we sometimes think that friends who are strong enough to aid us, and yet, declining our aid, take care of themselves, are brave enough to tell us the truth. The two friends of Lincoln here referred to are Joshua F. Speed and Leonard Swett. In quoting them I adhere strictly to their written statements now in my possession. The former, under date of December 6, 1866, says: "Mr. Lincoln was so unlike all the men I had ever known before or seen or known since that there is no one to whom I can compare him. In all his habits of eating, sleeping, reading, conversation, and study he was, if I may so express it, regularly irregular: that is, he had no stated time for eating, no fixed time for going to bed, none for getting up. No course of reading was chalked out. He read law, history, philosophy, or poetry ; Burns, Byron, Milton, or Shakespeare and the newspapers, retaining them all about as well as an ordinary man would any one of them who made only one at a time his study. I once remarked to him that his mind was a wonder to me ; that impressions were easily made upon it and never effaced. ‘ No,’ said he, ‘you are mistaken ; I am slow to learn, and slow to forget that which I have learned. My mind is like a piece of steel—very hard to scratch anything on it, and almost impossible after you get it there to rub it out.’ I give this as his own illustration of the character of his mental faculties ; it is as good as any I have seen from anyone.

“ The beauty of his character was its entire simplicity. He had no affectation in anything. True to nature, true to himself, he was true to everybody and everything around him. When he was ignorant on any subject, no matter how simple it might make him appear, he was always willing to acknowledge it. His whole aim in life was to be true to himself, and being true to himself he could be false to no one.

“ He had no vices, even as a young man. Intense thought with him was the rule and not, as with most of us, the exception. He often said that he could think better after breakfast, and better walking than sitting, lying, or standing. His world-wide reputation for telling anecdotes and telling them so well was in my judgment necessary to his very existence.   Most men who have been great students, such as he was, in their hours of idleness have taken to the bottle, to cards or dice.   He had no fondness for any of these.   Hence he sought relaxation in anecdotes.   So far as I now remember of his study for composition, it was to make short sentences and a compact style.   Illustrative of this it might be well to state that he was a great admirer of the style of John C. Calhoun.   I remember reading to him one of Mr. Calhoun's speeches in reply to Mr. Clay in the Senate, in which Mr. Clay had quoted precedent.   Mr. Calhoun replied (I quote from memory) that ' to legislate upon precedent is but to make the error of yesterday the law of to-day.'   Lincoln thought that was a great truth and grandly uttered.

" Unlike all other men, there was entire harmony between his public and private life.   He must believe he was right, and that he had truth and justice with him, or he was a weak man ; but no man could be stronger if he thought he was right.

" His familiar conversations were like his speeches and letters in this : that while no set speech of his (save the Gettysburg address) will be considered as entirely artistic and complete, yet, when the gems of American literature come to be selected, as many will be culled from Lincoln's speeches as from any American orator.   So of his conversation, and so of his private correspondence ; all abound in gems.

" My own connection or relation with Mr. Lincoln during the war has so often been commented on, and its extent so often enlarged upon, I feel impelled to state that during his whole administration he never requested me to do anything, except in my own State, and never much in that except to advise him as to what measures and policy would be most conducive to the growth of a healthy Union sentiment.

" My own opinion of the history of the Emancipation Proclamation is that Mr. Lincoln foresaw the necessity for it long before he issued it. He was anxious to avoid it, and came to it only when he saw that the measure would subtract from its labor, and add to our army quite a number of good fighting men. I have heard of the charge of duplicity against him by certain Western members of Congress. I never believed the charge, because he has told me from his own lips that the charge was false. I, who knew him so well, could never after that credit the report. At first I was opposed to the Proclamation, and so told him. I remember well our conversation on the subject. He seemed to treat it as certain that I would recognize the wisdom of the act when I should see the harvest of good which we would ere long glean from it. In that conversation he alluded to an incident in his life, long passed, when he was so much depressed that he almost contemplated suicide. At the time of his deep depression he said to me that he had 'done nothing to make any human being remember that he had lived,' and that to connect his name with the events transpiring in his day and generation, and so impress himself upon them as to link his name with something that would redound to the interest of his fellow man, was what he desired to live for.   He reminded me of that conversation, and said with earnest emphasis, ' I believe that in this measure [meaning his Proclamation] my fondest hope will be realized.'   Over twenty years had passed between the two conversations.

"The last interview but one I had with him was about ten days prior to his last inauguration.   Congress was drawing to a close; it had been an important session; much attention had to be given to the important bills he was signing; a great war was upon him and the country; visitors were coming and going to the President with their varying complaints and grievances from morning till night with almost as much regularity as the ebb and flow of the tide; and he was worn down in health and spirits.   On this occasion I was sent for, to come and see him.   Instructions were given that when I came I should be admitted.   When I entered his office it was quite full, and many more—among them not a few Senators and members of Congress —still waiting.   As soon as I was fairly inside, the President remarked that he desired to see me as soon as he was through giving audiences, and that if I had nothing to do I could take the papers and amuse myself in that or any other way I saw fit till he was ready.   In the room, when I entered, I observed sitting near the fireplace, dressed in humble attire, two ladies modestly waiting their turn.   One after another of the visitors came and went, each bent on his own particular errand, some satisfied and others evidently displeased at the result of their mission. The hour had arrived to close the door against all further callers. No one was left in the room now except the President, the two ladies, and me. With a rather peevish and fretful air he turned to them and said, 'Well, ladies, what can I do for you?' They both commenced to speak at once. From what they said he soon learned that one was the wife and the other the mother of two men imprisoned for resisting the draft in western Pennsylvania. 'Stop,' said he, 'don't say any more. Give me your petition.' The old lady responded, 'Mr. Lincoln, we've got no petition; we couldn't write one and had no money to pay for writing one, and I thought best to come and see you.' 'Oh,' said he, 'I understand your cases.' He rang his bell and ordered one of the messengers to tell General Dana to bring him the names of all the men in prison for resisting the draft in western Pennsylvania. The General soon came with the list. He enquired if there was any difference in the charges or degrees of guilt. The General replied that he knew of none. 'Well, then,' said he, 'these fellows have suffered long enough, and I have thought so for some time, and now that my mind is on the subject I believe I will turn out the whole flock. So, draw up the order, General, and I will sign it.' It was done and the General left the room. Turning to the women he said, 'Now, ladies, you can go.' The younger of the two ran forward and was in the act of kneeling in thankfulness. 'Get up,' he said; 'don't kneel to me, but thank God and go.' The old lady now came forward with tears in her eyes to express her gratitude. 'Good-bye, Mr. Lincoln,' said she; 'I shall probably never see you again till we meet in heaven.' These were her exact words. She had the President's hand in hers, and he was deeply moved. He instantly took her right hand in both of his and, following her to the door, said, 'I am afraid with all my troubles I shall never get to the resting-place you speak of; but if I do I am sure I shall find you. That you wish me to get there is, I believe, the best wish you could make for me. Good-bye.'

"We were now alone. I said to him, 'Lincoln, with my knowledge of your nervous sensibility, it is a wonder that such scenes as this don't kill you.' He thought for a moment and then answered in a languid voice, 'Yes, you are to a certain degree right. I ought not to undergo what I so often do. I am very unwell now; my feet and hands of late seem to be always cold, and I ought perhaps to be in bed; but things of the sort you have just seen don't hurt me, for, to tell you the truth, that scene is the only thing to-day that has made me forget my condition or given me any pleasure. I have, in that order, made two people happy and alleviated the distress of many a poor soul whom I never expect to see. That old lady,' he continued, ' was no counterfeit. The mother spoke out in all the features of her face. It is more than one can often say that in doing right one has made two people happy in one day. Speed, die when I may, I want it said of me by those who know me best, that I always plucked a thistle and planted a flower when I thought a flower would grow.'   What a fitting sentiment!   What a glorious recollection!"

The recollections of Lincoln by Mr. Swett are in the form of a letter dated January 17, 1866.   There is so much of what I know to be true in it, and it is so graphically told, that although there may be some repetition of what has already been touched upon in the preceding chapters, still I believe that the portrait of Lincoln will be made all the more life-like by inserting the letter without abridgment.

" Chicago, Ill., Jan. 17, 1866.

" Wm. H. Herndon, Esq.
 " Springfield, Ill.

" *Dear Sir:*   I received your letter to day, asking me to write you Friday.   Fearing if I delay, you will not get it in time, I will give you such hasty thoughts as may occur to me to-night.   I have mislaid your second lecture, so that I have not read it at all, and have not read your first one since about the time it was published.   What I shall say, therefore, will be based upon my own ideas rather than a review of the lecture.

" Lincoln's whole life was a calculation of the law of forces and ultimate results.   The whole world to him was a question of cause and effect.   He believed the results to which certain causes tended ; he did not believe that those results could be materially hastened or impeded.   His whole political history, especially since the agitation of the slavery question, has been based upon this theory.   He believed from the first, I think, that the agitation of slavery would produce its overthrow, and he acted upon the result as though it was present from the beginning.   His tactics were to get himself in the right place and remain there still, until events would find him in that place. This course of action led him to say and do things which could not be understood when considered in reference to the immediate surroundings in which they were done or said. You will remember, in his campaign against Douglas in 1858, the first ten lines of the first speech he made defeated him. The sentiment of the 'house divided against itself' seemed wholly inappropriate. It was a speech made at the commencement of a campaign, and apparently made for the campaign. Viewing it in this light alone, nothing could have been more unfortunate or inappropriate. It was saying just the wrong thing; yet he saw it was an abstract truth, and standing by the speech would ultimately find him in the right place. I was inclined at the time to believe these words were hastily and inconsiderately uttered, but subsequent facts have convinced me they were deliberate and had been matured. Judge T. L. Dickey says, that at Bloomington, at the first Republican Convention in 1856, he uttered the same sentences in a speech delivered there, and that after the meeting was over, he (Dickey) called his attention to these remarks.

" Lincoln justified himself in making them by stating they were true; but finally, at Dickey's urgent request, he promised that for his sake, or upon his advice, he would not repeat them. In the summer of 1859, when he was dining with a party of his intimate friends at Bloomington, the subject of his Springfield speech was discussed. We all insisted it was a great mistake, but he justified himself, and finally said, 'Well, gentlemen, you may think that speech was a mistake, but I never have believed it was, and you will see the day when you will consider it was the wisest thing I ever said.'

"He never believed in political combinations,

and consequently, whether an individual man or class of men supported or opposed him, never made any difference in his feelings, or his opinions of his own success. If he was elected, he seemed to believe that no person or class of persons could ever have defeated him, and if defeated, he believed nothing could ever have elected him. Hence, when he was a candidate, he never wanted anything done for him in the line of political combination or management. He seemed to want to let the whole subject alone, and for everybody else to do the same. I remember, after the Chicago Convention, when a great portion of the East were known to be dissatisfied at his nomination, when fierce conflicts were going on in New York and Pennsylvania, and when great exertions seemed requisite to harmonize and mould in concert the action of our friends, Lincoln always seemed to oppose all efforts made in the direction of uniting the party. I arranged with Mr. Thurlow Weed after the Chicago Convention to meet him at Springfield. I was present at the interview, but Lincoln said nothing. It was proposed that Judge Davis should go to New York and Pennsylvania to survey the field and see what was necessary to be done. Lincoln consented, but it was always my opinion that he consented reluctantly.

" He saw that the pressure of a campaign was the external force coercing the party into unity. If it failed to produce that result, he believed any individual effort would also fail. If the desired result followed, he considered it attributable to the great cause, and not aided by the lesser ones. He sat down in his chair in Springfield and made himself the Mecca to which all politicians made pilgrimages. He told them all a story, said nothing, and sent them away. All his efforts to procure a second nomination were in the same direction. I believe he earnestly desired that nomination. He was much more eager for it than he was for the first, and yet from the beginning he discouraged all efforts on the part of his friends to obtain it. From the middle of his first term all his adversaries were busily at work for themselves. Chase had three or four secret societies and an immense patronage extending all over the country. Frémont was constantly at work, yet Lincoln would never do anything either to hinder them or to help himself.

"He was considered too conservative, and his adversaries were trying to outstrip him in satisfying the radical element. I had a conversation with him upon this subject in October, 1863, and tried to induce him to recommend in his annual message a constitutional amendment abolishing slavery. I told him I was not very radical, but I believed the result of the war would be the extermination of slavery; that Congress would pass the amendment making the slave free, and that it was proper at that time to be done. I told him also, if he took that stand, it was an outside position, and no one could maintain himself upon any measure more radical, and if he failed to take the position, his rivals would. Turning to me suddenly he said, 'Is not the question of emancipation doing well enough now?' I replied it was. 'Well,' said he, 'I have never done an official act with a view to promote my own personal aggrandizement, and I don't like to begin now. I can see that emancipation is coming; whoever can wait for it will see it; whoever stands in its way will be run over by it.'

"His rivals were using money profusely; journals and influences were being subsidized against him. I accidentally learned that a Washington newspaper, through a purchase of the establishment, was to be turned against him, and consulted him about taking steps to prevent it. The only thing I could get him to say was that he would regret to see the paper turned against him. Whatever was done had to be done without his knowledge. Mr. Bennett of the *Herald*, with his paper, you know, is a power. The old gentleman wanted to be noticed by Lincoln, and he wanted to support him. A friend of his, who was certainly in his secrets, came to Washington and intimated if Lincoln would invite Bennett to come over and chat with him, his paper would be all right. Mr. Bennett wanted nothing, he simply wanted to be noticed. Lincoln in talking about it said, 'I understand it; Bennett has made a great deal of money, some say not very properly, now he wants me to make him respectable. I have never invited Mr. Bryant or Mr. Greeley here; I shall not, therefore, especially invite Mr. Bennett.' All Lincoln would say was, that he was receiving everybody, and he should receive Mr. Bennett if he came.

" Notwithstanding his entire inaction, he never for a moment doubted his second nomination. One time in his room discussing with him who his real friends were, he told me, if I would not show it, he would make a list of how the Senate stood. When he got through, I pointed out some five or six, and I told him I knew he was mistaken about them. Said he, 'You may think so, but you keep that until the convention and tell me then whether I was right.' He was right to a man. He kept a kind of account book of how things were progressing, for three or four months, and whenever I would get nervous and think things were going wrong, he would get out his estimates and show how everything on the great scale of action, such as the resolutions of legislatures, the instructions of delegates, and things of that character, were going exactly as he expected. These facts, with many others of a kindred nature, have convinced me that he managed his politics upon a plan entirely different from any other man the country has ever produced.

" He managed his campaigns by ignoring men and by ignoring all small causes, but by closely calculating the tendencies of events and the great forces which were producing logical results.

" In his conduct of the war he acted upon the theory that but one thing was necessary, and that was a united North. He had all shades of sentiments and opinions to deal with, and the consideration was always presented to his mind, how can I hold these discordant elements together?

" It was here that he located his own greatness as a President. One time, about the middle of the war, I left his house about eleven o'clock at night, at the Soldiers' Home. We had been discussing the discords in the country, and particularly the States of Missouri and Kentucky. As we separated at the door he said, ' I may not have made as great a President as some other men, but I believe I have kept these discordant elements together as well as anyone could.' Hence, in dealing with men he was a trimmer, and such a trimmer the world has never seen. Halifax, who was great in his day as a trimmer, would blush by the side of Lincoln; yet Lincoln never trimmed in principles, it was only in his conduct with men. He used the patronage of his office to feed the hunger of these various factions. Weed always declared that he kept a regular account-book of his appointments in New York, dividing his various favors so as to give each faction more than it could get from any other source, yet never enough to satisfy its appetite.

" They all had access to him, they all received favors from him, and they all complained of ill treatment ; but while unsatisfied, they all had ' large expectations,' and saw in him the chance of obtaining more than from anyone else whom they could be sure of getting in his place.   He used every force to the best possible advantage.   He never wasted anything, and would always give more to his enemies than he would to his friends; and the reason was, because he never had anything to spare, and in the close calculation of attaching the factions to him, he counted upon the abstract affection of his friends as an element to be offset against some gift with which he must appease his enemies. Hence, there was always some truth in the charge of his friends that he failed to reciprocate their devotion with his favors.   The reason was, that he had only just so much to give away—'He always had more horses than oats.'

"An adhesion of all forces was indispensable to his success and the success of the country; hence he husbanded his means with the greatest nicety of calculation.   Adhesion was what he wanted; if he got it gratuitously he never wasted his substance paying for it.

"His love of the ludicrous was not the least peculiar of his characteristics.   His love of fun made him overlook everything else but the point of the joke sought after.   If he told a good story that was refined and had a sharp point, he did not like it any the better because it was refined.   If it was outrageously vulgar, he never seemed to see that part of it, if it had the sharp ring of wit; nothing ever reached him but the wit.   Almost any man that will tell a very vulgar story, has, in a degree, a vulgar mind; but it was not so with him; with all his purity of character and exalted morality and sensibility, which no man can doubt, when hunting for wit he had no ability to discriminate between the vulgar and the refined substances from which he extracted it.   It was the wit he was after, the pure jewel, and he would pick it up out of the mud or dirt just as readily as he would from a parlor table.

"He had great kindness of heart. His mind was full of tender sensibilities, and he was extremely humane, yet while these attributes were fully developed in his character, and, unless intercepted by his judgment, controlled him, they never did control him contrary to his judgment. He would strain a point to be kind, but he never strained it to breaking. Most men of much kindly feeling are controlled by this sentiment against their judgment, or rather that sentiment beclouds their judgment. It was never so with him; he would be just as kind and generous as his judgment would let him be—no more. If he ever deviated from this rule, it was to save life. He would sometimes, I think, do things he knew to be impolitic and wrong to save some poor fellow's neck. I remember one day being in his room when he was sitting at his table with a large pile of papers before him, and after a pleasant talk he turned quite abruptly and said, 'Get out of the way, Swett; to-morrow is butcher-day, and I must go through these papers and see if I cannot find some excuse to let these poor fellows off.' The pile of papers he had were the records of courts martial of men who on the following day were to be shot. He was not examining the records to see whether the evidence sustained the findings; he was purposely in search of occasions to evade the law, in favor of life.

"Some of Lincoln's friends have insisted that he lacked the strong attributes of personal affection which he ought to have exhibited; but I think this is a mistake. Lincoln had too much justice to run a great government for a few favors; and the complaints against him in this regard, when properly digested, seem to amount to this and no more, that he would not abuse the privileges of his situation.

"He was certainly a very poor hater. He never

judged men by his like or dislike for them. If any given act was to be performed, he could understand that his enemy could do it just as well as anyone. If a man had maligned him or been guilty of personal ill-treatment, and was the fittest man for the place, he would give him that place just as soon as he would give it to a friend.

"I do not think he ever removed a man because he was his enemy or because he disliked him.

"The great secret of his power as an orator, in my judgment, lay in the clearness and perspicuity of his statements. When Mr. Lincoln had stated a case it was always more than half argued and the point more than half won. It is said that some one of the crowned heads of Europe proposed to marry when he had a wife living. A gentleman, hearing of this proposition, replied, how could he? 'Oh,' replied his friend, 'he could marry and then he could get Mr. Gladstone to make an explanation about it.' This was said to illustrate the convincing power of Mr. Gladstone's statement.

"Mr. Lincoln had this power greater than any man I have ever known. The first impression he generally conveyed was, that he had stated the case of his adversary better and more forcibly than his opponent could state it himself. He then answered that statement of facts fairly and fully, never passing by or skipping over a bad point.

"When this was done he presented his own case. There was a feeling, when he argued a case, in the mind of any man who listened to it, that nothing had been passed over; yet if he could not answer the objections he argued, in his own mind, and himself arrive at the conclusion to which he was leading others, he had very little power of argumentation. The force of his logic was in conveying to the minds of others the same clear and thorough analysis he had in his own, and if his own mind failed to be satisfied, he had little power to satisfy anybody else. He never made a sophistical argument in his life, and never could make one. I think he was of less real aid in trying a thoroughly bad case than any man I was ever associated with. If he could not grasp the whole case and believe in it, he was never inclined to touch it.

" From the commencement of his life to its close, I have sometimes doubted whether he ever asked anybody's advice about anything. He would listen to everybody; he would hear everybody; but he rarely, if ever, asked for opinions. I never knew him in trying a case to ask the advice of any lawyer he was associated with.

" As a politician and as President, he arrived at all his conclusions from his own reflections, and when his opinion was once formed, he never doubted but what it was right.

" One great public mistake of his character, as generally received and acquiesced in, is that he is considered by the people of this country as a frank, guileless, and unsophisticated man. There never was a greater mistake. Beneath a smooth surface of candor and apparent declaration of all his thoughts and feelings, he exercised the most exalted tact and the wisest discrimination. He handled and moved men remotely as we do pieces upon a chess-board. He retained through life all the friends he ever had, and he made the wrath of his enemies to praise him. This was not by cunning or intrigue, in the low acceptation of the term, but by far-seeing reason and discernment. He always told enough only of his plans and purposes to induce the belief that he had communicated all, yet he reserved enough to have communicated nothing. He told all that was unimportant with a gushing frankness, yet no man ever kept his real purposes closer, or penetrated the future further with his deep designs.

"You ask me whether he changed his religious opinions towards the close of his life. I think not. As he became involved in matters of the greatest importance, full of great responsibility and great doubt, a feeling of religious reverence, a belief in God and his justice and overruling power increased with him. He was always full of natural religion ; he believed in God as much as the most approved Church member, yet he judged of Him by the same system of generalization as he judged everything else. He had very little faith in ceremonials or forms. In fact he cared nothing for the form of anything. But his heart was full of natural and cultivated religion. He believed in the great laws of truth, and the rigid discharge of duty, his accountability to God, the ultimate triumph of the right and the overthrow of wrong. If his religion were to be judged by the lines and rules of Church creeds he would fall far short of the standard ; but if by the higher rule of purity of conduct, of honesty of motive, of unyielding fidelity to the right, and acknowledging God as the supreme ruler, then he filled all the requirements of true devotion, and his whole life was a life of love to God, and love of his neighbor as of himself.

"Yours truly,
"LEONARD SWETT."

CHAPTER X.

THE outlines of Mr. Lincoln's Presidential career
are alone sufficient to fill a volume, and his history
after he had been sworn into office by Chief Justice
Taney is so much a history of the entire country,
and has been so admirably and thoroughly told by
others, that I apprehend I can omit many of the
details and still not impair the portrait I have been
endeavoring to draw in the mind of the reader. The
rapid shifting of scenes in the drama of secession, the
disclosure of rebellious plots and conspiracies, the
threats of Southern orators and newspapers, all cul-
minating in the attack on Fort Sumter, brought
the newly installed President face to face with the
stern and grave realities of a civil war.* Mr. Lincoln's military knowledge had been acquired in the
famous campaign against the Indian Chief Black
Hawk on the frontier in 1832, the thrilling details

---

* " Lincoln then told me of his last interview with Douglas. ' One
day Douglas came rushing in,' he related, ' and said he had just got a
telegraph despatch from some friends in Illinois urging him to come
out and help set things right in Egypt, and that he would go, or stay
in Washington, just where I thought he could do the most good.
I told him to do as he chose, but that he could probably do best in
Illinois. Upon that he shook hands with me and hurried away to
catch the next train. I never saw him again.' "—Henry C. Whitney,
MS. letter, November 13, 1866.

of which he had already given the country in a Congressional stump-speech ; and to this store of experience he had made little if any addition.   It was therefore generally conceded that in grappling with the realities of the problem which now confronted both himself and the country he would be wholly dependent on those who had made the profession of arms a life-work.   Those who held such hastily conceived notions of Mr. Lincoln were evidently misled by his well-known and freely advertised Democratic manners.   Anybody had a right, it was supposed, to advise him of his duty ; and he was so conscious of his shortcomings as a military President that the army officers and Cabinet would run the Government and conduct the war.   That was the popular idea.   Little did the press, or people, or politicians then know that the country lawyer who occupied the executive chair was the most self-reliant man who ever sat in it, and that when the crisis came his rivals in the Cabinet, and the people everywhere, would learn that he and he alone would be master of the situation.

It is doubtless true that for a long time after his entry into office he did not assert himself ; that is, not realizing the gigantic scale upon which the war was destined to be fought, he may have permitted the idea to go forth that being unused to the command of armies he would place himself entirely in the hands of those who were.*   The Secretary of

---

* "I was in Washington in the Indian service for a few days before August, 1861, and I merely said to Lincoln one day, ' Everything is drifting into the war, and I guess you will have to put me in the

Edward D. Baker.

Stephen A. Douglas.

David Davis.

State, whose ten years in the Senate had acquainted him with our relations to foreign powers, may have been lulled into the innocent belief that the Executive would have no fixed or definite views on international questions. So also of the other Cabinet officers; but alas for their fancied security! It was the old story of the sleeping lion. Old politicians, eying him with some distrust and want of confidence, prepared themselves to control his administration, not only as a matter of right, but believing that he would be compelled to rely upon them for support. A brief experience taught them he was not the man they bargained for.

Next in importance to the attack on Fort Sumter, from a military standpoint, was the battle of Bull Run. How the President viewed it is best illustrated by an incident furnished by an old friend * who was an associate of his in the Legislature of Illinois, and who was in Washington when the engagement took place. "The night after the battle," he relates, "accompanied by two Wisconsin Congressmen, I called at the White House to get the news from Manassas, as it was then called, having failed in obtaining any information at Seward's office and elsewhere. Stragglers were coming with all sorts of wild rumors, but nothing more definite than that there had been a great engagement; and

---

army.' He looked up from his work and said, good-humoredly, ' I'm making generals now. In a few days I will be making quartermasters, and then I'll fix you.' "—H. C. Whitney, MS. letter, June 13, 1866.

* Robert L. Wilson, MS., Feb. 10, 1866.

the bearer of each report had barely escaped with his life. Messengers bearing despatches to the President and Secretary of War were constantly arriving, but outsiders could gather nothing worthy of belief. Having learned that Mr. Lincoln was at the War Department we started thither, but found the building surrounded by a great crowd, all as much in the dark as we. Removing a short distance away we sat down to rest. Presently Mr. Lincoln and Mr. Nicolay, his private secretary, came along, headed for the White House. It was proposed by my companions that as I was acquainted with the President I should join him and ask for the news. I did so, but he said that he had already told more than under the rules of the War Department he had any right to, and that, although he could see no harm in it, the Secretary of War had forbidden his imparting information to persons not in the military service. 'These war fellows,' he said, complainingly, 'are very strict with me, and I regret that I am prevented from telling you anything; but I must obey them, I suppose, until I get the hang of things.' 'But, Mr. President,' I insisted, 'if you cannot tell me the news, you can at least indicate its nature, that is, whether good or bad.' The suggestion struck him favorably. Grasping my arm he leaned over, and placing his face near my ear, said, in a shrill but subdued voice, 'It's d——d bad.' It was the first time I had ever heard him use profane language, if indeed it was profane in that connection; but later, when the painful details of the fight came in, I realized that, taking into consideration the time and the circumstances, no other term would have contained a truer qualification of the word ' bad.' "

" About one week after the battle of Bull Run," relates another old friend—Whitney—from Illinois, " I made a call on Mr. Lincoln, having no business except to give him some presents which the nuns at the Osage Mission school in Kansas had sent to him through me. A Cabinet meeting had just adjourned, and I was directed to go at once to his room. He was keeping at bay a throng of callers, but, noticing me enter, arose and greeted me with his old-time cordiality. After the room had been partially cleared of visitors Secretary Seward came in and called up a case which related to the territory of New Mexico. 'Oh, I see,' said Lincoln; ' they have neither Governor nor Government. Well, you see Jim Lane ; the secretary is his man, and he must hunt him up.' Seward then left, under the impression, as I then thought, that Lincoln wanted to get rid of him and diplomacy at the same time. Several other persons were announced, but Lincoln notified them all that he was busy and could not see them. He was playful and sportive as a child, told me all sorts of anecdotes, dealing largely in stories about Charles James Fox, and enquired after several odd characters whom we both knew in Illinois. While thus engaged General James was announced. This officer had sent in word that he would leave town that evening, and must confer with the President before going. 'Well, as he is one of the fellows who make cannons,' observed Lincoln, 'I suppose I must see him. Tell him

when I get through with Whitney I'll see him.'
No more cards came up, and James left about five
o'clock, declaring that the President was closeted
with 'an old Hoosier from Illinois, and was telling
dirty yarns while the country was quietly going to
hell.'   But, however indignant General James may
have felt, and whatever the people may have
thought, still the President was full of the war.
He got down his maps of the seat of war," continues Whitney, " and gave me a full history of the
preliminary discussions and steps leading to the
battle of Bull Run. He was opposed to the battle,
and explained to General Scott by those very maps
how the enemy could by the aid of the railroad re-
inforce their army at Manassas Gap until they had
brought every man there, keeping us meanwhile successfully at bay. 'I showed to General Scott our
paucity of railroad advantages at that point,' said
Lincoln, 'and their plenitude, but Scott was obdurate
and would not listen to the possibility of defeat.
Now you see I was right, and Scott knows it, I
reckon. My plan was, and still is, to make a strong
feint against Richmond and distract their forces
before attacking Manassas. That problem General McClellan is now trying to work out.' Mr.
Lincoln then told me of the plan he had recommended to McClellan, which was to send gunboats
up one of the rivers—not the James—in the direction of Richmond, and divert the enemy there
while the main attack was made at Manassas. I
took occasion to say that McClellan was ambitious
to be his successor. 'I am perfectly willing,' he

answered, 'if he will only put an end to this war.' " *

The interview of Mr. Whitney with the President on this occasion is especially noteworthy because the latter unfolded to him his idea of the general plan formed in his mind to suppress the rebellion movement and defeat the Southern army. "The President," continues Mr. Whitney, " now explained to me his theory of the Rebellion by the aid of the maps before him. Running his long forefinger down the map he stopped at Virginia. 'We must drive them away from here (Manassas Gap),' he said, 'and clear them out of this part of the State so that they cannot threaten us here (Washington) and get into Maryland. We must keep up a good and thorough blockade of their ports. We must march an army into east Tennessee and liberate the Union sentiment there. Finally we must rely on the people growing tired and saying to their leaders: 'We have had enough of this thing, we will bear it no longer.' "

Such was Mr. Lincoln's plan for heading off the Rebellion in the summer of 1861. How it enlarged as the war progressed, from a call for seventy-five thousand volunteers to one for five hundred thousand men and five hundred millions of dollars, is a matter now of well-known history. The war once inaugurated, it was plain the North had three things to do. These were: the opening of the Mississippi River; the blockade of the Southern ports; and

---

* This interview with Lincoln was written out during the war, and contains many of his peculiarities of expression.

the capture of Richmond. To accomplish these great and vital ends the deadly machinery of war was set in motion. The long-expected upheaval had come, and as the torrent of fire broke forth the people in the agony of despair looking aloft cried out, " Is our leader equal to the task ? " That he was the man for the hour is now the calm, unbiassed judgment of all mankind.

The splendid victories early in 1862 in the south-west, which gave the Union cause great advance toward the entire redemption of Kentucky, Tennessee, and Missouri from the presence of rebel armies and the prevalence of rebel influence, were counter-balanced by the dilatory movements and inactive policy of McClellan, who had been appointed in November of the preceding year to succeed the venerable Scott. The forbearance of Lincoln in dealing with McClellan was only in keeping with his well-known spirit of kindness ; but, when the time came and circumstances warranted it, the soldier-statesman found that the President not only comprehended the scope of the war, but was determined to be commander-in-chief of the army and navy himself. When it pleased him to place McClellan again at the head of affairs, over the protest of such a wilful and indomitable spirit as Stanton, he displayed elements of rare leadership and evidence of uncommon capacity. His confidence in the ability and power of Grant, when the press and many of the people had turned against the hero of Vicksburg, was but another proof of his sagacity and sound judgment.

As the bloody drama of war moves along we come now to the crowning act in Mr. Lincoln's career—that sublime stroke with which his name will be forever and indissolubly united—the emancipation of the slaves. In the minds of many people there had been a crying need for the liberation of the slaves. Laborious efforts had been made to hasten the issuance by the President of the Emancipation Proclamation, but he was determined not to be forced into premature and inoperative measures. Wendell Phillips abused and held him up to public ridicule from the stump in New England. Horace Greeley turned the batteries of the New York *Tribune* against him; and, in a word, he encountered all the rancor and hostility of his old friends the Abolitionists. General Frémont having in the fall of 1861 undertaken by virtue of his authority as a military commander to emancipate the slaves in his department, the President annulled the order, which he characterized as unauthorized and premature. This precipitated an avalanche of fanatical opposition. Individuals and delegations, many claiming to have been sent by the Lord, visited him day after day, and urged immediate emancipation. In August, 1862, Horace Greeley repeated the "prayer of twenty millions of people" protesting against any further delay. Such was the pressure from the outside. All his life Mr. Lincoln had been a believer in the doctrine of gradual emancipation. He advocated it while in Congress in 1848; yet even now, as a military necessity, he could not believe the time was ripe for the general liberation of the slaves. All the coercion from without, and all the blandishments from within, his political household failed to move him. An heroic figure, indifferent alike to praise and blame, he stood at the helm and waited. In the shadow of his lofty form the smaller men could keep up their petty conflicts. Towering thus, he overlooked them all, and fearlessly abided his time. At last the great moment came. He called his Cabinet together and read the decree. The deed was done, unalterably, unhesitatingly, irrevocably, and triumphantly. The people, at first profoundly impressed, stood aloof, but, seeing the builder beside the great structure he had so long been rearing, their confidence was abundantly renewed. It was a glorious work, " sincerely believed to be an act of justice warranted by the constitution upon military necessity," and upon it its author "invoked the considerate judgment of mankind and the gracious favor of Almighty God." I believe Mr. Lincoln wished to go down in history as the liberator of the black man. He realized to its fullest extent the responsibility and magnitude of the act, and declared it was "the central act of his administration and the great event of the nineteenth century." Always a friend of the negro, he had from boyhood waged a bitter unrelenting warfare against his enslavement. He had advocated his cause in the courts, on the stump, in the Legislature of his State and that of the nation, and, as if to crown it with a sacrifice, he sealed his devotion to the great cause of freedom with his blood. As the years roll slowly by, and the participants in the late war drop gradually out of the ranks of men, let us pray that we may never forget their deeds of patriotic valor; but even if the details of that bloody struggle grow dim, as they will with the lapse of time, let us hope that so long as a friend of free man and free labor lives the dust of forgetfulness may never settle on the historic form of Abraham Lincoln.

As the war progressed, there was of course much criticism of Mr. Lincoln's policy, and some of his political rivals lost no opportunity to encourage opposition to his methods. He bore everything meekly and with sublime patience, but as the discontent appeared to spread he felt called upon to indicate his course. On more than one occasion he pointed out the blessings of the Emancipation Proclamation or throttled the clamorer for immediate peace. In the following letter to James C. Conkling* of Springfield, Ill., in reply to an invitation to attend a mass meeting of " Unconditional Union " men to be held at his old home, he not only disposed of the advocates of compromise, but he evinced the most admirable skill in dealing with the questions of the day;

------

* " SPRINGFIELD, ILL., January 11, 1889.

" JESSE W. WEIK, Esq.

   " *Dear Sir:*

   " I enclose you a copy of the letter dated August 26, 1863, by Mr. Lincoln to me. It has been carefully compared with the original and is a correct copy, except that the words commencing ' I know as fully as one can know ' to the words ' You say you will fight to free negroes ' were not included in the original, but were telegraphed the next day with instructions to insert. The following short note in Mr. Lincoln's own handwriting accompanied the letter:

" EXECUTIVE MANSION,
WASHINGTON, August 26, 1863.

" HON. JAMES C. CONKLING.

" *My Dear Sir :*

" Your letter inviting me to attend a mass meeting of Unconditional Union men, to be held at the Capitol of Illinois, on the 3d day of September, has been received.

" It would be very agreeable to me to thus meet my old friends at my own home ; but I cannot, just now, be absent from here so long as a visit there would require.

" The meeting is to be of all those who maintain unconditional devotion to the Union ; and I am sure my old political friends will thank me for tendering, as I do, the nation's gratitude to those other noble men, whom no partisan malice, or partisan's hope, can make false to the nation's life.

" There are those who are dissatisfied with me. To such I would say : You desire peace ; and you blame me that we do not have it. But how can we attain it ? There are but three conceivable ways.

" First, to suppress the rebellion by force of arms. This I am trying to do. Are you for it ? If

---

[Private.]   " ' WAR DEPARTMENT,
" ' WASHINGTON CITY, D. C., August 27, 1862.

" ' *My Dear Conkling :*

" ' I cannot leave here now. Herewith is a letter instead. You are one of the best public readers. I have but one suggestion—read it very slowly. And now God bless you, and all good Union men.

" ' Yours as ever,
" ' A. LINCOLN.'

" Mr. Bancroft, the historian, in commenting on this letter, considers it addressed to me as one who was criticising Mr. Lincoln's policy. On the contrary, I was directed by a meeting of ' Unconditional Union ' men to invite Mr. Lincoln to attend a mass meeting composed of such men, and he simply took occasion to address his opponents through the medium of the letter.

" Yours truly,
" JAMES C. CONKLING."

you are, so far we are agreed. If you are not for it, a second way is, to give up the Union. I am against this. Are you for it? If you are, you should say so plainly. If you are not for *force*, nor yet for *dissolution*, there only remains some imaginable *compromise*. I do not believe any compromise, embracing the maintenance of the Union, is now possible. All I learn leads to a directly opposite belief. The strength of the rebellion is its military —its army. That army dominates all the country and all the people within its range. Any offer of terms made by any man or men within that range in opposition to that army is simply nothing for the present, because such man or men have no power whatever to enforce their side of a compromise, if one were made with them. To illustrate: suppose refugees from the South, and peace men of the North, get together in convention and frame and proclaim a compromise embracing a restoration of the Union; in what way can that compromise be used to keep Lee's army out of Pennsylvania? Meade's army can keep Lee's army out of Pennsylvania, and I think can ultimately drive it out of existence.

"But no paper compromise, to which the controllers of Lee's army are not agreed, can at all affect that army. In an effort at such compromise we should waste time, which the enemy would improve to our disadvantage; and that would be all. A compromise, to be effective, must be made either with those who control the rebel army, or with the people first liberated from the domination of that army by the success of our own army. Now allow me to assure you that no word or intimation from that rebel army or from any of the men controlling it, in relation to any peace compromise, has ever come to my knowledge or belief.

"All changes and insinuations to the contrary

are deceptive and groundless. And I promise you that, if any such proposition shall hereafter come, it shall not be rejected and kept a secret from you. I freely acknowledge myself the servant of the people, according to the bond of service—the United States Constitution, and that, as such, I am responsible to them.

"But to be plain, you are dissatisfied with me about the negro. Quite likely there is a difference of opinion between you and myself upon that subject.

"I certainly wish that all men could be free, while I suppose you do not. Yet I have neither adopted nor proposed any measure which is not consistent with even your view, provided you are for the Union. I suggested compensated emancipation; to which you replied you wished not to be taxed to buy negroes. But I had not asked you to be taxed to buy negroes, except in such way as to save you from greater taxation to save the Union exclusively by other means.

"You dislike the Emancipation Proclamation, and, perhaps, would have it retracted. You say it is unconstitutional—I think differently. I think the constitution invests its Commander-in-chief with the law of war in time of war. The most that can be said, if so much, is that slaves are property. Is there—has there ever been—any question that by the law of war, property, both of enemies and friends, may be taken when needed?

"And is it not needed wherever taking it helps us or hurts the enemy? Armies the world over destroy enemies' property when they cannot use it; and even destroy their own to keep it from the enemy. Civilized belligerents do all in their power to help themselves or hurt the enemy, except a few things regarded as barbarous or cruel.

"Among the exceptions are the massacre of vanquished foes and non-combatants, male and female.

" But the proclamation, as law, either is valid or is not valid.

" If it is not valid, it needs no retraction. If it is valid, it cannot be retracted any more than the dead can be brought to life. Some of you profess to think its retraction would operate favorably for the Union.

" Why *better* after the retraction than *before* the issue?

" There was more than a year and a half of trial to suppress the rebellion before the proclamation issued, the last one hundred days of which passed under an explicit notice that it was coming, unless averted by those in revolt returning to their allegiance.

" The war has certainly progressed as favorably for us since the issue of the proclamation as before.

" I know as fully as one can know the opinion of others that some of the commanders of our armies in the field who have given us our most important successes believe the emancipation policy and the use of the colored troops constituted the heaviest blow yet dealt to the Rebellion, and that at least one of these important successes could not have been achieved when it was but for the aid of black soldiers. Among the commanders holding these views are some who have never had any affinity with what is called abolitionism or with Republican party policies, but who held them purely as military opinions. I submit these opinions as being entitled to some weight against the objections often urged that emancipation and arming the blacks are unwise as military measures, and were not adopted as such in good faith.

" You say you will not fight to free negroes. Some of them seem willing to fight for you ; but no matter.

"Fight you, then, exclusively to save the Union. I issued the proclamation on purpose to aid you in saving the Union. Whenever you shall have conquered all resistance to the Union, if I shall urge you to continue fighting, it will be an apt time then for you to declare you will not fight to free negroes.

"I thought that in your struggle for the Union, to whatever extent the negroes should cease helping the enemy, to that extent it weakened the enemy in his resistance to you. Do you think differently? I thought that whatever negroes can be got to do as soldiers leaves just so much less for white soldiers to do, in saving the Union. Does it appear otherwise to you?

"But negroes, like other people, act upon motives. Why should they do anything for us, if we will do nothing for them? If they stake their lives for us, they must be prompted by the strongest motive—even the promise of freedom. And the promise being made, must be kept.

"The signs look better. The Father of Waters again goes unvexed to the sea. Thanks to the great North-west for it. Nor yet wholly to them. Three hundred miles up they met New England, Empire, Keystone, and Jersey, hewing their way right and left. The Sunny South too, in more colors than one, also lent a hand.

"On the spot, their part of the history was jotted down in black and white. The job was a great national one; and let none be barred who bore an honorable part in it. And while those who have cleared the great river may well be proud, even that is not all. It is hard to say that anything has been more bravely and well done than at Antietam, Murfreesboro, Gettysburg, and on many fields of lesser note. Nor must Uncle Sam's web-feet be forgotten. At all the watery margins they have been present. Not only on the deep sea, the broad bay, and the rapid river, but also up the narrow, muddy bayou, and wherever the ground was a little damp, they have been, and made their tracks, thanks to all. For the great republic—for the principle it lives by and keeps alive—for man's vast future—thanks to all.

" Peace does not appear so distant as it did. I hope it will come soon and come to stay, and so come as to be worth the keeping in all future time. It will then have been proved that, among free men, there can be no successful appeal from the ballot to the bullet; and that they who take such appeal are sure to lose their case and pay the cost. And then there will be some black men who can remember that, with silent tongue, and clenched teeth, and steady eye, and well-poised bayonet, they have helped mankind on to this great consummation; while I fear there will be some white ones, unable to forget that, with malignant heart and deceitful speech, they have strove to hinder it.

" Still, let us not be over-sanguine of a speedy final triumph. Let us be quite sober. Let us diligently apply the means, never doubting that a just God, in his own good time, will give us the rightful result.

"Yours very truly,
" A. LINCOLN."

The summer and fall of 1864 were marked by Lincoln's second Presidential campaign, he, and Andrew Johnson, of Tennessee, for Vice-President, having been nominated at Baltimore on the 8th of June. Frémont, who had been placed in the field by a convention of malcontents at Cleveland, Ohio, had withdrawn in September, and the contest was left to Lincoln and General George B. McClellan, the

nominee of the Democratic convention at Chicago,
The canvass was a heated and bitter one. Dissatisfied elements appeared everywhere. The Judge
Advocate-General of the army (Holt) created a
sensation by the publication of a report giving con-
clusive proof of the existence of an organized secret
association at the North, controlled by prominent
men in the Democratic party, whose objects were
the overthrow by revolution of the administration
in the interest of the rebellion.* Threats were rife

---

*" Mr. Lincoln was advised, and I also so advised him, that the
various military trials in the Northern and Border States, where the
courts were free and untrammelled, were unconstitutional and wrong;
that they would not and ought not to be sustained by the Supreme
Court; that such proceedings were dangerous to liberty. He said he
was opposed to hanging; that he did not like to kill his fellow-man;
that if the world had no butchers but himself it would go bloodless.
When Joseph E. McDonald went to Lincoln about these military
trials and asked him not to execute the men who had been con-
victed by the military commission in Indiana he answered that he
would not hang them, but added, 'I'll keep them in prison awhile to
keep them from killing the Government.' I am fully satisfied therefore that Lincoln was opposed to these military commissions, especially in the Northern States, where everything was open and
free."—David Davis, statement, September 10, 1866, to W. H. H.

"I was counsel for Bowles, Milligan, *et al.*, who had been con-
victed of conspiracy by military tribunal in Indiana. Early in 1865
I went to Washington to confer with the President, whom I had
known, and with whom in earlier days I had practised law on the circuit in Illinois. My clients had been sentenced, and unless the President interfered were to have been executed. Mr. Hendricks, who
was then in the Senate, and who seemed to have little faith in the
probability of executive clemency, accompanied me to the White
House. It was early in the evening, and so many callers and visitors had preceded us we anticipated a very brief interview. Much
to our surprise we found Mr. Lincoln in a singularly cheerful and
reminiscent mood. He kept us with him till almost eleven o'clock.

of a revolution at the North, especially in New York City, if Mr. Lincoln were elected. Mr. Lincoln went steadily on in his own peculiar way. In a preceding chapter Mr. Swett has told us how indifferent he appeared to be regarding any efforts to be made in his behalf. He did his duty as President, and rested secure in the belief that he would be re-elected whatever might be done for or against him. The importance of retaining Indiana in the column of Republican States was not to be overlooked. How the President viewed it, and how he proposed to secure the vote of the State, is shown in the following letter written to General Sherman :

"EXECUTIVE MANSION,
"WASHINGTON, September 19, 1864.

" MAJOR GENERAL SHERMAN :

"The State election of Indiana occurs on the 11th of October, and the loss of it to the friends of the Government would go far towards losing the whole Union cause. The bad effect upon the November election, and especially the giving the State government to those who will oppose the war in every

---

He went over the history of my clients' crime as shown by the papers in the case, and suggested certain errors and imperfections in the record. The papers, he explained, would have to be returned for correction, and that would consume no little time. 'You may go home, Mr. McDonald,' he said, with a pleased expression, 'and I'll send for you when the papers get back; but I apprehend and hope there will be such a jubilee over yonder,' he added, pointing to the hills of Virginia just across the river, 'we shall none of us want any more killing done.' The papers started on their long and circuitous journey, and sure enough, before they reached Washington again Mr. Lincoln's prediction of the return of peace had proved true."— Hon. Joseph E. McDonald, statement, August 28, 1888, to J. W. W.

possible way, are too much to risk if it can be avoided. The draft proceeds, notwithstanding its strong tendency to lose us the State. Indiana is the only important State voting in October whose soldiers cannot vote in the field. Anything you can safely do to let her soldiers or any part of them go home and vote at the State election will be greatly in point. They need not remain for the Presidential election, but may return to you at once. This is in no sense an order, but is merely intended to impress you with the importance to the army itself of your doing all you safely can, yourself being the judge of what you can safely do.

" Yours truly,

" A. LINCOLN." *

The election resulted in an overwhelming victory for Lincoln. He received a majority of over four hundred thousand in the popular vote—a larger majority than had ever been received by any other President up to that time. He carried not only Indiana, but all the New England States, New York, Pennsylvania, all the Western States, West Virginia, Tennessee, Louisiana, Arkansas, and the newly admitted State of Nevada. McClellan carried but three states : New Jersey, Delaware, and Kentucky. The result, as Grant so aptly expressed it in his telegram of congratulation, was " a victory worth more to the country than a battle won." A second time Lincoln stood in front of the great Capitol to take the oath of office administered by his former rival, Salmon P. Chase, whom he himself had appointed to succeed the deceased Roger B.

---

* Unpublished MS.

Taney. The problem of the war was now fast working its own solution. The cruel stain of slavery had been effaced from the national escutcheon, and the rosy morn of peace began to dawn behind the breaking clouds of the great storm.* Lincoln, firm

---

* Bearing on the mission of the celebrated Peace Commission the following bit of inside history is not without interest :

"I had given notice that at one o'clock on the 31st of January I would call a vote on the proposed constitutional amendment abolishing slavery in the United States. The opposition caught up a report that morning that Peace Commissioners were on the way to the city or were in the city. Had this been true I think the proposed amendment would have failed, as a number who voted for it could easily have been prevailed upon to vote against it on the ground that the passage of such a proposition would be offensive to the commissioners. Accordingly I wrote the President this note :

"'HOUSE OF REPRESENTATIVES,
"'January 31, 1865.

"'*Dear Sir :*
"'The report is in circulation in the House that Peace Commissioners are on their way or in the city, and is being used against us. If it is true, I fear we shall lose the bill. Please authorize me to contradict it, if it is not true.

"'Respectfully,
"'J. M. ASHLEY.'

To the President.

Almost immediately came the reply, written on the back of my note :

"'So far as I know there are no Peace Commissioners in the city or likely to be in it.   "'A. LINCOLN.'
January 31, 1865.

"Mr. Lincoln knew that the commissioners were then on their way to Fortress Monroe, where he expected to meet them, and afterwards did meet them. You see how he answered my note for my purposes, and yet how truly. You know how he afterwards met the so-called commission, whom he determined at the time he wrote this note should not come to the city. One or two gentlemen were present when he wrote the note, to whom he read it before sending it to me."—J. M. Ashley, M. C., letter, November 23, 1866, MS.

but kind, in his inaugural address bade his misguided brethren of the South come back. With a fraternal affection characteristic of the man, and strictly in keeping with his former utterances, he asked for the return of peace. "With malice towards none, with charity for all," he implored his fellow-countrymen, "with firmness in the right as God gives us to see the right, let us finish the work we are in, to bind up the nation's wounds, to care for him who shall have borne the battle and for his widow and his orphans, to do all which may achieve and cherish a just and a lasting peace among ourselves and with all nations." With the coming of spring the great armies, awakening from their long winter's sleep, began preparations for the closing campaign. Sherman had already made that grandest march of modern times, from the mountains of Tennessee through Georgia to the sea, while Grant, with stolid indifference to public criticism and newspaper abuse, was creeping steadily on through swamp and ravine to Richmond. Thomas had defeated Hood in Tennessee, sending the latter back with his army demoralized, cut in pieces, and ruined. The young and daring Sheridan had driven Early out of the Shenandoah Valley after a series of brilliant engagements. The "Kearsarge" had sunk the "Alabama" in foreign waters. Farragut had captured Mobile, and the Union forces held undisputed possession of the West and the Mississippi Valley from the lakes to the gulf. Meanwhile Sherman, undaunted by the perils of a further march through the enemy's country, returning from the sea, was aiming for Richmond, where Grant, with bull-dog tenacity, held Lee firmly in his grasp. Erelong, the latter, with his shattered army reduced to half its original numbers, evacuated Richmond, with Grant in close pursuit. A few days later the boys in blue overtook those in gray at Appomattox Court-house, and there, under the warm rays of an April sun, the life was at last squeezed out of the once proud but now prostrate Confederacy. "The sun of peace had fairly risen. The incubus of war that had pressed upon the nation's heart for four long, weary years was lifted; and the nation sprang to its feet with all possible demonstrations of joyous exultation."

Mr. Lincoln himself had gone to the scene of hostilities in Virginia. He watched the various military manœuvres and operations, which involved momentous consequences to the country; he witnessed some of the bloody engagements participated in by the army of the Potomac. Within a day after its surrender he followed the victorious Union army into the city of Richmond. In this unfortunate city—once the proud capital of Virginia—now smoking and in ruins, he beheld the real horrors of grim war. Here too he realized in a bountiful measure the earnest gratitude of the colored people, who everywhere crowded around him and with cries of intense exultation greeted him as their deliverer. He now returned to Washington, not like Napoleon fleeing sorrowfully from Waterloo bearing the tidings of his own defeat, but with joy proclaiming the era of Union victory and peace

among men. " The war was over. The great
rebellion which for four long years had been assail-
ing the nation's life was quelled. Richmond, the
rebel capital, was taken ; Lee's army had surrendered ; and the flag of the Union was floating in
reassured supremacy over the whole of the National
domain. Friday, the 14th of April, the anniversary
of the surrender of Fort Sumter in 1861 by Major
Anderson to the rebel forces, had been designated
by the Government as the day on which the same
officer should again raise the American flag upon
the fort in the presence of an assembled multitude,
and with ceremonies befitting so auspicious an
occasion. The whole land rejoiced at the return
of peace and the prospect of renewed prosperity
to the country. President Lincoln shared this common joy, but with a deep intensity of feeling which
no other man in the whole land could ever know.
He saw the full fruition of the great work which
had rested so heavily on his hands and heart for
four years past. He saw the great task—as
momentous as had ever fallen to the lot of man
—which he had approached with such unfeigned
diffidence, nearly at an end. The agonies of war
had passed away ; he had won the imperishable
renown which is the reward of those who save their
country; and he could devote himself now to the
welcome task of healing the wounds which war had
made, and consolidating by a wise and magnani-
mous policy the severed sections of our common
Union. His heart was full of the generous sentiments which these circumstances were so well cal-

culated to inspire. He was cheerful and hopeful of the success of his broad plans for the treatment of the conquered people of the South. With all the warmth of his loving nature, after the four years of storm through which he had been compelled to pass, he viewed the peaceful sky on which the opening of his second term had dawned. His mind was free from forebodings and filled only with thoughts of kindness and of future peace." But alas for the vanity of human confidence! The demon of assassination lurked near. In the midst of the general rejoicing at the return of peace Mr. Lincoln was stricken down by the assassin, John Wilkes Booth, in Ford's Theatre at Washington. The story of his death, though oft repeated, is the saddest and most impressive page in American history. I cannot well forbear reproducing its painful and tragic details here.*

" Mr. Lincoln for years had a presentiment that he would reach a high place and then be stricken down in some tragic way. He took no precautions to keep out of the way of danger. So many threats had been made against him that his friends were alarmed, and frequently urged him not to go out unattended. To all their entreaties he had the same answer: 'If they kill me the next man will be just as bad for them. In a country like this, where our habits are simple, and must be, assassina-

---

* For the details of the assassination and the capture and subsequent history of the conspirators, I am indebted to Mrs. Gertrude Garrison, of New York, who has given the subject no little study and investigation. J. W. W.

tion is always possible, and will come if they are determined upon it.'

" Whatever premonition of his tragic fate he may have had, there is nothing to prove that he felt the nearness of the awful hour. Doomed men rise and go about their daily duties as unoppressed, often, as those whose paths know no shadow. On that never-to-be-forgotten 14th of April President Lincoln passed the day in the usual manner. In the morning his son, Captain Robert Lincoln, breakfasted with him. The young man had just returned from the capitulation of Lee, and he described in detail all the circumstances of that momentous episode of the close of the war, to which the President listened with the closest interest. After breakfast the President spent an hour with Speaker Colfax, talking about his future policy, about to be submitted to his Cabinet. At eleven o'clock he met the Cabinet. General Grant was present. He spent the afternoon with Governor Oglesby, Senator Yates, and other friends from Illinois. He was invited by the manager of Ford's theatre, in Washington, to attend in the evening a performance of the play, 'Our American Cousin,' with Laura Keene as the leading lady. This play, now so well known to all play-goers, in which the late Sothern afterward made fortune and fame, was then comparatively unheralded. Lincoln was fond of the drama. Brought up in a provincial way, in the days when theatres were unknown outside of the larger cities, the beautiful art of the actor was fresh and delightful to him.

IIe loved Shakespeare, and never lost an opportunity of seeing his characters rendered by the masters of dramatic art. But on that evening, it is said, he was not eager to go. The play was new, consequently not alluring to him ; but he yielded to the wishes of Mrs. Lincoln and went. They took with them Miss Harris and Major Rathbone, daughter and stepson of Senator Harris, of New York.

" The theatre was crowded. At 9 : 20 the President and his party entered. The audience rose and cheered enthusiastically as they passed to the ' state box ' reserved for them. Little did anyone present dream that within the hour enthusiasm would give place to shrieks of horror. It was ten o'clock when Booth came upon the scene to enact the last and greatest tragedy of the war. He had planned carefully, but not correctly. A good horse awaited him at the rear of the theatre, on which he intended to ride into friendly shelter among the hills of Maryland. He made his way to the President's box—a double one in the second tier, at the left of the stage. The separating partition had been removed, and both boxes thrown into one.

" Booth entered the theatre nonchalantly, glanced at the stage with apparent interest, then slowly worked his way around into the outer passage leading toward the box occupied by the President. At the end of an inner passage leading to the box door, one of the President's " messengers " was stationed to prevent unwelcome intrusions. Booth presented a card to him, stating that Mr. Lincoln had sent for him, and was permitted to pass. After gaining an entrance and closing the hall door, he took a piece of board prepared for the occasion, and placed one end of it in an indentation in the wall, about four feet from the floor, and the other against the molding of the door panel a few inches higher, making it impossible for any one to enter from without. The box had two doors. He bored a gimlet hole in the panel of one, reaming it out with his knife, so as to leave it a little larger than a buckshot on the inside, while on the other side it was big enough to give his eye a wide range. Both doors had spring locks. To secure against their being locked he had loosened the screws with which the bolts were fastened.

" So deliberately had he planned that the very seats in the box had been arranged to suit his purpose by an accomplice, one Spangler, an attaché of the theatre. The President sat in the left-hand corner of the box, nearest the audience, in an easy arm-chair. Next him, on the right, sat Mrs. Lincoln. A little distance to the right of both, Miss Harris was seated, with Major Rathbone at her left, and a little in the rear of Mrs. Lincoln, who, intent on the play, was leaning forward, with one hand resting on her husband's knee. The President was leaning upon one hand, and with the other was toying with a portion of the drapery. His face was partially turned to the audience, and wore a pleasant smile.

" The assassin swiftly entered the box through the door at the right, and the next instant fired.

The ball entered just behind the President's left ear, and, though not producing instantaneous death, completely obliterated all consciousness.

"Major Rathbone heard the report, and an instant later saw the murderer, about six feet from the President, and grappled with him, but his grasp was shaken off. Booth dropped his pistol and drew a long, thin, deadly-looking knife, with which he wounded the major. Then, touching his left hand to the railing of the box, he vaulted over to the stage, eight or nine feet below. In that descent an unlooked-for and curious thing happened, which foiled all the plans of the assassin and was the means of bringing him to bay at last. Lincoln's box was draped with the American flag, and Booth, in jumping, caught his spur in its folds, tearing it down and spraining his ankle. He crouched as he fell, falling upon one knee, but soon straightened himself and stalked theatrically across the stage, brandishing his knife and shouting the State motto of Virginia, '*Sic semper tyrannis!*' afterward adding, 'The South is avenged!' He made his exit on the opposite side of the stage, passing Miss Keene as he went out. A man named Stewart, a tall lawyer of Washington, was the only person with presence of mind enough to spring upon the stage and follow him, and he was too late.

"It had all been done so quickly and dramatically that many in the audience were dazed, and could not understand that anything not a part of the play had happened. When, at last, the awful truth was known to them there ensued a scene, the like of which was never known in a theatre before. Women shrieked, sobbed, and fainted. Men cursed and raved, or were dumb with horror and amazement. Miss Keene stepped to the front and begged the frightened and dismayed audience to be calm. Then she entered the President's box with water and stimulants. Medical aid was summoned and came with flying feet, but came too late. The murderer's bullet had done its wicked work well. The President hardly stirred in his chair, and never spoke or showed any signs of consciousness again.

" They carried him immediately to the house of Mr. Petersen, opposite the theatre, and there, at 7:22 the next morning, the 15th of April, he died.

" The night of Lincoln's assassination was a memorable one in Washington. Secretary Seward was attacked and wounded while lying in bed with a broken arm.

" The murder of the President put the authorities on their guard against a wide-reaching conspiracy, and threw the public into a state of terror. The awful event was felt even by those who knew not of it. Horsemen clattered through the silent streets of Washington, spreading the sad tidings, and the telegraph wires carried the terrible story everywhere. The nation awakened from its dream of peace on the 15th of April, 1865, to learn that its protector, leader, friend, and restorer had been laid low by a stage-mad 'avenger.' W. O. Stoddard, in his ' Life of Lincoln,' says: ' It was as if there had been a death in every house throughout

THE PETERSEN HOUSE, WASHINGTON.
Building in which Lincoln died.

the land. By both North and South alike the awful news was received with a shudder and a momentary spasm of unbelief. Then followed one of the most remarkable spectacles in the history of the human race, for there is nothing else at all like it on record. Bells had tolled before at the death of a loved ruler, but never did all bells toll so mournfully as they did that day. Business ceased. Men came together in public meetings as if by a common impulse, and party lines and sectional hatreds seemed to be obliterated.

" The assassination took place on Friday evening, and on the following Sunday funeral services were held in all the churches in the land, and every church was draped in mourning."

The death of Mr. Lincoln was an indescribable shock to his fellow countrymen. The exultation of victory over the final and successful triumph of Union arms was suddenly changed to the lamentations of grief. In every household throughout the length and breadth of the land there was a dull and bitter agony as the telegraph bore tidings of the awful deed. The public heart, filled with joy over the news from Appomattox, now sank low with a sacred terror as the sad tidings from the Capitol came in. In the great cities of the land all business instantly ceased. Flags drooped half-mast from every winged messenger of the sea, from every church spire, and from every public building. Thousands upon thousands, drawn by a common feeling, crowded around every place of public resort and listened eagerly to whatever any public speaker

chose to say.   Men met in the streets and pressed
each other's hands in silence, and burst into tears.
The whole nation, which the previous day had been
jubilant and hopeful, was precipitated into the
depths of a profound and tender woe.   It was a
memorable spectacle to the world—a whole nation'
plunged into heartfelt grief and the deepest sorrow.

The body of the dead President, having been em-
balmed, was removed from the house in which the
death occurred to the White House, and there appropriate funeral services were held.   After the transfer
of the remains to the Capitol, where the body was exposed to view in the Rotunda for a day, preparations
were made for the journey to the home of the deceased in Illinois. On the following day (April
21) the funeral train left Washington amid the silent grief of the thousands who had gathered to witness its departure.   At all the great cities along the
route stops were made, and an opportunity was
given the people to look on the face of the illustrious
dead.   The passage of this funeral train westward
through country, village, and city, winding across
the territory of vast States, along a track of more
than fifteen hundred miles, was a pageant without a
parallel in the history of the continent or the world.
At every halt in the sombre march vast crowds, such
as never before had collected together, filed past the
catafalque for a glimpse of the dead chieftain's face.
Farmers left their farms, workmen left their shops,
societies and soldiers marched in solid columns,
and the great cities poured forth their population
in countless masses. From Washington the funeral

train moved to Baltimore, thence to Harrisburg, Philadelphia, New York, Albany, Buffalo, Cleveland, Columbus, Indianapolis, Chicago, and at last to Springfield.

As the funeral cortège passed through New York it was reverently gazed upon by a mass of humanity impossible to enumerate. No ovation could be so eloquent as the spectacle of the vast population, hushed and bareheaded under the bright spring sky, gazing upon his coffin. Lincoln's own words over the dead at Gettysburg came to many as the stately car went by: "The world will little note nor long remember what we say here, but it can never forget what they did here."

It was remembered, too, that on the 22d of February, 1861, as he raised the American flag over Independence Hall, in Philadelphia, he spoke of the sentiment in the Declaration of Independence which gave liberty not only to this country, but, "I hope," he said, "to the world for all future time. But if this country cannot be saved without giving up that principle, I was about to say I would rather be assassinated upon this spot than surrender it."

When he died the veil that hid his greatness was torn aside, and the country then knew what it had possesssed and lost in him. A New York paper, of April 29, 1865, said: "No one who personally knew him but will now feel that the deep, furrowed sadness of his face seemed to forecast his fate. The genial gentleness of his manner, his homely simplicity, the cheerful humor that never failed, are now seen to have been but the tender light that played around the rugged heights of his strong and noble nature. It is small consolation that he died at the moment of the war when he could best be spared, for no nation is ever ready for the loss of such a friend. But it is something to remember that he lived to see the slow day breaking. Like Moses, he had marched with us through the wilderness. From the height of patriotic vision he beheld the golden fields of the future waving in peace and plenty. He beheld, and blessed God, but was not to enter in."

In a discourse delivered on Lincoln on the 23d of that month, Henry Ward Beecher said:

"And now the martyr is moving in triumphal march, mightier than when alive. The nation rises up at every stage of his coming. Cities and states are his pall-bearers, and the cannon speaks the hours with solemn progression. Dead, dead, dead, he yet speaketh. Is Washington dead? Is Hampden dead? Is any man that was ever fit to live dead? Disenthralled of flesh, risen to the unobstructed sphere where passion never comes, he begins his illimitable work. His life is now grafted upon the infinite, and will be fruitful as no earthly life can be. Pass on, thou that hast overcome. Ye people, behold the martyr whose blood, as so many articu- late words, pleads for fidelity, for law, for liberty."

The funeral train reached Springfield on the 3d of May. The casket was borne to the State House and placed in Representative Hall—the very cham- ber in which in 1854 the deceased had pronounced that fearful invective against the sin of human slavery. The doors were thrown open, the coffin lid was removed, and we who had known the illustrious dead in other days, and before the nation lay its claim upon him, moved sadly through and looked for the last time on the silent, upturned face of our departed friend. All day long and through the night a stream of people filed reverently by the catafalque. Some of them were his colleagues at the bar; some his old friends from New Salem; some crippled soldiers fresh from the battle-fields of the war; and some were little children who, scarce realizing the impressiveness of the scene, were destined to live and tell their children yet to be born the sad story of Lincoln's death.

At ten o'clock in the morning of the second day, as a choir of two-hundred-and-fifty voices sang "Peace, Troubled Soul," the lid of the casket was shut down forever. The remains were borne outside and placed in a hearse, which moved at the head of a procession in charge of General Joseph Hooker to Oak Ridge cemetery. There Bishop Matthew Simpson delivered an eloquent and impressive funeral oration, and Rev. Dr. Gurley, of Washington, offered up the closing prayer. While the choir chanted "Unveil Thy Bosom, Faithful Tomb," the vault door opened and received to its final rest all that was mortal of Abraham Lincoln.

"It was soon known that the murder of Lincoln was one result of a conspiracy which had for its victims Secretary Seward and probably Vice-President Johnson, Secretary Stanton, General Grant, and perhaps others. Booth had left a card for Mr.

Johnson the day before, possibly with the intention of killing him. Mr. Seward received wounds, from which he soon recovered. Grant, who was to have accompanied Lincoln to the theatre on the night of the assassination, and did not, escaped unassailed. The general conspiracy was poorly planned and lamely executed. It involved about twenty-five persons. Mrs. Surratt, David C. Harold, Lewis Payne, Edward Spangler, Michael O'Loughlin, J. W. Atzerodt, Samuel Arnold, and Dr. Samuel Mudd, who set Booth's leg, which was dislocated by the fall from the stage-box, were among the number captured and tried.

" After the assassination Booth escaped unmolested from the theatre, mounted his horse, and rode away, accompanied by Harold, into Maryland. Cavalrymen scoured the country, and eleven days after the shooting discovered them in a barn on Garrett's farm, near Port Royal on the Rappahannock. The soldiers surrounded the barn and demanded a surrender. After the second demand Harold surrendered, under a shower of curses from Booth, but Booth refused, declaring that he would never be taken alive. The captain of the squad then fired the barn. A correspondent thus describes the scene:

" ' The blaze lit up the recesses of the great barn till every wasp's nest and cobweb in the roof were luminous, flinging streaks of red and violet across the tumbled farm gear in the corner. They tinged the beams, the upright columns, the barricades, where clover and timothy piled high held toward the hot incendiary their separate straws for the funeral pile. They bathed the murderer's retreat in a beautiful illumination, and, while in bold outlines his figure stood revealed, they rose like an impenetrable wall to guard from sight the hated enemy who lit them. Behind the blaze, with his eye to a crack, Colonel Conger saw Wilkes Booth standing upright upon a crutch. At the gleam of fire Booth dropped his crutch and carbine, and on both hands crept up to the spot to espy the incendiary and shoot him dead. His eyes were lustrous with fever, and swelled and rolled in terrible beauty, while his teeth were fixed, and he wore the expression of one in the calmness before frenzy. In vain he peered, with vengeance in his look ; the blaze that made him visible concealed his enemy. A second he turned glaring at the fire, as if to leap upon it and extinguish it, but it had made such headway that he dismissed the thought. As calmly as upon the battle-field a veteran stands amidst the hail of ball and shell and plunging iron, Booth turned and pushed for the door, carbine in poise, and the last resolve of death, which we name despair, set on his high, bloodless forehead.

" ' Just then Sergeant Boston Corbett fired through a crevice and shot Booth in the neck. He was carried out of the barn and laid upon the grass, and there died about four hours afterward. Before his misguided soul passed into the silence of death he whispered something which Lieutenant Baker bent down to hear. "Tell mother I die for my country," he said, faintly. Reviving a moment later he re peated the words, and added, " I thought I did for the best."

" His days of hiding and fleeing from his pursuers had left him pale, haggard, dirty, and unkempt. He had cut off his mustache and cropped his hair close to his head, and he and Harold both wore the Confederate gray uniform.'

" Booth's body was taken to Washington, and a post mortem examination of it held on board the monitor "Montauk," and on the night of the 27th of April it was given in charge of two men in a row-boat, who, it is claimed, disposed of it in secrecy—how, none but themselves know. Numerous stories have been told of the final resting-place of that hated dead man. Whoever knows the truth of it tells it not.

" Sergeant Corbett, who shot Booth, fired without orders. The last instructions given by Colonel Baker to Colonel Conger and Lieutenant Baker were: 'Don't shoot Booth, but take him alive.' Corbett was something of a fanatic, and for a breach of discipline had once been court-martialled and sentenced to be shot. The order, however, was not executed, but he had been drummed out of the regiment. He belonged to Company L of the Sixteenth New York Cavalry. He was English by birth, but was brought up in this country, and learned the trade of hat finisher. While living in Boston he joined the Methodist Episcopal Church. Never having been baptized, he was at a loss to know what name to adopt, but after making it a subject of prayer he took the name of Boston, in honor of the place of his conversion. He was ever undisciplined and erratic. He is said to be living in Kansas, and draws a pension from the Government.

"Five of the conspirators were tried, and four, Payne, Harold, Atzerodt and Mrs. Surratt, were hanged. Dr. Mudd was sent to the Dry Tortugas for a period of years, and there did such good work among the yellow-fever sufferers during an epidemic that he was pardoned and returned to this country. He died only about two years ago at his home in Maryland, near Washington. John Surratt fled to Italy, and there entered the Papal guards. He was discovered by Archbishop Hughes, and by the courtesy of the Italian government, though the extradition laws did not cover his case, was delivered over to the United States for trial. At his first trial the jury hung; at the second, in which Edwards Pierrepont was the Government counsel, Surratt got off on the plea of limitations. He undertook to lecture, and began at Rockville, Md. The *Evening Star*, of Washington, reported the lecture, which was widely copied, and was of such a feeble character that it killed him as a lecturer. He went to Baltimore, where, it is said, he still lives. Spangler, the scene-shifter, who was an accomplice of Booth, was sent to the Dry Tortugas, served out his term and died about ten years ago. McLoughlin, who was arrested because of his acquaintance with the conspirators, was sent to the Dry Tortugas and there died.

" Ford's Theatre was never played in after that memorable night. Ten or twelve days after the assassination Ford attempted to open it, but Stanton prevented it, and the Government bought the theatre for $100,000, and converted it into a medical museum. Ford was a Southern sympathizer. He ran two theatres until four years ago, one in Washington and one in Baltimore. Alison Naylor, the livery man who let Booth have his horse, still lives in Washington. Major Rathbone, who was in the box with Lincoln when he was shot, died within the last four years. Stewart, the man who jumped on the stage to follow Booth, and announced to the audience that he had escaped through the alley, died lately. Strange, but very few persons can now be found who were at the theatre that night. Laura Keene died a few years ago.

" Booth the assassin was the third son of the eminent English tragedian Junius Brutus Booth, and the brother of the equally renowned Edwin Booth. He was only twenty-six years old when he figured as the chief actor in this horrible drama. He began his dramatic career as John Wilkes, and as a stock actor gained a fair reputation, but had not achieved any special success. He had played chiefly in the South and West, and but a few times in New York. Some time before the assassination of Lincoln he had abandoned his profession on account of a bronchial affection. Those who knew him and saw him on that fatal Friday say that he was restless, like one who, consciously or unconsciously, was overshadowed by some awful fate.

He knew that the President and his party intended to be present at Ford's theatre in the evening, and he asked an acquaintance if he should attend the performance, remarking that if he did he would see some unusually fine acting. , He was a handsome man. His eyes were large and dark, his hair dark and inclined to curl, his features finely moulded, his form tall, and his address pleasing."

Frederick Stone, counsel for Harold after Booth's death, is authority for the statement that the occasion for Lincoln's assassination was the sentiment expressed by the President in a speech delivered from the steps of the White House on the night of April 11, when he said: "If universal amnesty is granted to the insurgents I cannot see how I can avoid exacting in return universal suffrage, or at least suffrage on the basis of intelligence and military service." Booth was standing before Mr. Lincoln on the outskirts of the crowd. "That means nigger citizenship," he said to Harold by his side. "Now, by God! I'll put him through." But whatever may have been the incentive, Booth seemed to crave the reprehensible fame that attaches to a bold and dramatically wicked deed. He may, it is true, have been mentally unhinged, but, whether sane or senseless, he made for himself an infamous and endless notoriety when he murdered the patient, forbearing man who had directed our ship of state through the most tempestuous waters it ever encountered.

In the death of Lincoln the South, prostrate and bleeding, lost a friend; and his unholy taking-off at the very hour of the assured supremacy of the Union cause ran the iron into the heart of the North. His sun went down suddenly, and whelmed the country in a darkness which was felt by every heart ; but far up the clouds sprang apart, and soon the golden light, flooding the heavens with radiance, illuminated every uncovered brow with the hope of a fair to-morrow. His name will ever be the watchword of liberty. His work is finished, and sealed forever with the veneration given to the blood of martyrs. Yesterday a man reviled and abused, a target for the shafts of malice and hatred : to-day an apostle. Yesterday a power : to-day a prestige, sacred, irresistible. The life and the tragic death of Mr. Lincoln mark an epoch in history from which dates the unqualified annunciation by the Amercan people of the great-est truth in the bible of republicanism—the very keystone of that arch of human rights which is des-tined to overshadow and remodel every government upon the earth. The glorious brightness of that upper world, as it welcomed his faint and bleeding spirit, broke through upon the earth at his exit—it was the dawn of a day growing brighter as the grand army of freedom follows in the march of time.

Lincoln's place in history will be fixed—aside from his personal characteristics—by the events and results of the war. As a great political leader who quelled a rebellion of eight millions of people, liberated four millions of slaves, and demonstrated to the world the ability of the people to maintain a government of themselves, by themselves, for themselves, he will assuredly occupy no insignificant place.

To accomplish the great work of preserving the Union cost the land a great price. Generations of Americans yet unborn, and humanity everywhere, for years to come will mourn the horrors and sacrifices of the first civil war in the United States; but above the blood of its victims, above the bones of its dead, above the ashes of desolate hearths, will arise the colossal figure of Abraham Lincoln as the most acceptable sacrifice offered by the nineteenth century in expiation of the great crime of the seventeenth. Above all the anguish and tears of that immense hecatomb will appear the shade of Lincoln as the symbol of hope and of pardon.

This is the true lesson of Lincoln's life: real and enduring greatness, that will survive the corrosion and abrasion of time, of change, and of progress, must rest upon character. In certain brilliant and what is understood to be most desirable endowments how many Americans have surpassed him. Yet how he looms above them all! Not eloquence, nor logic, nor grasp of thought; not statesmanship, nor power of command, nor courage; not any nor all of these have made him what he is, but these, in the degree in which he possessed them, conjoined to those qualities comprised in the term character, have given him his fame—have made him for all time to come the great American, the grand, central figure in American—perhaps the world's—history.

CHAPTER XI.*

Soon after the death of Mr. Lincoln Dr. J. G.
Holland came out to Illinois from his home in Massachusetts to gather up materials for a life of the
dead President. The gentleman spent several days
with me, and I gave him all the assistance that lay
in my power. I was much pleased with him, and
awaited with not a little interest the appearance of
his book. I felt sure that even after my long and
intimate acquaintance with Mr. Lincoln I never fully
knew and understood him, and I therefore wondered
what sort of a description Dr. Holland, after inter-
viewing Lincoln's old-time friends, would make of his
individual characteristics. When the book appeared
he said this: " The writer has conversed with mul-
titudes of men who claimed to know Mr. Lincoln
intimately : yet there are not two of the whole
number who agree in their estimate of him. The
fact was that he rarely showed more than one
aspect of himself to one man. He opened himself
to men in different directions. To illustrate the
effect of the peculiarity of Mr. Lincoln's intercourse
with men it may be said that men who knew him
through all his professional and political life offered
opinions as diametrically opposite to these, viz.:
that he was a very ambitious man, and that he was

---

* The substance of this chapter I delivered in the form of a lecture
to a Springfield audience in 1866. W. H. H.

without a particle of ambition; that he was one of the saddest men that ever lived, and that he was one of the jolliest men that ever lived; that he was very religious, but that he was not a Christian; that he was a Christian, but did not know it; that he was so far from being a religious man or a Christian that 'the less said upon that subject the better;' that he was the most cunning man in America, and that he had not a particle of cunning in him; that he had the strongest personal attachments, and that he had no personal attachments at all—only a general good feeling towards everybody; that he was a man of indomitable will, and that he was a man almost without a will; that he was a tyrant, and that he was the softest-hearted, most brotherly man that ever lived; that he was remarkable for his pure-mindedness, and that he was the foulest in his jests and stories of any man in the country; that he was a witty man, and that he was only a retailer of the wit of others; that his apparent candor and fairness were only apparent, and that they were as real as his head and his hands; that he was a boor, and that he was in all respects a gentleman; that he was a leader of the people, and that he was always led by the people; that he was cool and impassive, and that he was susceptible of the strongest passions. It is only by tracing these separate streams of impression back to their fountain that we are able to arrive at anything like a competent comprehension of the man, or to learn why he came to be held in such various estimation. Men caught only separate aspects of his character—only the fragments that were called into exhibition by their own qualities."

Dr. Holland had only found what Lincoln's friends had always experienced in their relations with him—that he was a man of many moods and many sides. He never revealed himself entirely to any one man, and therefore he will always to a certain extent remain enveloped in doubt. Even those who were with him through long years of hard study and under constantly varying circumstances can hardly say they knew him through and through. I always believed I could read him as thoroughly as any man, and yet he was so different in many respects from any other one I ever met before or since his time that I cannot say I comprehended him. In this chapter I give my recollection of his individual characteristics as they occur to me, and allow the world to form its own opinion. If my recollection of the man destroys any other person's ideal, I cannot help it. By a faithful and lifelike description of Lincoln the man, and a study of his peculiar and personal traits, perhaps some of the apparent contradictions met with by Dr. Holland will have melted from sight.

Mr. Lincoln was six feet four inches high, and when he left the city of his home for Washington was fifty-one years old, having good health and no gray hairs, or but few, on his head. He was thin, wiry, sinewy, raw-boned; thin through the breast to the back, and narrow across the shoulders; standing he leaned forward—was what may be called stoop-shouldered, inclining to the consumptive by build. His usual weight was one hundred and eighty pounds. His organization—rather his structure and functions—worked slowly.

His blood had to run a long distance from his heart to the extremities of his frame, and his nerve force had to travel through dry ground a long distance before his muscles were obedient to his will. His structure was loose and leathery; his body was shrunk and shrivelled; he had dark skin, dark hair, and looked woe-struck. The whole man, body and mind, worked slowly, as if it needed oiling. Physically he was a very powerful man, lifting with ease four hundred, and in one case six hundred, pounds. His mind was like his body, and worked slowly but strongly. Hence there was very little bodily or mental wear and tear in him. This peculiarity in his construction gave him great advantage over other men in public life. No man in America—scarcely a man in the world—could have stood what Lincoln did in Washington and survived through more than one term of the Presidency.

When he walked he moved cautiously but firmly; his long arms and giant hands swung down by his side. He walked with even tread, the inner sides of his feet being parallel. He put the whole foot flat down on the ground at once, not landing on the heel; he likewise lifted his foot all at once, not rising from the toe, and hence he had no spring to his walk. His walk was undulatory—catching and pocketing tire, weariness, and pain, all up and down his person, and thus preventing them from locating. The first impression of a stranger, or a man who did not observe closely, was that his walk implied shrewdness and cunning—that he was a tricky man; but, in reality, it was the walk of caution and firmness. In sitting down on a common chair he was

43

no taller than ordinary men. His legs and arms were abnormally, unnaturally long, and in undue proportion to the remainder of his body. It was only when he stood up that he loomed above other men.

Mr. Lincoln's head was long, and tall from the base of the brain and from the eyebrows. His head ran backwards, his forehead rising as it ran back at a low angle, like Clay's, and unlike Webster's, which was almost perpendicular. The size of his hat measured at the hatter's block was seven and one-eighth, his head being, from ear to ear, six and one-half inches, and from the front to the back of the brain eight inches. Thus measured it was not below the medium size. His forehead was narrow but high ; his hair was dark, almost black, and lay floating where his fingers or the winds left it, piled up at random. His cheek-bones were high, sharp, and prominent ; his jaws were long and up-curved ; his nose was large, long, blunt, and a little awry towards the right eye ; his chin was sharp and upcurved ; his eyebrows cropped out like a huge rock on the brow of a hill ; his long, sallow face was wrinkled and dry, with a hair here and there on the surface ; his cheeks were leathery ; his ears were large, and ran out almost at right angles from his head, caused partly by heavy hats and partly by nature ; his lower lip was thick, hanging, and under-curved, while his chin reached for the lip upcurved ; his neck was neat and trim, his head being well balanced on it ; there was the lone mole on the right cheek, and Adam's apple on his throat.

Thus stood, walked, acted, and looked Abraham

Lincoln. He was not a pretty man by any means, nor was he an ugly one; he was a homely man, careless of his looks, plain-looking and plain-acting. He had no pomp, display, or dignity, so-called. He appeared simple in his carriage and bearing. He was a sad-looking man; his melancholy dripped from him as he walked. His apparent gloom impressed his friends,* and created sympathy for him—one means of his great success. He was

---

* Lincoln's melancholy never failed to impress any man who ever saw or knew him. The perpetual look of sadness was his most prominent feature. The cause of this peculiar condition was a matter of frequent discussion among his friends. John T. Stuart said it was due to his abnormal digestion. His liver failed to work properly—did not secrete bile—and his bowels were equally as inactive. " I used to advise him to take blue-mass pills," related Stuart, " and he did take them before he went to Washington, and for five months while he was President, but when I came on to Congress he told me he had ceased using them because they made him cross." The reader can hardly realize the extent of this peculiar tendency to gloom. One of Lincoln's colleagues in the Legislature of Illinois is authority for the statement coming from Lincoln himself that this " mental depression became so intense at times he never dared carry a pocket-knife." Two things greatly intensified his characteristic sadness: one was the endless succession of troubles in his domestic life, which he had to bear in silence; and the other was unquestionably the knowledge of his own obscure and lowly origin. The recollection of these things burned a deep impress on his sensitive soul.

As to the cause of this morbid condition my idea has always been that it was occult, and could not be explained by any course of observation and reasoning. It was ingrained, and, being ingrained, could not be reduced to rule, or the cause arrayed. It was necessarily hereditary, but whether it came down from a long line of ancestors and far back, or was simply the reproduction of the saddened life of Nancy Hanks, cannot well be determined. At any rate it was part of his nature, and could no more be shaken off than he could part with his brains.

gloomy, abstracted, and joyous—rather humorous—
by turns ; but I do not think he knew what real joy
was for many years.

Mr. Lincoln sometimes walked our streets cheer-
ily, he was not always gloomy, and then it was that
on meeting a friend he greeted him with plain
" Howd'y ? " clasping his hand in both of his own,
and gave him a hearty soul-welcome.   On a winter's
morning he might be seen stalking towards the
market-house, basket on arm, his old gray shawl
wrapped around his neck, his little boy Willie or
Tad running along at his heels asking a thousand
boyish questions, which his father, in deep abstrac-
tion, neither heeded nor heard.*   If a friend met or

* " I lived next door to the Lincolns for many years, knew the
family well. Mr. Lincoln used to come to our house, his feet
encased in a pair of loose slippers, and with an old, faded pair of
trousers fastened with one suspender. He frequently came to our
house for milk. Our rooms were low, and he said one day, ' Jim,
you'll have to lift your loft a little higher ; I can't straighten out
under it very well.' To my wife, who was short of stature, he used
to say that little people had some advantages : they required less
' wood and wool to make them comfortable.' In his yard Lincoln
had but little shrubbery. He once planted some rose bushes, to
which he called my attention, but soon neglected them altogether.
He never planted any vines or fruit trees, seemed to have no fondness for such things. At one time, yielding to my suggestion, he
undertook to keep a garden in the rear part of his yard, but one
season's experience sufficed to cure him of all desire for another.
He kept his own horse, fed and curried it when at home ; he also
fed and milked his own cow, and sawed his own wood. Mr. Lincoln
and his wife agreed moderately well. Frequently Mrs. Lincoln's
temper would get the better of her. If she became furious, as she
often did, her husband tried to pay no attention to her. He would
sometimes laugh at her, but generally he would pick up one of the
children and walk off. I have heard her say that if Mr. Lincoln

passed him, and he awoke from his reverie, something would remind him of a story he had heard in Indiana, and tell it he would, and there was no alternative but to listen.

Thus, I repeat, stood and walked and talked this singular man. He was odd, but when that gray eye and that face and those features were lit up by the inward soul in fires of emotion, then it was that all those apparently ugly features sprang into organs of beauty or disappeared in the sea of inspiration that often flooded his face. Sometimes it appeared as if Lincoln's soul was fresh from its Creator.

I have asked the friends and foes of Mr. Lincoln alike what they thought of his perceptions. One gentleman of unquestioned ability and free from all partiality or prejudice said, "Mr. Lincoln's perceptions were slow, a little perverted, if not somewhat distorted and diseased." If the meaning of this is that Mr. Lincoln saw things from a peculiar angle of his being, and from this was susceptible to nature's impulses, and that he so expressed himself, then I have no objection to what is said.

---

had remained at home more she could have loved him better. One day while Mr. Lincoln was absent—he had gone to Chicago to try a suit in the United States Court—his wife and I formed a conspiracy to take off the roof and raise his house. It was originally a frame structure one story and a half high. When Lincoln returned he met a gentleman on the sidewalk and, looking at his own house and manifesting great surprise, inquired: 'Stranger, can you tell me where Lincoln lives?' The gentleman gave him the necessary information, and Lincoln gravely entered his own premises."—Statement, James Gourly, February 9, 1866.

Otherwise I dissent. Mr. Lincoln's perceptions were slow, cold, clear, and exact. Everything came to him in its precise shape and color. To some men the world of matter and of man comes ornamented with beauty, life, and action; and hence more or less false and inexact. No lurking illusion or other error, false in itself and clad for the moment in robes of splendor, ever passed undetected or unchallenged over the threshold of his mind—that point which divides vision from the realm and home of thought. Names to him were nothing, and titles naught—assumption always standing back abashed at his cold, intellectual glare. Neither his perceptions nor intellectual vision were perverted, distorted, or diseased. He saw all things through a perfect mental lens. There was no diffraction or refraction there. He was not impulsive, fanciful, or imaginative; but cold, calm, and precise. He threw his whole mental light around the object, and, after a time, substance and quality stood apart, form and color took their appropriate places, and all was clear and exact in his mind. His fault, if any, was that he saw things less than they really were; less beautiful and more frigid. He crushed the unreal, the inexact, the hollow, and the sham. He saw things in rigidity rather than in vital action. He saw what no man could dispute, but he failed to see what might have been seen.

To some minds the world is all life, a soul beneath the material; but to Mr. Lincoln no life was individual that did not manifest itself to him. His mind was his standard. His mental action was deliberate, and he was pitiless and persistent in pursuit of the truth. No error went undetected, no falsehood unexposed, if he once was aroused in search of the truth. The true peculiarity of Mr. Lincoln has not been seen by his various biographers; or, if seen, they have failed wofully to give it that importance which it deserves. Newton beheld the law of the universe in the fall of an apple from a tree to the ground ; Owen saw the animal in its claw; Spencer saw evolution in the growth of a seed ; and Shakespeare saw human nature in the laugh of a man. Nature was suggestive to all these men. Mr. Lincoln no less saw philosophy in a story and an object lesson in a joke. His was a new and original position, one which was always suggesting something to him. The world and man, principles and facts, all were full of suggestions to his susceptible soul. They continually put him in mind of something. His ideas were odd and original for the reason that he was a peculiar and original creation himself.

His power in the association of ideas was as great as his memory was tenacious and strong. His language indicated oddity and originality of vision as well as expression. Words and language are but the counterparts of the idea—the other half of the idea ; they are but the stinging, hot, leaden bullets that drop from the mould ; in a rifle, with powder stuffed behind them and fire applied, they are an embodied force resistlessly pursuing their object. In the search for words Mr. Lincoln was often at a loss. He was often perplexed to give proper expression to his ideas; first, because he was not master of the English language; and secondly, because there were, in the vast store of words, so few that contained the exact coloring, power, and shape of his ideas. This will account for the frequent resort by him to the use of stories, maxims, and jokes in which to clothe his ideas, that they might be comprehended. So true was this peculiar mental vision of his that, though mankind has been gathering, arranging, and classifying facts for thousands of years, Lincoln's peculiar standpoint could give him no advantage over other men's labor. Hence he tore down to their deepest foundations all arrangements of facts, and constructed new ones to govern himself. He was compelled from his peculiar mental organization to do this. His labor was great and continuous.

The truth about Mr. Lincoln is that he read less and thought more than any man in his sphere in America. No man can put his finger on any great book written in the last or present century that he read thoroughly. When young he read the Bible, and when of age he read Shakespeare; but, though he often quoted from both, he never read either one through. He is acknowledged now to have been a great man, but the question is what made him great. I repeat, that he read less and thought more than any man of his standing in America, if not in the world. He possessed originality and power of thought in an eminent degree. Besides his well established reputation for caution, he was concentrated in his thoughts and had great continuity of reflection. In everything he was patient and enduring. These are some of the grounds of his wonderful success.

Not only were nature, man, and principle suggestive to Mr. Lincoln, not only had he accurate and exact perceptions, but he was causative; his mind, apparently with an automatic movement, ran back behind facts, principles, and all things to their origin and first cause—to that point where forces act at once as effect and cause. He would stop in the street and analyze a machine. He would whittle a thing to a point, and then count the numberless inclined planes and their pitch making the the point. Mastering and defining this, he would then cut that point back and get a broad transverse section of his pine-stick, and peel and define that. Clocks, omnibuses, language, paddle-wheels, and idioms never escaped his observation and analysis. Before he could form an idea of anything, before he would express his opinion on a subject, he must know its origin and history in substance and quality, in magnitude and gravity. He must know it inside and outside, upside and downside. He searched and comprehended his own mind and nature thoroughly, as I have often heard him say. He must analyze a sensation, an idea, and run back in its history to its origin, and purpose. He was remorseless in his analysis of facts and principles. When all these exhaustive processes had been gone through with he could form an idea and express it; but no sooner. He had no faith, and no respect for "say so's," come though they might from tradition or authority. Thus everything had to run through the crucible, and be tested by the fires of his analytic mind; and when at last he did speak, his utterances rang out with the clear and keen ring of gold upon the counters of the understanding. He reasoned logically through analogy and comparison. All opponents dreaded his originality of idea, his condensation, definition, and force of expression; and woe be to the man who hugged to his bosom a secret error if Lincoln got on the chase of it. I repeat, woe to him! Time could hide the error in no nook or corner of space in which he would not detect and expose it.

Though gifted with accurate and acute perception, though a profound thinker as well as analyzer, still Lincoln's judgment on many and minor matters was oftentimes childish. By the word judgment I do not mean what mental philosophers would call the exercise of reason, will—understanding; but I use the term in its popular sense. I refer to that capacity or power which decides on the fitness, the harmony, or, if you will, the beauty and appropriateness of things. I have always thought, and sometimes said, Lincoln lacked this quality in his mental structure. He was on the alert if a principle was involved or a man's rights at stake in a transaction; but he never could see the harm in wearing a sack-coat instead of a swallow-tail to an evening party, nor could he realize the

offense of telling a vulgar yarn if a preacher happened to be present.*

As already expressed, Mr. Lincoln had no faith.
In order to believe, he must see and feel, and thrust
his hand into the place. He must taste, smell, and
handle before he had faith òr even belief. Such a
mind manifestly must have its time. His forte and
power lay in digging out for himself and securing
for his mind its own food, to be assimilated unto
itself. Thus, in time he would form opinions and
conclusions that no human power could overthrow.
They were as irresistible as the rush of a flood; as
convincing as logic embodied in mathematics. And
yet the question arises: "Had Mr. Lincoln great,
good common-sense?" A variety of opinions suggest themselves in answer to this. If the true test

---

* Sometime in 1857 a lady reader or elocutionist came to Springfield and gave a public reading in a hall immediately north of the
State House. As lady lecturers were then rare birds, a very large
crowd greeted her. Among other things she recited "Nothing to
Wear," a piece in which is described the perplexities that beset
"Miss Flora McFlimsey" in her efforts to appear fashionable. In
the midst of one stanza, in which no effort is made to say anything
particularly amusing, and during the reading of which the audience
manifested the most respectful silence and attention, some one in the
rear seats burst out into a loud, coarse laugh—a sudden and explo-
sive guffaw. It startled the speaker and audience, and kindled a
storm of unsuppressed laughter and applause. Everyone looked
back to ascertain the cause of the demonstration, and was greatly
surprised to find that it was Mr. Lincoln. He blushed and squirmed
with the awkward diffidence of a schoolboy. What prompted him
to laugh no one was able to explain. He was doubtless wrapped up
in a brown study, and, recalling some amusing episode, indulged in
laughter without realizing his surroundings. The experience mortified him greatly.

is that a man shall judge the rush and whirl of human actions and transactions as wisely and accurately as though indefinite time and proper conditions were at his disposal, then I am compelled to follow the logic of things and admit that he had no great stock of common-sense ; but if, on the other hand, the time and conditions were ripe, his common-sense was in every case equal to the emergency. He knew himself, and never trusted his dollar or his fame in casual opinions—never acted hastily or prematurely on great matters.

Mr. Lincoln believed that the great leading law of human nature is motive. He reasoned all ideas of a disinterested action out of my mind. I used to hold that an action could be pure, disinterested, and wholly free from selfishness; but he divested me of that delusion. His idea was that all human actions were caused by motives, and that at the bottom of these motives was self. He defied me to act without motive and unselfishly ; and when I did the act and told him of it, he analyzed and sifted it to the last grain. After he had concluded, I could not avoid the admission that he had demonstrated the absolute selfishness of the entire act. Although a profound analyzer of the laws of human nature he could form no just construction of the motives of the particular individual. He knew but little of the play of the features as seen in the " human face divine." He could not distinguish between the paleness of anger and the crimson tint of modesty. In determining what each play of the features indicated he was pitiably weak.

The great predominating elements of Mr. Lincoln's peculiar character were: first, his great capacity and power of reason; second, his conscience and his excellent understanding; third, an exalted idea of the sense of right and equity; fourth, his intense veneration of the true and the good. His conscience, his heart and all the faculties and qualities of his mind bowed submissively to the despotism of his reason. He lived and acted from the standard of reason—that throne of logic, home of principle—the realm of Deity in man. It is from this point Mr. Lincoln must be viewed. Not only was he cautious, patient, and enduring; not only had he concentration and great continuity of thought; but he had profound analytical power. His vision was clear, and he was emphatically the master of statement. His pursuit of the truth, as before mentioned, was indefatigable. He reasoned from well-chosen principles with such clearness, force, and directness that the tallest intellects in the land bowed to him. He was the strongest man I ever saw, looking at him from the elevated standpoint of reason and logic. He came down from that height with irresistible and crashing force. His Cooper Institute and other printed speeches will prove this; but his speeches before the courts —especially the Supreme Court of Illinois—if they had been preserved, would demonstrate it still more plainly. Here he demanded time to think and prepare. The office of reason is to determine the truth. Truth is the power of reason, and Lincoln loved truth for its own sake. It was to him reason's food.

Conscience, the second great quality of Mr. Lincoln's character, is that faculty which induces in us love of the just. Its real office is justice; right and equity are its correlatives. As a court, it is in session continuously; it decides all acts at all times. Mr. Lincoln had a deep, broad, living conscience. His reason, however, was the real judge; it told him what was true or false, and therefore good or bad, right or wrong, just or unjust, and his conscience echoed back the decision. His conscience ruled his heart; he was always just before he was generous. It cannot be said of any mortal that he was always absolutely just. Neither was Lincoln always just; but his general life was. It follows that if Mr. Lincoln had great reason and great conscience he must have been an honest man; and so he was. He was rightfully entitled to the appellation " Honest Abe." Honesty was his polar star.

Mr. Lincoln also had a good understanding; that is, the faculty that comprehends the exact state of things and determines their relations, near or remote. The understanding does not necessarily enquire for the reason of things. While Lincoln was odd and original, while he lived out of himself and by himself, and while he could absorb but little from others, yet a reading of his speeches, messages, and letters satisfies us that he had good understanding. But the strongest point in his make-up was the knowledge he had of himself; he comprehended and understood his own capacity—what he did and why he did it—better perhaps than any man of his day. He had a wider and deeper comprehension of his environments, of the political conditions especially, than men who were more learned or had had the benefits of a more thorough training.

He was a very sensitive man,—modest to the point of diffidence,—and often, hid himself in the masses to prevent the discovery of his identity. He was not indifferent, however, to approbation and public opinion. He had no disgusting egotism and no pompous pride, no aristocracy, no haughtiness, no vanity. Merging together the qualities of his nature he was a meek, quiet, unobtrusive gentleman.

As many contradictory opinions prevail in reference to Mr. Lincoln's heart and humanity as on the question of his judgment. As many persons perhaps contend that he was cold and obdurate as that he was warm and affectionate. The first thing the world met in contact with him was his head and conscience; after that he exposed the tender side of his nature—his heart, subject at all times to his exalted sense of right and equity, namely his conscience. In proportion as he held his conscience subject to his head, he held his heart subject to his head and conscience. His humanity had to defer to his sense of justice and the eternal right. His heart was the lowest of these organs, if we may call them such—the weakest of the three. Some men have reversed this order and characterized his heart as his ruling organ. This estimate of Mr. Lincoln endows him with love regardless of truth, justice, and right. The question still is, was Lincoln cold and heartless, or warm and affectionate? Can a man be all heart, all head, and all conscience? Some of these are masters over the others, some will be dominant, ruling with imperial sway, and thus giving character to the man. What, in the first place, do we mean by a warm-hearted man? Is it one who goes out of himself and reaches for others spontaneously, seeking to correct some abuse to mankind because of a deep love for humanity, apart from equity and truth, and who does what he does for love's sake? If so, Mr. Lincoln was a cold man. If a man, woman, or child approached him, and the prayer of such an one was granted, that itself was not evidence of his love. The African was enslaved and deprived of his rights; a principle was violated in doing so. Rights imply obligations as well as duties. Mr. Lincoln was President; he was in a position that made it his duty, through his sense of right, his love of principle, the constitutional obligations imposed upon him by the oath of office, to strike the blow against slavery. But did he do it for love? He has himself answered the question: "I would not free the slaves if I could preserve the Union without it." When he freed the slaves there was no heart in the act. This argument can be used against his too enthusiastic friends.

In general terms his life was cold—at least characterized by what many persons would deem great indifference. He had, however, a strong latent capacity to love : but the object must first come in the guise of a principle, next it must be right and true—then it was lovely in his sight. He loved humanity when it was oppressed—an abstract love

as against the concrete love centered in an individual. He rarely used terms of endearment, and yet
he was proverbially tender and gentle. He gave
the key-note to his own character when he said:
"With malice towards none, with charity for all."
In proportion to his want of deep, intense love he
had no hate and bore no malice. His charity for
an imperfect man was as broad as his devotion to
principle was enduring.

"But was not Mr. Lincoln a man of great humanity?" asks a friend at my elbow; to which I reply,
"Has not that question been answered already?"
Let us suppose it has not. We must understand
each other. What is meant by his humanity? Is
it meant that he had much of human nature in
him? If so, I grant that he was a man of humanity.
If, in the event of the above definition being unsatis-
factory or untrue, it is meant that he was tender
and kind, then I again agree. But if the inference
is that he would sacrifice truth or right in the
slightest degree for the love of a friend, then he
was neither tender nor kind; nor did he have any
humanity. The law of human nature is such that it
cannot be all head, all conscience, and all heart in
one person at the same time. Our Maker so constituted things that, where God through reason blazed
the way, we might boldly walk therein. The glory
of Mr. Lincoln's power lay in the just and magnificent equipoise of head, conscience, and heart; and
here his fame must rest or not at all.

Not only were Mr. Lincoln's perceptions good;
not only was nature suggestive to him; not only

was he original and strong; not only had he great reason, good understanding; not only did he love the true and the good—the eternal right; not only was he tender and sympathetic and kind;—but, in due proportion and in legitimate subordination, he had a glorious combination of them all. Through his perceptions—the suggestiveness of nature, his originality and strength; through his magnificent reason, his understanding, his conscience, his tenderness, quick sympathy, his heart; he approximated as nearly as human nature and the imperfections of man would permit to an embodiment of the great moral principle, " Do unto others as ye would they should do unto you."

Of Mr. Lincoln's will-power there are two opinions also: one that he lacked any will; the other that he was all will. Both these contradictory views have their vehement and honest champions. For the great underlying principles of mind in man he had great respect. He loved the true first, the right second, and the good last. His mind struggled for truth, and his soul reached out for substances. He cared not for forms, ways, methods—the non-substantial things of this world. He could not, by reason of his structure and mental organization, care anything about them. He did not have an intense care for any particular or individual man— the dollar, property, rank, orders, manners, or similar things; neither did he have any avarice or other like vice in his nature. He detested somewhat all technical rules in law, philosophy, and other sciences

—mere forms everywhere—because they were, as a general thing, founded on arbitrary thoughts and ideas, and not on reason, truth, and the right. These things seemed to him lacking in substance, and he disregarded them because they cramped the originality of his genius. What suited a little narrow, critical mind did not suit Mr. Lincoln any more than a child's clothes would fit his father's body. Generally he took no interest in town affairs or local elections; he attended no meetings that pertained to local interests. He did not care—because by reason of his nature he could not—who succeeded to the presidency of this or that society or railroad company; who made the most money; who was going to Philadelphia, and what were the costs of such a trip; who was going to be married; who among his friends got this office or that—who was elected street commissioner or health inspector. No principle of truth, right, or justice being involved in any of these things he could not be moved by them.* He could not understand why men struggled so desperately for the little glory or lesser salary the small offices afforded. He made

---

* A bitter, malignant fool who always had opposed Lincoln and his friends, and had lost no opportunity to abuse them, induced Lincoln to go to the Governor of Illinois and recommend him for an important office in the State Militia. There being no principle at stake Lincoln could not refuse the request. When his friends heard of it they were furious in their denunciation of his action. It mortified him greatly to learn that he had displeased them. " And yet," he said, a few days later, dwelling on the matter to me in the office, " I couldn't well refuse the little the fellow asked of me."

this remark to me one day in Washington: "If ever this free people—this Government—is utterly demoralized, it will come from this human struggle for office—a way to live without work." It puzzled him a good deal, he said, to get at the root of this dreaded disease, which spread like contagion during the nation's death struggle.

Because he could not feel a deep interest in the things referred to, nor manifest the same interest in those who were engaged in the popular scramble, he was called indifferent—nay, ungrateful—to his friends. This estimate of the man was a very unjust as well as unfair one. Mr. Lincoln loved his friends with commendable loyalty: in many cases he clung to them tenaciously, like iron to iron welded; and yet, because he could not be actively aroused, nor enter into the spirit of their anxiety for office, he was called ungrateful. But he was not so. He may have seemed passive and lacking in interest; he may not have measured his friendly duties by the applicant's hot desire; but yet he was never ungrateful. Neither was he a selfish man. He would never have performed an act, even to promote himself to the Presidency, if by that act any human being was wronged. If it is said that he preferred Abraham Lincoln to anyone else in the pursuit of his ambition, and that because of this he was a selfish man, then I can see no impropriety in the charge. Under the same conditions we should all be equally guilty.

Remembering that Mr. Lincoln's mind moved logically, slowly, and cautiously, the question of his

The St. Gaudens Statue of Lincoln,
In Lincoln Park, Chicago.

will and its power is easily solved. Although he cared but little for simple facts, rules, and methods, he did care for the truth and right of principle. In debate he courteously granted all the forms and non-essential things to his opponent. Sometimes he yielded nine points out of ten. The nine he brushed aside as husks or rubbish; but the tenth, being a question of substance, he clung to with all his might. On the underlying principles of truth and justice his will was as firm as steel and as tenacious as iron. It was as solid, real, and vital as an idea on which the world turns. He scorned to support or adopt an untrue position, in proportion as his conscience prevented him from doing an unjust thing. Ask him to sacrifice in the slightest degree his convictions of truth *—as he was asked to do when he made his "house-divided-against-itself speech"—and his soul would have exclaimed with indignant scorn, "The world perish first!"

Such was Lincoln's will. Because on one line of questions—the non-essential—he was pliable, and on the other he was as immovable as the rocks, have arisen the contradictory notions prevalent regarding him. It only remains to say that he was inflexible and unbending in human transactions when it was

---

* "Mr. Lincoln seems to me too true and honest a man to have his eulogy written, and I have no taste for writing eulogies. I am sure that, if he were alive, he would feel that the exact truth regarding himself was far more worthy of himself and of his biographer than any flattering picture. I loved the man as he was, with his rugged features, his coarse, rebellious hair, his sad, dreamy eyes; and I love to see him, and I hope to describe him, as he was, and not otherwise."—Robert Dale Owen, January 22, 1867, MS.

necessary to be so, and not otherwise. At one moment he was pliable and expansive as gentle air; at the next as tenacious and unyielding as gravity itself.

Thus I have traced Mr. Lincoln through his perceptions, his suggestiveness, his judgment, and his four predominant qualities: powers of reason, understanding, conscience, and heart. In the grand review of his peculiar characteristics, nothing creates such an impressive effect as his love of the truth. It looms up over everything else. His life is proof of the assertion that he never yielded in his fundamental conception of truth to any man for any end.

All the follies and wrong Mr. Lincoln ever fell into or committed sprang out of these weak points: the want of intuitive judgment; the lack of quick, sagacious knowledge of the play and meaning of men's features as written on the face; the want of the sense of propriety of things; his tenderness and mercy; and lastly, his unsuspecting nature. He was deeply and sincerely honest himself, and assumed that others were so. He never suspected men; and hence in dealing with them he was easily imposed upon.

All the wise and good things Mr. Lincoln ever did sprang out of his great reason, his conscience, his understanding, his heart, his love of the truth, the right, and the good. I am speaking now of his particular and individual faculties and qualities, not of their combination or the result of any combinations. Run out these qualities and faculties abstractly, and see what they produce. For instance, a tender heart, a strong reason, a broad understanding, an exalted conscience, a love of the true and the good must, proportioned reasonably and applied practically, produce a man of great power and great humanity.

As illustrative of a combination in Mr. Lincoln's organization, it may be said that his eloquence lay in the strength of his logical faculty, his supreme power of reasoning, his great understanding, and his love of principle ; in his clear and accurate vision ; in his cool and masterly statement of principles around which the issues gather ; and in the statement of those issues and the grouping of the facts that are to carry conviction to the minds of men of every grade of intelligence. He was so clear that he could not be misunderstood or long misrepresented. He stood square and bolt upright to his convictions, and anyone who listened to him would be convinced that he formed his thoughts and utterances by them. His mind was not exactly a wide, broad, generalizing, and comprehensive mind, nor yet a versatile, quick, and subtle one, bounding here and there as emergencies demanded ; but it was deep, enduring, strong, like a majestic machine running in deep iron grooves with heavy flanges on its wheels.

Mr. Lincoln himself was a very sensitive man, and hence, in dealing with others, he avoided wounding their hearts or puncturing their sensibility. He was unusually considerate of the feelings of other men, regardless of their rank, condition, or station. At first sight he struck one with his plainness, simplicity of manner, sincerity, candor, and truthfulness. He had no double interests and no overwhelming dignity with which to chill the air around his visitor. He was always easy of approach and thoroughly democratic. He seemed to throw a charm around every man who ever met him. To be in his presence was a pleasure, and no man ever left his company with injured feelings unless most richly deserved.

The universal testimony, " He is an honest man," gave him a firm hold on the masses, and they trusted him with a blind religious faith. His sad, melancholy face excited their sympathy, and when the dark days came it was their heart-strings that entwined and sustained him. Sympathy, we are told, is one of the strongest and noblest incentives to human action. With the sympathy and love of the people to sustain him, Lincoln had unlimited power over them; he threw an invisible and weightless harness over them, and drove them through disaster and desperation to final victory. The trust and worship by the people of Lincoln were the result of his simple character. He held himself not aloof from the masses. He became one of them. They feared together, they struggled together, they hoped together; thus melted and moulded into one, they became one in thought, one in will, one in action. If Lincoln cautiously awaited the full development of the last fact in the great drama before he acted, when longer waiting would be a crime, he knew that the people were determinedly at his back. Thus, when a blow was struck, it came with the unerring aim and power of a bolt from heaven. A natural king—not ruling men, but lead-

The Lincoln Monument in Springfield.

ing them along the drifts and trends of their own tendencies, always keeping in mind the consent of the
governed, he developed what the future historian
will call the sublimest order of conservative statesmanship.

Whatever of life, vigor, force, and power of eloquence his peculiar qualities gave him ; whatever
there was in a fair, manly, honest, and impartial
adminstration of justice under law to all men at all
times ; whatever there was in a strong will in the
right governed by tenderness and mercy ; whatever
there was in toil and sublime patience ; whatever
there was in these things or a wise combination of
them, Lincoln is justly entitled to in making up the
impartial verdict of history. These limit and define
him as a statesman, as an orator, as an executive of
the nation, and as a man. They developed in all
the walks of his life ; they were his law; they were
his nature , they were Abraham Lincoln.

This long, bony, sad man floated down the Sangamon river in a frail canoe in the spring of 1831.
Like a piece of driftwood he lodged at last, without
a history, strange, penniless, and alone. In sight of
the capital of Illinois, in the fatigue of daily toil he
struggled for the necessaries of life. Thirty years
later this same peculiar man left the Sangamon
river, backed by friends, by power, by the patriotic
prayers of millions of people, to be the ruler of the
greatest nation in the world.

As the leader of a brave people in their desperate
struggle for national existence, Abraham Lincoln
will always be an interesting historical character.

His strong, honest, sagacious, and noble life will always possess a peculiar charm. Had it not been for his conservative statesmanship, his supreme confidence in the wisdom of the people, his extreme care in groping his way among facts and before ideas, this nation might have been two governments to-day. The low and feeble circulation of his blood; his healthful irritability, which responded so slowly to the effects of stimuli; the strength of his herculean frame; his peculiar organism, conserving its force; his sublime patience; his wonderful endurance ; his great hand and heart, saved this country from division, when division meant its irreparable ruin.

The central figure of our national history, the sublime type of our civilization, posterity, with the record of his career and actions before it, will decree that, whether Providence so ordained it or not, Abraham Lincoln was the man for the hour.

APPENDIX.

UNPUBLISHED FAMILY LETTERS.

THE following letters by Mr. Lincoln to his relatives were at one time placed in my hands. As they have never before been published entire I have thought proper to append them here. They are only interesting as showing Mr. Lincoln's affection for his father and step-mother, and as specimens of the good, sound sense with which he approached every undertaking. The list opens with a letter to his father written from Washington while a member of Congress:

"WASHINGTON, Dec. 24, 1848.

"*My Dear Father :*

"Your letter of the 7th was received night before last. I very cheerfully send you the twenty dollars, which sum you say is necessary to save your land from sale. It is singular that you should have forgotten a judgment against you—and it is more singular that the plaintiff should have let you forget it so long, particularly as I suppose you have always had property enough to satisfy a judgment of that amount. Before you pay it, it would be well to be sure you have not paid, or at least that you cannot prove you have paid it.

"Give my love to Mother and all the Connections.

"Affectionately, your son,

"A. LINCOLN."

His step-brother, John D. Johnston, for whom Mr. Lincoln always exhibited the affection of a real brother, was the recipient of many letters. Some of them were commonplace, but

321

between the lines of each much good, homely philosophy may be read. Johnston, whom I knew, was exactly what his distinguished step-brother charged—an idler. In every emergency he seemed to fall back on Lincoln for assistance. The aid generally came, but with it always some plain but sensible suggestion. The series opens as follows:

"SPRINGFIELD, Feb. 23, 1850.

"*Dear Brother:*

"Your letter about a mail contract was received yesterday. I have made out a bid for you at $120, guaranteed it myself, got our P. M. here to certify it, and send it on. Your former letter, concerning some man's claim for a pension, was also received. I had the claim examined by those who are practised in such matters, and they decide he cannot get a pension.

"As you make no mention of it, I suppose you had not learned that we lost our little boy. He was sick fifteen days, and died in the morning of the first day of this month. It was not our *first*, but our second child. We miss him very much.

"Your Brother, in haste,

"A. LINCOLN."

"To JOHN D. JOHNSTON."

Following is another, which, however, bears no aate:

"*Dear Johnston:*

"Your request for eighty dollars I do not think it best to comply with now. At the various times when I have helped you a little you have said to me, 'We can get along very well now,' but in a very short time I find you in the same difficulty again. Now this can only happen by some defect in your conduct. What that defect is, I think I know. You are not *lazy*, and still you are an *idler*. I doubt whether, since I saw you, you have done a good whole day's work in any one day. You do not very much dislike to work, and still you do not work much, merely because it does not seem to you that you could get much for it. This habit of uselessly wasting time is the whole difficulty; and it is vastly important to you, and still more so to your children, that you should break the habit. It is more important to them because they have longer to live, and can keep out of an idle habit, before they are in it, easier than they can get out after they are in.

" You are in need of some ready money, and what I propose is that you shall go to work 'tooth and nail' for somebody who will give you money for it. Let father and your boys take charge of things at home, prepare for a crop, and make the crop, and you go to work for the best money wages, or in discharge of any debt you owe, that you can get,—and to secure you a fair reward for your labor, I now promise you that for every dollar you will, between this and the first of next May, get for your own labor, either in money or as your own indebtedness, I will then give you one other dollar. By this, if you hire yourself at ten dollars a month, from me you will get ten more, making twenty dollars a month for your work. In this I do not mean you shall go off to St. Louis, or the lead mines, or the gold mines in California, but I mean for you to go at it for the best wages you can get close to home in Coles County. Now if you will do this, you will be soon out of debt, and, what is better, you will have a habit that will keep you from getting in debt again. But if I should now clear you out, next year you would be just as deep in as ever. You say you would give your place in heaven for $70 or $80. Then you value your place in heaven very cheap, for I am sure you can, with the offer I make, get the seventy or eighty dollars for four or five months' work.

" You say, if I will furnish you the money, you will deed me the land, and if you don't pay the money back you will deliver possession. Nonsense! If you can't now live with the land, how will you then live without it? You have always been kind to me, and I do not mean to be unkind to you. On the contrary, if you will but follow my advice, you will find it worth more than eight times eighty dollars to you.

" Affectionately,

" Your brother,

" A. LINCOLN."

The following, written when the limit of Thomas Lincoln's life seemed rapidly approaching, shows in what esteem his son held the relation that existed between them :

"SPRINGFIELD, Jan'y 12, 1851.

"*Dear Brother :*

"On the day before yesterday I received a letter from Harriett, written at Greenup. She says she has just returned from your house; and that Father is very low, and will hardly recover. She also says that you have written me two letters; and that although you do not expect me to come now, you wonder that I do not write. I received both your letters, and although I have not answered them, it is not because I have forgotten them, or [not] been interested about them, but because it appeared to me I could write nothing which could do any good. You already know I desire that neither Father or Mother shall be in want of any comfort either in health or sickness while they live ; and I feel sure you have not failed to use my name, if necessary, to procure a doctor, or anything else for Father in his present sickness. My business is such that I could hardly leave home now, if it were not, as it is, that my own wife is sick a-bed (it is a case of baby-sickness, and I suppose is not dangerous). I sincerely hope Father may yet recover his health ; but at all events tell him to remember to call upon and confide in our great, and good, and merciful Maker, who will not turn away from him in any extremity. He notes the fall of a sparrow, and numbers the hairs of our heads ; and He will not forget the dying man who puts his trust in Him. Say to him that if we could meet now it is doubtful whether it would not be more painful than pleasant ; but that if it be his lot to go now he will soon have a joyous meeting with many loved ones gone before, and where the rest of us, through the help of God, hope ere long to join them.

"Write me again when you receive this.

"Affectionately,

"A. LINCOLN."

Lincoln's mentor-like interest in his step-mother and his shiftless and almost unfortunate step-brother was in no wise diminished by the death of his father. He writes:

"SPRINGFIELD, Aug. 31, 1851.

"*Dear Brother:*

"Inclosed is the deed for the land. We are all well, and have nothing in the way of news. We have had no cholera here for about two weeks.

"Give my love to all, and especially to Mother.

"Yours as ever,

"A. LINCOLN."

No more practical or kindly-earnest advice could have been given than this:

"SHELBYVILLE, Nov. 4, 1851.

"*Dear Brother:*

"When I came into Charleston day before yesterday I learned that you are anxious to sell the land where you live, and move to Missouri. I have been thinking of this ever since, and cannot but think such a notion is utterly foolish. What can you do in Missouri better than here? Is the land richer? Can you there, any more than here, raise corn and wheat and oats without work? Will anybody there, any more than here, do your work for you? If you intend to go to work, there is no better place than right where you are; if you do not intend to go to work you cannot get along anywhere. Squirming and crawling about from place to place can do no good. You have raised no crop this year, and what you really want is to sell the land, get the money and spend it. Part with the land you have, and, my life upon it, you will never after own a spot big enough to bury you in. Half you will get for the land you spend in moving to Missouri, and the other half you will eat and drink and wear out, and no foot of land will be bought. Now I feel it is my duty to have no hand in such a piece of foolery. I feel that it is so even on your own account, and particularly on *Mother's* account. The eastern forty acres I intend to keep for Mother while she lives;

if you *will not cultivate it*, it will rent for enough to support her; at least it will rent for something. Her dower in the other two forties she can let you have, and no thanks to me.

" Now do not misunderstand this letter. I do not write it in any unkindness. I write it in order, if possible, to get you to *face* the truth, which truth is, you are destitute because you have idled away all your time. Your thousand pretences for not getting along better are all nonsense; they deceive nobody but yourself. *Go to work* is the only cure for your case.

" A word for Mother : Chapman tells me he wants you to go and live with him. If I were you I would try it awhile. If you get tired of it (as I think you will not) you can return to your own home. Chapman feels very kindly to you ; and I have no doubt he will make your situation very pleasant.

" Sincerely your son,

" A. LINCOLN."

The list closes with this one written by Lincoln while on the circuit :

" SHELBYVILLE, Nov. 9, 1851.

"Dear Brother :

" When I wrote you before, I had not received your letter. I still think as I did ; but if the land can be sold so that I get three hundred dollars to put to interest for Mother, I will not object if she does not. But before I will make a deed, the money must be had, or secured beyond all doubt at ten per cent.

" As to Abraham, I do not want him *on my own account ;* but I understand he wants to live with me so that he can go to school and get a fair start in the world, which I very much wish him to have. When I reach home, if I can make it convenient to take, I will take him, provided there is no mistake between us as to the object and terms of my taking him.

" In haste, as ever,

" A. LINCOLN."

AN INCIDENT ON THE CIRCUIT.

" In the spring term of the Tazewell County Court in 1847, which at that time was held in the village of Tremont, I was detained as a witness an entire week. Lincoln was employed in several suits, and among them was one of Case *vs.* Snow Bros. The Snow Bros., as appeared in evidence (who were both minors), had purchased from an old Mr. Case what was then called a " prairie team," consisting of two or three yoke of oxen and prairie plow, giving therefor their joint note for some two hundred dollars ; but when pay-day came refused to pay, pleading the minor act. The note was placed in Lincoln's hands for collection. The suit was called and a jury im-panelled. The Snow Bros. did not deny the note, but pleaded through their counsel that they were minors, and that Mr. Case knew they were at the time of the contract and convey-ance. All this was admitted by Mr. Lincoln, with his peculiar phrase, ' Yes, gentlemen, I reckon that's so.' The minor act was read and its validity admitted in the same manner. The counsel of the defendants were permitted without question to state all these things to the jury, and to show by the statute that these minors could not be held responsible for their con-tract. By this time you may well suppose that I began to be uneasy. ' What!' thought I, 'this good old man, who con-fided in these boys, to be wronged in this way, and even his counsel, Mr. Lincoln, to submit in silence!' I looked at the court, Judge Treat, but could read nothing in his calm and dig-nified demeanor. Just then, Mr. Lincoln slowly got up, and in his strange, half-erect attitude and clear, quiet accent began : *'Gentlemen of the Jury*, are you willing to allow these boys to begin life with this shame and disgrace attached to their char-acter ? If you are, *I* am not. The best judge of human char-acter that ever wrote has left these immortal words for all of us to ponder :

45

> "Good name in man or woman, dear my lord,
>   Is the immediate jewel of their souls:
>   Who steals my purse steals trash: 'tis something, nothing;
>   'Twas mine, 'tis his, and has been slave to thousands;
>   But he that filches from me my good name
>   Robs me of that which not enriches him
>   And makes me poor indeed." '

"Then rising to his full height, and looking upon the defendants with the compassion of a brother, his long right arm extended toward the opposing counsel, he continued: 'Gentlemen of the jury, these poor innocent boys would never have attempted this low villany had it not been for the advice of these lawyers.' Then for a few minutes he showed how even the noble science of law may be prostituted. With a scathing rebuke to those who thus belittle their profession, he concluded: 'And now, gentlemen, you have it in *your* power to set these boys right before the world.' He plead for the young men only; I think he did not mention his client's name. The jury, without leaving their seats, decided that the defendants must pay the debt; and the latter, after hearing Lincoln, were as willing to pay it as the jury were determined they should. I think the entire argument lasted not above five minutes."—*George W. Minier*, statement, Apr. 10, 1882.

LINCOLN'S FELLOW LAWYERS.

Among Lincoln's colleagues at the Springfield bar, after his re-entry into politics in 1854, and until his elevation to the Presidency, were, John T. Stuart, Stephen T. Logan, John A. Mc-Clernand, Benjamin S. Edwards, David Logan, E. B. Herndon, W. I. Ferguson, James H. Matheney, C. C. Brown, N. M. Broadwell, Charles W. Keyes, John E. Rosette, C. S. Zane, J. C. Conkling, Shelby M. Cullom, and G. W. Shutt. There were others, notably John M. Palmer and Richard J. Oglesby, who came in occasionally from other counties and tried suits with and against us, but they never became members of our bar, strictly speaking, till after the war had closed.—W. H. H.

THE TRUCE WITH DOUGLAS.—TESTIMONY OF IRWIN.

" The conversation took place in the office of Lincoln & Herndon, in the presence of P. L. Harrison, William H. Herndon, Pascal Enos, and myself. It originated in this way: After the debate at Springfield on the 4th and 5th of October, 1854, William Jayne, John Cassiday, Pascal Enos, the writer, and others whose names I do not now remember, filled out and signed a written request to Lincoln to follow Douglas until he 'ran him into his hole' or made him halloo ' Enough,' and that day Lincoln was giving in his report. He said that the next morning after the Peoria debate Douglas came to him and flattered him that he knew more on the question of Territorial organization in this government than all the Senate of the United States, and called his mind to the trouble the latter had given him. He added that Lincoln had already given him more trouble than all the opposition in the Senate, and then proposed to Lincoln that if he (Lincoln) would go home and not follow him, he (Douglas) would go to no more of his appointments, would make no more speeches, and would go home and remain silent during the rest of the campaign. Lincoln did not make another speech till after the election."—*B. F. Irwin*, statement, Feb. 8, 1866, unpublished MS.

See *ante*, pp. 368-369.

THE BLOOMINGTON CONVENTION.

Following is a copy of the call to select delegates to the Bloomington Convention held May 29, 1856, when the Republican party in Illinois came into existence. It will be remembered that I signed Lincoln's name under instructions from him by telegraph. The original document I gave several years ago to a friend in Boston, Mass.:

" We, the undersigned, citizens of Sangamon County, who are opposed to the repeal of the Missouri Compromise, and the present administration, and who are in favor of restoring to the general government the policy of Washington and Jefferson, would suggest the propriety of a County Convention, to be held in the city of Springfield on Saturday, the 24th day of May, at 2 o'clock, P. M., to appoint delegates to the Blooming-ton Convention.

" A. LINCOLN,
" W. H. HERNDON and others."

The decided stand Lincoln took in this instance, and his speech in the Convention, undoubtedly paved the way for his leadership in the Republican party.—W. H. H.

AN OFFICE DISCUSSION—LINCOLN'S IDEA OF WAR.

One morning in 1859, Lincoln and I, impressed with the probability of war between the two sections of the country, were discussing the subject in the office. " The position taken by the advocates of State Sovereignty," remarked Lincoln, "always reminds me of the fellow who contended that the proper place for the big kettle was inside of the little one." To me, war seemed inevitable, but when I came to view the matter squarely, I feared a difficulty the North would have in controlling the various classes of people and shades of senti-ment, so as to make them an effective force in case of war : I feared the lack of some great head and heart to lead us on-ward. Lincoln had great confidence in the masses, believing that, when they were brought face to face with the reality of the conflict, all differences would disappear, and that they would be merged into one. To illustrate his idea he made use of this figure : " Go to the river bank with a coarse sieve and fill it with gravel. After a vigorous shaking you will observe that the small pebbles and sand have sunk from view and fallen to the ground. The next larger in size, unable to slip between

the wires, will still be found within the sieve.   By thorough and
repeated shakings you will find that, of the pebbles still left in
the sieve, the largest ones will have risen to the top.   Now,"
he continued, " if, as you say, war is inevitable and will shake
the country from centre to circumference, you will find that the
little men will fall out of view in the shaking.   The masses will
rest on some solid foundation, and the big men will have climbed
to the top.   Of these latter, one greater than all the rest will
leap forth armed and equipped—the people's leader in the conflict."   Little did I realize the strength of the masses when
united and fighting for a common purpose ; and much less did
I dream that the great leader soon to be tried was at that very
moment touching my elbow !—W. H. H.

LINCOLN AND THE KNOW-NOTHINGS.

Among other things used against Lincoln in the campaign of
1860 was the charge that he had been a member of a Know-
Nothing lodge.   When the charge was laid at his door he
wrote the following letter to one of his confidential political
friends.   I copy from the original MS.:

[Confidential.]

"SPRINGFIELD, ILLS., July 21, 1860.

" Hon. A. JONAS.

"*My Dear Sir :*

" Yours of the 20th is received.   I suppose as
good, or even better, men than I may have been in American
or Know-Nothing lodges ; but, in point of fact, I never was in
one, at Quincy or elsewhere.   I was never in Quincy but one
day and two nights while Know-Nothing lodges were in existence, and you were with me that day and both those nights.
I had never been there before in my life ; and never afterwards,
till the joint debate with Douglas in 1858.   It was in 1854,
when I spoke in some hall there, and after the speaking you,

with others, took me to an oyster saloon, passed an hour there, and you walked with me to, and parted with me at, the Quincy House quite late at night. I left by stage for Naples before daylight in the morning, having come in by the same route after dark the evening previous to the speaking, when I found you waiting at the Quincy House to meet me. A few days after I was there, Richardson, as I understood, started the same story about my having been in a Know-Nothing lodge. When I heard of the charge, as I did soon after, I taxed my recollection for some incident which could have suggested it; and I remembered that, on parting with you the last night, I went to the office of the Hotel to take my stage passage for the morning, was told that no stage office for that line was kept there, and that I must see the driver before retiring, to insure his calling for me in the morning; and a servant was sent with me to find the driver, who, after taking me a square or two, stopped me, and stepped perhaps a dozen steps farther, and in my hearing called to some one, who answered him, apparently from the upper part of a building, and promised to call with the stage for me at the Quincy House. I returned and went to bed, and before day the stage called and took me. This is all.

"That I never was in a Know-Nothing lodge in Quincy I should expect could be easily proved by respectable men who were always in the lodges, and never saw me there. An affidavit of one or two such would put the matter at rest.

"And now, a word of caution. Our adversaries think they can gain a point if they could force me to openly deny the charge, by which some degree of offence would be given to the Americans. For this reason it must not publicly appear that I am paying any attention to the charge,

"Yours truly,

"A. LINCOLN."

LINCOLN'S VIEWS ON THE RIGHTS OF SUFFRAGE.

At one time, while holding the office of attorney for the city of Springfield, I had a case in the Supreme Court, which involved the validity or constitutionality of a law regulating the matter of voting. Although a city case, it really abridged the right of suffrage. Being Lincoln's partner I wanted him to assist me in arguing the questions involved. He declined to do so, saying : " I am opposed to the limitation or lessening of the right of suffrage ; if anything, I am in favor of its extension or enlargement. I want to lift men up—to broaden rather than contract their privileges."—W. H. H.

THE BURIAL OF THE ASSASSIN BOOTH.

" Upon reaching Washington with the body of Booth—having come up the Potomac—it was at once removed from the tug-boat to a gun-boat that lay at the dock at the Navy Yard, where it remained about thirty-six hours. It was there examined by the Surgeon-General and staff and other officers, and identified by half a score of persons who had known him well. Toward evening of the second day Gen. L. C. Baker, then chief of the 'Detective Bureau of the War Department,' received orders from Secretary of War Stanton to dispose of the body. Stanton said, ' Put it where it will not be disturbed until Gabriel blows his last trumpet.' I was ordered to assist him. The body was placed in a row-boat, and, taking with us one trusty man to manage the boat, we quietly floated down the river. Crowds of people all along the shore were watching us. For a blind we took with us a heavy ball and chain, and it was soon going from lip to lip that we were about to sink the body in the Potomac. Darkness soon came on, completely concealing our movements, and under its cover we pulled slowly back to the old Penitentiary, which during the war was used as an arsenal.　The body was then lifted from the boat and carried through a door opening on the river front.　Under the stone floor of what had been a prison cell a shallow grave was dug, and the body, with the United States blanket for a 'winding-sheet,' was there interred.　There also it remained till Booth's accomplices were hanged.　It was then taken up and buried with his companions in crime.　I have since learned that the remains were again disinterred and given to his friends, and that they now rest in the family burial-place in Baltimore, Md."—*From MS. of L. B. Baker, late Lieut. and A. Q. M. 1st D. C. Cav.*

A TRIBUTE TO LINCOLN BY A COLLEAGUE AT THE BAR.

"The weird and melancholy association of eloquence and poetry had a strong fascination for Mr. Lincoln's mind.　Tasteful composition, either of prose or poetry, which faithfully contrasted the realities of eternity with the unstable and fickle fortunes of time, made a strong impression on his mind.　In the indulgence of this melancholy taste it is related of him that the poem, *'Immortality,'* he knew by rote and appreciated very highly.　He had a strange liking for the verses, and they bear a just resemblance to his fortune.　Mr. Lincoln, at the time of his assassination, was encircled by a halo of immortal glory such as had never before graced the brow of mortal man.　He had driven treason from its capital city, had slept in the palace of its once proud and defiant, but now vanquished leader, and had saved his country and its accrued glories of three-quarters of a century from destruction.　He rode, not with the haughty and imperious brow of an ancient conqueror, but with the placid complacency of a pure patriot, through the streets of the political Babylon of modern times.　He had ridden over battle-fields immortal in history, when, in power at least, he was the leader.　Having assured the misguided citizens of the South that he meant them no harm beyond a determination to maintain the government, he returned buoyant with hope to the Executive Mansion where for four long years he had been held, as it were, a prisoner.

" Weary with the stories of state, he goes to seek the relaxation of amusement at the theatre; sees the gay crowd as he passes in; is cheered and graciously smiled upon by fair women and brave men; beholds the gorgeous paraphernalia of the stage, the brilliantly lighted scene, the arched ceiling, with its grotesque and inimitable figuring to heighten the effect and make the occasion one of unalloyed pleasure. The hearts of the people beat in unison with his over a redeemed and ransomed land. A pause in the play—a faint pistol shot is heard. No one knows its significance save the hellish few who are in the plot. A wild shriek, such as murder wrings from the heart of woman, follows: the proud form of Mr. Lincoln has sunk in death. The scene is changed to a wild confusion such as no poet can describe, no painter delineate. Well might the murdered have said and oft repeated:

> ' 'Tis the wink of an eye, 'tis the draught of a breath,
> From the blossom of health to the paleness of death,
> From the gilded saloon to the bier and the shroud,—
> Oh, why should the spirit of mortal be proud?' "

[*From a speech by Hon. Lawrence Weldon, at a bar-meeting held in the United States Court at Springfield, Ills., in June,* 1865.]

LINCOLN AT FORT MONROE.

An interesting recollection of Lincoln comes from the pen of Colonel LeGrand B. Cannon, of New York. One cannot fail to be impressed with the strength of the side-light thrown by these reminiscences on a life as peculiar, in some respects, as it was grand and unique in others:

" It was my great good fortune," relates Colonel Cannon, " to know something of Mr. Lincoln distinct from his official life. Intensely in earnest I entered the service at the opening of the Rebellion as a staff officer in the regular army and was assigned to the Department of Virginia, with headquarters at Fort Monroe. Major-General Wool was in command of the Department, and I was honored by him as his chief of-staff, and enjoyed his entire confidence. It was the only gate open for communication with the rebel government, and General Wool was the agent for such intercourse.

"In the early stages of the war there was a want of harmony between the army and navy about us which seriously embarrassed military operations, resulting in the President and Secretaries Chase and Stanton coming to Fort Monroe to adjust matters. Domestic comforts were limited at headquarters, and the President occupied my room. I was (in accordance with military etiquette) assigned to him as 'Aide-in-Waiting' and Secretary. Although I had frequently met the President as 'Bearer of Dispatches,' I was not a little prejudiced, and a good deal irritated, at the levity which he was charged with indulging in. In grave matters, jesting and frolicking seemed to me shocking, with such vital matters at stake, and I confess to thinking of Nero.

"But all this changed when I came to know him; and I very soon discerned that he had a sad nature; but that, although a terrible burden, his sadness did not originate in his great official responsibilities. I had heard that his home was not pleasant, but did not know that there was more beyond it.

"The day after Mr. Lincoln came to us he said to me: 'I suppose you have neither a Bible nor a copy of Shakespeare here?' I replied that I had a Bible, and the General had Shakespeare, and that the latter never missed a night without reading it. 'Won't he lend it to me?' inquired the President. I answered, 'Yes,' and, of course, obtained it for him.

"The day following he read by himself in one of my offices, two hours or more, entirely alone, I being engaged in a connecting room on duty. He finally interrupted me, inviting me to rest while he would read to me. He read from *Macbeth, Lear,* and finally, *King John.* In reading the passage where Constance bewails to the King the loss of her child, I noticed that his voice trembled and he was deeply moved. Laying the book on the table he said:

" ' Did you ever dream of a lost friend and feel that you were having a sweet communion with that friend, and yet a consciousness that it was not a reality ? '

" ' Yes,' I replied, ' I think almost any one may have had such an experience.'

" ' So do I,' he mused; ' I dream of my dead boy, Willie, again and again.'

" I shall never forget the sigh nor the look of sorrow that accompanied this expression. He was utterly overcome ; his great frame shook, and, bowing down on the table, he wept as only such a man in the breaking down of a great sorrow could weep. It is needless to say that I wept in sympathy, and quietly left the room that he might recover without restraint.

" Lincoln never again referred to his boy, but he made me feel that he had given me a sacred confidence, and he ever after treated me with a tenderness and regard that won my love.

" Again, some days later, I had been absent on a reconnoissance, and returned late in the afternoon. I was in my room dressing for dinner (which was a very formal affair, as, besides the Administration, we had, almost daily, distinguished foreigners to dine) when the President came in. Seeing me in full uniform he said:

" ' Why, Colonel, you're fixing up mighty fine. Suppose you lend me your comb and brush, and I'll put on a few touches, too.'

" I handed the desired articles to him and he toyed with the comb awhile and then laid it down, exclaiming :

" ' This thing will never get through my hair. Now, if you have such a thing as they comb a horse's tail with, I believe I can use it.' After a merry laugh, he continued : ' By the way, I can tell you a good story about my hair. When I was nominated, at Chicago, an enterprising fellow thought that a great many people would like to see how Abe Lincoln looked, and, as I had not long before sat for a photograph, this fellow having seen it, rushed over and bought the negative. He at once got out no end of wood-cuts, and, so active was their circulation, they were selling in all parts of the country. Soon after they reached Springfield I heard a boy crying them for sale on the streets. 'Here's your likeness of Abe Lincoln!' he shouted. 'Buy one; price only two shillings! Will look a good deal better when he gets his hair combed!'"

INDEX.

THE END.